All She Ever Wanted

Books by
Lynn Austin
FROM BETHANY HOUSE PUBLISHERS

All She Ever Wanted

Eve's Daughters

Hidden Places

Wings of Refuge

REFINER'S FIRE

Candle in the Darkness

Fire by Night

A Light to My Path

CHRONICLES OF THE KINGS

Gods and Kings

Song of Redemption

The Strength of His Hand

www.lynnaustin.org

LYNN
AUSTIN

All She Ever Wanted

BETHANYHOUSE

MINNEAPOLIS, MINNESOTA

To my family

Ken, Joshua, Benjamin, and Maya

LYNN AUSTIN is a three-time Christy Award winner for her historical novels *Hidden Places, Candle in the Darkness,* and *Fire by Night.* In addition to writing, Lynn is a popular speaker at conferences, retreats, and various church and school events. She and her husband have three children and make their home in Illinois.

". . . give me neither poverty nor riches, but give me only my

daily bread. Otherwise, I may have too much and disown you

and say, 'Who is the Lord?' Or I may become poor and steal,

and so dishonor the name of my God."

— P R O V E R B S   3 0 : 8 — 9

Part
I

KATHLEEN AND JOELLE

2004

Chapter

1

This wouldn't be the first time Kathleen Seymour left home and never returned. But after the day she'd had, she was sorely tempted to pack all her clothes, climb into her Lexus, and drive as far away as a tank of gas would take her. Judging by what little she knew of her ancestors, it was almost a family tradition to leave home when things got rough and start life all over again in a new town. In fact, if the bigwigs who ran the federal Witness Protection Program wanted a few pointers on creating a new identity in a new location, they could consult Kathleen's family. They were experts.

"I'm leaving home and never coming back!" Her sixteen-year-old daughter, Joelle, yelled, echoing Kathleen's thoughts. Joelle stomped dramatically up the stairs to her bedroom, but the thick carpeting muffled the impact of her tantrum.

"Don't bother!" Kathleen called up to her. "I'll leave first!"

Joelle slammed her bedroom door in reply, rattling the teacups on the dining room shelf below her room.

"You know, I've had about all I can take, Joelle," Kathleen shouted, then clapped her hand over her mouth. She'd used the same phrase, in the same tone of voice, that her own mother had always used. When had Kathleen turned into her mother?

She sank down at the kitchen table, her legs too unsteady to hold her any longer. They had begun to tremble during the confrontation with her boss a few hours ago and had barely been strong enough to carry her out to the parking lot as she'd stormed from her office building. It was a good thing that she'd been sitting down in her car, removing her high heels, when the police called on her cell phone. She might have collapsed on the spot.

"Mrs. Seymour? This is Officer Marks of the city police department. We have your daughter, Joelle Marie Seymour . . . in custody. . . ."

Kathleen couldn't remember much after that. Somehow she'd driven to the mall, found the security office, and sweated through an agonizing meeting with Officer Marks and the undercover cop who had caught Joelle shoplifting a seven-dollar tube of lipstick from the cosmetics counter. It had seemed like a bad dream, especially Joelle's reaction to it all. She had shown no remorse as she'd slouched in the chair with her arms folded, refusing to make eye contact and coolly swinging her foot—beautiful Joelle, with the cinnamon-colored hair that reminded Kathleen so much of her own father's. But the last thing Kathleen needed in this situation was to be reminded of her father.

Thankfully, she was able to persuade the store manager not to press charges since it was Joelle's first offense, but she would be banned from shopping at the mall for one year and a second offense would earn her a trip to the police station and a juvenile record. Kathleen had practically kissed Officer Marks on both cheeks.

"Where are your friends?" Kathleen asked Joelle when the police finally allowed them to leave. "Didn't you come to the mall with Colleen and Stacey?"

Joelle shrugged. "They ditched me when I got caught."

"Some friends."

"Can you drop me off at Colleen's house?" Joelle asked when they reached the car.

Kathleen stared at her in disbelief. "Are you out of your mind?"

Joelle sank into the passenger's seat and slammed the door, ignoring her seat belt and the annoying *ping* of the warning bell. When she reached to crank up the volume on the car radio, Kathleen shoved aside her hand.

"Leave that off—and put your seat belt on!"

"Like you care what happens to me!"

Kathleen felt herself losing control. She started the engine and pulled out of the mall parking lot, tires squealing. "Why would you do such a stupid thing, Joelle? What were you thinking? I give you fifty dollars a week for your allowance—what would possess you to steal a seven-dollar lipstick?"

Joelle shrugged. "It's no big deal. They let me go."

After that the ride home degenerated into a screaming match, ending with Joelle's threat to leave home and never return. Kathleen had made the very same threat—how many years ago? But she had followed through on it.

Kathleen's hands were still trembling as she reached across the kitchen table for the portable phone to call her husband. Thankfully, she got Mike himself instead of his voice mail. "What's up, Kath?"

"You need to come home," she said, her voice breaking.

"Can you tell me more than that? I'm kinda busy—"

"Joelle was arrested for shoplifting." Her tears started to fall then, tears of rage and incomprehension and grief. At first she made no sound as they trickled down her face, but when she glanced up at the refrigerator door and saw the note reminding her that Joelle needed to bring a snack to the youth group meeting at church tonight, she began to sob.

"I'll be right home," Mike said quietly.

He arrived in time to stop Joelle as she dragged her backpack and an overstuffed suitcase down the stairs. "I'm not letting you run away, sweetie," he soothed. "Let's go upstairs and talk about this."

Kathleen wondered if Mike would have tried to stop her if she'd been the one with the suitcase instead of Joelle. She listened to their voices drifting down from upstairs, envying the relationship they had, aware that she had blown it once again. She and Joelle fought just like Kathleen and her own mother used to fight—maybe more. Kathleen kept promising herself that she would try harder to be a better, more caring mother, but she didn't know how or where to begin.

She reached for the framed snapshot—taken last winter on their skiing trip to Colorado—that she kept on her desk in the kitchen. All three of them were smiling as they squinted in the glare of winter sun, their faces scrunched together in a rare moment of bonding, a picture-perfect family. Mike's habitual worry lines were relaxed into smile lines, and his bristly, steel-gray hair was hidden beneath a ski cap, making him look younger than his fifty-eight years. Kathleen herself was used to being told that she didn't look fifty-four—thanks to regular workouts at the health club and a creative hairdresser who kept Kathleen's light-brown hair fashionably styled and free from encroaching gray. She had been thirty-eight when Joelle was born, after years of medical procedures and countless prayers. She'd vowed to stay young looking for her daughter's sake, but today she felt like the wicked old crone in a bad fairy tale.

In the photograph Joelle's reddish-brown hair was a mass of natural curls, framing a face that still held a child's softness and innocence, yet hinted at the promise of womanly beauty and sensuality. "Lord, help us," Kathleen breathed, closing her eyes. Joelle was only sixteen and already in trouble—God only knew what lay ahead.

"I've got her settled down," Mike said when he came downstairs an hour later. He had loosened his tie and rolled up the sleeves of his starched, white shirt. "But I think you should go up and talk to her. Let her know you still love her."

"I'm very, very angry with her right now," Kathleen said in a tight voice. She had finally summoned the energy to push her chair away from the table and start heating up leftovers in the microwave for their supper—although the last thing she felt like doing was eating. She hadn't taken off her suit coat or her shoes and panty hose, as if still toying with the idea of leaving home.

"We've given her everything she could ever want, Mike, yet she's so ungrateful. I longed for a life like hers when I was her age. I can't believe she'd toss it all away for a stupid tube of lipstick. Why would she do such a dumb thing? We give her an enormous allowance. She could buy a dozen lipsticks."

"Maybe she's trying to get your attention."

His words felt like a slap in the face. "How dare you say that to me? You're away from home for weeks at a time! I'm the one who has always been here for her!" She yanked her purse off the table, fishing out her car keys as she headed for the back door.

"Don't walk out, Kathleen. This is one problem that you'd better not run away from."

She whirled to face him. "I'm not running away—although I'll admit I'm tempted! I'm just going outside for some air!"

He snatched the keys from her hands. "Don't get behind the wheel. You're in no condition to drive."

"Fine!"

She stalked down to the end of the block, then back again, her high heels too painful to take her any farther. The upscale neighborhood was quiet, not at all the sort of place where children rode their bikes or played stickball in the street on a warm summer night. She didn't have to worry about nosy neighbors overhearing her screaming match with Joelle or wondering why she was stomping up and down the street in her business suit. The houses sat isolated from each other on their half-acre lots, shielded behind bushes and trees, all outside noises muffled by the whir of air-conditioners and the hum of swimming-pool filters.

Kathleen stopped at her mailbox on the way back to the house and pulled out a wad of catalogues, flyers, and junk mail. Finding a handwritten letter among the junk was such a rare occurrence these days that the lone envelope seemed to jump out at her. She looked at the return address and saw her sister's name and an address in Riverside, New York, where they had grown up. Why was Annie writing? Kathleen tore open the envelope.

Inside she found a gaudy invitation decorated with balloons and party hats. It looked as though it had come from a dollar store. She scanned the details, then read them again to make sure she hadn't misunderstood: Her sister was throwing a party for their father. *Please try to come, Kathy,* she had printed across the bottom. *It would mean so much to Daddy.*

"This is the last straw," Kathleen muttered. She strode up the driveway and into the house, trying not to picture her father's infectious grin, trying not to remember the happiness she felt every time he scooped her up in his freckled arms and called her "my Kathy." Happy-go-lucky Daddy with his cinnamon-colored hair. For all she knew, he could be bald by now. After all, it had been thirty-five years since she'd seen him.

But she couldn't go home—not now, not ever. Just the thought of returning to Riverside made her want to cover her head in shame. She would have to drive past her old high school, where she'd spent four years walking around with her head down, hoping no one would notice her, hoping no one would call her "Cootie Kathy" or, worse, "Kathy the Commie." No, she'd run away once before and would never go back . . . least of all for her father.

Kathleen threw the invitation into the trash can beneath the sink and tossed the rest of the mail onto the table in front of Mike. He was digging into a plate of leftover Chinese takeout and reading the *Washington Post.* "I'm going to bed," she told him. "I want to forget that today ever happened."

"Hey, hey, wait a minute, Kath. Don't you want to eat something, first?"

"I'm not hungry." She walked as far as the kitchen door, then turned around to add, "By the way, I had a fight with my boss this afternoon— before the incident with Joelle. I walked out on him. I think I might be unemployed."

She didn't wait for Mike's response but continued upstairs to their master suite and took a long hot shower. This was much worse than just a bad day. Kathleen's carefully constructed life was falling apart all around her, and she didn't know how to fix it. She thought of the Bible character, Job, who'd lamented that the thing he'd feared the most had come upon him. Kathleen's greatest fear was much the same as his: that everything she'd worked for, everyone she loved, would be snatched away from her.

She let her tears fall freely as she showered. When she came out, Mike was sitting on their bed. "I found this in the garbage," he said, waving the balloon-covered invitation. "Did you mean to throw it away?"

She exhaled. "I would have run it through a paper shredder if we had one."

Chapter 2

Kathleen sank into the driver's seat of her car the following day and leaned her head against the steering wheel, allowing her tears to fall. She had worked for the Impost Corporation for more than twenty years, clawing her way up from accountant to comptroller to CFO—and now her career with them was over. Grief overwhelmed her as she slowly comprehended all that she had just lost. As she relived this morning's meeting with her boss, searching for some way that it might have had a different outcome, Kathleen remained convinced that she had done the right thing. There were moral issues at stake, but being right didn't ease the pain.

At last she sat up, worried that someone in the parking lot might see her, and wiped her eyes with her fingertips, careful not to smudge her mascara. She drew a deep breath as if air could suffocate her grief, then released it with a sigh. When she felt in control again, she pulled her cell phone out of her purse and speed-dialed Mike. She knew he had been waiting for her call when he answered on the first ring.

"Hi, it's me," she said, swallowing a knot of sorrow. "Well, I'm officially unemployed."

He was silent for a long moment. Kathleen could tell from the background noise that he was at a work site, not his office. She pictured him wearing a yellow hard hat, closing his eyes and lowering his head in grief as she had done. "I'm so sorry, Kath," he finally murmured. "Are you okay? Where are you?"

"In the parking lot at work. I should go back inside and pack all my stuff, but . . ."

"Leave it for now," he said when her voice broke. "You can get it another day. Tell me what happened."

She leaned her head against the headrest and switched the cell phone to her other ear while she removed her earrings. She and Mike had talked about her dilemma at length last night, and they had agreed that standing up to her young boss was the right thing to do. If only she'd been able to convince her boss to see the situation the same way they did.

"Well, I explained to him that things have changed since the new corporate accounting laws were put into practice, and that I couldn't, in good conscience, sign off on the Danbury project. He forced me to admit that, yes, technically speaking, he wasn't breaking any laws—so in the end, it came down to my Christian convictions. We reached an impasse. He told me he would accept my resignation."

"You did the right thing," Mike said quietly.

"Yeah—well, it sure doesn't feel like it. This never would have happened if his father was still the CEO . . . but . . ." Kathleen stared through the windshield, her tears blurring the pink and red impatiens that lined the median strip. She drew another shaky breath, knowing that she had to stop crying long enough to drive home. "I guess I'd better call that corporate headhunting firm your friend used last year. It looks like I'll be needing another job."

"I think you should wait, Kath. Take some time off. Impost will give you a severance package, and you have some vacation time coming, don't you? Maybe it's better if Joelle isn't home alone all summer."

Kathleen had managed to push aside her problems with Joelle as she'd focused on her problems at work. But the pain of what her daughter had done suddenly sprang from hiding, like an intruder waiting behind a closed door, and hit Kathleen squarely in the gut.

"So, I get to be Joelle's prison warden from now on? Great. What are we supposed to do together all day? Shopping at the mall is out."

Mike didn't react to her sarcasm. "They were asking for volunteers at church last Sunday for vacation Bible school. Why don't you and Joelle—"

"Right. We're wonderful role models. I'm sure the other mothers would love to have me teaching their children when I can't even control my own."

Mike's long silence made her regret her bitter words. She was sorry for using him as an outlet for her anger and grief, but so very grateful that he was willing to listen. She heard him sigh.

"I know you're hurting, Kathleen, but don't take it out on Joelle."

"I'm sorry . . . but I'm just so scared for her! I'm afraid of what she'll become. . . ." The tears that she thought were under control started falling again.

"Hey, hey, listen to me. I'm worried, too, but she's hardly a career criminal."

Yet. Kathleen barely stopped herself from voicing the thought out loud.

"I talked to Al Lyons from my men's prayer group about Joelle this morning," Mike continued. "He works at the Christian Counseling Center and—"

"You didn't! I don't want everyone at church to know our business!" Kathleen was appalled. She knew that the body of Christ was supposed to offer help and consolation in times of trial and loss, but she would sooner die than share her needs and fears with her fellow church members. She was known as a mature believer, a woman who was strong and in control, a woman of unquestioning faith. It horrified her to think that people might learn what Joelle had done.

"Al is a professional," Mike said calmly. "He knows all about patient confidentiality. He thinks a few sessions with a therapist might help her, and I agree. He said they'd assign someone who isn't a family acquaintance. I already set up an appointment for her."

"Fine. If you think it will help."

"I'm sure it will." Mike sighed. "It'll be okay, Kathleen. Drive safely. I'll see you when I get home."

When Kathleen hung up, she felt as if she'd worked a full day of hard labor on a chain gang. She drove the familiar route home in a daze, wondering how Joelle would react to the news that Kathleen had lost her job at Impost—and that Joelle had an appointment with a shrink. What on earth would they do together all day? Joelle had long outgrown craft projects and trips to the children's museum.

Kathleen arrived home to find her daughter still in bed. In fact, she discovered over the next few days that she needn't have worried at all about what they would do together. Joelle rarely awoke before one-thirty in the afternoon, and after eating a bowl of cereal, she spent most of the day watching soap operas or sitting by the pool slathered in oil, talking to her friends on her cell phone. Kathleen began to wonder if Joelle had shoplifted out of sheer boredom. The thought was somehow comforting. Maybe her daughter wasn't a sociopath or a kleptomaniac after all.

Kathleen certainly wasn't going to stay in bed until one-thirty every day, but she had no idea what to do with all her free time, either. She returned to Impost and cleared out her office, read a novel she'd been wanting to finish, and then spent a few hours on her home computer doing a halfhearted job search on the Internet. The prospect of facing a job interview made her quickly decide that Mike was right: she should take some time off. She was much too depressed to act perky for a bunch of Donald Trump wannabes in a grueling series of job interviews.

It was almost a relief when Joelle's twice-weekly therapy sessions began, giving both of them a reason to get up and get dressed. Joelle's therapist, Dr. Marie Russo, was short and round with graying brown hair that she wore pulled back in an untidy bun. She wore sensible shoes and drab brown suits that looked as though they'd been purchased at a garage sale in some eastern European country. After Joelle's fourth visit, Dr. Russo called Kathleen into her office.

"I would like to spend part of our next session with you, Mrs. Seymour, instead of Joelle."

Kathleen stared. "Me! Why?"

"I think it would help if I got a sense of your family dynamics. Your daughter's behavior didn't occur in a vacuum."

"Right. The mother's always to blame," Kathleen said, only half-joking. "And here I was hoping it would turn out to be something simple, like peer pressure."

Dr. Russo didn't smile. She poked at her sagging hair to no effect. "I'll see you on Thursday, Mrs. Seymour."

When Kathleen woke up on Thursday morning, she immediately understood why Joelle had cried and argued and pleaded with Mike when he'd told her she would be going to a therapist. It was very disconcerting to think that a stranger might try to pry open doors that had been carefully locked and secured all these years—like a computer hacker cracking your secret codes and gaining access to your private files. She sat stiffly in the chair across from Dr. Russo, her feet flat on the floor, her palms sweating as she gripped the armrests. It wouldn't take an expert psychologist to interpret Kathleen's body language. Dr. Russo didn't waste any time coming to the point. She was the type of woman, Kathleen decided, who rips off bandages in a single jerk.

"Joelle tells me that the two of you never talk," the doctor began. She says she finds it very hard to communicate with you."

"Isn't that typical of teenagers?" Kathleen asked with a nervous laugh. The doctor didn't smile.

"When I asked her to describe you—to give me her perception of you as a person—she couldn't do it. She doesn't know who you really are when you aren't wearing the obvious hats of wife or successful businesswoman."

Kathleen couldn't reply. She had worked very hard to make sure that no one knew the real her. And the last thing she ever wanted to do was look too closely at herself.

"I can tell from your expression that Joelle's comments have upset you," Dr. Russo said, leaning forward slightly. "I think it would be helpful if you shared what you're thinking." When Kathleen still didn't reply, the doctor said, "I know this is your first session with me, but you can trust me, Mrs. Seymour."

Kathleen cleared her throat. "I'm sorry. But trust is a real big issue with me."

"Would you like to tell me why that is?"

She shook her head. She remembered reading in a self-help book that when a child's trust in her parents was breached at an early age, it made it difficult for her to trust anyone else—including God. But the reason for her lack of trust was a Pandora's box that she certainly wasn't going to open now. "I thought this was about Joelle, not me," Kathleen finally said. Dr. Russo didn't miss a beat.

"Would you say Joelle's assessment of your relationship is a fair one?"

"You mean, that we don't communicate very well? Yes, that's fair. I majored in mathematics and business administration in college. I'm a CPA with an MBA. I never was much good at all that touchy-feely kind of stuff or expressing my *inner feelings*."

But she wasn't a total failure at communicating, she wanted to add. She and Mike communicated very well and seldom argued. They had married when they were both in their mid-thirties, both comfortable with their single status and with the lives they lived apart from each other. Kathleen wasn't the sort of wife who needed a man to "complete" her or who demanded long, introspective talks about every issue. What business was it of hers what Mike was thinking or feeling every minute of the day?

"Joelle is a very sensitive young woman," Dr. Russo said, interrupting her thoughts. "She *wants* to express her feelings—to you, not just to her friends. But she needs to feel like you're giving something of your inner self in return. You see, she's trying to discover who she is, and part of that exploration includes the need to know where she came from—where her parents came from."

"Whoa!" Kathleen held up both hands. Alarm bells and warning sirens began to shrill in her mind like a four-alarm fire. She half-expected the sprinkler system to kick in, or for the secretary to burst through the door shouting "Call 9-1-1!" Kathleen wanted to bolt from the room and never return, but her concern for Joelle was stronger, deeper, than her fear. She still wasn't convinced that exposing her carefully hidden self would save Joelle from a life of crime, but she knew that she would face a raging inferno for her daughter's sake.

"Look, I'll be honest, Dr. Russo. I brought Joelle here because she was caught shoplifting. I don't understand how talking about my past is going to prevent her from doing it again."

"You're approaching this as if Joelle has a problem and you want me to 'fix' her so you can be a perfect family again."

"You're wrong. I've never had a perfect family. I wouldn't know what one looked like, much less how to live with one."

The doctor tucked back a loose strand of hair—and three more long, graying strands fell down in its place. Kathleen bit her lip, resisting the urge to say "For crying out loud, get it cut!"

"Well, to answer your question," Dr. Russo continued, "yes, I do believe that talking about your past will help Joelle. I believe that the shoplifting incident was a cry for your attention."

"I'm home with her all day now! She can talk to me for twelve hours straight if she wants to." Although Kathleen would never admit that the idea terrified her.

"I'd like both of you to come to our next session," Dr. Russo said calmly. "I'll provide a safe place for self-expression and act as a moderator as we work through some effective communication strategies."

Why did she make it sound like something much more complicated than a mother talking with her daughter?

Kathleen spent the next few days dreading the joint therapy session. When the time came, she sat facing Joelle with the same sweaty-palmed fear she'd felt when facing Dr. Russo alone. Kathleen might have been strapped into an electric chair, waiting for the first bolt of electricity to hit her.

Then it did.

Joelle pulled the balloon-covered invitation—now splattered with sweet-and-sour sauce—out of her purse and waved it at Kathleen. Did that thing have a boomerang attached to it? How did it keep returning from the trash can to haunt her?

"I found this in the garbage," Joelle said accusingly. "Why don't you ever talk about your family, Mom? Why don't I even know my aunt—" she glanced at the smudged writing—"my aunt Annie? Don't I have a right to know her or my own grandparents?"

"I want nothing to do with them, and they want nothing to do with me," Kathleen replied in a tight voice. "Believe me, you're better off not knowing them—not having them around as part of your life."

"Why?" Joelle glared at her, demanding an answer.

Kathleen turned to Dr. Russo, pleading silently for help. She couldn't do this. It was too upsetting. She longed to talk to the doctor alone, to explain everything to her without Joelle listening. But she also knew that if she sent her daughter away now, without an answer, it might be a mortal blow to their already shaky relationship. She gripped the armrests, hanging on for dear life.

"I made the decision to cut myself off from my family a long time ago," she finally replied. "It was in the interest of self-preservation."

"Your *sister* is giving a *party* for your *dad*," Joelle said dramatically. "How can you be so cold and unfeeling?"

The electric chair delivered a second jolt. "Is that what you think? That I'm cold and unfeeling?"

Joelle didn't reply. She didn't need to. She slumped back in her chair, staring at the ceiling to keep her tears from falling.

Dr. Russo finally intervened. "I think what Joelle is trying to express is that she sometimes finds it difficult to understand you or to feel close to you. Is that a fair assessment, Joelle?"

She nodded, swiping at a tear that had slipped past her defenses.

Kathleen exhaled. She was running out of ways to avoid the question. "I came from a terrible background," she said. "No one in my family was a Christian, and I am. That created a lot of tension. We have nothing in common with each other. I chose to walk away—and I've stayed away."

"But when you cut yourself off from your family," Dr. Russo said, "then you also severed a part of yourself. If you're a Christian, then you must understand the principles of forgiveness—"

"I *did* forgive my family," Kathleen interrupted. "A long time ago. But I've stayed away to avoid being hurt all over again. I had to establish safe boundaries and all of that."

"Boundaries are helpful as long as they're not an excuse to avoid issues of forgiveness. And as long as they're not at the expense of your own feelings."

"I've trained myself not to feel anything at all as far as my family is concerned—as if I never had a family. It was the only way I could get on with my life and start all over again." She turned to Joelle. "I'm sorry if that makes me appear cold and unfeeling. You must know that I . . . I love your father and you . . . very, very much."

Joelle didn't reply, wouldn't look up, and the icy distance between them terrified Kathleen.

Dr. Russo finally stepped into the silence. "Joelle, wasn't there another question you wanted to ask your mother?" Joelle shrugged and wiped her nose with a tissue. When she didn't reply, the doctor said, "Mrs. Seymour, Joelle wondered what your relationship with your own mother was like when you were Joelle's age."

"Terrible," Kathleen replied. "We fought constantly. About everything."

"How are things between you and your mother now?"

Kathleen's heart started to thump. It was as if the doctor was probing her wounds, inching closer and closer to the part of her that was broken and bruised. When she finally touched it, Kathleen knew there would be unbearable pain. She glanced frantically around the room, searching for an oil painting or a college diploma to focus on—anything to replace the image of her mother that was beginning to crystallize in her mind. "My mother is dead," she said softly.

"I'm sorry. Was there closure? Reconciliation before she died?"

Far from it. The last words Kathleen had ever spoken to her mother were angry ones—words that could never be taken back. The doctor was waiting for an answer.

"My mother died very . . . suddenly. Unexpectedly." Kathleen couldn't explain any further. "I don't see how this helps anybody."

Dr. Russo smiled. Kathleen supposed that she was trying to look sympathetic, but under the circumstances, with Kathleen's life unraveling all around her, the doctor looked like a disheveled Mrs. Santa Claus. "Maybe if you talked with Joelle about some of the difficulties you had with your own mother," she said in a kindergarten-teacher voice, "then Joelle would feel more connected to you."

"And see me as human, instead of cold and unfeeling? Tell me, when will it be my husband's turn to come in and have his past excavated?"

"Of course I'll want to talk with Mr. Seymour, too. All three of you together, in fact. I know that digging into the past can be painful, but I like to picture it as winding a broken strand of yarn backward to see where it leads. Once we understand what it was once a part of, we can begin to reweave it into a beautiful new pattern."

Who was this woman, Mr. Rogers in drag?

Kathleen had brought Mike into the conversation deliberately, hoping he would deflect some of the heat she was feeling. But once she was finally out of the doctor's office and off the hot seat, she began to wish that she had left Mike out of it. She knew exactly what he would say; they'd had this conversation before. Mike would tell her that she should try to make amends with her family before it was too late. He would remind her of the Scripture verse that said if you have a grudge against your brother you should go and be reconciled before you came to the Lord for forgiveness. He would ask her how she would feel if Joelle walked away from home, the way Kathleen had, and never came back.

Kathleen suddenly remembered the stupid invitation that wouldn't stay in the garbage pail where it belonged. Should she go to the party for her father? She certainly couldn't use her job as an excuse.

On the drive home, Kathleen stole glances at her daughter's perfect profile and shining corona of hair. Memories of her as a baby brought tears to Kathleen's eyes. Why had she never been able to convey her love to Joelle adequately? She longed to draw Joelle close and fasten her securely to her own heart, yet she was prevented from doing so by the terrible fear that she would let her down, destroy her trust . . . as her own trust had been so cruelly destroyed. She saw Joelle drifting away and ached to pull her back before it was too late. But how? If digging into her own past was the only way to save Joelle, then Kathleen decided she would do it. She pulled the car into the garage and turned off the ignition.

"Why are you looking at me like that?" Joelle asked when she noticed Kathleen staring at her. Kathleen cleared her throat, blinked away tears. Why was this so hard?

"I love you, Joelle."

"I know," she mumbled. They got out of the car and walked into the kitchen in silence.

"Could I have my invitation back, please?" Kathleen asked in a near whisper. "I'm going to do it. I'm going to go." Joelle wouldn't look at her as she handed it over. She fled upstairs to her room.

Kathleen picked up the phone before she had a chance to change her mind. If she called her sister in the daytime, maybe Annie would be at work and Kathleen wouldn't have to talk to her. She could leave a message on the answering machine. It upset her to realize that she wouldn't have known her sister's phone number if it hadn't been printed on the invitation.

Annie's phone rang four times . . . five times . . . *"You've reached Annie and Bob. Leave a message. . . ."*

Thank God.

Kathleen gripped the receiver. Her voice shook. "Hi, Annie, this is Kathleen. Yeah, I know, you're probably surprised to hear from me. Don't faint. . . . Anyway, I'm going to try to make it to the . . . um . . . get-together next week for Daddy." She couldn't call it a party. Wouldn't. "So . . . I guess I'll see you then? Bye." She carefully set the receiver on the kitchen counter as if it might jump up and bite her.

What in the world was she doing?

Chapter
3

The phone rang at 4:13 A.M., startling Kathleen awake. She felt the bed shake as Mike groped in the dark for the receiver, then heard him mumbling into it in a sleep-thickened voice: "Hello . . . Yes . . . Really. . . ? How far behind?"

Kathleen groaned and rolled over with her back to him. Mike's engineering firm did consulting work all over the world; wasn't anyone on his staff bright enough to figure out what time it was in America before calling him?

He hung up and climbed out of bed—a bad sign. She pulled the pillow over her head when she heard the water running in the shower. Then she remembered that she was leaving today to drive to New York for her sister's party and a wave of nausea washed through her. It had taken two hours and a sleeping pill for her to fall asleep the first time. She would never get back to sleep now. Kathleen still wasn't sure how this sacrifice—and there was no other word for it—would help Joelle. She only hoped that her daughter would see it as a gesture of love.

She was wide awake, staring at the ceiling, when Mike finished his shower. He tiptoed to his closet with a towel tied around his waist, drying his bristly hair with another towel. "Who was on the phone?" she asked.

"Our client in South Africa. I'm sorry he woke you. It looks like I'll have to fly over there."

She scrambled to sit up. "To South Africa? When?"

"Well, if I hurry I can catch a morning flight and be home again by the middle of next week."

"But . . . but I'm supposed to go to my sister's get-together this weekend. I'm leaving today, remember?"

"So?" He looked at her blankly. Was he that dense?

"I can't leave Joelle here all alone. And it's too late now to make other arrangements for her."

Even as she said the words, Kathleen felt relieved. Maybe she would be spared this ordeal after all. Maybe her willingness to go would be proof enough that she loved Joelle.

"Take her with you," Mike said. "She can meet your family."

"You've got to be kidding! *I* don't even want to be with those people—how can I inflict them on my daughter? I'm so ashamed to show her where I came from, how I lived, who my family is. . . ." Tears cut off her words. Mike sat on the bed in his wet towel and pulled her into his arms.

"Hey, hey . . . there's no reason for you to feel ashamed. Your past wasn't your fault. Maybe Joelle would cut you some slack if she knew about it."

"I don't want her pity—or anyone else's."

He sighed as he released her. "Do you want me to call the office back and cancel South Africa?"

"You would do that?"

He nodded—reluctantly—and she was stunned to realize that he loved her enough to change his plans for her. She saw how her own act of self-denial might send a similar message to Joelle.

"Thanks. But you'd better go. One of us needs to stay employed if we want to keep a roof over our heads."

He smiled, his hair sticking up like a punk rock star. "Will you at least consider taking Joelle with you before you call your sister and bow out?" he asked. "All those hours in the car would give you a lot of quality time together."

"Goody. Six hours of listening to Jessica Simpson CDs. I can hardly wait."

She woke Joelle at seven o'clock to invite her to come along, hoping that her daughter's enthusiasm for meeting her relatives would fade when she found out that it meant getting out of bed before noon.

"I'll go, but do we have to leave this early?" Joelle moaned.

"Yes. It's a long drive. Believe me, I'm not happy about going there, either," Kathleen told her. "But I want us to be—" What? The perfect family she never had? "I would really like you to come with me," she finished.

Joelle gave a faint, mischievous smile, one that Kathleen hadn't seen since she was a toddler. "What about my appointment with Dr. Russo?"

Kathleen felt a smile tugging at her mouth, too. "Dr. Russo can go analyze herself."

"Yes!" Joelle pumped her fist in the air and climbed out of bed.

Kathleen poured herself another cup of coffee while she waited, then quickly dumped it down the drain. Her nerves were already jumping around like a flea circus. She made a quick tour through the house, checking to make sure that everything was turned on or off that needed to be on or off. She called Dr. Russo's office to reschedule the appointment, studied the road map one last time, and dug out some loose change for tolls.

Joelle shook her head at the offer of breakfast, grabbing a granola bar and a cola instead. They finally climbed into the Lexus at ten minutes past eight.

"So how long is this trip gonna take?" Joelle asked when they were on the highway. All the lanes heading into the city were clogged with rush-hour traffic, but the congestion wasn't bad at all in the direction they were going, away from the city.

"I'm guessing six or seven hours," Kathleen said. "Depends on the traffic." They were nervous with each other, no doubt about it. In the past, Kathleen would have switched on the radio or put in a CD—anything to fill up the uncomfortable silence—but today she didn't.

"So, am I finally going to meet my grandmother and grandfather?" Joelle asked after awhile.

"My mother died when I was eighteen, right after I left home to go to college."

"Oh. Sorry. I forgot." Joelle's expression looked soft and childlike, as if imagining her own mother dying and feeling sad about it. "What about your father? Do you have any brothers and sisters besides Aunt Annie?"

Kathleen took a deep breath, letting the question about her father slide for the moment. "I have two brothers, JT and Poke, and —"

"Poke? What kind of a name is that?"

"His real name is Donald, like my father, but he was always a dawdler—a slow poke—so the nickname stuck. JT's real name is John Thomas, which sounds much too dignified, seeing as his favorite pastime was torturing insects and small animals. And Annie is my only sister."

"Are they older than you or younger?"

"I'm the oldest. I was four when Poke was born, six when JT was born, and eight when Annie was born." She glanced at Joelle and saw her smiling. "What?"

"I'll bet it was fun to have a baby sister. Like having a real-live baby doll to play with."

"You would think so. But Annie spent every waking minute of her life crying. It's a wonder she didn't grow up to be all leathery and dehydrated like that awful yuppie fruit leather your dad buys. Poke and JT were like the James Brothers reincarnated."

"Who are the James Brothers?"

"You know . . . Jesse James, the famous outlaw, and his brother Frank. My brothers probably drive motorcycles and are covered with tattoos and piercings by now. It'll be a miracle if they aren't incarcerated. They were always into some deviltry or other."

"Like what?"

She searched her memory for one of their more harmless escapades. "Well, there was the time they got tired of watching our sister, Annie, so they hog-tied her with the belt of my mother's bathrobe and stuffed her in a closet." Joelle's girlish giggles spurred Kathleen on. "And one time they got mad at the neighbor lady so they stuck the nozzle of her garden hose down her dryer vent and turned it on."

"Oh no!" Joelle laughed. "That's awful!"

"Yeah, they were well on the road to becoming criminals at a pretty young age, and—" She froze when she remembered Joelle's recent brush with the law. Joelle quickly turned away, as if studying the passing scenery, but her cheeks had turned pink. She and Kathleen had been doing so well, and now it was as if a door had slammed shut, and Kathleen didn't know how to open it again. She would welcome some help from frumpy Dr. Russo right about now, but the doctor wasn't here. Kathleen was about to turn on the radio in self-defense when Joelle broke the silence.

"Daddy told me you had a hard childhood."

"He did? What else did he say?" She felt as if she were sitting on a box of vipers, trying to keep the lid on and all the ugliness inside.

"He said it was up to you, not him, to tell me about it. But only if you wanted to. He said it was traumatic."

"Yeah—well, for one thing I grew up very poor. I spent my youth hunched over with my mousy brown hair hanging in my eyes, hoping no one would notice me. And you know those run-down slum houses you see in the movies with sagging roofs and rusting cars in the driveway and little kids running around outside half-naked, covered with filth?"

Joelle stared at her as if to see if she was joking.

"It's true. That's how I grew up. Of course, I didn't know we were poor when I was really young. But I clearly remember the day I first realized that we were. I was nine years old that summer. . . ."

Part

2

KATHLEEN

1959 — 1968

Chapter
4

The first rumblings of a summer thunderstorm sounded in the distance as a brand-new 1959 Cadillac pulled to a stop outside our house. The car was so shiny and important-looking that I scooped up my baby sister from the tumbledown porch where we'd been sitting and raced into the house, hollering, "Mommy! Mommy, come quick!"

There was no answer. I quickly searched the bungalow's two bedrooms, then ran outside to the backyard outhouse. The baby howled in my ear as I stood on tiptoe to peer through the crescent-moon window. "Mommy. . . ? Are you in there?"

"What do you want now, Kathleen? Can't you see I'm busy?" What I saw was my mother sitting on a broken kitchen chair, paging through the Montgomery Ward catalogue.

"Mommy, there's a fancy black car stopping out in front of our house—"

"Chariots of the bourgeoisie," she huffed in disgust. I had no idea what a "bourgeoisie" was, but from the tone of my mother's voice, she might have been talking about a breed of rodents. "Tell whoever it is I'm not home."

"You want me to *lie*, Mommy?"

"It's not a lie. I'm not home—I'm out here. Does this look like my home? Now go find out what they want."

Raindrops sprinkled my bare arms as I hurried back to the house, thunder grumbling in the distance. "Oh, shut *up*, Annie!" I told my wailing sister, "or I'll give you something to cry about!" She had smelly pants again and a slimy face.

By the time I returned to the house, the slender, blond woman who'd driven the car had already picked her way across the littered yard and was rapping on our screen door, calling, "Hello? Is anyone home?"

My two brothers, dressed only in dingy underpants, stared back at her through the torn screen. The woman looked as though she'd walked right out of the Ward's catalogue with her crisp, navy linen dress, high-heeled spectator pumps, and pillbox hat. I wished my mom was as pretty as she was. Mommy didn't seem to care about her appearance at all. She dressed in baggy cotton housedresses that zipped up the front, and she pulled her dark brown hair back in a ponytail. I set Annie on the floor beside Poke and JT, then stepped hesitantly toward the door.

"My mom isn't . . . here." The words felt like a lie. I found it hard to say them. "She's not here in the house with us, I mean."

"I'm Cynthia Hayworth. Will your mother be back soon, dear?"

I shrugged. A shrug wasn't a lie, was it? Besides, I really didn't know how long my mom would stay locked in the outhouse—her *sanctuary,* as she sometimes called it. I had no idea why she spent so much time in there. I certainly would never choose to stay inside that cobweb-y, spider-filled place one second longer than I had to—and even then only in an emergency, like when the indoor toilet was plugged.

"Well, I can just as easily leave the things with you, dear," the woman said. "I—"

The loud clap of thunder made both of us jump. Out in the street, the car door suddenly flew open and a pudgy little girl about the same age as me bolted for the house, ran up the sagging porch steps, and clung to her mother like macaroni to cheese. She wore pink shorts and a perfectly matched pink-flowered blouse. Even the bows in her pale blond hair and the lace around her ankle socks were pink.

"Why, May Elizabeth! You needn't be frightened," the woman soothed. "That's just the angels in heaven, rearranging their furniture again."

I had never heard that explanation for thunder before, but I liked it. I couldn't help smiling as I pictured white-robed angels with feathery wings, shoving sofas and chairs and TV sets across the bare wooden floors of heaven. Then my smile faded as the new little girl looked beyond me into the front room and said, "P-yew! What happened to your house?"

"Hush, May!" her mother chided.

"But it stinks, and the ceiling is all falling down, and—"

The woman touched her ruby-tipped fingers to May's lips to silence her, then turned to me again with a kind smile. "I brought some clothes and things I thought your family could use. If you and your brothers would like to come out to the car and help us carry them, maybe we can get everything inside before it starts to pour."

I couldn't imagine who this stranger was or what she was bringing us or why, but I gave my brother Poke a nudge and pulled him to his feet. "Come on, she needs your help. JT, you stay here with Annie. Make sure she doesn't crawl away."

The hard-packed dirt felt hot beneath my feet as I followed Mrs. Hayworth across the yard to the Cadillac, towing a reluctant Poke behind me. The girl in pink kept pace with me, whispering in my ear so Mrs. Hayworth wouldn't hear her.

"Did you just move into your house or something? Is that why you don't have any curtains or rugs?"

"No," I answered with a proud lift of my chin. "We just don't want any, that's all. We like our house the way it is."

"Come on, girls. Quickly!" Mrs. Hayworth called. "Run between the drops!"

I looked at her in surprise, then glanced up into the darkening skies. "But . . . but how can I do that? I can't see the raindrops coming."

Mrs. Hayworth smiled, tilting her head to one side as if she were watching a puppy. "Of course you can't, dear. It's just an expression." She opened the trunk of her car and handed me a paper grocery sack. "Here are some clothes that May Elizabeth has outgrown. You look as though you might be a size or two smaller than she is." She reached inside for another bag and handed it to Poke. "And here are some toys that my son, Ronnie, doesn't play with anymore. Do you think you can carry them, honey?"

Poke nodded solemnly as he accepted the bag, but I saw a sparkle of excitement in his eyes as he glimpsed a bright red fire truck sticking out of the top. He trotted across the lawn with the bag, his bare bottom peeking from his sagging underpants.

We all followed him, carrying more grocery sacks, but the car's huge trunk held still more treasures. I saw garden produce, boys' corduroy pants, and striped T-shirts, colorful sweaters and winter jackets, and a Barbie doll in a black-and-white bathing suit, with tiny high heels to match.

"Why can't I wait in the car?" May Elizabeth grumbled as we returned to the Cadillac for another load. "I'm getting wet!"

"No, dear. You won't melt," Mrs. Hayworth said.

I looked at May Elizabeth in horror, recalling the melting wicked witch in *The Wizard of Oz*. "What do you mean?" I asked. "Why would she melt?"

"What I mean," Mrs. Hayworth explained, "is that even though she's as sweet as sugar, she won't melt in water the way sugar does."

I loved the way this beautiful woman talked: *"Angels moving furniture . . . running between the drops . . . sweet enough to melt like sugar."* I couldn't imagine Mrs. Hayworth ever shouting things like "I've had about all I can take," the way my own mother did, or spending hours at a time seeking "sanctuary" in the outhouse.

Mrs. Hayworth handed her daughter a bag with tomatoes on top, then gave me the bag with the Barbie doll. Poke hadn't returned to help us. I could hear him in the house making siren noises as Annie shrieked and JT shouted, "Let me see it, let me see it!"

By the time we'd carried the last bag to the porch, the storm was nearly upon us. May Elizabeth sprinted back to the car, leaped in, and slammed the door closed. Mrs. Hayworth pulled a leaflet from her purse and handed it to me. There was a picture on it of the church we always passed when I walked with my brothers to the village park to play.

"Will you give this to your mother, please, dear? Tell her you're all welcome to visit Park Street Church any time. And we have Sunday school classes for you and your brothers, too. Would you like to attend with May Elizabeth some time?"

"Okay," I said. But I was pretty sure that my mother would never allow it.

"Well, I'd better run!" Mrs. Hayworth said as a flash of lightning lit the street. "Bye, bye, dear." She didn't really run, though. Instead, she glided back to her Cadillac like a movie star walking down a red carpet.

I dragged all the bags into the living room, then sat cross-legged on the floor to examine the clothes May Elizabeth had outgrown. I pulled out pretty plaid dresses for school with matching knee socks; shorts and blouse sets that matched; and even a blue-flowered nightgown, all carefully ironed and neatly folded. Everything had a sweet, flowery scent. I didn't realize I was crying until Poke suddenly asked, "What's wrong? Why are you crying?"

I didn't know why. I longed to run into my bedroom and try on all those beautiful new clothes—yet I hated myself for wanting them. I'd seen the way Mrs. Hayworth had looked at Poke and JT in their raggedy underwear, and I was old enough to recognize that look for what it was—pity.

I stood, suddenly angry, and scooped the clothing back into the bag. "Nothing's wrong!" I kicked the bag with my bare foot, knocking it over, then ran into the bedroom to hide my tears.

Chapter
5

The next time I saw May Elizabeth Hayworth was on the first day of school that fall. I liked school and I was always a good student. I even enjoyed the long walk to Riverside Elementary, crossing the bridge, hiking through the tiny downtown district and up the hill to the school. The modern one-story building had been constructed after the war to accommodate the baby boom, and it had a long central hallway and huge picture windows in each classroom that overlooked the grassy school grounds and play yards. I loved the way the halls smelled on the first day, like fresh paint and disinfectant. The linoleum floors were slippery-shiny, the desks freshly sanded and clean. They never stayed that way for very long.

After taking care of my siblings all summer, I was glad to be out of the house and away from them—although I did have to hold Poke's hand and walk him to his kindergarten classroom that fall. He walked agonizingly slow, too, looking all around at everything as if he'd just hatched from an egg that morning and had never seen the world before. His arms must have stretched two inches that first day from me pulling on them as I tugged him along. When we finally arrived, I pushed him through the door of the kindergarten room, then fled so I wouldn't have to watch Poke destroy the place.

My fourth-grade classroom was two-thirds of the way down the hall, and the handful of kids who had arrived before me were milling around, looking things over. I found a desk with my name taped to it—*Kathleen G.*—and slid into the seat, swiveling it back and forth a few times and opening and closing the hinged desktop to try it out. The lid squeaked. I liked the scary, haunted house sound of it so I did it a few more times. Then May Elizabeth Hayworth sailed into the room.

Even at the tender age of nine, she had already perfected the art of making a grand entrance. She waved her hand like Mamie Eisenhower and called out, "Hello-oo, I'm here-ere," as if we had been holding our breath, waiting for her to arrive. You would have thought she was Elvis Presley the way the other girls gathered around her. May and I had never been in the same class before, but the rest of the kids already knew that if a Hayworth was your classmate, you could expect a small truckload of treats at all the class parties. The Hayworths were the richest family in town. May's brother, Ron, who was two years older than May, ruled the playground the way Jimmy Hoffa ruled the Teamsters.

"So this is my room!" May said breathlessly. Her blond curls bounced as she looked all around. "I was hoping I'd be in Miss Powell's room across the hall. She's young and pretty and does the funnest things in her class. Oh, well. I'll just have to make the best of it, I guess."

She was flying high, talking nonstop, commanding attention. The other girls, who had been laughing and talking before May arrived, fell silent in awe. The boys practically bowed down to her. I was watching her performance from a distance, content to be a silent bystander, when, to my horror, May Elizabeth Hayworth suddenly singled me out.

"I know you," she said, pointing. "You're the girl we gave all our old clothes to, aren't you?"

I ducked my head inside my desk like a turtle trying to crawl inside its shell, clinging to the forlorn hope that no one had heard her. May walked closer, and I unconsciously curled my legs beneath the seat in an attempt to appear smaller—maybe even to disappear. No such luck.

"That dress used to be mine," she announced to the class. "I didn't want it anymore because it's ugly and I hate the color green. The knee socks used to be mine, too."

I felt my cheeks turn hot with embarrassment and anger. Each year since I'd started kindergarten, every kid in Riverside except me had arrived for the first day of school in a new outfit. This fall I finally had new clothes to wear—well, they were almost new—and that loudmouth May Elizabeth had to go and ruin everything. Nobody would have known that my dress was secondhand if she had kept her stupid mouth shut. Why did she have to go and spoil it?

"You can have this dress, too, when I'm tired of it," she said, pinching the fabric between two fingers, then flinging it away like Uncle Leonard flicking ash off his cigar.

I gritted my teeth, wishing she would move to China—or at least transfer to "fun" Miss Powell's class. But no, May found the desk with her name on it and plopped her plump bottom down in the seat right beside me. I would have crawled inside my desk and closed the lid, but I was afraid I would get stuck. It would only add to my humiliation if the Riverside Volunteer Fire Department had to be summoned to pry me out.

"Want to see my new school supplies?" May asked the throng of worshipers who had assembled around her. I glanced over as she opened a beautiful red-plaid schoolbag with leather trim and brass buckles. It was jammed full of new things: scissors, gum erasers, brightly colored number-two pencils, a flowered pencil case with a zipper, ruler, protractor and compass set, and a brand new box of crayons—the kind that came in sixty-four colors and had a crayon sharpener on the side. I loved to color, but I always had to use the school's crayons—dirty, broken bits of wax with the paper all torn off. They made my fingers feel grubby after I'd used them.

I watched May arrange her arsenal of supplies, noticing that her desktop opened silently, and I had to turn away as my cheeks turned from pink to green with envy. I lifted my own desktop, but all the fun had gone out of the squeak; it sounded old and broken to me now. I held it open with my head and quickly shoved my "new" pencil case—one of Uncle Leonard's used cigar boxes—deep inside where no one could see it.

Then our teacher marched through the door. "Good morning," she announced in her husky, smoker's voice. "I'm Mrs. Wayne." She was so tall and massive that generations of students before me had speculated that she was John Wayne's twin sister. She was certainly built like him. Older, wiser kids like Ron Hayworth whispered that she had begun life as the Duke's twin brother but had gone to Scandinavia for a sex-change operation like Christine Jorgensen.

Mrs. Wayne had a bosom the size of Mt. Everest, and it seemed to create a chronic problem with her brassiere straps. She spent hours of class time groping inside her blouse to haul the errant straps back into place on her shoulders. She made it look like such a tiresome chore—as hopeless as shoveling sand against the tide—that I was glad I wouldn't have to worry about such a complicated thing as a bra for a few more years. When I finally did get my first bra I always remembered Mrs. Wayne's troubles and was careful not to make any embarrassing adjustments in public. Of course, by that time smart women were burning their bras in protest—and I would have wagered that Mrs. Wayne was among the first to light a match to hers.

But I liked Mrs. Wayne in spite of her brassiere woes. She wasn't a warm, motherly person, but that was okay with me. She ran her classroom with equal justice for all, rich or poor, boy or girl, and she never failed to give praise where it was due. I would smile as I read the succinct notes she wrote on my papers—*Nice work, Excellent*—and in my mind I could hear her praising me in her gravelly man's voice.

The first morning of school passed quickly, with no more embarrassing announcements about my wardrobe from May Elizabeth, and at noon we filed down the hall to the cafeteria. May was rich enough to buy a meal ticket, good for an entire month of lunches from the school cafeteria. I went through the line to collect my free carton of milk, courtesy of the public assistance program, then sat down alone at an empty table in the corner. A moment later, May sank down beside me with a gray plastic tray of food: a gooey tomato and macaroni dish called "Roman Holiday," a dinner roll, red Jell-O made with fruit cocktail, and chocolate pudding with a button-sized dollop of whipped cream on top.

I kept my wrinkled paper lunch bag on my lap, busying myself with my carton of milk as May glanced over at me. I was ashamed to open my lunch in front of anyone, let alone a Hayworth. I'd made the sandwich myself with the only things I could find in the cupboard that morning—two leftover ends from a loaf of white bread and a layer of peanut butter from welfare, all wrapped up in a square of used tin foil. I ate with my head down, my sandwich concealed in my lap, taking furtive bites from it as May gobbled forkfuls of "Roman Holiday." When I finished, I carefully folded up the foil and the paper bag so I could use them again.

"Want this?" May suddenly asked, pointing to her chocolate pudding. "I'm full." She puffed out her cheeks as if struggling to hold back all that she had eaten. I gave an indifferent shrug, trying to disguise my yearning. I loved chocolate pudding. May stuck a spoon through the pudding's rubbery skin and slid the dish in front of me. "Here. My mother doesn't like it when I waste food. She says, 'Think of all the children in the world who are starving.'"

I ignored the implication that I was among the world's starving children, knowing full well that I probably was. I devoured the pudding, skin and all, then licked the bowl and spoon. I think it was May Elizabeth's lunchtime gesture of charity that made me decide to come to her rescue when Danny Reeves tried to bully her on the playground during recess.

Danny was a ruffian who should have been in junior high but had flunked a year or two. He roamed around our neighborhood of run-down houses like he owned the whole world, helping himself to whatever he wanted, whenever he wanted it. Anything that wasn't chained to someone's house, he considered his—and I wouldn't have been surprised if he carried bolt cutters in his back pocket, just in case. I'd stood up to him once before when he'd tried to snatch Poke's fire truck away from him, and I'd learned that Danny was really a coward at heart. I stood up to him this time, too, when he grabbed the chain of May's swing in midflight, nearly flinging her off.

"Time's up," Danny growled. "Get off." May was clearly frightened, not only because she'd nearly been thrown to the ground, but because Danny had a menacing, escaped-convict face, and a skinny, tough-dog stance, as if he ate barbed wire for breakfast and land mines for lunch. His favorite phrase was "You wanna make something of it?" In the hierarchy of the school playground, Danny stood a notch lower than May's brother, Ron, and I wondered if he'd decided to take out his frustration on Ron's pudgy sister in retaliation.

I strode over to face Danny head on. "You get out of here, Danny Reeves, and leave her alone. You're not the boss."

"You wanna make something of it?"

"Mrs. Wayne might want to. She's our teacher."

"So? Who cares," he sneered. But he sauntered away all the same, obviously aware of Mrs. Wayne's reputation for law and justice—not to mention her formidable size. I was shaking in my sneakers, but it was the good kind of shaking, the kind that comes from a rush of adrenaline, not fear. May gazed at me in awe.

"Wow! You *saved* my *life*!" she said in her overly dramatic way. "Thanks!"

"You're welcome." I walked away as she began pumping her legs again, trying to resume her lofty height. "Saving her life" might have been an overstatement, but I felt good about my actions just the same. To my mind, I had evened the score and erased the stigma of charity, making the hand-me-down clothes she had given me truly mine. I'd earned them. I'd stood up to Danny Reeves, of all people. I'd repaid the debt.

Later that afternoon, when Mrs. Wayne told us to choose a partner for an art project, May turned to me first and said, "I choose Kathleen G." I usually ended up paired with kids like Charlie Grout, who lived next door to us and was almost as poor as we were. Charlie had been the butt of everyone's jokes since first grade when he'd wolfed down half a jar of white paste before the teacher caught him. But I didn't have to be Charlie's partner today. The class queen had chosen me.

"My best friend used to be Suzanne Clark," May informed me, "but she moved to New Jersey last summer. You can be my new best friend."

I hesitated, not sure I wanted to be the runner-up. I felt like the girl in the Miss America pageant who has to stand beside the winner and watch her cry tears of joy as they put the crown on her head. Then I remembered my showdown with Danny Reeves, and I knew that May's offer of friendship wasn't based on charity; I'd earned it. I slid my desk across the aisle toward hers until they touched. We were partners.

"Does anyone need crayons?" Mrs. Wayne asked. She approached my desk waving a carton of broken-down crayons that might have been new when George Washington was president. Our town was small enough for Mrs. Wayne to know that I was one of the kids who always needed to borrow the school's crayons. She stopped beside me, holding the tattered box in one hand, groping for her bra strap with the other. This time May saved me.

"Here," she said, pulling her glorious, brand-new, sixty-four-count box of Crayola crayons from her desk. "You can share mine."

I decided it was going to be a wonderful year.

Being May Elizabeth Hayworth's new best friend created a chain reaction of problems that started as soon as my mother learned of our friendship. "Hayworth!" she grumbled, making the name sound like a curse word. "I don't want you associating with those stuck-up rich people. Stay away from her."

My uncle Leonard—president, founder, and sole member of the Tri-County Communist party—was especially gloomy in his analysis. "Just because the Hayworths own the factory, they think they own the entire town and everyone in it. Nothing good can come of this liaison, Kathleen. Whenever the proletariat tries to consort with the bourgeoisie, it's the poor working man that always ends up exploited. These arrangements always favor the rich and are always to their advantage. Do you see how this underscores the need for a society in which the resources are evenly distributed and shared rather than—"

"May Elizabeth shares her crayons with me," I said, rising to her defense. Uncle Leonard shook his head.

"I'm not impressed with such pseudo-generosity. In a true Communist society, the Hayworth girl would *give* the crayons away, dividing them equally among all the students."

I quickly did the arithmetic in my head: There were sixty-four crayons in the box and twenty-six kids in my class, which meant we would each get two-and-a-half crayons. I'd be no better off in Uncle Leonard's Communist society than I was using the school's box of broken pieces. No, I liked things just the way they were. I sat beside May Elizabeth in class and she shared all her school supplies with me—her new best friend. On the playground, I was her guardian, keeping bullies like Danny Reeves at bay.

When I brought home an invitation to May's birthday party in October, my mother was furious. "Absolutely not, Kathleen! You don't belong with those people."

Fortunately, my father was home from his wanderings for once, right when I needed him. He rushed to my rescue, like Superman saving Lois Lane. "Aw, they're just kids, Eleanor. Don't blame the Hayworth girl for her parents' shortcomings. Let them have their fun." He turned to me, grinning. "Do you want to go to her party, Kathy?"

I had never been to a birthday party in my life—not even my own, or my brothers' or sister's. Mommy might bake us a packaged cake if she remembered what day it was—and if she had enough powdered eggs on hand from welfare. I glanced at my mother and saw that she was fuming.

"Yes," I answered softly, hoping Mommy wouldn't hear me. "I want to go."

"Then go you shall!" Daddy laughed and swept me up in his freckled arms. I loved him. No one could hug me the way Daddy could. Whenever Mommy hugged me it was quick and efficient, not warm and lingering like Daddy's hugs. During those wonderful days when my father was home, I was Daddy's girl, his princess.

My daddy was the kindest, gentlest man in the whole world and as happy-go-lucky as a circus clown. He would get right down on the floor and play with the boys and me, and we'd tickle each other and laugh until the tears ran. Daddy never lost his temper or spanked us, even when the boys deserved it, even when Daddy had been drinking. And he treated my mom like she was the queen of the world. Too bad he was away more often than he was home.

When I was old enough to ask Mom about his long absences, she told me that he was a long-distance truck driver. Later she changed her story and said he was a traveling salesman. I never asked what Daddy trucked or sold. My melancholy, Communist uncle lived with us whenever Daddy was away, staying with us for months at a time, so at least there was a man around the house.

Uncle Leonard was Mom's older brother and Daddy's best friend. He was very tall and stoop-shouldered with a droopy, bloodhound face and Brylcreemed black hair. He slept on our living room couch and stored his clothing in boxes stuffed behind it. He had hundreds of books, piled in stacks in every room of our house. The boys used them like bricks to build forts. Uncle Leonard spent his evenings sitting at our chrome dining table, scribbling manifestos on yellow, legal-size note pads. The stacks of his Communist rantings left no place for us to sit down and eat, but that didn't matter; we never sat down for a meal anyway.

Our car belonged to Uncle Leonard and so did our TV, purchased secondhand, Mom said, so that he could watch the McCarthy hearings. He watched the news every night, and I'm sure our neighbors two blocks away could hear Uncle Leonard arguing with Walter Cronkite. I'd learned to accept my uncle and his billowing cigars as part of the furnishings, but he made me mad that day when he put in his two-cents' worth about May Elizabeth's birthday party.

"What about a present?" he asked. "A spoiled, bourgeois rich kid like her is going to expect a present—and a nice one, too."

Daddy's grin never wavered. "Then we'd better go shopping for one, right, Kathy?"

"Shopping!" Mom said with a huff. "You think the Hayworths are worth six more months, Donald?"

It seemed as though his smile faded slightly at her question, but he quickly recovered. "My Kathy is certainly worth it."

I had no idea what they were talking about, but a few days before the party, Daddy loaded Poke, JT, and me into Uncle Leonard's decaying 1950 Ford sedan and took us shopping. Not at Brinkley's Drugstore in downtown Riverside, mind you; we drove all the way to Bensenville to shop at Woolworth's. Daddy carried JT in his arms as we perused the aisles, looking for something May Elizabeth would like. He had Annie's misshapen diaper bag slung over his shoulder, which seemed a little odd seeing as Annie had stayed home and three-year-old JT didn't wear diapers. Besides, Daddy never would have volunteered to change a diaper even if JT had worn one. But there wasn't time to ask questions. I quickly became distracted by so many choices.

"I don't know what to buy her," I moaned.

"Well, you're her best friend," Daddy coached. "Just pick something you would like to have, and she's sure to like it, too."

There were lots of things I liked. Daddy watched me gaze at packages of hair barrettes, a magic slate that you could draw on then lift to erase, a plastic doll bottle that seemed to magically empty when you tilted it upside down, and so much more. Poke lingered near the Davy Crockett stuff: coonskin caps, rubber tomahawks, and plastic six-shooters with holsters. I finally decided on a box of Play-Doh in four different colors for May Elizabeth's present.

Once I'd made up my mind, Daddy led us to the nickel-and-dime counter and told us we could each have a quarter to spend. "I need to look at something for your mother," he said, setting JT down beside Poke and me. Daddy disappeared, leaving us to contemplate the colorful array of ten-cent toys.

There were so many to choose from! Of course my brothers wanted everything in sight. They didn't understand the value of a quarter and kept reaching their grubby fists into the bins and pulling out items as if Daddy had told them to buy one of each thing. I was exhausted from tugging toys out of their hands and telling them that all the plastic whistles and rubber soldiers and toy cars they were trying to stuff into their pockets cost more money than they were allowed, then listening to them scream in protest. The storeowner hovered close to the three of us, and I saw sweat form on his brow as he tried to make sure that everything the boys stuffed into their pockets made it out again.

Finally my father reappeared and took over, helping JT choose a rubber snake and Poke a plastic dagger. I had settled on a pop-bead necklace. Daddy lifted JT up on the counter while he paid for our treats and for a box of dusting powder that he had chosen for Mom. We were back in the car and on our way home before I realized that we had forgotten the very thing we'd come for: May Elizabeth's birthday present.

"Daddy, stop! We forgot the present! Go back! We have to go back!"

"I didn't forget it, honey," he said, laughing. "It's right here in the bag."

"Where? Which bag?" I peered over the front seat, searching frantically. The only thing in the Woolworth's bag was Mom's dusting powder. I didn't see a box of Play-Doh anywhere. "Where is it, Daddy? Where?"

"It's right here. . . ." Daddy slowed the car down a bit, driving with one hand while he fished Annie's diaper bag off the floor and set it on the seat. Sure enough, May Elizabeth's present was inside—and also the magic drawing slate and the plastic doll bottle that I'd admired, and a coonskin cap for each of the boys. I also saw a bottle of cologne for Mom to go with the dusting powder, and a shiny three-piece screwdriver set that I figured Daddy had bought for himself.

"Are all of these things for us?" I asked in surprise.

"You bet they are. Why should that Hayworth kid be the only one who gets presents?"

It felt like Christmas as I gave the boys their new hats and sat back to draw on my magic slate. The boys took turns annoying me with their furry raccoon tails. It wasn't until later that afternoon that I began to wonder exactly when Daddy had paid for all of those surprises. He hadn't put them on the counter when he'd stood in line at the cash register. And why had the clerk put everything in the diaper bag instead of in a Woolworth's bag? I could have used some extra bags for my lunches.

I got such a funny feeling in my stomach the more I thought about it, that I finally had to go think about something else.

Chapter
6

Compared to our house, the Hayworths lived in a mansion. Uncle Leonard drove me there on the day of May Elizabeth's party, and he started shaking his gloomy head as soon as he turned the car into her long, curving driveway. "Do you know how many proletariat apartments could be carved out of that bourgeois palace?" he asked.

I didn't wait for him to finish calculating. I gave the car door a slam—you had to or it wouldn't stay closed—and ran up the steps to ring the doorbell. The first thing I noticed when Mrs. Hayworth invited me inside was that everyone was dressed in fancy clothes. I felt bedraggled. The other girls all wore crinkly crinolines under their party dresses and ribbons in their Shirley Temple curls. My mousy brown hair hung in limp strands, and I was the only one wearing sneakers instead of patent leather shoes. My gift, wrapped in cheesy, dime-store paper, looked forlorn beside all the others trimmed with glitter and curling ribbons and shiny bows. Several times I noticed the adults looking at me, and I knew they were whispering about me behind their hands.

The food was wonderful. Mr. Hayworth cooked hot dogs on his

charcoal grill beside the swimming pool, and he let me eat as many as I wanted. I ate four, on squishy white buns with mustard, catsup, and relish. I ate potato salad that day for the first time in my life, and hard-boiled eggs that May said had been "deviled," and a heavenly treat she called ambrosia salad. There was a towering mold of Jell-O in striped layers and Pepsi-Cola to drink. The cake came from a bakery and had huge icing flowers on it and ten candles for May to blow out. She gave everyone a goody bag full of candy and a brand-new Hula-Hoop to take home as a present.

The house was very modern and clean, with thick carpets and a sunken living room with Danish-modern furniture. The only other house I'd ever been inside was Charley Grout's house, next door, so May's house seemed like something from a dream or a TV show. She had her own bedroom with a canopy bed, a fluffy comforter, hundreds of stuffed animals, dozens of dolls. Even her bathroom was all ruffly and clean, with a shining turquoise sink and toilet, and a mosaic-tile floor that was so spotless you could have eaten off it. I peeked under the princess doll that was sitting on the toilet tank and saw that she hid an extra roll of toilet paper beneath her ruffled skirt.

Later we played games like pin the tail on the donkey and musical chairs, but I didn't win any prizes. I walked around in a daze all afternoon, the way Poke always did, just trying to take everything in. The party seemed to speed by so quickly that the next thing I knew, Mrs. Hayworth was driving me home.

"Would you like to come to Sunday school tomorrow with May Elizabeth and our family?" she asked as her Cadillac glided to a halt in front of my house.

"I guess so. . . ." That was my standard reply whenever I felt shy and didn't know what else to say. Either that or "I don't know . . ."

"Why don't you ask your parents, okay? Sunday school starts at nine-thirty. We'll wait for you out front. You know where Park Street Church is, don't you, honey?"

"Uh huh." Mommy and Uncle Leonard would say that religion was a crutch for the weak-minded masses, but I really wanted to go. I wanted to be anywhere but home. "Thank you for inviting me to the party," I remembered to say as I climbed from the car.

"You're very welcome, honey. I hope you'll come and visit us again."

There is always a natural letdown whenever you return home from a party, but what I felt that afternoon when I walked up our sagging porch steps was much, much worse. I saw my house with new eyes and noticed for the first time how foul it smelled—like dirty diapers and too many cats. Our living room floors were made of bare plywood; the linoleum in the kitchen was stained and torn; the bathroom floor was rotting beneath our leaky toilet. All of our furniture sagged and reeked, and the picture on our black-and-white TV skipped so badly that you had to nod your head up and down like those dolls that ride in the rear windows of cars as you tried to watch a program. Our bedrooms didn't even have beds, just mattresses on the floor. All four of us kids slept in the same room, Poke and JT on one mattress, Annie and me on the other.

When I walked through the front door that afternoon, Daddy lay sprawled on the couch, nodding his way through a World Series baseball game. He had the volume turned way up so he could hear it above the sound of Annie's wailing. "How was the party?" he asked.

"Good."

"Good? That's all—just 'good'? Did she like the present we got her?"

"Yeah, I guess so. I had fun," I said without enthusiasm. "Look at all the stuff she gave me."

I had the Hula-Hoop slung around my neck, and I was holding the goody bag high above my head to keep it away from my brothers. They could smell candy the way sharks scented blood, and they had moved in quickly for the kill, circling around me. I wished I had a secret hiding place where I could stash it. The boys were forever taking my stuff and ruining it. They'd already busted open my doll bottle to see how it worked and ripped the cellophane off my magic drawing slate so they could stick it on the TV screen and scribble over their favorite cartoons. My dolls had suffered so much abuse from Poke and JT that Betsy Wetsy looked more like a disaster victim than a baby. Barbie had barely survived her lobotomy before being scalped. If I didn't eat all of my goody-bag candy before sundown today, I could kiss it good-bye.

"I'll bet the Hayworths have a big house, huh?" Daddy asked. "And lots of fancy things, like a color TV?"

"Yeah. It's really nice." I sat down beside him on the couch, stuffing candy in my cheeks like a squirrel. He chased Poke and JT away and started asking me a lot more questions about the Hayworth home, ending with the unfathomable one: "Do they have a dog?"

I didn't want to think about their house anymore, but Daddy seemed to be the only person who was interested in hearing about the party, so I snuggled up beside him, sharing all the details. I even dared to ask him if I could go to Sunday school with May Elizabeth and her family tomorrow.

"So they're religious people, are they?" Daddy asked. "What church do they belong to? Do they all go, even Mr. Hayworth? Every Sunday? What time?"

He sounded so interested that I wondered if he wanted to come, too. His smile grew broader and broader as I answered all his questions. Then he hugged me and said, "Sure, honey. I think it would be a wonderful idea for you to go to Sunday school." He turned off the TV and hurried next door to borrow the neighbors' telephone. We didn't have a phone because Uncle Leonard didn't want the FBI listening in on his conversations.

I felt weary from all the excitement of the party and nauseated from eating so much candy. I went to my room, still clutching my Hula-Hoop, wondering where on earth I could hide it. But when I saw my musty-smelling mattress that never seemed to have a sheet and remembered May Elizabeth's puffy, canopied bed, I ran outside to the backyard and cried.

I walked to Park Street Church by myself the next day and stood out front for a long time watching for the Hayworth's Cadillac. "Kathleen, you came," May's mother said when she spotted me. She sounded overjoyed. May Elizabeth seemed less than pleased as she looked me up and down. Her mother took my hand and led me inside as if I were part of the family. Sunday school was about to start.

Students from all grades met in a group in the church basement. We sang songs with a lot of hand motions, and the kids tossed quarters and dimes into an offering basket. When it was time to divide into smaller groups for our lesson, the room dissolved into chaos as kids scraped chairs across the cement floor and the teachers unfolded screens to make partitions.

"We're in a class with the fourth through sixth graders," May told me above the din. "We meet upstairs in the sanctuary."

I stared at her, dumbfounded. I thought of my mom's sanctuary and knew I must have misunderstood. "What? The *sanctuary*?"

"Yeah," she nodded. "Upstairs."

I pictured everyone crowding inside a smelly old outhouse behind the church, and I backed away. "There's no way I'm sitting in a sanctuary!" I said as I bolted toward the door. May ran after me.

"Wait . . . wait . . . where are you going?"

"Sanctuaries smell horrible, and they have spiders and flies."

"What are you talking about? There aren't any spiders. And it smells real nice. Come and see."

I remembered how different my house was from May's, and I thought maybe the rich people's sanctuaries were nicer, too. I let her lead me upstairs. The church sanctuary was beautiful, with stained-glass windows and polished wood pews. It smelled like flowers and candle wax. I didn't see any spiders—or any holes to pee in, either. But I was still confused by the word "sanctuary," and for years I thought God had a pretty nice outhouse.

The lesson that first morning was about Jesus and the lepers. At first I thought the teacher was saying "leopards," and I wondered how anyone dared leave home in Jesus' day with packs of wild cats wandering around. Then the teacher explained that lepers were people who had a terrible disease that made their body parts turn rotten and fall off. This gruesome piece of news delighted all of the boys, and Ron Hayworth started to sing: "Leprosy is crawling all over me. . . . There goes my eyeball into my highball. . . ."

The white-haired teacher, Miss Trimble, had to repeat, "Boys . . . boys . . ." over and over in her shaky voice until order was finally restored. When I learned about the fruit of the Spirit a few years later, I decided that Miss Trimble must have had patience the size of a watermelon.

When she finally managed to quiet everyone down, she explained that the disease was contagious and anyone who touched a leper was very likely to start losing a thumb or a nose, too. To avoid this disaster, the lepers had to stand at a distance and shout "Unclean . . . unclean!" so people would know to stay away from them.

"But Jesus walked right up to those lepers and touched them," Miss Trimble told us happily. Ron and the other boys fell silent momentarily, impressed with Jesus' courage. Then the teacher told us that not only did all of Jesus' fingers and toes stay where they belonged, but the leprosy magically disappeared from the lepers' bodies when He touched them, just like the pictures on my magic drawing slate disappeared when I lifted the plastic.

I didn't understand all the deep, spiritual principles the teacher was trying to make that first day, but I certainly understood that there were two very different classes of people involved—lepers and non-lepers. Uncle Leonard had drilled the truth about class distinctions into me ever since I was as small as Annie, and I knew that the ruling elite always picked on the underdogs—the lepers. When I looked at the Sunday school lesson in those terms, I liked Jesus. He was for the little guy—sort of a kindly, magical union negotiator.

The teacher gave each of us a colorful, eight-page newspaper to take home and reminded us not to forget our memory verse for next week. Then she prayed for us in her shaky voice and dismissed us. The moment she did, the boys turned their newspapers into airplanes and held a contest to see who could land theirs on the organ pipes first. May Elizabeth and I went out into the hallway, where Mr. and Mrs. Hayworth were waiting for us.

"Would you like to stay and go to church with us, Kathleen?" she asked.

The hallway and sanctuary were filling up with families, and I could see that, once again, I wasn't dressed like everyone else. For one thing, every girl in sight had on black patent leather shoes shined with Vaseline, and I had on sneakers without any socks because I hadn't been able to find any clean ones that morning. The ladies and girls all wore hats and white gloves, including May Elizabeth and her mother. It seemed to be required attire. One family with three daughters was wearing hats that resembled a set of dishes: the mother wore the dinner plate, the oldest daughter the soup bowl, the middle one the salad plate, and the youngest one the tea cup.

"No, thank you," I mumbled. "I have to go home."

"Are you sure?" Mrs. Hayworth asked, smiling. "We'd love to have you." I shook my head and shuffled toward the door. "Maybe you can worship with us next week," she called after me as I hurried away.

I spent all afternoon searching for a place to store my Sunday school paper where the boys wouldn't wreck it. I wanted to learn the memory verse for next week so I could win a prize. I could think of only one place to hide it where the boys would never go: Mom's sanctuary. Somehow, it seemed appropriate.

On Monday morning May Elizabeth burst into our classroom with shocking news. "Our house got broken into yesterday!" she told us breathlessly. "The thieves stole Ron's transistor radio and his reel-to-reel tape recorder and Daddy's new color TV and some money and a couple of kitchen appliances and a whole bunch of Mommy's jewelry and her fur coat. . . ." She paused to gulp another breath. "They even took the liquor bottles right out of Daddy's cabinet!"

We stared at her in slack-mouthed horror. This was just like a TV show. If only Perry Mason or the cops from *Dragnet* were around to solve this terrible crime. We all felt bad for her family's losses, but I could tell that May Elizabeth was reveling in the drama of it all.

"They broke in while we were at *church*!" she huffed, as if that was the lowest blow of all. She had everyone's attention as she finished with, "Daddy says we're going to get a watchdog!"

Suddenly I had the same funny feeling in my stomach that I had on the day we went shopping for May's birthday present. I couldn't help wondering about my daddy's detailed questions after the party and why he had particularly asked about a dog. I wanted to talk to him about it so that the funny feeling would go away, but when I got home from school that afternoon Daddy wasn't there.

"He left for work yesterday while you were at church," Mommy said. "He'll be on the road all week. Why?"

"I just wondered . . . never mind." I felt scared and angry at the same time, and I didn't know why. I went into our bedroom to try to think things through and discovered that my Hula-Hoop was gone. I heard my brothers laughing maliciously in the backyard, and I ran outside.

"Stop! Give that back!" I yelled. "You'll break it!" The boys had tied my Hula-Hoop to a tree branch with a piece of rope and were about to use it as a swing. I raced across the yard but was too late. The hoop snapped in two beneath Poke's weight, and he tumbled to the ground on top of JT. I walked away in tears, hoping the collision had broken both of their necks.

That Halloween, May Elizabeth invited me to go trick-or-treating in her neighborhood. The rich people on her side of town actually gave out treats; our side of town was better known for its tricks.

"You can go with her," Mommy said, "but you have to take Poke and JT."

"Mommy, no!" I wailed. "I won't have any fun if I have to drag them all over town with me."

"Well, someone has to take them. They're too little to go trick-or-treating by themselves."

"Can't you or Daddy or Uncle Leonard take them?" I didn't think it would require much make-up to dress up my uncle as Frankenstein.

"Fine," Mom said in a voice that told me it wasn't. "Your brothers don't have to go trick-or-treating this year. But you'll have to share all your candy with them when you get home."

I took the boys.

May Elizabeth dressed up as a fairy princess in a long, glittery gown with feathery wings on her back. She wore a rhinestone tiara on her golden curls and carried a magic wand with silver streamers. Mommy said that the boys and I could dress up as hobos, but I didn't see a whole lot of difference between our costumes and the way we usually dressed. Poke and JT didn't care about costumes, anyway—they were after the free candy. They each carried a paper bag to collect their loot, but they walked up and down the streets eating the candy as fast as people handed it to them, scattering a trail of Milky Way and Tootsie Roll wrappers behind them like dead leaves. JT had three lollipops sticking out of his mouth at the same time. They gorged themselves until their faces turned green.

We saved May Elizabeth's house for last because her mother was going to give us hot cocoa and a ride home. We rang the doorbell as if it was any other house, and May and I stood giggling on the doorstep as we waited for our treats. Poke was suspiciously tranquil.

"Trick or treat!" we chorused when Mrs. Hayworth opened the door.

"Oh, my! Who do we have here?" she asked. She was pretending to be surprised, but a moment later her expression changed to genuine shock as Poke leaned inside the doorway and threw up on her gold shag carpeting. JT, who mimicked everything Poke did, promptly threw up alongside him. May Elizabeth screamed.

I closed my eyes, wishing May could wave her magic fairy princess wand and make me disappear.

Chapter
7

Did you write up your list for Santa, yet?" May Elizabeth asked a few days before Christmas vacation. Nearly four months had passed since school had started, and amazing as it seemed, we were still best friends.

"No . . . not yet," I mumbled. She must have noticed that I quickly ducked my head, and she knew me well enough by then to know that I was avoiding the question.

"What's wrong, Kathy?"

"Santa Claus doesn't come to our house." I gave what I hoped was an indifferent shrug so she'd know I wasn't asking for pity. "Uncle Leonard called him a fraud and the creation of greedy capitalists, so I think Santa's mad at us."

"Santa doesn't get mad, silly. He only cares if you've been naughty or nice."

"Yeah, well, my brothers were born naughty," I said hopelessly. "They would have set the hospital nursery on fire if they could have gotten their tiny little fingers on some matches. The word *nice* isn't in their vocabulary."

"But you're nice, Kathleen."

I shook my head. Santa seemed to avoid our whole neighborhood every Christmas. I had always figured that there weren't enough "nice" kids on the block for him to put his sleigh and reindeer at risk. Danny Reeves would have climbed up on the roof of the house as soon as Santa's back was turned and hijacked his bag of toys. And Charlie Grout would probably make reindeer burgers out of Dasher and Dancer.

"Well, you never know . . ." she said, giving me her dimpled smile. "Maybe he'll come this year."

I wasn't holding my breath.

I had been attending Sunday school regularly with May, and I decided to go to the Christmas program with her on the Sunday night before Christmas. She played baby Jesus' mother, Mary, in the pageant—a wonderfully poignant and dramatic performance. When the innkeeper turned her away, sending her to the stable to sleep, May got so carried away with her role that she wept real tears and asked, "Can't we even come in for a drink of water?"

The innkeeper wasn't the experienced performer that May Elizabeth was; he shook his head and said, "No! That isn't in the script."

May was outraged. "You'd better not get leprosy," she yelled, "because I'll tell Jesus not to cure you!"

I wasn't very familiar with the original version of the story, so I thought the altercation was quite gripping. The rest of the audience found it hilarious.

After the program, the Sunday school superintendent passed out candy and oranges to all the kids, and Miss Trimble gave everyone in our class a present. Mine was a necklace with a little gold cross on it. I couldn't seem to keep the tears out of my eyes when I thanked her for it, especially when she patted my hand and said, "Jesus loves you, Kathleen." Her eyes looked a little watery, too, but it might have been because she was old.

The church looked so pretty with all the decorations and colored lights that I made up my mind to ask Daddy if we could buy a Christmas tree for once. I sat down beside him on the couch when I got home from the pageant, and he got very quiet when I showed him my new necklace. May Elizabeth had helped me put it on, and I'd already decided that I would never, ever take it off.

"That's real pretty," Daddy said. "Looks like good quality, too. It shouldn't turn your neck green." His words were meant to reassure me, but I was so alarmed at the thought of my neck turning as green as a Martian's that I almost forgot what I wanted to ask him.

"Can we get a Christmas tree this year, Daddy?"

He sighed. "A tree is only half the problem. We'd need lights and decorations and all that malarkey . . . and then people might expect to find some presents underneath it, too. No, we don't have that kind of money, Kathy. Things are pretty tight, right now."

I was disappointed but not surprised. If we did get a tree, Poke and JT would probably demolish it faster than you could say "Kris Kringle." And what good was a tree without any presents? But later that night, after Daddy and Uncle Leonard had polished off a six-pack of beer, he suddenly changed his mind.

"Get your coat on, Kathleen. I think I know where I can get a tree—and lights."

We jumped into my uncle's car, and Daddy let me sit up front with him. Our crummy neighborhood looked festive with a handful of Christmas lights twinkling and all the trash and junked cars buried under a layer of snow. We took the road to Bensenville for a ways, then turned off on a side road and headed out to the country where the farms were. As the houses and barns got farther and farther apart, Daddy slowed the car and turned off his headlights. My stomach began to make sickening little flips as we drove another mile in the dark.

"What do you think of that one?" Daddy suddenly asked, pointing to a little pine tree at the end of a farmer's driveway.

He had lowered his voice to a near whisper, so I answered in a hushed voice, "Isn't that someone's front yard?"

"That tree has a nice shape to it, don't you think? And see? It even has lights." He pulled the car to a halt beside it and left the engine running.

"I don't think those people will like us taking their tree, Daddy. . . ."

"Shh . . . Let's listen a minute and see if they have a dog." He opened the car door and stepped out, scanning the quiet farmyard, listening. "All clear," he whispered. "Come on."

He pulled an axe and a saw out of the trunk and motioned for me to follow him. I didn't know what to do. Getting a Christmas tree had been my idea, so I could hardly back out now. Even so, I was pretty sure that whoever had decorated the row of trees and bushes at the end of this driveway had never intended for people to come along and chop one down. But I couldn't disobey my father, could I?

I zipped up my coat all the way to my chin and tried to scrunch down inside it as I stepped from the car. The words to "Silent Night" kept playing over and over in my mind as I tried to summon the peace and contentment I'd felt in church earlier that night: *All is calm . . . all is bright. . . .*

"Stick your hand through the branches, Kathy, and hang on to the trunk for me. Like this . . ." Neither of us wore gloves, and the pine needles pricked me like pins as Daddy guided my hands through the branches and showed me where to hang on. The trunk felt cold and sticky. "Try to hold it steady, honey. This should only take a minute."

Daddy crouched down and started chopping away at the trunk of the tree. I wanted to burrow into a snowbank and hide. I kept my eyes glued to the farmhouse at the end of the driveway, waiting for the front door to burst open and a shotgun-wielding farmer to run out with his pack of snarling Dobermans.

. . . *Sleep in heavenly peace. . . .* Why had I ever mentioned a Christmas tree?

"We've almost got it now," Daddy said cheerfully. "Hang on tight." The trunk vibrated beneath my hands as he switched from the axe to the saw. My toes were starting to go numb.

Hur-ry up, I silently sang to the tune of "Silent Night." *Please, hurry up. . . .* I was afraid I might wet my pants.

"Wait!" Daddy said at the last minute, "the lights are still plugged in." He crawled around searching for the extension cords, and the lights abruptly blinked off—not only the lights on our tree but on all the trees and bushes to the left of it.

"Oops!" Daddy said, stifling a laugh. "Guess we'd better hurry!"

I wished he would stop saying "we."

Daddy sawed as if he were in a race with Paul Bunyan, and suddenly the tree started to fall over, pulling me with it. "Daddy, help!" I squeaked. He grabbed hold of it just in time, saving the tree and me from crashing to the ground. He started to laugh, and it was such a rollicking, joyful sound that I couldn't help giggling along with him. My laughter verged on the hysterical side at first, but once we'd finished stuffing the tree into the trunk of the car and had roared off down the road, I felt genuinely happy. We had a Christmas tree! With lights!

We were flying high, and my wonderful, happy-go-lucky daddy began to sing: "Dashing through the snow, in a one horse open sleigh. . . ."

I joined him on the chorus and we roared into Riverside with a Christmas tree bouncing in our trunk, singing at the top of our lungs: "Jingle bells, jingle bells . . . jingle all the way. . . ." We were still laughing and singing as Daddy carried his prize up the porch steps, and we crammed it through the front door.

"Merry Christmas!" Daddy crowed. He set the tree trunk down on the floor with a triumphant thump. Poke and JT started dancing around the tree like two little pagans. The commotion set Annie wailing.

"It's covered with snow, Donald!" Mommy said. "You're getting the floor all wet." As if that would be a disaster in *our* house.

"How are you going to keep it up without a tree stand?" Uncle Leonard asked. "Or are you planning to stand there until Christmas is over?"

"It even came with lights," Daddy said with a grin. "Plug them in, Kathy. Show everybody how nice it looks."

I got down on all fours and groped around for the plug, then crawled over to the wall socket. It was already overflowing with wires and plugs and extension cords, and I hoped we wouldn't blow a fuse. That was a regular occurrence at our house. I unplugged a floor lamp, just to be on the safe side, and a moment later our glorious tree sprang to life.

"Ta-da!" Daddy sang.

"The capitalists at the power company will be delighted," Uncle Leonard said. "That's why they invented this pseudo-holiday."

I refused to let my uncle spoil this great moment. "Christmas is Jesus' birthday," I told him.

"Then he must be a capitalist, too."

Eventually, Daddy got tired of holding up the tree, and he and my uncle rigged a stand out of scrap lumber. It looked as dilapidated as everything else in our house, but at least we had a Christmas tree. It seemed like a miracle.

On Christmas Eve, an even bigger miracle happened. I was lying in bed, trying to fall asleep, when I heard someone knocking on our front door. My heart began to pound. If Santa Claus did decide to venture into our neighborhood, he would have to use the front door since we didn't have a fireplace. I heard voices, and I crept out to the hall for a peek. It wasn't Santa, but the man in our doorway was carrying an armload of brightly wrapped presents. I wondered if he was Santa's bodyguard. Then I recognized the second man—the Sunday school superintendent—and he had an armful of presents, too.

"What's all this?" Uncle Leonard asked. He had been getting ready for bed and had answered the door in his undershirt and boxers.

"Some presents for your children," the superintendent said. "Merry Christmas!" The two men piled their packages beneath our stolen tree and left as quickly as they had come. I was so overwhelmed that I didn't know whether to laugh or cry. I had to pinch myself the way they do in stories to see if I was dreaming.

When I finally crept back to bed, Uncle Leonard was still standing in front of the tree in his boxer shorts, slowly shaking his head.

Spring brought flowers—and another stomach-churning crisis. The entire school had to undergo a head-lice inspection. Mrs. Wayne made everybody in our class line up and walk down to the nurse's office in a single file. The nurse wore rubber gloves as she examined us one by one. When she lifted the hair on the nape of my neck with a wooden tongue depressor, I heard her gasp.

"Look here," she told the high school girl from the Future Nurses' Club who had volunteered to help. "Those are *nits!*"

The future nurse leaped backward so fast that she tripped over the scale and brought it crashing to the floor with a loud clang. Charlie Grout, who stood in line behind me yelled, "Kathy has cooties!" and Mrs. Wayne's orderly line dissolved in chaos. The boys hooted with laughter and the girls shrieked in fear as if the Russians were attacking us.

I was hustled home from school, thoroughly humiliated. They sent my brother Poke home with me. We slept in the same room and used the same comb and brush, so naturally we all got the same lice infestation. We were a perfect example of an equitable society with a free distribution of goods, just like Uncle Leonard wanted. Even Annie had lice in her matted snarl of hair.

Mommy gave the boys crew cuts, which solved their problems. I'd always worn my hair long, but she had to cut it all off and throw it into the burning can along with our comb and brush. When I glanced in the mirror, my hair looked as though Mommy had plopped a mixing bowl on my head and trimmed around it. Afterwards she scrubbed me down with a special shampoo that smelled terrible and burned like fire. It was powerful stuff. Then she wrapped what was left of my hair inside one of our threadbare towels for fifteen minutes to make sure all of the nits died. I'd seen photographs of the devastation that followed a nuclear explosion, and I was certain that my poor head would remain bald for the next fifty or sixty years from the fallout.

When the school officials finally allowed me to come back—following a preliminary inspection in the nurse's office, of course—I learned that I had been rechristened. "Cootie Kathy . . . Cootie Kathy," the boys chanted on the playground. The girls ran from me whenever I got too close, squealing, "Watch out! You'll catch Kathy's cooties!"

Nobody wanted me on her team in gym class. Anybody who had to stand in line next to me was careful to leave a wide buffer of uncontaminated space between us. All the kids who sat in neighboring desks scooted them away from mine until I looked like the sole survivor on a deserted island. I thought of Miss Trimble's Sunday school lesson on lepers and wondered if I would have to shout, "Unclean!" for the rest of my life. Even May Elizabeth kept me at arm's length.

"What's it like to have cooties?" she asked, her eyes wide with fascination. "Can you feel them crawling around on your head?"

I walked away from her.

As I headed home from school at the end of that terrible week, May's mother pulled her Cadillac to a stop alongside me and rolled down the window. "Kathleen, hop in a minute. I have something for you." She gestured to the place beside her on the front seat. May Elizabeth sat safely huddled in the back.

I climbed in, careful not to let my head touch the car in case I still had a nit or two hiding in the stubble waiting to hop out and contaminate someone.

"Kathleen, honey, I heard that some of the other kids have been teasing you about having lice, and I wanted to tell you not to listen to them. You don't need to feel ashamed about something that wasn't your fault."

I stared at my lap, nodding, unsure what to say.

"Here, this is for you. . . ." Mrs. Hayworth said. She handed me a Macy's bag. Inside were two brand-new packages of barrettes and a little gift box with three bottles of pink liquid: one was shampoo, one was cologne, and one was hand lotion. They all smelled like strawberries. I gazed up at her, too moved to speak.

"You have beautiful hair," Mrs. Hayworth told me, and she reached out to touch it, her bejeweled fingers gently caressing my head. A tear slipped down my cheek.

I knew how the lepers felt when Jesus touched them and made them whole again.

Chapter
8

Once school got out for the summer, I didn't see May Elizabeth again until the fall. Her family went on vacations to exciting places every year and also spent time at their cottage on the Finger Lakes. And, of course, May and Ron spent a week or two at summer camp. I had to stay home and try to keep my brothers from killing themselves, each other, or the neighbor kids.

That was the summer Poke and JT convinced Charlie Grout's little brother, Larry, that he was Superman and got him to fly off the roof of his house. Luckily, Larry survived with only a broken leg. And my brothers' feud with Mrs. Garvey began that year, too. Poke and JT, who were always hungry, stole produce out her garden and fruit off her trees as fast as it ripened. The resulting enmity rivaled the legendary battle between Peter Rabbit and Farmer McGregor—although I don't think Mrs. Garvey would have actually baked them into a pie. When Mrs. Garvey called them "stinking little thieves" and chased after them with a hoe, they decided to get even by sticking the nozzle of her garden hose down her dryer vent and turning it on.

When they weren't tormenting Mrs. Garvey or trying to kill Larry Grout, my brothers were busy setting things on fire. I couldn't take my eyes off of them for one minute. They could burn down someone's shed in the time it took me to run inside and use the bathroom. They also took great delight in hiding aerosol cans in the neighbors' burning barrels and waiting for the explosions. Most kids loved summer vacation and hated returning to school, but I was just the opposite. I couldn't wait for school to start again.

I was thrilled to discover that May and I were in the same fifth-grade class that fall, with Mr. Standish as our teacher. Once again, May chose me as her best friend, but this time it was because she was flunking mathematics and needed my help.

I loved numbers. They were so neat and precise and easy to control, while the rest of my life was always in chaos: I never knew when we would eat or when I'd have to go to bed hungry; when my father would be home so we'd all be happy or when I'd wake up to find Uncle Leonard snoring on the sofa; when my mother would wash my clothes or when she would be holed up in her sanctuary; when Annie would wet our bed in the middle of the night or when I'd get a good night's sleep.

I lived a disorganized life that was never predictable, but numbers—ah, numbers behaved in an orderly fashion: One plus one always equaled two. I could memorize the multiplication and addition tables, knowing they would never change. I loved long division, even with remainders. I liked nothing better than solving a crisp page of word problems, especially the ones with trains coming from different directions at different speeds, or the ones where I had to figure out how many pounds of tomatoes I could buy at thirty-nine cents a pound if I only had two dollars. Other kids would groan when Mr. Standish handed out a work sheet on fractions, but I looked forward to finding common denominators. They offered a glimpse of Uncle Leonard's perfect society where all differences would be equalized and collectivized. Best of all, no one else in my class came close to challenging me as a math whiz. I scored A's on all my tests. Mr.

Standish took me aside and told me I was the best math student he'd ever had. He said I had a gift.

May Elizabeth, on the other hand, still didn't know her times tables and needed to drill with flash cards. Mr. Standish asked me to coach her. We'd find a quiet corner in the back of the room and I'd hold up a card with *6 X 8* on it, for example, and she'd say, "I don't know . . . forty-something?"

I would tell her what my daddy always said: "Close doesn't count except with hurricanes and hand grenades." He had fought in the war, so he knew about things like that.

"Let's do our homework together," May begged. "You can come to my house after school."

It was a dream come true. I would have to walk Poke home first, but then I would circle back to May's neighborhood to do homework with her. Her mother gave us snacks to eat after school, things like Hostess cupcakes and Pepsi-Cola and potato chips—treats that were unheard of at my house. I got to watch all of my favorite after-school TV shows in living color, and the picture on the screen never even budged.

"I hate math," May Elizabeth groaned, lying beside me on the shag carpet in front of the TV. I could do a page of math homework in the time it took May to do the first problem.

"It would be a lot easier if you learned your times tables," I told her, scooping the filling out of another Twinkie with my tongue.

May sighed, pouting. "I know, but please, *please*, just tell me what answer you got for number one? *Please?* Just this once?"

Of course it never was "just once." She copied my homework every single night, then wondered why she got Ds and Fs on her tests. I didn't care; I was eating Cheez Doodles every afternoon until my tongue turned orange. My life seemed almost happy for the first time that I could ever recall, and I was so afraid that it wouldn't last.

It didn't.

That year, 1960, was an election year, and the race for the White House was heating up between Vice President Richard M. Nixon and

Senator John F. Kennedy. Our teacher thought we should learn more about politics and government, so he decided we would attend the presidential debates. Not the real ones, of course. The debate club at Riverside High School was holding a mock debate in the school auditorium between the local leaders of the two political parties. Our class was going to walk three blocks to the high school for a field trip and watch the proceedings.

Everything would have been fine if my dad had been home, but he wasn't. I had to give the field trip permission slip to Uncle Leonard to sign.

"This is outrageous!" he bellowed, his face turning as red as his politics.

"It's okay, Uncle Leonard. It's just a dumb assembly in the auditorium." I tried to pull the permission slip out of his hands. "Never mind, Mommy can sign it for me." The only reason I had asked him in the first place was because I hadn't wanted to venture outside to the outhouse to look for my mother. Now I was sorry I hadn't. Uncle Leonard wouldn't be silenced.

"This is America!" He banged his fist on the chrome table so hard he made a pile of his yellow legal tablets slide to the floor. "I thought we had freedom of speech in America."

"We do, Uncle Leonard. Our teacher explained it to us. That's why they're having this debate."

"Well, I demand to know why the Communist Party wasn't invited to debate the issues like any other political party?"

I was only ten, but I could have told him why they hadn't been invited. America was fighting the Cold War. Everyone hated the Communists. Our fathers had just fought a war against the Nazis, and now the Communists were trying to take over the world. The Russians were going to rain down missiles on America and nuke us in our sleep and take over our lives. From cradle to grave, those stinking Commies would get to decide everything we did: who went to school and who didn't, what we studied, who we married, where we worked—just like they did in the USSR and Red China. Children would be raised in communes—which was fine with me as long as I wasn't on the same commune as Poke and JT and Annie. The Communists would force us to dress alike and live in identical houses—again, fine with me as long as the houses and clothes looked like May Elizabeth's and not mine.

The Communists would take away our freedom—along with our TVs and our cars and our professional baseball teams. But first there would be a nuclear war and all the horrors that went with it. Ever since the Russians launched *Sputnik* in 1957 and got a head start in the space race, everyone knew that the Communists were just a day or two away from launching their bombs from outer space. We had air raid drills in class every couple of months. The town siren would go off and Mr. Standish would holler, "Duck and cover!" and we had to huddle beneath our desks, turning our backs away from the huge picture windows and covering our eyes to shield them from the blast. But even if you were lucky enough to survive the mushroom cloud, you still had to worry about radiation poisoning. The water would be unsafe to drink and the air unsafe to breathe, and you would have to stay in your fallout shelter—if you were rich enough to have one—until it was safe to come out in three or four years. Yes, everyone hated the Communists. And my uncle was one.

"I have some phone calls to make," Uncle Leonard said. He hurried next door to use the Grouts' telephone, still carrying my permission slip. I had to ask Mr. Standish for a new one and give it to Mom to sign.

On the day of the mock Kennedy-Nixon debate, our class walked the three blocks to the high school beneath gorgeous blue skies. The air was fragrant with the smell of burning leaves, and the trees scattered a trail of red and orange and yellow leaves in our path. Life seemed wonderful.

Then I walked into the auditorium and saw Uncle Leonard sitting up on the stage between the Democrat and the Republican, and I knew that my peaceful life was over. The infamous lice infestation would be nothing compared to the humiliation I was about to face.

The Kennedy man was introduced first, but I didn't hear a word he said above the sound of fear roaring in my ears. What was my uncle doing up there? In what new way was I about to be mocked and blackballed? My stomach writhed into knots. The Democrat finished his speech and sat down. The president of the debate club walked to the podium again.

"Next we will hear from Mr. Leonard Bartlett, president of the Tri-County Communist Party. . . ." The rest of the introduction was drowned out by a chorus of booing. There was no applause for my uncle as there had been for the first speaker. I slid further down in my seat.

Uncle Leonard ambled to the podium, his face gloomier than I'd ever seen it. He was such a gangly, awkward man that he walked like a marionette being controlled by a three-year-old. He held up his hands for silence and the booing grew louder still. He gripped the microphone and spent four or five painful minutes trying to talk about the Communist Party while the catcalls in the auditorium became progressively louder and wilder. Kids fired spitballs and threw stuff at him. I slithered so far down in my seat that I was nearly on the floor.

Finally the principal stood and tried to restore order, banging on the podium with his fist. "Use your shoe, like Khrushchev at the UN," someone yelled. After that the assembly turned into a free-for-all and the debate had to be cancelled. Uncle Leonard smiled, probably because the Republican hadn't had a chance to speak yet. My uncle hated Richard Nixon.

No one dared to walk beside me on the trip back to class. Even though my last name was Gallagher, everyone knew that the town Communist was my uncle. I acquired a new nickname: "Kathy the Commie." I thought it was an improvement over "Cootie Kathy" until pranksters splashed red paint all over the front of our house. Someone painted a crude hammer and sickle on the trunk of my uncle's car, too. If Daddy had been home he would have just laughed and painted over it, but Uncle Leonard refused to hide the red paint. He was proud of being "Red."

"Leave it on there," he told my mother. "I want these kids to see what kind of a country they're growing up in. This would never happen in Russia."

Of course not, I wanted to say. The Russians sent dissidents to Siberia where paint froze in July. I crept into my mother's bedroom later that night to have a talk with her.

"Mommy, when is Daddy coming home?"

She blew out a stream of cigarette smoke. "Three to six months."

"Can't you make Uncle Leonard move out? Please? The kids are all making fun of me at school again, just like they did when I had lice."

Being called a Communist was worse, though. There was no shampoo to wash away that shame. Mom stared at her lap, not at me.

"You don't know what shame is," she murmured. "When I was growing up, my mother . . . Never mind."

"Why does Uncle Leonard have to live here? Why can't he get his own house?"

"Uncle Leonard is a good man," she said fiercely. "And America is a free country. He's entitled to believe whatever he wants."

The mocking and teasing I received after the debate lasted even longer than after the cootie episode. May Elizabeth stopped needing my help with her homework. No more Twinkies and potato chips. I hated my uncle.

Then one day May came to school with another dramatic announcement: "Guess what! My daddy had a fallout shelter built in our backyard, so now we can survive a nuclear war!"

I was certain that a Commie like me would never be allowed anywhere near it, but when the dismissal bell rang at the end of the day, May turned to me and said, "Want to come over to my house and see it? Maybe Mommy will let us do our homework inside it. Won't that be fun?"

The Hayworths' fallout shelter was the most impressive thing I'd ever seen. They had bought the deluxe luxury model, of course, so May's family would be safe even if a hydrogen bomb exploded twenty miles away in Bensenville. The shelter was a fourteen-by-eight-foot steel cylinder buried four feet beneath the Hayworths' backyard.

"It comes with everything," May gushed as she gave me the grand tour. "See? Canned food and water, a fold-down bed with an air mattress for each of us, and a radio so we'll know when it's safe to come out."

"I hope you bought extra batteries in case the electricity goes out," I said, always the practical one.

"We don't need batteries. Daddy says we can make our own electricity with this." She pointed to a brand new generator.

"Won't you go crazy locked in here for years and years?" I asked. I hadn't had a chance to calculate the volume of a fourteen-by-eight-foot cylinder yet, but the thought of being stuck in this tank with my family for even one hour made me feel like screaming. May shook her head.

"We've stashed away lots of books and puzzles and board games to play. And the shelter comes with protective suits so we can walk around outside afterward. And see this?" she asked, brandishing a small yellow box with lots of wires and dials. "This is our very own Geiger counter so we can measure the radiation."

"It looks like your father thought of everything," I said wistfully. The fallout shelter was sturdier and better stocked and waterproofed than our house. I didn't see any toilet facilities, but I was sure Mr. Hayworth had thought of that, too—and hopefully a can opener.

May was quiet for a long moment before saying, "Can I ask you a question?"

My stomach rolled over like a trained dog, but I shrugged and said, "Okay. . . ."

"Are you really a Communist?"

"No! Of course not! I hate the Commies as much as everyone else does. It's just my stupid uncle who likes them—and I don't think I'm really related to him. I keep hoping they'll tell me I was adopted or they'll find out that someone gave Mommy the wrong baby at the hospital, so I can go live with normal people."

"Oh, I hope so, too!" May said in her dramatic way. She gripped my hands in both of hers and gave them a little squeeze. "Maybe they'll find out that we're really sisters! Maybe they got you and Ron mixed up and my brother will have to go live at your house and you can live here."

"It would be pretty hard to get us mixed up," I said, sounding practical again. "For one thing, Ron is two years older than me. And for another thing . . . well . . ." I paused, reluctant to get into a discussion of "basic equipment."

"Oh. Yeah. I forgot about the two years," May said with a theatrical sigh. "See? You're so good at numbers, Kathy. Do you think you could help me with my math homework?"

"Sure . . . Does the fallout shelter come with potato chips?"

I began attending both Sunday school and church after kids started calling me "Kathy the Commie." Everyone knows that real Communists are atheists, so going to church seemed like the best way to prove to everyone in Riverside that I didn't share my uncle's beliefs. Mrs. Hayworth had been inviting me to attend with her family all along, but I knew I would feel out of place sitting in a pew with them. I still didn't have a hat or gloves or patent leather shoes.

On the Sunday after the mock debate was canceled, I was on my way home after Sunday school when I suddenly decided that I couldn't face returning to our red-splotched house. I turned around. The weather was warm, the church door open, and I heard beautiful organ music coming from inside. I crept through the door and sat down alone, in a pew in the back.

I knew quite a lot about Jesus by that time, enough to know that He would welcome me into His house even if no one else was thrilled to see me. He liked lepers and poor people and outcasts like me whom everybody else avoided. I had learned memory verses like "Blessed be ye poor: for yours is the kingdom of God," and had sung songs like "Jesus Loves Me." In fact, our Sunday school lesson that very morning had been the story of the poor widow whom Jesus praised for putting her meager penny into the offering box, giving a larger percent of her income than all the rich people who could well afford it. The story had been memorable, combining two things I knew a lot about: class differences and percentages.

The church service that first Sunday was memorable, too. I loved the music and the serenity and the beauty of everything—and that, in itself, was enough to make me want to come back. Then the minister read the Scripture verse: "Ho, every one that thirsteth, come ye to the waters, and he that hath no money; come ye, buy, and eat; yea, come, buy wine and milk without money and without price."

He began talking about Jesus' death on the cross—which I had learned about but had never thought of as being for me—and he said that God's invitation was to everyone, rich or poor. Salvation—which I imagined as a sort-of cosmic fallout shelter, protecting the lucky ones from hell—came from God as a free gift. If I believed in Jesus and told Him about all the things I'd done wrong, then God would hand out salvation for free, just like Halloween candy. It didn't matter where I lived or who my parents were; Jesus was everyone's common denominator.

All the money in the world couldn't buy God's love. And it had nothing to do with hats and white gloves and patent leather shoes. "God so loved the world, that He gave His only begotten Son. . . ." God loved *me*.

"He that cometh to me," Jesus said, "shall never hunger. . . ." And I was starving for love. I couldn't work hard and earn it like an A on a test at school or by memorizing my times table or Sunday school verses. All I had to do was tell God I was sorry; sorry for all the rotten things I'd done, like hating my uncle and my mother and my brothers and sister. God's forgiveness was free. Jesus loved me.

I bowed my head that morning and became a Christian.

When I arrived home I felt different. My sin had been as ugly as the red paint stains on the front of our house, but Jesus had washed them all away. I went to the outhouse and unearthed my hidden packet of Sunday school papers. Then I sat down on the splintered wooden bench and reread every single one of them.

Chapter

9

I discovered Nancy Drew mystery books during the summer between fifth and sixth grade. Nancy was a sleuth who could solve any mystery, even the ones that baffled all the adults. She had "Titian" hair, a best friend named Bess, and drove a convertible. I wanted to be just like her. I could think of a few mysteries that I would have liked to clear up in my own life, such as why Mommy didn't take care of us the way other mothers did. And why we always seemed to have more money when Daddy was home than when he was away at work. And why Daddy hadn't figured this out by now and quit going away for months at a time.

I wanted to read every Nancy Drew mystery in the Riverside Public Library so I could become a super-sleuth like her. But my brothers discovered trains that summer. The railroad tracks angled through the vacant lot a block and a half from our house, and we'd grown up with freight trains rumbling though our neighborhood three times a week, whistles shrieking. But this was the first summer that Poke and JT figured out all the creatively dangerous things they could do around trains. Combined with their fascination with fire, their new hobby didn't leave me much leisure time for reading.

I got May Elizabeth hooked on Nancy Drew when we returned to school in the fall, and we took turns devouring every book that the school library owned. Our sixth-grade teacher that year was Miss Pfister. Her name was hard to pronounce without spitting, especially if you had a lisp like Patty DeMarco. Miss Pfister was new and young and very beautiful. The boys all fell in love with her, and they behaved themselves in class, for once, just to impress her. The girls all wanted to be like her, and some of them grew their hair long and began teasing it into a bouffant hairdo like hers. I liked Miss Pfister because she gave a ton of homework every night, and once again, May Elizabeth invited me over to her house after school so we could do it together—which usually meant that I'd do the work and she'd copy mine. Then May and I would sit in her fluffy pink bedroom, sip Pepsi Colas, and read Nancy Drew.

The school year passed quickly and uneventfully, for which I was grateful. With May Elizabeth as my best friend, the other kids seemed to forgive me for having lice and a Communist uncle, and they left me alone for the most part. Both of my brothers attended Riverside Elementary now and were regular guests in the principal's office. They were rumored to be the culprits who had waxed the playground slide, causing multiple injuries to dozens of little kids who shot off the end of it like bullets out of a gun. Bobby Peters broke his arm in two places. But my brothers' reputation seemed to inspire more awe than ridicule among the other students. After all, JT—who was in kindergarten—held the school record as the youngest student ever to be suspended.

By April of 1962, May and I had read every Nancy Drew book in both the school and public libraries. "I'm getting real good at solving the mystery before Nancy does," May bragged one night as we sat in her bedroom. "I figured out the mystery of the moss-covered mansion while Nancy was still driving around in her roadster having luncheon."

"How come we have to eat lunch in the cafeteria instead of luncheon?" I asked thoughtfully. As a mature sixth grader, all of twelve years old, I had become very philosophical. "Why doesn't anyone eat 'luncheon' anymore?"

"My mom and her friends go to luncheons all the time," May replied.

I should have known that it would turn out to be a matter of social class. I don't think my mother even ate lunch, let alone luncheon.

"Hey! You know what?" May said suddenly. "We should open our own detective agency and solve mysteries. I'll be Nancy Drew and you can be Bess. I'll bet we could make a lot of money."

The ease with which May Elizabeth embraced capitalism amazed me. I felt a rush of gratitude for her friendship and for the free exchange of ideas that she offered me after being brainwashed by my uncle all my life. Even so, I didn't think Uncle Leonard would object to our starting a business as long as May and I gave away any treasure we found, like Nancy Drew always did—or if we at least split the profits equally.

"I'll bet there's a mystery or two we could solve right here in Riverside," I replied. "Where should we start?"

"Well-ll . . ." May said, stretching out the word to heighten the suspense, "we could find out the truth about your Uncle Leonard. Everyone in Riverside thinks he's a Soviet spy."

"Uncle *Leonard*? A *spy*? You've got to be kidding! For one thing, I don't think the Russians would be interested in any secrets that came from this dumpy old town. And for another thing, he's much too loud to be a spy. He crashes all around with his huge, clunky feet, and he's always yelling at everything, especially the television."

"What about his girlfriend? She's a Communist, too, isn't she?"

"You mean Connie Miller? She works at the Valley Food Market, for pete's sake." I didn't add that she was as fluffy and dumb as a Pekinese, but I could have.

"Where does your uncle work?" May Elizabeth asked, and I could tell that she was still playing the part of Nancy Drew, ferreting out the truth.

"He works for the Teamster's Union over in Bensenville. He sits in an office all day hoping the workers go on strike so he can make picket signs and yell out slogans. We can follow him around if you want to, but I don't think it'll be much fun."

May appeared crestfallen—but only for a moment. "I know! We can track down the thieves who broke into our house and stole all our stuff while we were at church that time. The police never did solve that crime."

My stomach felt as if I'd crested a hill in a car without brakes. "No, that's too boring," I said, trying desperately to sound nonchalant. "Nancy and Bess would never take such a boring case. Besides, that was two years ago."

"How about a missing person, then?" May asked.

"That's *much* better." I felt like I could breathe again. But to be honest, I figured that if anyone had been lucky enough to disappear from boring old Riverside, they probably wouldn't be too happy if we found them again. I didn't say so out loud, though, for fear that May Elizabeth would go back to the unsolved break-in. "Now, who do we know that's missing?" I prompted, stroking my chin.

"My dad."

"Your dad isn't missing. I saw him in church yesterday. *My* dad is the one who goes away for months at a time. He hasn't been home since the end of January."

"No, my dad is never home, either," May insisted. "We eat supper without him almost every night. And when he does come home for supper, he always has to run off again."

"Where does he go?"

"That's the mystery!" she said, spreading her palms. "Maybe *he's* the spy instead of your uncle! Wouldn't that be cool?"

I had my doubts, but we decided to start with May's dad since he was only "missing" here in Riverside. We could work on finding my dad once we gained a little more experience—and maybe learned to drive a car.

I was home watching TV two nights later when Charlie Grout knocked on our door and said I had a phone call over at his house. It was May Elizabeth. At first I thought we had a bad connection since I could hardly understand her; then I realized she was whispering.

"Now's our chance, *Bess*," she said, using my code name. "My dad just left. He said he had to go back to the office, but I'll bet he's picking up secret documents from a Russian defector."

I felt a wonderful shiver of excitement. "What's your plan, *Nancy?*"

She didn't reply. As the silence lengthened I realized that it was going to be up to me to devise a plan, just like it was up to me to do all the homework. "We have to follow him," I decided.

"Should I ask my mom to drive us?"

I rolled my eyes. "No, she might be in on the spy ring. We'll have to ride bikes."

"But you don't have a bike—"

"I know, I *know*. I was hoping I could borrow your brother's." I glanced at Charlie Grout. I could tell by the way he was eyeing me that he was eavesdropping. I cupped my hand over the receiver. "Sneak the bicycles out of your garage, okay? I'll be right over."

"Should I dress all in black?" May asked.

"If you want to—but I don't think Nancy Drew ever does."

"Yes, she did in *The Clue in the Old Stagecoach,* remember?"

I suppressed a sigh of impatience. Mr. Hayworth could have driven all the way to Bensenville, exchanged his secret documents, and driven home again in the time it was taking us to get organized. "You can wear black if you want to," I said. "I don't think I have any black clothes."

"Isn't this fun?" she asked with a giggle.

Half an hour later, May and I rode our bicycles to the top of the rise overlooking the gravel parking lot at Hayworth Industries. Her father's car was sitting in his reserved parking spot close to the main door of the sprawling brick building. I felt terribly disappointed that we had found him so easily.

"Now what?" I asked. "Should we go down and sneak inside and see what he's doing?"

"We can't!" she said, clutching my arm. "They have a security guard!" My skin prickled at the idea of encountering a real-live gunman. I felt like a genuine detective.

"What would Nancy and Bess do?" I whispered. May didn't reply. We stood looking down at the peaceful scene, pondering our next move, when the main door suddenly opened and Mr. Hayworth strode through it. He walked straight to his car and climbed in.

"Let's follow him!" May said. She hopped onto her bike, ready to give chase. I had a harder time leaping into action on a boy's bicycle, but I eventually caught up with her.

Chasing a car on a bicycle was not as impossible as it sounds—especially in Riverside. The village speed limit was twenty-five miles per hour, and stop signs sprouted at nearly every intersection to slow things down further. County highway officials had decided that our town was too small and insignificant to merit a real stoplight, so the village trustees had retaliated by erecting a multitude of stop signs—mostly to annoy the county snowplow drivers. Those signs would make them stop and take notice of Riverside.

Mr. Hayworth was an excellent driver. He never broke the speed limit, and he stopped at every sign. I was disappointed. I would have expected a spy on an important mission to drive more recklessly. But when he reached the edge of town, May's father suddenly did a very spy-like thing: He pulled into the cemetery without using his turn signal and doused his headlights. My heart began to speed up. The cemetery was the perfect place for spies to exchange secret documents!

May Elizabeth's brakes squealed as she skidded to a stop near the pillared entrance. It was growing dark, and the wooded, unlit cemetery looked spooky. Some of the graves were one hundred and fifty years old, including that of Sarah Hawkins, whose ghost was rumored to haunt the grounds at night. Even spookier, Sarah had been our age when she'd died.

"We'd better go home," May said. Her voice sounded shaky. "My mom gets mad if I ride my bike after dark, even with a headlight and reflectors."

"What kind of a detective would be afraid of an old graveyard?" I asked, cutting to what I figured was the heart of the problem. "Nancy Drew wouldn't be afraid of ghosts. Remember *The Haunted Bridge*? Come on."

I pedaled through the entrance and followed the winding dirt road deep into the cemetery, using the dust cloud from Mr. Hayworth's car as a clue to guide me. I was pretending to be brave, but I was trembling inside. It was a very delicious feeling.

May's father had pulled his car to a halt way in the back, parking near the edge of the cemetery where the woods began. Another car was parked in front of his—a Volkswagen Beetle. I slowed to a stop a short distance away, half-hidden behind the Moore family's giant monument. My heart thumped with fear and excitement. I signaled for May to halt, too, and held my fingers to my lips to warn her to be quiet, but her mouth hung so slackly that she looked incapable of speech. I wondered if I looked as wide-eyed as she did.

Mr. Hayworth opened his car door and climbed out, nervously glancing around. The spy in the Volkswagen got out, too. I could tell that it was a woman by her shape and her bouffant hairdo—and there was something familiar about her, even at this distance. I figured the pair would quickly exchange documents and hurry away, but instead they did a very surprising thing. They wrapped their arms all around each other just like lovers do at the end of a good movie—and they kissed! Right there in the cemetery! I heard May Elizabeth gasp.

When the kiss ended, Mr. Hayworth glanced all around again, then opened the rear door of his car. He guided the woman spy into the back seat, then climbed in beside her and closed the door. A moment later their heads sank out of sight.

I tried to make sense of the scene, adding all the clues together just like Nancy Drew would do when solving a mystery. I thought I remembered seeing someone driving a Volkswagen Beetle all around town. Then it came to me: It was my teacher, Miss Pfister. Yes! That's who the familiar-looking woman had been! But Miss Pfister wasn't a Russian spy. She was a young, pretty, unmarried, sixth-grade teacher at Riverside Elementary School. What was she doing at the cemetery in the back of a car with May Elizabeth Hayworth's father?

Then I realized what.

May Elizabeth must have put all the clues together at the same moment that I did, because I heard a crash as her bicycle fell over. I turned in time to see her sink to the ground as if all the strength had gone out of her legs. She covered her face with her hands and wept. I didn't know what to do.

It seemed like hours passed as May huddled in the road, crying uncontrollably, and I stood beside her, twisting my hands.

"May Elizabeth. . . ?" I finally whispered. "May? We better go home."

She drew a deep, shuddering breath, as if preparing to scream—but she didn't. Instead, she leaped to her feet, grabbed her fallen bicycle and jumped on it, pedaling out of the cemetery as if Sarah Hawkins and all of the other dead people had risen from their graves and were chasing after her. I don't know how May could see where she was going through her tears.

She didn't say one word to me all the way home, and when we reached her house she dropped her bicycle on the front lawn and ran inside, slamming the door behind her. I gazed numbly at her house for a long time, wondering if I should go inside and talk to her or not. What on earth would I say?

I finally wheeled Ron's bike around to the garage and put it away, then went back for May Elizabeth's bike. I felt like a criminal and didn't know why. I was slinking down the driveway, heading home, when I heard Mrs. Hayworth calling me.

"Kathleen! Kathleen, wait!" I turned around but couldn't meet her gaze. "What happened to May Elizabeth? Why is she crying like that? Kathleen, please. You have to tell me what's wrong."

"I don't know. . . ." I said with a shrug. But when I remembered how Mr. Hayworth and Miss Pfister had kissed, I began to cry, too. Mrs. Hayworth gently gripped my shoulders.

"I think you do. Please, honey. I'm not angry with you, I just want to help you and May. But I can't help if I don't know what's wrong. Please . . . did someone hurt you or her?"

Oh, yes. We were hurt. My throat felt so tight that I could barely get the words out. "We were pretending to be detectives. . . ." I began. I told her how we had followed Mr. Hayworth's car from the factory. I told her where he had gone and what we had seen. It was the hardest thing I'd ever done. When I finished I felt sick inside.

Mrs. Hayworth's face had turned very white. Her eyes were bright with unshed tears. "Please don't mention this to anyone else, Kathleen. Please," she begged.

"I won't. I promise." She drew me into her arms for a long hug. Then she went back inside.

My mother started yelling at me as soon as I got home. "Since when do you take off without telling anyone where you're going? Where have you been?"

I let myself get angry in return so I wouldn't cry. If I did, Mom might start asking questions that I didn't want to answer. Besides, as soon as Mommy started yelling, Annie had started crying loudly enough for both of us. After a lifetime of practice, my brothers had learned to ignore any and all yelling, even when it was directed at them. They appeared catatonic as they sat on the floor, staring at the bobbing TV.

"I was with May Elizabeth," I said, sounding sullen. "Since when do you care?"

"You watch your mouth, young lady. You're grounded for staying out until after dark. What are you doing running around until all hours of the night, anyway?" She snuffed out her cigarette then reached into the pack for another one.

I looked her straight in the eye, my anger building. I needed to know the truth. "Where's Daddy?" I asked. Mommy looked surprised by the sudden change of subject.

"He's away on business. And that's too bad for you, isn't it? He's not around to take your side and spoil you rotten like he always does."

"Where does he work?"

"I told you—he's a traveling salesman. . . . Listen, you leave your father out of this. You're still grounded. You can't go over to your rich friend's house for a week. You hear me?"

"You told me before that Daddy was a trucker."

"Well . . . he was. Now he's in sales."

I could tell by the way that my mother glanced away as she blew smoke toward the ceiling that she wasn't telling the truth. I was furious with Mr. Hayworth for lying to May and her mother, and furious with my parents for lying to me. I made up my mind to solve the mystery of my missing dad all by myself, no matter how ugly the truth turned out to be.

"What company does Daddy work for? What does he sell?"

"Don't you take that tone with me. I've had about all I can take from you, Kathleen."

"I want to write him a letter. What's his address?"

My mother wrote a letter to him once a week, and she always made me fill a page of lined notebook paper, telling him what I was doing in school. Daddy sent letters back to us, and Mommy would read parts of them out loud to us, but Daddy never said anything that would provide a clue to his whereabouts. I had to find out his return address.

Mommy shook her finger at me, and the ribbon of ash on the end of her cigarette dribbled onto the couch. "If you think you're going to get out of trouble by writing a letter, you've got another think coming! Now, go to your room!"

"*My* room? Ha! That's a joke!" I stomped away, longing to vent my anger by slamming the bedroom door. I didn't dare. It would probably fall off its hinges.

I pulled out a piece of notebook paper and started composing a letter to my father: *Dear Daddy, How are you? Fine, I hope.* I had to be careful not to mention being grounded or to plead with him to take my side against my mother because I knew she would read it—and she would never send it to him if I did. *School is fine. I'm still getting A's. . . .* My tears started falling again when I remembered Miss Pfister's betrayal, but I kept writing, determined to solve this mystery. *I miss you, Daddy. When are you coming home?*

When I finished, I walked out to the living room and handed the letter to my mother. "I'm sorry I stayed out after dark," I said. It was the truth. I was also sorry I had decided to become a detective and follow Mr.

Hayworth into the cemetery, so my heartfelt apology came easily. "Will you mail this to Daddy for me?"

"Fine." She took the letter from me. Her eyes never left the drifting TV screen.

"If you want, I can print the envelope myself," I told her. "We learned how to do it in school last year."

"You don't have to. I'll put your letter in with mine."

This dead end frustrated me. I went back to my room and racked my brain for another idea. If I could just keep my mind focused on finding Daddy, I wouldn't have to picture Miss Pfister kissing May's father. I wouldn't have to remember how devastated May had been or how Mrs. Hayworth's arms had trembled as she'd hugged me.

I was still thinking about how to find my dad when Annie drifted into the bedroom a little while later and lay down on our bed, yawning. None of us had a fixed bedtime. My brothers might sleep in their bed at night or they might sleep on the living room floor in front of the TV. In our house, you slept wherever you fell asleep and nobody ever bothered to move you.

"You need to brush your teeth before you go to bed," I told Annie.

"I don't want to," she whined. Annie couldn't even say "hello" or "good-bye" without whining.

"Well, at least put your pajamas on," I said.

"I don't want to." She turned toward the wall and fell asleep.

I kept the light on, still trying to plan my strategy. When I heard Uncle Leonard come home a little while later, I crept down the hallway toward the living room so I could hear what he and my mother were saying. At first they made a lot of stupid small talk, but when Mommy said, "Will you mail this for me tomorrow?" I hurried into the room as if I were on my way to the kitchen to scrounge something to eat. I saw him take an envelope from my mother and put it into the pocket of his ratty overcoat. He tossed the coat over the back of a dining room chair.

I hoped that he wasn't going to stay up all night writing manifestoes because I was exhausted from the evening's traumatic events and I wasn't sure how much longer I could remain awake. My mom went to bed while I was fixing myself a can of tomato soup. I couldn't find a clean bowl and there was no room at the table to sit down, so I leaned against the sink and ate the soup out of the pot. By the time I finished, my uncle had turned off the TV and was pulling his blanket and pillow from behind the couch to make his "bed." He tossed the unraveling afghan that Daddy got at the thrift store over my sleeping brothers on the floor.

"Good night, Uncle Leonard," I said on my way back to my room.

"Night," he grunted. Nothing was "good" when you were a Communist living in a capitalistic society.

I put on my nightgown and brushed my teeth, then turned off the light and stood near my bedroom door, waiting for my uncle to fall asleep. I knew that if I got comfortable I'd fall asleep myself, and I couldn't allow that to happen.

After a very long time, I heard Uncle Leonard snoring. The house was dark and shadowy, reminding me of my earlier trip into the cemetery. I almost changed my mind when I remembered what we had discovered there. But I was May Elizabeth's best friend, and it was only fair that we both find our missing fathers on the same night. I tiptoed into the living room, careful not to make a sound, and fished the letter from my uncle's coat pocket. It was too dark to read the address. I went into the kitchen and opened the refrigerator door a crack so the light would come on. The odor of sour milk drifted out as I read the envelope:

Donald Gallagher
K21633–277
County Correctional Center
Bensenville, New York

I slammed the refrigerator door shut as if that would make the horrible truth vanish with the light and the stench. My daddy was in *jail*? He had a *number*?

For a long moment I stood frozen, trying to comprehend it. Then the envelope fluttered to the floor as I fled to the bathroom and threw up the tomato soup I'd eaten. I felt as though my heart had died and turned to stone. My wonderful, laughing daddy really, truly was a thief. He had been caught and sent to prison. How many other times had he been locked away behind bars when he'd gone missing? I understood why May Elizabeth hadn't been able to stop crying, because for a long time I couldn't stop, either. In fact, I cried myself sick and couldn't go to school the next day.

When I did return, I felt so ashamed of who I was that I kept my chin tucked against my chest, unable to meet anyone's gaze. May Elizabeth missed three days of school, and when she came back, I found out she'd transferred into the other sixth-grade classroom across the hall. I saw her on the playground at recess, standing alone near the jungle gym. She was usually so animated, but now she looked like a windup toy with a broken spring. I went over to stand alongside her.

"You okay?" I asked.

"No . . . I'm afraid my parents are going to get a *divorce*," she said tearfully.

I remained silent for a moment as we both grieved, then I said, "Don't feel bad. I found my missing dad, too. . . . He's in jail."

"Oh, Kathleen!" May gave me a hug—a long, shaky one like her mother's—then we walked away from each other so we both wouldn't start bawling.

We never discussed it, but we scrapped our plans to open a detective agency after solving our first case. I never read another Nancy Drew mystery, either. We both grew up that spring of 1962, our innocence gone, our childhood at an end.

Chapter

10

I was glad that I had become a Christian when World War III almost started. For six tense days in October of 1962, it seemed like the world was about to come to an end in a fiery nuclear holocaust.

My family was watching TV one Monday night when President Kennedy appeared during prime time and told us that the Russians were building nuclear missile bases in Cuba, a mere ninety miles from the United States. The president had photographs to prove it, taken from a U.S. spy plane. To stop the buildup, he was placing an air and sea quarantine around the island of Cuba.

"He can't do that!" Uncle Leonard shouted. "A naval blockade in international waters is an act of war!"

"Shh . . . Be quiet and listen, Len," Mommy said.

I didn't understand all the big words the president used, and it was hard to concentrate when his face kept disappearing into the top of the screen then reappearing at the bottom, like soap bubbles rising into the air and bursting. But I understood the gist of the matter: President Kennedy had told the Communists to tear down the missile bases—or else. If

Khrushchev's reaction was anything like my uncle's, there was sure to be war.

"What gives Kennedy the right to tell Castro what to do?" Uncle Leonard sprang from his chair, unable to remain seated in the face of such an outrage. He paced around our tiny living room shouting, "The Cuban people have every right to purchase arms to defend themselves. Remember the Bay of Pigs invasion? If the U.S. can build missile bases all over the world, why can't the Soviets?" He shook his fist at the TV set, which showed Castro and Khrushchev acting all chummy. "Don't give in to Kennedy!" he told them. "If he wants a war, then give him one!"

The Russians took Uncle Leonard's advice. They not only refused to stop building missile bases in Cuba, they told President Kennedy that if he tried to launch another invasion like the Bay of Pigs or if he interfered with Cuban shipping, the United States would be starting a nuclear war. Russia and the U.S. both went on full military alert. The next few days would be critical ones, deciding the fate of mankind.

The fact that we hovered on the brink of World War III upset a lot of people in Riverside. My uncle, the town Communist, made a convenient scapegoat for everyone's fear and anger, a visible target to hate. The splotches of red paint that still set our house apart from all the others began to spread around to the sides and rear like poison ivy. If this kept up, our entire house would wind up red. Things grew so tense that Uncle Leonard decided to pack up and leave town for a few days.

May Elizabeth was the only person I knew who seemed excited about the idea of a nuclear war. "Guess what! My family is getting ready to live in our bomb shelter," she told our seventh-grade class. "Daddy said we're going to wait it out where it's safe." Her parents hadn't divorced after all. In fact, they showed up together in church every week as if nothing had ever happened.

"Do you think there might be room in your fallout shelter for me, too?" I asked hopefully. "I don't mind sleeping on the floor. And I don't eat very much. You can copy all my math homework while we're waiting for the smoke to clear. And any other homework you want to copy, too." I knew I sounded desperate. I was.

May shook her head. She had been acting snooty and indifferent toward me ever since our first day in seventh grade. Debbie Harris was her new best friend now. "There's only enough air and food for four people," May told me.

I couldn't bear the thought of being locked in our mouse-infested, dirt-floored cellar with Poke and JT—not to mention having to listen to Annie scream until the radiation count was safe. I decided to cast my lot with my uncle. I figured that maybe he had an "in" with his comrades Khrushchev and Castro, and we would be spared when the missiles started falling because of my uncle's faithful devotion to the party.

"Can I leave town with you, Uncle Leonard? Please?" I begged. "I'll join the Communist Party and come to all of the meetings, if you want."

"No, you need to stay home and help your mother with the kids."

"Oh, let her come, for goodness' sake," his girlfriend, Connie, said. She had been dating my uncle for more than two years, but there didn't seem to be any wedding plans in sight. The membership rolls of the Tri-County Communist Party had doubled when Connie converted to the cause. I was offering to increase it by fifty percent.

I never understood what Connie saw in my uncle. They were opposites in every conceivable way: She was small and round and fair, he was tall and thin and dark; she was always smiling and happy, he was perennially doleful; she never finished high school, he considered himself an intellectual. In every way, Connie's glass was always half full, Uncle Leonard's would forever be half empty.

"Let her come, Lennie," she coaxed. "She deserves to have a little fun before the world comes to an end."

That weekend we drove to Pennsylvania in my uncle's twelve-year-old Ford. It didn't have a muffler or a heater, and the car's body had more rust than metal, but you could still see the crude hammer and sickle daubed in red paint on the trunk.

"Where are we going?" I asked as we chugged along the highway. Not that it mattered; anyplace was better than home.

"Deer Falls," he said, as if I should know exactly where that was.

"Where?"

"It's the town where your mother and I grew up. We're staying with your grandmother."

Grandmother? I had a grandmother? The astonishing news made me feel a little dizzy. I'd had no idea that she even existed. I began imagining a cozy cottage in the woods and a sweet little white-haired woman who would bake cookies and hug me a lot.

"How come we never visited her before?" I asked, but my uncle didn't seem to hear me. He was too busy explaining to Connie about the battle of wills that was taking place between President Kennedy and Premier Khrushchev, and how the United States had no right to dictate foreign policy to Cuba or anyone else. Connie smiled and nodded and made comforting noises whenever Uncle Leonard paused for breath, but nothing seemed to soothe him.

After the first hour my ears throbbed from the missing muffler and the nonstop drone of my uncle's voice. I started to regret my decision to come. But when we finally pulled into town, I knew it had been worth suffering through two-and-a-half hours of Communist rhetoric to come to this enchanting place.

Deer Falls was such a beautiful little town that I couldn't imagine why Mommy and Uncle Leonard would ever want to leave it—especially to live in a nowhere place like Riverside. The village sat at the edge of a secluded lake, nestled among the Pocono Mountains, and there were all sorts of things to do: fishing, sailing, water skiing, or just walking around town and looking at all the quaint little shops and inns. Connie told me that Deer Falls was a very popular tourist destination during the summer. And it was surprisingly crowded that weekend, too. Thousands of city people who didn't own bomb shelters had evidently fled to the mountains, hoping to escape the holocaust when the Russians flattened New York and Philadelphia and Washington. Traffic had been very heavy on the highway. Everyone, including me, wanted to forget all about the Cuban missile crisis, and Deer Falls offered a perfect refuge from all the tension and worry.

The woods in the state park on the edge of town were the stuff of fairy tales: dense and green and mysterious. The weather was too cold for swimming and we didn't have a boat, but Uncle Leonard parked the car down by the lake, and Connie and I went for a walk along the shoreline to stretch our legs.

"Just imagine, Kathleen, this might be the very last time we ever see trees," she said with a happy smile. "And look at that sky! We may never see such a brilliant blue sky again, so let's just soak it up!" Coming from someone other than optimistic Connie, those words might have sounded morbid. She made the threat of global annihilation seem like an exciting adventure.

"Are we all going to die?" I asked her.

She smiled, her eyes bright with excitement, and I waited to hear words of comfort and reassurance. They didn't come. "Yes, I believe we are," she said happily. "But I'm not afraid, and you shouldn't be, either. Death will be a wonderful surprise."

I swallowed a knot of fear. "Our Sunday school teacher said we'll go to heaven when we die if we know Jesus."

"Oh, what a sweet thought," Connie said. "You hold on to those words if they help you, sweetie. Leonard's always telling me that religion is a drug for the masses, and I can see how he's right. It *has* given you a happy feeling, hasn't it, wiping out all your fears. You go ahead and use that drug, Kathleen."

Connie rambled on and on about nuclear war and "darling Leonard," and the more she talked, the more I began to doubt that she was the committed Communist that my uncle believed her to be. I got the feeling she was more interested in marrying Leonard than in helping the Communists take over the world. I wouldn't mind having cheerful Connie for an aunt, but I couldn't see how she and my uncle would both fit on our sofa at night. She was fairly plump.

Connie had been a Girl Scout, and as we walked along she reassured me that she knew how to survive in the woods. "If the nuclear fallout doesn't kill us or poison all this wonderful vegetation," she said, "I'll show you how to live off the land. It'll be so much fun. I can make a lean-to and cook over a campfire, and I know how to use leaves and herbs to cure common ailments, too."

I wanted to ask her if she had a home remedy for radiation sickness, but she seemed so happy and carefree as we ambled along the path, hand-in-hand, that I hated to spoil her mood with a dose of reality.

When we got back to the car, Uncle Leonard had his transistor radio pressed to his ear and was listening to the news. "Has the nuclear war started, honey?" Connie asked as she slid across the seat to cuddle beside him. "We didn't hear any missiles falling, did we, Kathleen? But then, I'm not really sure what a nuclear missile sounds like."

"I never heard one fall, either," Uncle Leonard said, "but I guarantee we'll know it when it does."

Connie laughed and squeezed his arm. "Oh, you know so many things, Lenny."

We drove down the picturesque main street of the village and parked in front of a florist's shop. Uncle Leonard shut off the engine, and the car shuddered to a stop. "This is it," he said.

"You're buying flowers for your mother?" Connie asked. "What a sweet idea, Lenny."

"No, I'm not buying flowers. This is where she lives. It used to be a hat shop. Mother ran it when Eleanor and I were kids, and we lived in the apartment upstairs. She still lives there."

This was news. Not only did I have a grandmother but she was a cap-italist. No wonder Uncle Leonard left home. We took our grocery sack "suitcases" out of the trunk and walked around to the rear entrance, climb-ing a rickety set of wooden stairs to a tilting porch on the second floor.

Grandma Fiona met us at the door, enveloping my uncle in a long, warm embrace. "It's so lovely to see you, Leonard . . . so lovely. I've missed you so!"

I had never seen my uncle behave so tenderly. His eyes misted over, and he looked almost human as he hugged her in return and said, "I've missed you, too, Mother." Then he cleared his throat and he was grumpy old Uncle Leonard again. "I've brought company. This is my comrade, Connie Miller . . . and this is Eleanor's daughter Kathleen."

My grandmother's face lit up when she heard who I was, and she moved right past poor Connie to take me into her arms. Her hug was even more wonderful than one of my daddy's hugs because it lasted so much longer, and she made a contented purring sound as she rocked me back and forth in her embrace.

"Kathleen . . ." she murmured. "Oh, Kathleen . . ."

Grandma Fiona had a creamy Irish accent, and I loved the musical sound of it. She did something wonderful with her tongue when she said my name—"Kathleen." It seemed to roll from her mouth like a marble on glass. She was beautiful and elegant, even at age sixty, with the same air of money and privilege that I saw in Cynthia Hayworth. I'd call it class. Fiona had class. I couldn't believe that my frumpy, bedraggled mother was her daughter. How could two such opposite people be related?

Fiona was slender and graceful and sweet-smelling. She dressed in silky dresses and feathery, gossamer shawls and satin slippers. She wore tinkling bracelets and sparkling earrings and bright red lipstick, even when she wasn't leaving the house. Her lips made a mark on my cheek when she kissed me.

Her apartment was as lovely as she was, filled with beautiful, delicate trinkets made of porcelain and crystal and silver, expensive-looking things that seemed as though they came from another era. It didn't take a genius to understand why my brothers had never been invited for a visit.

Fiona must have been expecting us because she had prepared roast beef for dinner. We sat down to eat it at her dining-room table, which had been set with china and silver on a white damask tablecloth. I felt like I was dining in Buckingham Palace with the queen. It was the best meal I'd eaten in my whole life—even better than the food at May Elizabeth's house—and I ate it slowly, reverently, the way people do in dreams. If the world did come to an end tomorrow, at least my final meal had been a wonderful one.

Afterward, I helped Grandma and Connie wash and dry the dishes while my uncle switched on his transistor radio again so he could hear the latest news of the missile crisis.

"Turn that noisy old thing off," Fiona scolded when we were finished. "Why do you want to be upsetting yourself and everyone else by listening to that nonsense?"

"We're in the middle of a world crisis, Mother."

"Well, take your blooming world crisis outside. I don't want to be hearing about it, and neither does Kathleen."

He retreated to the second-floor back porch, taking a reluctant Connie with him.

"Now then, luv," Fiona said with a girlish smile. "Let's you and me listen to some music, shall we?"

She didn't own a television set, but she did have a wonderful old phonograph and stacks and stacks of records. The music had an old-fashioned, muffled sound, as if the orchestra had been seated inside May Elizabeth's fallout shelter for the recording session. Some of the records were so scratchy from overuse they sounded as if the musicians were playing in the shower.

"Can you dance, Kathleen?" I shook my head, and Fiona's beautiful smile faded. "If I were younger I would teach you all the old dances: the waltz, the foxtrot, the Charleston. . . ."

"I'm really clumsy, Grandma. Even my gym teacher says so."

"Nonsense. A willowy lass like you? Why, I'll bet you would make a wonderful dancer with a few lessons."

"Did you used to dance when you were young, Grandma?"

"Aye, you should have seen me, Kathleen. I was the belle of New York. And Arthur had *wings* on his feet. He could glide across the dance floor so smoothly that his feet barely touched the floor. I could have danced with him all night. And I did, too."

"Who's Arthur?"

Fiona looked indignant. "Didn't your mother teach you anything about your ancestors? Shame on her! And what's wrong with Leonard that he doesn't tell you these things?" I shrugged, not knowing where to begin when it came to describing what was wrong with my loony uncle.

"Anyway, Arthur is your grandfather," Fiona continued. "We lived in Manhattan at the time, and we used to take a boat out to where the ships would anchor—miles offshore—so you could get something to drink. It was Prohibition, you see. And there would be music and food on board and . . . well, never mind. But we would dance beneath the stars until the band played the very last note."

I could see it all in my mind, and when she put more music on the record player, I closed my eyes and pretended that I was on that boat, dancing with Arthur with the wings on his feet.

Later, Grandma brought out an album filled with sepia-toned photographs and showed me pictures of her and Arthur. He looked old, even back when Grandma looked young. He always wore a suit and tie, and Grandma wore fancy jewelry and furs. I could see expensive cars and elegant furnishings in the background.

I saw photos of my mom and uncle when they were fat-cheeked babies, being pushed in a "pram," as Grandma called it, in Central Park. Near the end of the album, I saw my mom and Uncle Leonard as older children, living here in Deer Falls. My uncle looked just as morose when he was a child as he did as an adult, but Mommy looked young and pretty—and happy. I never knew she had such a nice smile. I saw pictures of her sitting beside the lake in a bathing suit, laughing with her friends, and I wondered how she had changed into the woman I lived with.

The life that Grandma Fiona showed me in that album was so different from my family's life now that it seemed made up. I wondered where that beautiful world had gone—because it had certainly vanished, as surely as our present world would vanish if the Russians dropped their bombs.

Grandma Fiona sipped sherry while we talked, and after a while she got weepy. "You have Arthur's eyes," she told me as she took my chin in her hand and gazed into them. "Such deep, deep brown eyes. Looking into them was like looking down a well."

"Did Arthur die?" I asked her.

She nodded sadly. "Aye, a long time ago, luv."

Connie and Uncle Leonard finally turned off the radio and came inside when the night air got too cold. He saw Grandma reminiscing and frowned. "That's enough of the past, Mother. You can't get it back."

"I can bring it back in my memories." She smiled faintly, and for a fleeting second I saw the beautiful young woman my grandmother had once been beneath the aging skin and faded hair.

"It's almost midnight," Leonard said, shutting off the phonograph. "We should go to bed."

I slept in Grandma Fiona's bed with her that night. The sheets were soft with age, just like her skin; they both smelled of lavender. But before we turned off the light for the night, she let me try on some of her costume jewelry—necklaces and bracelets and rings that were too big for my fingers.

"Aye, you're a lovely girl," she said. And as I sat at her dressing table and gazed at myself in her wavy, age-cracked mirror, I almost believed it.

I never wanted to go home. Grandma Fiona looked right into my eyes when she talked to me instead of looking through half-closed eyes, the way Mommy always did. Grandma listened to me—really listened—as if what I had to say was the most fascinating thing she'd ever heard. And the way that she caressed me—touching my face, stroking my hair, rubbing my back, holding my hand—made me feel more cherished than I had ever felt in my life.

But after a six-day standoff, the Russians backed down. President Kennedy had played the highest-stakes poker game of his life and won. I was probably one of the very few people in the world who hated to see the Cuban missile crisis come to an end. It meant that I had to leave my grandmother and the charming village of Deer Falls and go home to my miserable, unhappy family in Riverside.

"Come and visit me again, luv," Grandma Fiona begged as she hugged me good-bye. She stood on her back porch with tears in her eyes, waving to us with a lace handkerchief.

"I will," I promised. "I will come again!" I meant it, too.

But that was the last time I ever saw her.

Chapter

11

I endured yet another loss that autumn of 1962; the Cuban missile crisis dealt the final blow to my friendship with May Elizabeth. The crisis intensified the hatred and fear that people felt toward Communists, so even though a nuclear war had been averted, May acted as if it had been my fault that she'd spent a long weekend in her fallout shelter.

There were plenty of other reasons, too. We were in junior high now, and she had much more in common with Debbie Harris, who teased her hair and flirted with boys and listened to Peter, Paul and Mary records—than she did with me. May and I attended most of the same classes and our lockers stood right next to each other, but she acted as if I didn't exist. I should have known that our friendship couldn't survive. Hadn't I heard anything Uncle Leonard had tried to preach to me all these years about the proletariat and the bourgeoisie? Sometimes I wished that the world had come to an end while I was eating roast beef in Deer Falls with my grandmother.

Our regional school district bussed kids into town for junior high and high school from all the neighboring villages. We now had 101 kids in our grade instead of forty-seven. May Elizabeth found a whole new set of friends to hang out with, cool girls who wore training bras and garter belts and nylons. Her Sunday shoes had tiny little heels on them now. I went back to being "Cootie Kathy" because I didn't dress in the right clothes or wear my hair in a flip. It was hard to get my hair to do much of anything since we were always running out of shampoo and I had to wash my hair with a bar of soap in the rust-stained bathroom sink.

My daddy made parole that winter, and he stayed home for the longest period of time that I could ever recall. He supposedly had a job in Bensenville and rode there with Uncle Leonard every day. I didn't ask him where he worked. I didn't want to know. I was still mad at him for being an ex-convict, and I refused to cuddle up with him or let him try to cheer me up. Besides, he had a full-time job trying to cheer up Annie. Whatever Daddy's day job was, I don't think he liked it very much because he came home tired and sad every night. It seemed like we all walked around for the next few years acting gloomy and woebegone. Mommy, Uncle Leonard, and Annie had always been morose, but now Daddy and I joined their pity party.

The gloom deepened a year later when President Kennedy was assassinated in November of 1963. I remember walking home from eighth grade and finding my mother sitting in front of the TV set, crying. "Somebody just shot President Kennedy," she said.

I couldn't believe it. "Why?" I asked.

That question continued to occupy the nation for years. We were all sad, even Uncle Leonard, who had disliked President Kennedy long before the Bay of Pigs invasion. "Still, it's a shocking thing," he murmured. "Shocking."

We watched TV for days it seemed, feeling numb and listening to the news commentators talk on and on about the Texas Book Depository and the grassy knoll and Lee Harvey Oswald. We saw rerun after rerun of Jackie Kennedy in her pillbox hat and blood-splattered pink suit, looking grief-stricken and hollow. When Lee Harvey Oswald's Communist ties were discovered, Uncle Leonard feared a backlash and worried that he would have to leave town again.

I went to church one Sunday morning and came home to find Daddy wild-eyed and raving, pointing to the TV set and shouting, "Somebody just shot Lee Harvey Oswald! I sat right here and saw it live on TV! They shot him right in front of me!"

We watched the president's funeral procession, deeply moved by the riderless black horse with the empty boots turned around in the stirrups. The poise and courage of his young widow, Jacqueline, inspired us; the tragedy and poignancy of little John-John's salute touched us. I mourned, not only for John F. Kennedy, but for all that he had represented. He had been a man of power, handsome and strong, blessed with a beautiful wife, adorable children, wealth, and respect. My family was nothing at all like his, and I would never have any of the things he had. But for a little while, I had almost felt as if I did. The Kennedys were the all-American ideal, our nation's shining First Family, and in them we had tasted perfection. Now that ideal had been violently destroyed, the perfect life I so longed for cruelly snatched away by an assassin's bullet. It had been only a dream.

For most of the young people in Riverside, the gloom finally lifted a few months later when the Beatles landed in America in February of 1964. By then, our TV was so decrepit that Ed Sullivan looked as though he was stranded in a raging blizzard, buffeted by gale-force winds that blew him up to the top of the screen, then tossed him to the bottom again. But when I watched his show one Sunday night and saw the Beatles singing "I Want to Hold Your Hand," I fell in love with Ringo Starr. Yeah, yeah, yeah!

The next day, all the boys came to school with their hair combed down over their foreheads. The girls starting buying Beatles records and listening to their music on transistor radios and reading all about John, Paul, George, and Ringo in fan magazines. I didn't have a record player or a radio, let alone money for fan magazines. Any knowledge I had of the Fab Four had to come secondhand through the scraps of information I overheard in the school hallways. I lay on my mattress at night, fantasizing about how I would miraculously meet Ringo Starr and be whisked away to live happily ever after in his mansion in England. But I would be magnanimous with my newfound wealth; I would buy my family a new TV set as a parting gift.

I started high school in 1964 and entered an entirely different world from junior high. Nevertheless, it was still a world in which I was shunned and excluded. During our high school years May Elizabeth's life and mine took two entirely different courses, as if we lived in parallel universes on *The Twilight Zone*. May and her friends were cheerleaders and had boyfriends and went steady. She was voted homecoming queen and rode to the football field in a convertible, holding a bouquet of roses and waving her gloved hand like the Queen of England. I didn't actually see this performance since I never went to football games, but her picture appeared in the school newspaper.

May's brother, Ron, was the star quarterback, the captain of the basketball team, the prom king. He drove a red V–8 Mustang, and pretty girls swarmed all around him. My brothers drove the town constable to drink, and the only things that swarmed around Poke and JT were allegations. If anything was missing, demolished, dented, looted, or burned, the blame fell on the Gallagher boys. They had turned into regular hoodlums: shooting out streetlights with slingshots, soaping car windows, exploding firecrackers in mailboxes, stealing candy and comic books and squirt guns from the Valley Food Market and Brinkley's Drugstore.

"The nut doesn't fall far from the tree," I heard people saying. "The father is no good and neither are the sons." And they were right. I was old enough and wise enough to understand what was going on when Poke and JT would go "shopping" in Bensenville with Daddy. He had trained them well. The poor store clerks were so busy keeping an eye on the two little street toughs that no one noticed Donald Gallagher stuffing all kinds of things up his sleeves and inside his coat.

"You need anything from the store, Kathleen?" he would ask as he and the boys piled into the rusted Ford.

"No, thanks." My hair always felt dirtier when I washed it in stolen shampoo.

While the other kids went to football games and basketball games, I worked in the Riverside Diner washing dishes. With my mousy brown hair and skinny body and flat chest, I wasn't cute enough or perky enough at age sixteen to be a waitress, so they kept me hidden in the back. The diner was the town hangout, and all the kids congregated there after the games for hamburgers and French fries and milk shakes. Sometimes I would hear May Elizabeth's tinkling laughter above the roar of the dishwasher, and I'd catch a glimpse of her through the pass-through window when I brought the cook a stack of clean plates.

She was beautiful now, blonde and fair-skinned. Her pudginess had shifted around on her growing body and settled into voluptuous curves. She was always the center of attention, always animated and dramatic. I wished her well. I envied her. I knew I could never be like her.

I hated myself so much that I finally stopped looking in the mirror. I hated my scrawny, underdeveloped body and my stringy hair and my baggy, thrift-store clothes. I hated the way my clothes smelled and the way my house smelled and the way I smelled after working a shift in the diner's greasy kitchen. I had no girlfriends, let alone boyfriends. I went to school, sat in class without ever saying a word, ate lunch alone in the cafeteria, and walked home alone. No one noticed that I never attended a school dance or a football game or hung around the diner afterward. No one said, "Hey, where's Kathleen Gallagher? We should see if she wants to come along." No one noticed that I stopped attending Sunday school and didn't join the confirmation class and never went to church anymore. No one cared.

I hated my life.

I fought with my mother constantly. For as long as I could recall, she had taken my brothers' side in every argument and had looked the other way while they wrecked everything I owned. But the last straw came when the boys stole my new padded training bra and let Charlie Grout see it for a dollar. Thanks to Poke and JT, everyone in Riverside High School knew that Cootie Kathy wore falsies.

"I don't have any privacy!" I screamed at my mother. "I'm sick and tired of sharing a bedroom with my perverted brothers!" I had entered woman-hood, and I wanted to be able to shave my legs in peace without my brothers charging admission so their friends could peek through the hole where the bathroom doorknob should be.

"What do you expect me to do about it?" my mother said. "Build another room?"

I knew she would never take any action, so I took action myself. Uncle Leonard had moved in with his girlfriend after Daddy came home, so I decided that Poke and JT should sleep in our uncle's old "bedroom" in the living room. I dragged their mattress and pillows down the hall and stuffed all their clothes, slingshots, matches, and other stolen loot in Uncle Leonard's cardboard "closet" behind the couch. The boys didn't seem to care in the least that they had been relocated. They slept on the living room floor half the time, anyway. A mattress simply made it more comfortable.

I had a small measure of privacy at last, and to celebrate I bought a hook-and-eye lock at the cluttered Village Hardware Store and installed it myself with Daddy's screwdriver. Not that a lock had ever stopped my brothers, but I hoped it would slow them down a bit.

During my junior year of high school my figure finally began to change, and I outgrew most of my clothes. I barely had adequate clothing to begin with, but the fact that my mother didn't have the money or the energy to go to the Laundromat on a regular basis made the situation critical most of the time.

"Look at this," I told her, modeling the gaping buttons of my "good" cotton blouse. "I need new clothes."

"I'll ask Leonard to drive you to the thrift store in Bensenville."

"I *hate* thrift-store clothes. They stink like wet sheep dogs! Why can't I buy something new just once in my life?"

"You think you're better than the rest of us? You think you deserve to have new clothes while we have to make do with secondhand?"

"You could buy some new clothes once in a while, too," I griped. "Why do you have to look like a bag lady all the time? Why can't you be like other mothers?"

"I've had about all I can take from you," she said. "I don't think you deserve a trip to the thrift shop. You can go without until you change your attitude."

I might have gotten more sympathy from Daddy, but I refused to ask him. I knew how he "shopped," and I didn't want it on my conscience if he wound up back in the county correctional center because I needed new clothes. Besides, I would feel even more ashamed walking around in stolen clothes than if I wore clothes from the thrift store. As time passed, my wardrobe became more and more meager, my arguments with my mother fiercer and more frequent.

"Can you please sign this?" I asked her one afternoon. "I want to take driver's ed next semester." I showed her the consent form, holding my breath as she reached the bottom line and saw the enrollment fee and learner's permit fee.

"No. We can't afford it."

"I'll pay for it out of the money I make at the diner. Please . . . all you have to do is sign the permission slip."

"I already said no. It's a waste of time and money since we don't have a car for you to drive."

"Maybe Uncle Leonard will let me drive his car."

"I've gotten by just fine without a driver's license all these years, and so can you."

The helplessness and hopelessness I felt enraged me. "I hate living here and I hate this family and I hate you!" I screamed. "I'm going to go live with Connie and Uncle Leonard." I never thought I would say that; it was a measure of my desperation that I'd choose to live with my Communist uncle and his common-law wife. By now they had dated for almost seven years and had lived together at least half of that time. If Connie was still hoping for wedding bells to ring, she was in for a big disappointment. Uncle Leonard said marriage was for fools and capitalists.

My mother was unmoved by my declarations of hatred or my threats to move away. "That's out of the question," she said. "Connie Miller is a simpleton. There's only one reason why men are attracted to women like her."

I had a pretty good idea what that reason was.

I had to blame someone for the rotten life I lived, and since my mother was handy, I decided that it was all her fault. We had learned about alcoholism in health class, and I had begun to wonder if my mother secretly drank. Maybe that's what she'd been doing in the outhouse all these years—although it remained a mystery to me how she could afford to buy alcohol when we couldn't even afford groceries. Mom was always weak and exhausted, and her eyes drooped half-shut no matter how much sleep she got. She never had enough energy to cook a meal or clean the house or keep my brothers out of trouble.

I decided that if she wasn't such a frumpy recluse, maybe I wouldn't be ostracized in school. If she still lived in Deer Falls with Grandma Fiona, at least I would have a nice apartment that smelled like lavender instead of mold and urine. I was sullen and mouthy and bitter. No matter what Mom said to me, I had three standard replies: "Why should I?" or "What do you care?" or "I wish you weren't my mother."

Her response rang through our bungalow in a monotonous refrain: "I've had about all I can take from you. . . ."

I hated my life. I would sit in my room for hours, crying and crying, unable to stop. No one came in to ask me what was wrong. I thought about running away at least three times a week. One of those times was because she refused to let me go to Washington, DC, on our senior class trip—even if I paid for it with my own money.

"I'm leaving home and never coming back!" I yelled.

"Go ahead. How far do you think you'll get?"

"I'll go to Deer Falls and live with Grandma Fiona."

My mother got a funny look on her face. At first I couldn't figure out what it was, then I saw tears glistening in her eyes just before she turned her head away, and I realized that it was grief.

"Your grandmother's dead." I heard bitterness in her voice.

I had only met Fiona that one time, but when I thought of my beautiful, elegant grandmother sipping sherry and listening to her scratchy phonograph records, I felt her loss as keenly as if I had visited her only yesterday.

"No! You're lying! How did she die? Why didn't you tell me? Why didn't we ever go visit her again before it was too late?" My voice rose in volume and pitch with each question. But my mother simply shook her head and went outside to her sanctuary, slamming the kitchen door. I went out the front door, slamming it, too.

I crossed the bridge and walked through Riverside, not caring where I ended up. I felt like lying down on the grass in the cemetery and waiting to die like Sarah Hawkins. I would have done it, too, but we didn't own a cemetery plot and the groundskeeper would probably run me off for trespassing.

Tears spilled down my cheeks. My grandmother had made me feel loved and loveable and now she was gone forever. I was so mad that I wanted to beat somebody up. When I saw my uncle's car in the street outside their apartment, I ran upstairs and banged on the door. They lived in two cramped rooms above the Valley Food Market, where Connie worked.

I confronted Uncle Leonard with the question the moment Connie invited me inside. "When did Grandma Fiona die?"

Uncle Leonard exhaled and all the life seemed to go out of his gangly body, as if the puppeteer had dropped the strings. He leaned against the sink in Connie's tiny kitchenette. "More than four years ago—a few months after we visited her, in fact."

"Why didn't you tell me?"

"You hardly knew her," he said defensively.

"I did too know her! She was my grandmother! I would've gone to her funeral!"

"There was no funeral. They're a waste of money. Funerals are for fools who believe in God and an afterlife."

That was more than I could take. To think of lovely Fiona, unmourned, unloved, thrown into the garbage bin—or wherever Communists stashed their dead loved ones—was a bitter blow.

"How could you do that?" I yelled. I was trembling with fury and grief. "Grandma Fiona believed in God, and so do I!"

"For goodness' sake, sweetie. Calm down," Connie said. She looked worried. "Take a deep breath, have a drink of water."

"No! I want my grandma!"

Fiona had been the only person who had ever loved me. I could tell that she did by the way she looked into my eyes when she talked to me, and by the way she touched my hair and cupped her soft, wrinkled hand on my cheek. I remembered all the pretty things she'd had and how she had let me try on her necklaces and rings. Now she was gone forever, and I didn't have anything to remember her by.

"What did you do with all her stuff?"

"I took care of it," Uncle Leonard said coldly.

"Isn't there anything of hers left? A bracelet . . . something. . . ?" My eyes burned and my face was slick with tears, but I couldn't stop crying.

"It was all useless junk, Kathleen. It's gone."

"I hate you!" I screamed. I went after him with my fists, pummeling his chest, trying to hurt him as much as he had hurt me. He was stronger than he looked. He gripped my wrists so tightly they ached, as he held me away from him.

"I think I'd better take you home."

"No, I don't ever want to go home again," I sobbed. "Especially with you!"

Connie did the best thing anyone could have done. She nudged my uncle away and pulled me into her arms and let me cry. "Go away, Leonard," she said over my shoulder. "Can't you see she's heartbroken? Leave the poor girl with me."

Uncle Leonard left. Connie made soothing noises as she held me tightly, listening as I vented all of my hatred and rage. When I finally calmed down, she made me a cup of hot chocolate and a grilled cheese sandwich. I slept on her couch that night.

The next day was a Saturday, and she made French toast with butter and syrup. She put a rock-and-roll station on the radio just for me, and we danced to the Beatles in our bare feet.

"Can I live here with you, Connie?" I asked when it was time for her to go downstairs to work. "I don't ever want to go home again."

"I would love to say yes, sweetie. I've always wanted children of my own, you know. But you need to go home to your family."

"Why don't you get married and have some, then?"

She smiled sadly as she slipped her shop apron over her head and tied it around her ample waist. "The only man I've ever loved is your Uncle Leonard. And he doesn't want any children." I could see that this was a painful subject for her, so I let it go.

"I may not see you again," I told her as I hugged her good-bye. "I'm going to run away."

"Please don't do that," she said softly. "I quit school and ran away when I was sixteen, and now I wish I hadn't. I never finished my education, so I can never better myself. I'm forty-three years old, and all I have to show for it is a tiny apartment, a job in a grocery store, and a man who doesn't love me enough to marry me. But you're a bright girl, Kathleen—a pretty girl. You can get a college education and get out of this nowhere town and make something of yourself. That's the best way to show them, honey . . . not by running away."

I knew deep inside that Connie was right. Besides, I doubted that my family would even come looking for me if I disappeared. The nearsighted town constable would be no help, either. He'd be overjoyed to have one less thieving Gallagher in town. Not knowing what else to do or where to go, I returned home to my miserable life.

I used the money I earned at the diner to apply to colleges. I had straight A's in algebra, trigonometry, geometry and calculus, and my math teacher, Mr. Mueller, encouraged me to apply to Albany State University and major in mathematics.

"Your Regents' exam scores make you eligible for a New York State Regents' Scholarship," Mr. Mueller told me. "Depending on your family's financial need, you might qualify for full tuition." I assured him that I would qualify. The only problem would be paying for my room and board.

I was going to graduate third in my class, and with high SAT scores, I was easily accepted at Albany State. My goal was within sight. This would be the last year I would ever have to spend in Riverside, walking around with my head down. All I ever wanted was to leave home and never return.

Only one last detail remained, and I avoided taking care of it for as long as I possibly could, hoping for a miracle. No matter how many ways I added up my financial aid package from Albany State, there was still a gap between what I owed and what I had managed to save on my own. I had been awarded the mathematics prize at graduation and a small student council scholarship, but I was still short for room and board, plus books and various activity fees. The financial aid officer at the college had included student loan forms for me to fill out to cover the difference. All I needed was someone to cosign them for me.

I didn't ask Daddy. The signature of a paroled felon probably wouldn't carry much weight, and I was afraid that Daddy would be dumb enough to rob a bank for me if he knew that I needed money. After all, the last time that I had asked him for something, he had stolen a Christmas tree. I didn't ask Uncle Leonard, either, because I already knew what he thought of the capitalistic public education system.

"It ought to be free, like it is in Communist countries," he'd said a dozen times. In his mind a free education was more important than freedom of thought or freedom of speech or freedom of worship. Yes, I knew better than to ask him. Or Connie. She was a sweet soul, but she would never defy Uncle Leonard. That left my mother as my only resource. I waited until she was home alone, then went to where she lay sprawled on the couch and handed her the loan papers and a pen.

"I need you to sign this for me. It's for college."

"What is it?" She looked at it through sleepy, half-closed eyes. She couldn't seem to muster the energy to hold the pen much less sign her name.

"It's for a loan that I can pay back after I graduate."

"I thought you had a scholarship?"

"I do—for full tuition. And I can pay for most of my room and board with a campus job. But I need a loan to make up the difference." She started slowly shaking her head, and I felt my temper flare. "I'll pay it all back! I just need your signature!"

"Why do you want to go to a snooty, expensive school like that? What's wrong with the community college over in Bensenville?"

"Mom, *please*! Albany State is a much better school!"

"You'll be out of place there. It's a school for rich kids. The boys you'll meet there would never marry someone from our background. At least at the community college there will be others like you. You could live at home and save room and board."

"No!" I wailed. I sank down on the living room floor in front of the couch. "I don't want to marry someone from our background. I'd rather not get married at all! And I don't want to live in Riverside for one more minute. Don't you understand that? I know Daddy is a convicted criminal." She appeared startled. "I learned the truth a long time ago," I continued. "And I hate the way everyone looks at us and whispers about us behind our backs. I want to get out of here and go as far away as I can and start a new life all over again—like you did."

"You don't know a thing about me—" she began, but I shouted her down.

"I know that you left Grandma Fiona and ran away from Deer Falls and never went back! All my life people have been telling me to get good grades and get a college education so I could make something of myself— and now I'm so close! If you would just cosign this loan for me, you'll never have to see me again as long as you live!"

My mother closed her eyes and slowly tore the form in half.

"No!" I screamed.

"I'll get you the money," she said quietly. I scrambled to my feet and pulled the mangled papers out of her hands.

"How? Are you going to steal it, like Daddy? Well, don't bother! I'm leaving home and never coming back!"

I packed my meager belongings in the suitcase Connie had given me for a graduation present, and left. I was so angry and frustrated that I walked out to the county highway and hitched a ride to Bensenville with a car full of hippies. They dropped me off at the Greyhound station, and I caught a bus to Albany the next day. By the time I reached the campus, I had pieced the loan form together with tape and forged my mother's signature on it. A receptionist guided me to an information board, and within two days I had found a house full of hippies who were looking for another roommate, and a summer job at a coffee shop close to campus. My working hours were from five-thirty in the morning until one-thirty in the afternoon, so I was able to work a second job washing dishes at a restaurant from four o'clock in the afternoon until closing. I worked myself to exhaustion every day that summer, but I didn't care. Nobody knew the old Kathleen Gallagher who'd had cooties and a Communist uncle and a thieving father. I was starting life all over again.

Two weeks after moving to Albany, I came home to my apartment after a long shift at the restaurant and saw Uncle Leonard's beat-up car parked at the curb. It could have been any one of my family members, since they all used his car. Even Poke took it for joyrides whenever he felt like it, never caring that he was only fourteen.

But when I got closer I saw Uncle Leonard himself sitting on the front stoop with his head in his hands. He looked like a cadaver in the yellow-green light of the street lamp. He saw me approaching and stood.

"Kathleen . . . something terrible has happened," he said. He gripped my arms, and I wasn't sure if he was holding me up or leaning on me for support. I waited the longest moment of my life.

"Your mother is dead."

Part

3

KATHLEEN AND JOELLE

2004

Chapter

12

By the time Kathleen finished telling her story to Joelle, she felt as though she had aged thirty years. She could feel the tension in her shoulders and neck, the writhing knot in her stomach from reliving her past. And she hadn't even told Joelle the worst of it. Sooner or later she would want to know how her grandmother had died, but right now, Kathleen couldn't bring herself to say the words out loud.

Why did she still feel as though her mother's sudden death was her fault, even though it had happened after she left home? She would have to tell Joelle the details before someone else in the family did, but she had raked up enough muck for one morning.

"I have to stop for gas," Kathleen said, switching on the turn signal to exit the highway. "Do you need to get out and stretch? Want a sandwich or something?"

"Sure. . . . Mom, don't you want to just drive into Riverside and find all those horrible people who laughed at you and show them how rich and successful you are now?"

Kathleen's answer was quick: "No. I don't."

"Why not?"

The truth was that no matter how hard Kathleen had worked or how successful she'd become, the shame would never go away. She may have changed, but the town's perception of her probably hadn't, and after all this time she still feared their scorn.

"No one will believe it's true," she said quietly.

"Mom, you're driving a Lexus, for crying out loud."

It was on the tip of Kathleen's tongue to say: *They'll assume I stole it.*

She pulled the car to a halt beside the gas pump, and Joelle hopped out with the grace and energy of youth; Kathleen climbed out as if she were eighty-four instead of fifty-four. She filled the gas tank, and when she went inside to pay for the gas and buy sandwiches and drinks, Joelle set a package of Hostess Twinkies on the counter.

"These are for you, Mom. To make up for all those times you couldn't afford them."

Kathleen was so touched she could only manage to say, "Thanks."

She waited until she'd negotiated the entrance ramp and they were back on the highway before she said, "Do you understand why I wanted a different life for you?" *And why I was so upset with you for shoplifting?* she wanted to add.

"I guess so. . . ."

"And now that you know a little more about my past, do you understand why I resigned from my job at Impost? They weren't asking me to break the law, exactly, but it was much too close to the line for me to feel comfortable."

"What about Grandma's story?" Joelle asked after a moment.

A shadow of dread passed over Kathleen. "What do you mean?"

"Well, you wanted me to hear your story so I could understand you better—and I do, now that I know what a lousy childhood you had and everything. So . . . what about your mother? Why did she spend so much time in the outhouse? What was *her* story—what was *her* childhood like?"

"My mother would never talk about herself." Even as she said the words, Kathleen realized that she had never talked about herself, either, for all these years. But what if Joelle was right? What if there was something in her mother's past that would explain her behavior? Kathleen knew that she needed to forgive her mother for the mistakes she'd made, just as she hoped Joelle would forgive her. But had she ever bothered to try to understand her mother?

"You don't know *anything* about your mom?" Joelle persisted.

"Not much. . . . Just a few family stories that have been passed down over the years. My great-grandfather supposedly left Ireland in the 1920s and started all over again in America with my grandmother."

"You mean your *great*-grandmother."

"No, his wife stayed behind in Ireland with the rest of the children. Only my grandmother Fiona and her father came over."

"That's weird."

"Yes, I suppose it is. Anyway, Grandma Fiona left New York City at some point and started all over again with my mother and Uncle Leonard in Deer Falls, that little resort town in the Pocono Mountains."

"What about Fiona's husband?"

"I don't know anything about him. I think he might have died around that time. Anyway, my mother left home during World War II and started all over again in Riverside—where we're going."

And Kathleen had left there in 1968, starting all over again in Albany. What a legacy! Running away from life's problems.

"Why did everyone keep leaving home?" Joelle asked.

"I guess for the same reasons that I did—they wanted to take control of their lives, change the direction they were heading, get out of whatever rut their parents were in."

Joelle nodded, looking thoughtful. Kathleen felt a little thrill—they were communicating. And without any help from homely Dr. Russo, thank you very much. Kathleen had a question for Joelle, but she proceeded carefully, as if one false move would send them sliding all the way back to where they'd started, like a tiresome game of Chutes and Ladders.

"What do you want your life and your future to be, Joelle?"

"I want . . ." She stopped, shaking her head. "Whatever. Never mind."

"No, I'd really like to know."

"It will only make you mad."

"That's okay. I still want to hear it—not so I can talk you out of it, I promise. But so that we can get to know each other a little better. Please?"

Joelle exhaled, and when she finally spoke, her words came out bitter and tight. "I *hate* my life."

Her words stunned Kathleen. How often had Kathleen voiced the same thoughts when she was growing up—hating her life, hating her poverty and shame. But Joelle had everything Kathleen had dreamed of and longed for. How could she say she hated her life?

"Why?" Kathleen managed to ask.

"Because it's so phony and plastic. I can't stand the way you and Daddy and all my friends' parents live—it's like you're not really living at all! You're just making money and spending it—and not even enjoying it. And you're all so *boring*. At least your father and your Uncle Leonard sounded like interesting people."

Kathleen wanted to interrupt, to argue that being a criminal or a Communist made life difficult, not interesting. She wanted to defend herself and prove that she really *was* living and enjoying her life. It was the life she'd chosen and worked for. But she held her tongue and allowed Joelle to finish.

"I don't want to live the way you and Daddy do. I want to do something that *matters*."

"Don't we all?" Kathleen murmured.

"I mean, I don't care if I have a job that makes a lot of money. I want to do something to *help* people."

So many thoughts came to Kathleen's mind: how Joelle had been pampered and catered to since the day she'd been born; how she'd never even helped out around the house, much less helped strangers; how she was accustomed to nice stuff, expensive stuff, and lots of it. Joelle had no idea what it was like to have to scrimp and save just to buy a bottle of shampoo, or how disgusting your clothes smelled when you bought them at the thrift store, or what it was like to go to bed on a bare mattress with an empty stomach. Joelle threw more food into the garbage every day than Kathleen used to eat in a week when she was a child. Her daughter was rich and spoiled and dearly loved, and she took it all for granted.

But Kathleen didn't say any of those things. Instead, she pulled out to pass a slow-moving truck, and waited until she was sure her voice would sound encouraging, not critical or sarcastic. "You don't have to wait to help people, Joelle. Why don't you go to Mexico on the youth group mission trip this summer?"

"Mexico!" Joelle's expression of disgust was priceless, as if she was imagining what it would be like to sleep on the floor or to sacrifice her daily shower and her favorite TV shows or to eat mystery food. And how it would be to rise at dawn to do manual labor all day, coming home sweaty and dirty. Kathleen fought to suppress a smile.

Joelle eyed Kathleen carefully, as if suspicious of her motives. Kathleen hoped her face didn't betray her amusement.

Finally Joelle lifted her chin and looked away. "Maybe I *will* go to Mexico."

Kathleen finally grinned. "My uncle Leonard would be proud of you."

They pulled into a motel in Bensenville a little after three o'clock. Joelle had been dozing. Kathleen rubbed her shoulder. "Joelle, we're here."

She opened her eyes and gazed around, still groggy. "Is this the town where you grew up?"

"Not quite. There aren't any hotels in Riverside. This is the closest town that has one."

"Why aren't we staying with your family?"

"Um . . . no room." Hadn't she been listening? Didn't Kathleen just explain how poor her family was, what a dilapidated house she'd lived in? Kathleen wanted a clean bathroom and a firm mattress—and as little contact with her family as possible. Joelle should thank her for it.

They checked into the hotel, and Joelle flopped onto one of the beds with the TV remote. Kathleen couldn't seem to relax. Retelling the story of her past had reminded her of how much Mrs. Hayworth had once meant to her, and she was sorry they'd lost contact. On impulse, Kathleen pulled the phone book out of the nightstand drawer to see if there was a listing for her. There was, and it was at the same street address in Riverside where she'd always lived. Kathleen quickly dialed the number before she lost her nerve. She found herself half-hoping Mrs. Hayworth wouldn't answer, afraid of the memories that would be unearthed if she did. Cynthia answered on the second ring.

"Why, Kathleen Gallagher!" she said after Kathleen identified herself. "How are you? I was just thinking about you the other day when I read about your brother in the newspaper."

A shudder passed through Kathleen at the mention of her brother. She wondered what crime he'd committed this time to get his name in the paper. She could barely answer Mrs. Hayworth's question as she fought the urge to leap into her car and flee home to Maryland.

"Um . . . good. I'm good. I'm here in town, actually. Well, in Bensenville."

"Wonderful! Why don't you come over for a visit?"

"I'd hate to bother you if you're busy . . ."

"Nonsense. I'm a seventy-nine-year-old widow. How busy do you imagine I could be? I'd love to see you." Kathleen didn't feel right about accepting Cynthia's invitation to dinner, but she finally agreed to stop by afterward for coffee.

"Isn't Mrs. Hayworth your friend May Elizabeth's mother?" Joelle asked when Kathleen told her where she was going.

"Yes. She invited me to come over later. You don't have to come with me if you don't want to. I won't stay long. The hotel pool looks nice."

Joelle shrugged. "I'll come." She punched the TV remote lazily, flipping through the channels, then suddenly sat up. "Hey, do you suppose they still have their bomb shelter? It would be awesome to see it!"

Cynthia Hayworth met them at the front door, struggling to quiet a yapping little dog named Fluff. Kathleen thought of the break-in forty-odd years ago and wondered if it would have happened if the Hayworths had owned Fluff back then.

The Hayworth house, which had once seemed so huge and modern and glamorous to Kathleen, now looked small and outdated, like something from a 1960s museum. The sunken living room looked unchanged after all this time and even had the same brocade sofa she remembered. The pastel bathroom fixtures hadn't been updated, either, but the little doll that once hid the roll of toilet paper had disappeared, replaced by a bowl of potpourri. Kathleen glanced at the floor as she entered the front foyer, looking for the spot on the carpet where Poke and JT had thrown up, but the shag carpeting had been replaced.

Kathleen never would have recognized Cynthia if they had passed each other on the street. But when she looked closely, she could still see the glamorous woman she remembered underneath the aging exterior. Cynthia was still elegant—a classy lady—wearing a dress and jewelry and nylons, even on a warm summer evening. Her silvery hair looked freshly done. Kathleen felt a jolt of surprise to realize that her own mother would be in her late seventies, too, if she had lived. In Kathleen's mind, her mother would always look the way she had the last time she had seen her, remaining forty-four forever.

They chatted comfortably as they sipped coffee and lemonade, catching up on each other's lives. Kathleen was touched by the kind way that Cynthia drew Joelle into the conversation.

"How are May Elizabeth and Ron?" Kathleen asked after awhile.

"May is on her third husband, I'm sorry to say. She has three children, one from each, and lives in Atlanta. Ron went into his father's business, of course. He runs the factory now. He married Debbie Harris—remember her? They have three children, too, and their second grandchild is on the way." The idea of Ron Hayworth as a grandfather made Kathleen feel very old.

"I was telling Joelle on the way here what it was like growing up in Riverside, and I realized that I've never thanked you for helping me. You always made me feel welcome in your home, and you took an interest in our family and helped us out with clothes and things. You put your faith into action. And it's thanks to you that I'm a Christian today."

"Oh, dear," Cynthia said with a worried look. "I have a confession to make. I'm afraid that my motives weren't entirely unselfish, years ago. You see, I knew your mother before you were born, before she married your father. We were once best friends."

Kathleen couldn't reply. She couldn't picture it. How could classy

Cynthia Hayworth be best friends with frumpy Eleanor Gallagher? No. Cynthia might as well have told Kathleen that her mother had once been best friends with the Queen of England. But then, hadn't Kathleen and May Elizabeth once been unlikely friends, too?

"I always felt guilty about how differently things turned out for your mother and me," Cynthia continued, nervously stroking the dog's fur. "So I decided to help Eleanor and her family—behind the scenes, so to speak. Then I grew very fond of you, of course. I felt so bad when you stopped coming to church. I know it was partly because May Elizabeth treated you so badly once you girls got to junior high and high school, and I still feel so sorry about it all."

Kathleen barely heard Cynthia's apology as a hundred questions swirled through her mind. "When did you know my mother?" she asked. "Where did you meet her? I know Mom left Deer Falls and came here, but do you know when or why? We were just wondering about that, weren't we, Joelle? My mother never talked much about herself."

"I wish now that I would have told you about my friendship with your mother when you were growing up. Maybe it would have helped you understand her better if you'd known a little bit more of her story. But then again, May Elizabeth knew all about me, and it didn't seem to help our relationship."

"How did you and Mom meet?"

"Eleanor and I both came to town after Pearl Harbor to work in my husband's factory. Of course, it wasn't his factory back then, and he wasn't my husband. It was called Riverside Electronics, not Hayworth Industries. They had converted it into a defense plant during the war to manufacture electrical components and things like that. Eleanor and I were very, very different—yet we also had a lot in common. We were both born during the Roaring Twenties, spent our childhood under the cloud of the Great Depression, and came of age during the worst war the world had ever seen. And then we both applied for a job on the very same day. . . ."

Part

4

ELEANOR AND CYNTHIA

1942 — 1947

Chapter

13

Cynthia Weaver waited in the crowded front office at Riverside Electronics, wondering where she could go and what she would do if they didn't hire her. It hadn't taken very long to fill out the employment form since her only work experience had been on her family's farm. She hoped it would count for something. Women filled the tiny office: most of them older than Cynthia, many of them housewives in calico shifts and no-nonsense shoes, all of them looking for work. She felt out of place dressed in her Sunday best, but compared to the young woman sitting in the chair across from her, Cynthia felt like she'd just fallen off the turnip truck.

The girl looked Cynthia's age, but her obvious poise and confidence as she flipped through an old copy of *Life* magazine made her appear more mature. She wore her dark glossy hair perfectly styled in a pageboy, her lipstick and nail polish were the same shade of red as the stripe in her blouse, and she was the only woman in the office wearing slacks. She looked like she'd just stepped out of the pages of a fashion magazine. And in a town as small as Riverside, that meant she looked out of place.

The door leading into the factory opened suddenly, and a portly man in a drab, ill-fitting suit emerged, clutching a sheaf of papers. "Eleanor Bartlett?" he called. The stylish girl stood. "And Cynthia Weaver?" She scrambled to her feet. "I'm Ralph Jackson. This way, please, girls."

He led them down a cramped hallway, past piles of boxes and wooden pallets, and into the factory itself. The building hummed with the drone of machines and the buzz of fluorescent lighting, while in the background pounding hammers and screeching power saws added to the clamor. Cynthia glimpsed rows of workers intent on their labor and wondered how they could concentrate with such a racket.

"Pardon the noise," Mr. Jackson said as he steered them into his cubicle. "We're expanding the plant, retooling for war production." The tiny office had a wall of glass so he could see out onto the factory floor when he sat behind his desk. He shut the door, reducing the noise somewhat, and gestured to two chairs. "Have a seat, girls."

Cynthia sat stiffly on the edge of her chair, wondering what to do with her purse and with her fluttering hands, hoping she didn't look too fidgety as she straightened her skirt. The girl named Eleanor made herself comfortable almost effortlessly, managing to look ladylike, even in trousers, as she crossed her legs.

"What sort of electronics do you manufacture here?" she asked.

"Various gauges, switches for bombs."

Cynthia knew that her shock must have shown on her face when Mr. Jackson laughed. Hadn't her mother always warned her not to wear her heart on her sleeve for the whole world to see? She wished she could mask her emotions better.

"Don't worry, Miss Weaver," he said. "There aren't any explosives here. We assemble the switches, but they're wired to the actual bombs someplace else." He cleared his throat, as if to signal that the time had come to get down to business, and scanned the pile of papers in front of him. "Now, then, girls. First of all, I appreciate your willingness to do your patriotic duty by applying for a job in the defense industry. You've both listed your ages as eighteen and stated that you're high school graduates. Is that correct? Did you bring proof of that?"

Cynthia dug her birth certificate and high school diploma from her purse and passed them across the desk to him. The other girl's purse wasn't any larger than Cynthia's, but her papers looked remarkably crisp and unwrinkled as she pulled them out.

"Very good," he said when he'd finished examining them. "Congratulations, girls. You're hired. You can both start tomorrow. Training will take about two weeks, depending on how quickly you catch on. You'll be paid thirty-five dollars a week."

Cynthia broke into a wide grin, then squelched her enthusiasm when she saw Eleanor nodding calmly.

"Now I also see on your applications that neither of you has listed a local address as your place of residence."

"That's right," Eleanor said. "I planned to look for housing once I was certain that I had a position here. Perhaps I'll start searching this afternoon." She seemed so confident and poised. Cynthia would have stammered an inadequate apology. When she realized that she was nodding in agreement like a trained horse, she spoke up.

"Yes . . . me, too. I'll look today, too."

"Housing is scarce near almost all of the defense plants, as you've probably heard," Mr. Jackson said. "But I'm a lifelong resident of Riverside, and I could suggest a few places, if you want."

Eleanor smiled. "That would be very kind of you, Mr. Jackson."

"Yes. Yes, it would, Mr. Jackson." Cynthia hated the way she sounded. She wouldn't have remembered Mr. Jackson's name if Eleanor hadn't addressed him by it. She wondered if everyone could tell what a hick she was.

Mr. Jackson pulled out a list from a desk drawer and looked it over. "The most economical housing is a modest bed/sitting room above Montgomery's Funeral Home for twelve dollars a month. It so happens that Ada Montgomery is my sister-in-law, and I've seen the place. It's very nice. You would share a bath with two other boarders, and—"

"I'll take it," they both said simultaneously. Cynthia looked at Eleanor in alarm, but Eleanor laughed.

"No need to fight over it," Mr. Jackson said jovially. "Ada says it's large enough to accommodate two girls. I was about to add that whoever takes it will need to find a roommate."

"I'm game if you are," Eleanor said.

"Sure." Cynthia couldn't believe her good luck—she had landed a job and a roommate on the same day.

"You girls aren't squeamish about living above all the caskets and dead bodies and so forth, are you?" Mr. Jackson asked.

"I grew up on a farm," Cynthia said, then could have kicked herself. What a stupid thing to say. It made no sense. Should she explain what she'd meant? That she was accustomed to the sight of slaughtered hogs and chickens—or would that make matters worse?

"The funeral home isn't hard to find," he continued. "Did you see the stainless steel diner on Main Street as you came into town? The funeral home is right across the road from it. It sits back from the street a ways, behind some trees, so you might have missed it."

"Thank you for the suggestion, Mr. Jackson," Eleanor said smoothly. "I'm sure we'll have no trouble finding it."

He took them on a brief tour of the factory floor, and Cynthia had to resist the urge to shade her eyes from the glare of the thrumming fluorescent lights. The laborers stood in long rows behind workstations, assembling a complicated collage of wires and gadgets. Cynthia knew absolutely nothing about wiring and electricity, and she felt a ripple of anxiety, wondering how she could possibly get the hang of constructing such intricate devices. Mr. Jackson introduced them to their supervisor, Mr. Tomacek, a swarthy man in his sixties who smelled like cooked cabbage and looked as though he'd immigrated to America onboard a pirate ship. He glowered at them suspiciously, giving Cynthia the feeling that he disliked women in the workplace—especially brazen women like Eleanor who wore slacks.

"You'll need to wear a kerchief to cover your hair," Tomacek growled. "Keep your fingernails short, no polish. No jewelry allowed, either. And you'll be standing all day, so wear sturdy shoes."

Cynthia glanced at Eleanor. She wore a mischievous expression on her face, as if tempted to salute the old grouch and say "Aye, aye, sir!"

"The girls' locker room is through that door," Mr. Jackson said as he resumed the tour. "We just opened it about a month ago. There didn't used to be a girls' locker room or bathroom anywhere in this building, but after so many of our men enlisted following Pearl Harbor, well, three-quarters of our employees are girls now. Glad you two are coming forward to do your part."

"Mr. Jackson," Eleanor said, "no offense, but most of us would prefer to be called women, not girls."

Her frankness appalled Cynthia. Where she came from, a woman never spoke her mind to a man that way, especially if he was her boss. But she was even more surprised by Mr. Jackson's response. He laughed!

"No offense taken, Miss Bartlett. I'll try to remember that." They returned to his cubicle, the tour completed. "Well, that's about it, *ladies,*" he said, emphasizing the word. "If you have no further questions, I'll expect you here for work tomorrow at seven o'clock."

Eleanor held out her hand like a man and shook Mr. Jackson's. "Thank you so much for all your help," she told him. "I look forward to working here at Riverside Electronics."

"Yes . . . me, too," Cynthia squeaked. She felt like Eleanor's dimwitted sidekick.

"Well, it looks like we're in like Flynn," Eleanor said when they'd exited the building. "Shall we go check out our new room at the Cadaver Hotel?"

"I . . . um . . . sure. But I left my suitcases and things in a locker at the bus station." The summer day had turned out to be hot and humid, the kind of day that stole your energy and left you feeling wilted and boneless. Cynthia dreaded the prospect of dragging all her worldly goods across town in such heat.

"My things are at the station, too," Eleanor said. "Although it wasn't much of a station, was it? More like a hut. But, then, this isn't much of a town. Let's go claim our room first—before someone else comes along and pinches it. We can get our stuff later."

By the time they'd walked across town to Montgomery's Funeral Home, Cynthia felt as sticky and worn down as a discarded lollipop. They went to the front door of the rambling Victorian house and rang the bell. Mrs. Montgomery answered it, her withered lips already pursed in disapproval.

"Ralph Jackson called and said I could expect you two girls. Listen, you'll have to use the rear entrance from now on. This front door is only for our clients and the loved ones of the deceased. But you may as well come in, since you're already here, and I'll show you around. We aren't holding any services today."

She turned her broad back and led the way inside, the aged wooden floors creaking beneath her ample weight. The foyer and the three large rooms that had once been the parlor, morning room, and dining room had been turned into public areas for the funeral home's patrons. The rooms, like Mrs. Montgomery's clothing, were tastefully gloomy, with drab wallpaper, dark woodwork, somber drapes, and inadequate lighting. Wooden folding chairs stood in sedate rows facing a rickety podium and an empty casket stand. Modern plumbing and heating had obviously been later additions, judging by the pipes that climbed the walls in plain sight. A small room near the back served as the mortician's office. The house had a funny, medicinal odor that made Cynthia's nose itch.

"You'll be given a key to *this* outside door," Mrs. Montgomery informed them when they reached the rear of the house. "Kindly use these back stairs to the second and third floors. This other door leads to the basement, but you'll have no need to go downstairs where the embalming is done, unless there's an air raid. It goes without saying that gentlemen callers are not allowed inside at any time, for any reason."

Cynthia felt Eleanor nudge her in the ribs as they followed their landlady up the narrow steps. She turned and saw Eleanor mimicking Mrs. Montgomery's prim expression and heavy-footed tread. Cynthia quickly turned around, covering her mouth to stifle a giggle.

"These two rooms on the third floor were once the servants' quarters," Mrs. Montgomery continued. "We've added a good-sized bathroom in recent years. Two other young ladies, Miss Doris Henderson and Miss Lucille Kellogg, occupy the room across the hall from yours. They work at the electronics plant, as well. Since you'll be sharing the bathroom with them, you'll need to cooperate in preparing a schedule for baths and so on." She turned to unlock the bedroom door, and Eleanor quietly clicked her heels and gave a Nazi salute behind Mrs. Montgomery's back.

The room was surprisingly large and comfortable-looking, painted a cheery yellow, with flowered curtains on the windows and a colorful rag rug on the floor. There was a porcelain sink in one corner and two iron radiators that promised to deliver plenty of steam heat come wintertime. A dormer window overlooked the broad front lawn and Main Street beyond the row of trees.

The bedroom area had two twin beds with homey, mismatched quilts, a three-drawer dresser they could share, and a closet under the eaves with wire hangers in it. The sitting area had a lumpy, slip-covered loveseat, an overstuffed armchair, and an old wooden schoolmaster's desk. Cynthia imagined herself sitting at the desk, writing long impassioned letters to the soldier she would one day fall in love with.

"If you want towels and bed linens, it will be fifty cents extra each week," Mrs. Montgomery said. "You're allowed to use a hotplate for boiling water, but no other cooking, please. Kindly draw the blackout curtains at dusk. Any other questions, girls?"

"Yes," Eleanor said. "Miss Weaver and I both have baggage waiting at the bus station. Would it be possible for you to arrange transportation to get it here?"

Again, Eleanor's boldness surprised Cynthia—and pleased her. She never would have asked for such a favor on her own and would have hauled all her luggage down Main Street in the stifling heat and humidity, her arms aching, her body soaked with sweat.

"Certainly, Miss Bartlett," Mrs. Montgomery replied. "I'll ask our employee, William, to help you. Go ahead and have a look around your new room. I'll call you when he's ready to leave."

"Let's hope he doesn't drive us to the bus station in the hearse," Eleanor said when Mrs. Montgomery was gone. Cynthia's face must have betrayed her surprise because Eleanor added, "That was a joke, Cynthia. Don't take anything I say too seriously."

"Oh." She smiled nervously. "I guess I'm . . . uh . . ."

"Well, this place looks homey enough, don't you think?" Eleanor asked. "We'll get a hotplate and a pan for heating up some soup and we'll be all set." She kicked off her shoes and settled effortlessly onto the couch, stretching languidly. "So tell me all about yourself, Cynthia. Where are you from?"

Cynthia perched on the edge of the overstuffed chair as if Eleanor were interviewing her for a job. "You probably never heard of the town. It's upstate a ways, and it's even smaller than Riverside, if you can believe that. My folks have a little farm there with an orchard and stuff. My father was determined to marry me off to another farmer, but I didn't want anything to do with farm life—slaving from dawn to dusk and raising a litter of children. Ugh! I kept seeing advertisements everywhere for defense workers—*Do Your Part* and *We Can't Win the War Without Women*, and all that. They made it sound much more exciting than being a farmer's wife, so here I am." Cynthia didn't know why she had gone on and on like a windup toy, but it felt good after parroting one-syllable answers all morning. "Where are you from, Eleanor? What brings you here?" she asked.

"The same thing. I wanted to do my part. My older brother, Leonard, enlisted in the army right after they passed the Selective Service Bill in the fall of 1940. He was fresh out of high school and too young to be drafted but he wanted to serve his country. I'm just trying to keep up with him."

"I'll bet you're glad he didn't enlist in the Navy after what happened at Pearl Harbor, huh? Wasn't that terrible, all those men dying?"

"Yes. Very glad. That attack was one reason I decided to get a defense job. I saw the same advertising you did, about how patriotic it is to build planes and tanks and how women should support men like my brother who are off fighting the war. But the other reason was that I could make a lot more money working in a factory than doing the traditional women's jobs of waitress or sales clerk. I'm going to save my money and go to college someday."

"Do you have a boyfriend in the service?"

"Heavens, no." Eleanor made a face, as if a boyfriend was the last thing on her mind.

"Me, either, but I'd like one. Do you have family close by?"

She shook her head, then quickly asked, "Why did you pick Riverside?"

"I wanted to work in a defense plant but not one that might be attacked." Cynthia twisted her fingers as she talked. "I figured Riverside was far enough away from New York City and the coast that I'd be safe if the Japanese decided to bomb us again. Doesn't it scare you that we're in a war? It does, me."

"I didn't give the war much thought until Pearl Harbor. Leonard has been paying much closer attention than I have. He seemed to know that all this was coming, even way back in 1939 when Hitler invaded Poland. When Britain and France declared war, I was too busy watching *Gone With the Wind*—I went to see it four times—and I wanted America to stay neutral, just like everybody else did. But Leonard said, 'We'll be in this war, too, before long. Mark my words.' Then all those countries got overrun by the Nazis: Denmark, Norway, Belgium, Luxembourg, the Netherlands—boom, boom, boom. By the time France fell and Italy sided with Germany, Leonard had me convinced that he was right, and that we should get involved. Those stupid 'America First' people who oppose the war are so naïve—Lindbergh and Alice Longworth and that whole crowd. It's irresponsible to remain neutral as long as there is evil in the world."

The more Eleanor talked, the more Cynthia felt like a Dumb Dora. "How can you remember all those names and dates and things?" she asked.

Eleanor shrugged. "Leonard used to read newspapers and listen to the radio all the time. There wasn't much else to do, so I got in the habit, too. We used to listen to Edward R. Murrow broadcasting live from London, and we could hear air raid sirens and bombs going off in the background and the rumble of antiaircraft fire. It would give me the creeps because I knew people were dying. So when the same thing happened at Pearl Harbor, it was the last straw. I couldn't sit still anymore. I had a summer job as a lifeguard back home, but I made up my mind to do my part as soon as I finished high school. I would have joined the army if they'd let me fight, but I didn't want a stupid desk job. That's all they allow women to do in the army."

"We had a radio, too," Cynthia said, "but to be honest, I'd rather listen to Jack Benny or The Lux Radio Theater than the news. I've never been to the movies because my father is dead-set against them—because of our church, you know? Well, there weren't any theaters in town, anyway, so it didn't really matter. And we hardly ever went anyplace else. Coming here was the first time I ever rode on a bus."

"That's the only disappointing thing about Riverside," Eleanor said. "No movie theaters. But I hear there are a couple in Bensenville. Maybe we can take a bus there sometime—unless you're dead-set against movies, too."

"No! I'm dying to see one!"

"Girls?" Mrs. Montgomery called up the stairs. "William can drive you now."

"Thank you, ma'am. We'll be right down," Eleanor replied. She stood and slipped into her shoes. "Doesn't it gripe your middle kidney when people call us *girls*? After all, I'll be nineteen next month, for crying out loud."

Chapter
14

Cynthia gritted her teeth and braced for more pain. "Hold still," Eleanor commanded as she hovered over her with a pair of tweezers.

"Ouch!" The needle-like sting brought tears to Cynthia's eyes. "Why does plucking out tiny little eyebrow hairs have to hurt so much?"

Eleanor leaned back to study her work. "Pain is the price you pay for beauty. Hold still again."

"Maybe I'll just stay homely."

"You're beautiful, Cynthia. I mean it. Look in the mirror. It never lies."

If Cynthia looked closely, she could tell that she was the same old Cynthia beneath the layer of makeup. But if she squinted her eyes and looked at herself from a distance, the way you'd view a stranger, Cynthia saw that Eleanor was right. She had fair hair and perfect skin and beautiful features, not to mention a shapely body with curves in all the right places. She only lacked the confidence and grace to pull off the transformation from plain Cinderella to dazzling princess.

"I wish I didn't walk like I just came in from the barn," she complained.

"Practice walking with a book on your head," Eleanor said. "It's all a matter of attitude, you know. If you act cool, calm, and sophisticated long enough, you'll start to believe it."

Is that what Eleanor was doing? Cynthia didn't know how to read her new friend, sometimes. She admired Eleanor and wanted to be like her— but was everything about her really an act? No, Cynthia was certain that Eleanor had grown up with wealth and privilege. It showed in her clothes. But she rarely talked about herself and would change the subject if Cynthia started prying.

It hadn't taken long for either of them to unpack once they'd retrieved their luggage from the bus station. Eleanor didn't have a lot of clothes, but the ones she had were very nice, made from quality fabric in the latest styles. All of Cynthia's clothes were homemade or purchased from the Sears catalogue.

They soon established a routine in their new life together, washing out their laundry in the sink in their room and hanging it to dry on the clothesline they'd rigged under the eaves. Eleanor was a fanatic with a clothes iron, making sure everything she wore was relentlessly well pressed. "It doesn't matter if your clothes are a little worn," she told Cynthia. "If they're well pressed and your hair is clean and your shoes are shined, you'll always look good."

Eleanor seemed to know so much about fashions and manners—and not only how to dress and wear makeup but how to carry herself with style and poise. "How did you learn all these things?" Cynthia asked her. "Will you teach me?"

"I'd love to." Eleanor had taken Cynthia to Brinkley's Drugstore after they cashed their first paycheck and helped her pick out foundation, rouge, lipstick, and mascara.

"My father would have a fit if he could see me wearing all of this," Cynthia said. But Eleanor had such good taste that Cynthia never felt overdone—just pretty . . . for the first time in her life. Eleanor trimmed Cynthia's hair and taught her how to rinse it with hydrogen peroxide to lighten her natural honey shade to a ravishing blonde. They bought bobby pins, and Cynthia learned how to set her hair in pin curls.

In return, Cynthia did most of the cooking for the two of them, making bologna or egg salad or tuna sandwiches to pack in their lunch boxes and hot coffee for their thermoses. Eleanor had finally convinced Cynthia to ignore the rule about no cooking in their room. "Mrs. Montgomery is probably related to the guy who owns the diner across the street," Eleanor said, "and she probably wants to drum up business for him. Everyone is related to everyone else in a small town like this one. But we'll never save any money if we eat over there every night." Their suppers were simple meals—beans and franks or Spam with pineapple or a can of Campbell's soup.

Cynthia took great pride in their contributions to the war effort, donating their empty tin cans to the scrap metal drive and their used nylons to make parachutes. Since meat was among the rationed items, the girls did their part by eating at least one meatless meal a week—meatless Mondays—although many of their other meals were meatless, as well.

They would walk past the Valley Food Market on their way home from work every day and buy something for their supper that night and their lunch the next day. Eleanor always bought a newspaper, too, to keep up with the war. She had befriended the Montgomery's hired hand, William, and he allowed her to sneak down to the basement when Mrs. Montgomery wasn't around and use the funeral home's refrigerator to keep their milk and other things cold. Cynthia marveled at how Eleanor charmed and befriended everyone she met and soon had them eating out of her hand. Cynthia wouldn't have been surprised if Eleanor managed to crack Mrs. Montgomery's tough veneer one of these days, too.

The work at Riverside Electronics turned out to be easier than Cynthia feared, much easier than a lot of so-called "women's work," like knitting socks and gloves or following a complicated dress pattern. Once she got the hang of wiring and soldering, Cynthia found the repetitious job boring. But the inspectors never rejected her work, or Eleanor's, as second-rate.

"Tomacek would never admit it," Eleanor whispered to her one day, "but I'll bet we do a better job than the men did. Our nimble fingers can connect all these wires much better than their big, fat ones ever could."

On weekends Cynthia and Eleanor took the bus to Bensenville to go to the movies. It didn't take Cynthia long to push aside her guilt at enjoying this forbidden pleasure and become an avid fan of Clark Gable. As she glanced through the newspaper one evening, searching for the movie listings, she spotted the article about the USO.

"Hey, did you read this?" she asked Eleanor, who sat on the bed giving herself a pedicure. "They're opening a hangout in Bensenville for all the servicemen who are stationed at the army base west of the city."

"What kind of a hangout? A sleaze joint, no doubt?"

"No, it sounds very respectable. It's run by a group called the United Service Organization, or USO for short. The YMCA and Salvation Army started it for homesick draftees. It says that these USO places have sprung up all across the country, near military bases and transit points. They try to boost morale by offering movies, dances, hot food, a place to write a letter home—that sort of thing." She lowered the paper to see Eleanor's reaction. She looked unimpressed.

"We should go," Cynthia said. "I'm dying to meet a handsome serviceman."

"What for?"

"Don't you want a boyfriend?"

"Not particularly." Eleanor blew on her freshly polished toenails to dry them. "I don't need to be taken care of by a man like the women in my mother's generation did. If I do become involved in a relationship, I want it to be as equals. I don't ever want to be a housewife."

"What else is there to do if you don't have a husband and a house and kids?"

"Didn't you ever hear of a career, Cynthia?"

"For *women*?" she asked in surprise. "I've heard of women being schoolteachers and nurses, but they're usually women who haven't found a husband yet—or who never do find one."

"Some women find a career much more fulfilling than getting married," Eleanor said with conviction.

"Well, I sure wouldn't. I want every American woman's dream—a home and a husband. As long as he isn't a farmer, that is. All farmers are married to their land." She paused for a moment, wondering if she dared to share what she was really thinking. "I'll tell you the truth, Ellie, if you promise you won't think less of me. . . . I want to marry a wealthy husband. I want to live in a beautiful, modern house and wear all the latest styles and have everything that money can buy."

"You'll be sorry. Rich men don't have time to spend with their families. They're always too busy making money."

"Who cares? That's better than having your husband around all the time and being poor."

Eleanor stopped fussing with her nails and looked up at Cynthia, her expression serious. "I get the feeling you don't know very much about men, do you? Did you date a lot of fellas in high school?"

"Are you kidding?" Cynthia laughed. "If my father was too strict to allow us to go to the movies, you can imagine what he thought about dating. I don't think he and my mother ever kissed until the minister said, 'You may kiss the bride' at their wedding. My high school was too small to hold dances and things. Besides, farm boys needed to work after school and on weekends, not run around with girls. I grew up in a family of five sisters, so what I know about men would fit on the head of a pin. I don't even know how to dance."

"I can teach you."

"Really? You mean, teach me to dance or teach me about men?"

"Both."

"That would be super! Then we can go to the USO dances together."

"I don't know about that. . . ."

"Why aren't you keen to go, Eleanor?"

"Listen, those dances are going to be a bad deal for women. The GIs are going to be here today and gone tomorrow. But while they're here, they'll try to bamboozle everything they can from a woman. You can't fall for any of their malarkey, because they won't keep their promises. Some of those guys have a girl in every port and near every military base where they've been stationed—and they'll swear undying love to all of them, just so they can have their own way."

"Gee, you're really down on men. They're not all that bad, are they?"

"No. But there's something wrong with the ones who aren't. Listen, I'd hate to see someone as naïve as you get hurt, that's all. I have enough experience to know how to put my armor on. I'm pretty thick-skinned when it comes to men, but you would be easy prey for these guys."

"Then come with me. Teach me what to do. Please?" It took a good bit of wheedling on Cynthia's part, but she finally convinced her.

"All right, but let's make a deal—we'll only go on double dates with servicemen. It'll be safer that way."

True to her promise, Eleanor taught Cynthia to dance. She had used part of her first paycheck to buy a small radio for their room, spotting it in a department store window in Bensenville on their way to the movies one Saturday night. Every evening they would listen to dance-band music until bedtime, and Cynthia quickly learned all the latest steps. By the time the USO opened for business in Bensenville, Cynthia had been transformed from a plain, old-fashioned farm girl into a fashionable blonde who could tear up the dance floor. She felt great. Excited.

Eleanor was very pretty, too, slender and lively and animated, the kind of girl who lit up a room not because she was a ravishing beauty but because she was fun. When she and Cynthia went to their first dance at the USO, Eleanor didn't openly flirt like most of the other women did. Instead, she seemed to always have her guard up, as if afraid of being hurt. Her manner said, "I'll be your pal but that's all."

On the night that Cynthia met Rick Trent, Eleanor had chosen a table with a view of the door so she could get a good look at all the soldiers who came in and out. "Men do look handsome in a uniform," Eleanor admitted. "I could watch them all night."

"I sure wish I could meet a rich one," Cynthia sighed.

"You'll be sorry. The richer they are, the more they'll lie to you."

Cynthia studied her friend, never sure when she was serious and when she was pulling her leg. This time Eleanor looked serious. "Really? How do you know they're all liars?"

"I just do. And I can spot a rich, prep-school boy a mile away."

"Well, I can spot the country bumpkins a mile away," Cynthia said. "After all, I grew up with enough of them. See those guys over there?" she asked, pointing to a leering, whispering group in the corner. "Farm boys— every one of them. They're so nervous they need to chum together like Siamese quadruplets. They'll laugh a lot to boost their courage, and the louder they laugh, the more inexperienced they are. They're scared to death to ask a girl to dance because they don't know how to go about it for one thing, and for another they know they'll be shot down."

Eleanor rested her chin on her hand, eyeing the farm boys appreciatively. "Some of them have pretty nice physiques, though."

"Yeah—from tossing hay bales all day. All the muscles in the world can't make up for a homely face, in my book. I'll bet none of them has ever kissed a girl."

Eleanor smiled wryly. "Have you ever been kissed, Cynthia?"

"With a dad as strict as mine? What do you think?" She didn't need to ask Eleanor if she'd been kissed. Eleanor knew everything.

She had a wistful look on her face as she said, "They're homely, Cynthia, but they're probably very sweet. Girls won't even look twice at my brother, Leonard, but he has a lot of great qualities."

Cynthia had seen a picture of Leonard on Eleanor's nightstand. He would need an awful lot of great qualities to attract Cynthia's attention. Suddenly Eleanor tapped her arm.

"See that guy who just came in. . . ? Filthy rich."

"Do you know him?"

"No. I never saw him before in my life. But look at him. He's strutting around like he owns the room and smiling like he's God's gift to women. If you danced with him you'll discover that he has smooth hands."

"You can see his hands from way over here?"

"No, but rich boys never do any work, so their hands are always smooth. Now, watch him carefully. You know how your bumpkins all hang together for moral support? Look at rich-boy. He doesn't need moral support. He's the lone wolf, trolling the field for innocent lambs. Those guys trailing behind him are just his hangers-on. They're drawing courage from him, not the other way around. And see how well his uniform fits? He probably had it custom tailored. Only rich guys can afford that. Look how cocky he is. He's looking around for the prettiest woman, confident that there isn't a female in the room who would turn him down."

"I know I wouldn't," Cynthia said with a sigh. The GI was unbelievably good-looking—tall and broad-shouldered with slender hips and sandy hair and dimples. Cynthia could find fault with every guy in the room—his ears stuck out or his nose was too big or his teeth were crooked or he was too short, too tall, too fat, too gangly. But like in the story of Goldilocks and the Three Bears, this guy was *just* right. Cynthia still didn't know too many movie stars' names, but he looked as though he could be one.

"And he's got a really nice—what do you call it?—physique," she told Eleanor.

"That comes from playing sports at prep school, not from real work. Act indifferent, Cynthia. He's checking us out."

"Really? Why is he doing that?"

"Because you're a gorgeous blonde, that's why. Here he comes." Suddenly Eleanor laughed out loud as if Cynthia had just told a hilarious joke. She leaned close to Cynthia and whispered, "Don't look like you've been waiting for him to arrive. Act like we've been having fun without him and he's interrupting us. Don't seem too eager."

That wouldn't be easy to do. Cynthia was very eager. Her heart was thumping, her palms sweating. She nodded her head at Eleanor and smiled, trying to remember that it was all an act.

"Care to share the joke, girls?" The handsome GI grabbed a chair and swung it around to straddle it, as if they'd saved that place at their table just for him.

"It's too involved to explain," Eleanor said, waving his question away. "And besides, we're *women*, not girls." She was always so composed. Cynthia envied her.

"My name's Rick. Which one of you gorgeous dolls would like to dance with me first?"

"Cynthia will. I don't know how to dance," Eleanor said. Cynthia's mouth fell open at her lie. Then she caught herself and quickly tried to hide her surprise.

"Really?" the GI asked Eleanor with a bemused grin. "A classy-looking doll like you can't dance? Not even one step?"

"Nope. I was born with two left feet."

"I could teach you." He stood and held out his arms. His million-dollar smile displayed perfect teeth. Cynthia could almost hear Eleanor saying "That's another way you can tell a rich boy—perfect teeth."

"No thanks," Eleanor said with a yawn. "Go ahead and dance with Cynthia." She gestured to her, then turned away as if she had better things to do than talk to the handsomest GI in the room. Cynthia was so stunned by Eleanor's rebuff that she couldn't move a muscle. Eleanor kicked her beneath the table.

"Ouch! What. . . ?"

Rick turned to her and grabbed her hand. "All right—your loss is Cynthia's gain. Besides, I'll take a blonde over a brunette any day. Come on, gorgeous." He pulled her to her feet and led her to the dance floor as if she were a new car he'd just purchased and had every right to drive. He was too confident, too possessive. Cynthia knew she was still a farm girl at heart, too new at this acting business. Rick scared her to death.

She tried making small talk and learned that he was twenty-two years old and a city boy from Albany. He smelled every bit as good as he looked: spicy and masculine, good enough to eat. She couldn't take her eyes off him, laughing at all his jokes, agreeing with everything he said—behaving much too eagerly, as Eleanor would say. When he pulled her close for a slow song—closer than she'd ever been to any man—she couldn't seem to think straight.

From time to time she caught Rick glancing over at Eleanor. The mirror told Cynthia that she was the prettier of the two, but she couldn't deny that Eleanor's cool confidence made her very desirable, especially to a man like Rick who was used to getting whatever he wanted. Cynthia danced with him to the next three tunes, drank some lemonade, then danced a few more times. His cockiness began to grate on her. Rick held her too closely. He moved her around the dance floor as if she were a piece on a chessboard and he were the grand master. She didn't like that. And Eleanor had been right about another thing: His hands were as soft as her own.

"Let's you and me step outside for a while," he said when they'd been together about an hour. "My friends and I have something a little stronger than lemonade out in the jeep." He was moving much too fast for her. She knew he was way out of her league.

"No thanks," she said. "I really should go see if my friend—" She gestured to their table but Eleanor was gone. Cynthia spotted her a moment later, tearing up the dance floor with an awkward, big-eared guy who was even homelier than Eleanor's brother was. The GI couldn't dance to save his life, but Eleanor was swinging and moving as if she'd been born to it. Rick's face showed surprise, then anger.

"Hey, what gives? I thought your left-footed friend couldn't dance?" He dropped Cynthia's hand and strode over to where the pair was dancing, then stood with his hands on his hips, watching her. Eleanor was so dynamic on the dance floor that other people stopped to watch her, as well. Before long, everyone in the hall had gathered around Eleanor and her partner as if they were the last two contestants in a dance marathon. When the gangly soldier saw everyone watching, he began to blush and seemed to become even clumsier. Eleanor took her audience in stride. She bowed to the cheers and applause when the song ended, then whirled into her partner's arms for a brief hug.

"Thanks, Harry. That was great fun," she said, laughing. His face turned a fierce shade of red, and he slunk back to his corner to recover. Eleanor returned to their table and fell into her chair, then picked up a napkin to fan herself. Rick ignored Cynthia completely as he sank down beside Eleanor.

"What was that all about? I thought you said you couldn't dance."

"Harry was a *great* teacher, wasn't he?"

"Well, I could teach you a few steps that old Harry probably never heard of. Come on." He extended his hand.

"Not now—I'm bushed."

"Why don't you want to dance with me?"

Cynthia didn't wait to hear Eleanor's reply. Rick had forgotten she even existed. She hurried off to the ladies' room to take a powder, unwilling for either of them to see how hurt she was at being dumped like yesterday's newspaper. She didn't understand how she could feel angry that he'd rejected her and, at the same time, feel so relieved to be rid of him. Rick was too fast for her. She was too inexperienced. Hadn't she just turned down his offer to step outside? But he was undoubtedly attracted to Eleanor, and Cynthia was jealous.

She stayed in the ladies' room awhile, freshening her lipstick, touching up her mascara and rouge. When she studied her reflection, she barely recognized the beautiful girl she'd become. The transformation had been amazing. Cynthia took a deep breath to gather her courage before exiting the ladies' room. *It's all an act,* she told herself.

Rick still sat at the table beside Eleanor. Cynthia could tell by the animated way he talked, smiling and leaning close, that he was working very hard to impress her. Eleanor remained cool and unimpressed. Was that an act? Or did she truly dislike rich men that much?

Cynthia wasn't ready to give up on men and go home, yet. But she knew that she needed to start her new life as a gorgeous blonde much more slowly than with a guy like Rick. She spotted a group of bumpkins, huddled together for safety on the fringes of the dance floor, and decided to practice her acting skills on them. She sauntered over to them, swaying her hips and flashing her best smile.

"Hi, fellas," she said. "Where are you all from?"

She savored their appreciative "hubba-hubbas" and drew courage from their nervousness. Eventually they worked up enough gumption to take turns dancing with her. She began to relax and have a good time.

Much too soon, the time came to catch the last bus home to Riverside. Eleanor was still talking to Rick—or was it the other way around? Cynthia said good-night to her bumpkin friends and pasted on her best smile as she walked over to the table.

"Hey, Eleanor. We'd better get going. We don't want to miss our bus."

Eleanor looked at her watch, then pushed back her chair to stand up. "You're right. See you around, Rick."

He scrambled to his feet. "Whoa, whoa, wait a minute. You ladies need a ride? I might be able to help you out."

"No, thanks," Eleanor said. "The bus is fine. See you." She gave a lazy wave as if he'd been no one special, as if she hadn't just spent the last two hours talking with him.

Cynthia still felt hurt that Rick had dropped her so quickly for Eleanor, but she didn't say anything, determined not to let her know. After all, it hadn't been Eleanor's fault. They hurried to the bus station, barely making it in time to catch the last bus home. But when they were finally in their seats, the bus windows open and the warm night air streaming in, Cynthia could no longer remain quiet.

"For someone who hates rich boys as much as you do, you sure spent a lot of time talking to one tonight."

"In case you didn't notice, he was doing all the talking. I was trying to discourage him, but he was very persistent. For a while there, it looked like you two were hitting it off. What happened?"

"He moves too fast for me. He wanted me to go outside with him after a couple of dances. Said he had something stronger to drink than lemonade. I told him no."

"Good for you, Cynthia. You did exactly the right thing. Guys like Rick are used to getting their own way. I'm glad you stood your ground. You watch and see, he'll pick a different girl every week from now until he finishes his training. Nine out of ten women will be too dumb or too dazzled to turn him down the way you did."

"He sure was good-looking, though," Cynthia said with a sigh. "Why can't farm boys be as cute as he is?"

"Because God knows that handsome guys like Rick would never stay home and work on a farm—and then what would we all eat?"

Chapter 15

For the first time that Cynthia could recall, Eleanor was wrong. Rick Trent didn't choose a different girl the following week. He headed straight for Eleanor like a cow racing to the barn at milking time. Eleanor had been dancing to a slow song with another GI when Rick tapped the fellow on the shoulder and cut in, forcing Eleanor to dance with him. He never left her side after that, and they talked and danced together all evening.

"I've never known you to be wrong before," Cynthia told her on the bus ride home. "But you sure were wrong about Rick. He made a beeline for you the moment he stepped through the door tonight. Then he acted as if you were the only girl there."

Eleanor smiled faintly. "I might have misjudged him."

"So he's not a spoiled rich guy, after all?"

"Oh, he's loaded, all right. Very upper class. His father owns a couple of businesses or factories or something up in Albany. Rick could have gotten a deferment to help run them since they're defense industries, but he ran off and enlisted instead. Made his father madder than a bag of wet cats. He likes to rile his father."

Cynthia hadn't learned any of this in the time she'd spent dancing with him.

"Evidently there's some society girl back home that his parents wanted him to marry," Eleanor continued. "Old family money and all that. She was another reason why he bolted."

"So you've changed your opinion of him?"

"I have. He comes on like a dumb playboy, but he's actually very well-educated. Prep school at Andover, college degree from Princeton. The girl he's supposed to marry is a Dumb Dora—charm school alumnus, if you know what I mean. She's a real-live debutante with one of those cutesy names like Trixie or Pinky or Binny. Rick wants a wife he can converse with. He's one of the first guys I ever met who didn't run the other way when I told him I wanted an education and a career."

"Are you falling for him?"

"Of course not. I'm being very careful. It might be an act on his part. Time will tell. But for now, he's not as bad as I thought he was."

Cynthia noticed a change in both Rick and Eleanor as time passed. Rick lost his cocky swagger and seemed much more pleasant to be around without his playboy veneer. But even more surprising was when Eleanor began to let down her guard, and Cynthia caught a glimpse of what the real Eleanor was like—softer, more vulnerable—as she opened up to Rick. They both seemed gloriously happy, laughing a good portion of the time that they spent together. And it looked like genuine happiness, too, not an act. Eleanor sizzled like a Fourth of July sparkler as she waltzed around the dance floor in Rick's arms. They moved as one, not like a chess master manipulating a game piece. Cynthia hoped Eleanor wouldn't get hurt.

Before long, Eleanor and Cynthia began to double date with Rick and a string of his friends. One GI named Steve seemed to like Cynthia a lot, but she was waiting for fireworks, and they didn't happen. He was a nice guy and fun to be with, but she saw excitement and sparks between Eleanor and Rick, and she envied them. They looked into each other's eyes as if the secrets of the universe were written there, and so much electricity passed between them it was a wonder their hair didn't stand on end.

One wintry Friday night, Eleanor came down with a cold. "Go to the dance without me," she insisted. "All I want to do is crawl into bed and sleep." Cynthia didn't want to go at first, but Doris and Lucille from across the hall were going, and she decided to go with them. It would give her a chance to observe Rick and see if he was really serious about Eleanor, or if he would two-time her behind her back.

Cynthia was sitting at their usual table, watching the door, when Rick came in. "I'm going to take a powder," she told the other two girls. "If Rick asks where Eleanor is, tell him the truth—that she has a cold. Don't let him know I'm here."

But Rick sat at a table with a group of guys all night, ignoring the music and all the pretty women. He looked lost without Eleanor. When he spotted Cynthia later in the evening, he hurried over to talk to her.

"Doris said that Eleanor is sick. Is she okay?"

"Yeah, it's just a cold. She'll probably go to work on Monday."

"If I write her a note, will you take it to her?"

"Sure. As long as you get it to me before my bus leaves."

Rick raced out of the door as if the building were on fire. Cynthia wondered where on earth he was going for writing paper. The USO provided it for free to servicemen who wanted to write letters home. She and the other girls had just put on their coats, preparing to leave for the bus station, when Rick came racing back—with a bouquet of flowers!

"I've been running all over town trying to buy these," he said breathlessly. "And here's the note to go with them."

Eleanor was asleep when Cynthia returned home. She left the door to the hallway open a crack so she could find her way in the dark and sat down on her friend's bed, shaking her gently.

"Eleanor. . . ? Ellie, I'm sorry to wake you up, but you've got to see these. They're from Rick."

"What?" she asked sleepily, squinting in the thin beam of light. Cynthia laid the flowers on Eleanor's lap as she slowly sat up.

"He spent all night running around town trying to buy them. And he sent you this note, too." Cynthia crossed the room to turn on the desk light, then filled a pitcher with water for the flowers. When she looked back at her friend, Eleanor was wiping away a tear as she refolded the note.

"That was the nicest thing anybody ever did for me," she sniffed.

"Rick is a very nice guy," Cynthia said softly. "Even if he is rich."

The following night Cynthia's throat felt a little scratchy, too. The previous evening hadn't been much fun without Eleanor, so Cynthia decided to skip the dance at the USO and stay home. They were both sitting up in bed, listening to the radio with their pajamas on, when they heard something strike their bedroom window.

"What was that?" Cynthia asked. "Turn the radio down a minute." They heard the noise again.

"Someone is throwing rocks at our window!" Eleanor said. They climbed out of bed and ran to the front window, lifting the blackout curtain. Rick stood below, preparing to throw another rock. He had his friend Steve with him.

Eleanor slid the window open. "Go around to the back, you idiots! We'll be right down." She put her coat on over her pajamas and slipped into her shoes. Her face beamed like a searchlight. "Come on, Cynthia."

"Like this? I'm in my pj's!"

"Put your coat on. They won't know." She shoved Cynthia's coat into her hands and they ran down the back stairs. Rick pulled Eleanor into his arms and whirled her around, laughing.

"What are you doing here? How'd you find us?" she asked.

"Detective work, my dear! I overheard you mention catching a bus to Riverside. And you've told me several times that you lived in the Cadaver Hotel. I simply put two and two together and decided to come to Riverside's only funeral home."

"That's amazing!" Cynthia said, truly impressed.

Eleanor gave her a nudge in the ribs. "Don't be so gullible. They probably asked Doris and Lucille where we lived."

"But how did you know which window was ours?" Cynthia asked.

"We've been pitching rocks at all the ones with lights on," Rick said with a grin. "Hey, it's cold out here, and Eleanor's already sick. Invite us up."

"We can't!" Cynthia said, horrified at the idea. "Mrs. Montgomery said no gentlemen callers!"

Rick laughed again, mischievously. "That's okay. We're not gentlemen."

Cynthia shook her head. "It's really not a good idea. . . ."

"Oh, come on, Cynthia," Eleanor said. "They came this far. The least we can do is let them come in and get warm." She was looking at Rick as if he were the medicine she needed to cure her. Cynthia was still unsure.

"But . . . I don't want to get into trouble. What if we get kicked out?"

"We'll be *really* quiet. Right, guys?" Eleanor held her finger to her lips and tiptoed to the door with exaggerated stealth. Rick and Steve mimicked her, laughing and shushing each other. Against Cynthia's wishes—and better judgment—the two men sneaked upstairs to her room.

"Ta-da! Here it is," Eleanor said. "Welcome to the Presidential Suite at the Cadaver Hotel. Want some hot chocolate?"

"Ellie!" Cynthia quickly shut the door.

"What?"

"They were only going to stay a minute. We're in our pajamas!"

"You're welcome to take them off if you're uncomfortable," Rick said. Steve gave a wolf whistle, and Cynthia felt herself blushing clear to her toes. Everyone laughed except her, and she suddenly felt as prudish and uptight as an old spinster. She laughed in spite of herself and made up her mind to relax and enjoy their visitors.

"I'll make hot chocolate," she said, "but somebody else will have to go down to the dungeon and get the milk out of the refrigerator. I'm not going down there at night! It's spooky enough in the daytime."

"We don't need hot chocolate," Rick said. "How about a game of cards?"

They didn't have a table and there weren't enough chairs, so they all sat on the floor on the rag rug and played gin rummy, the girls still wearing their coats over their nightclothes. It was the best Saturday night that Cynthia had spent since coming to Riverside. Steve was a nice guy and a fun date, but his charm paled compared to his friend Rick. As Cynthia had gotten to know Rick better, she understood what Eleanor saw in and liked about him. Too bad he hadn't been this much fun when she had danced with him.

Eleanor seemed to have a gift for tearing down people's facades and bringing out the best in them. She'd certainly transformed Cynthia from a boring, ugly duckling into a beautiful swan. And the change in Rick was no less miraculous. He told hilarious stories, some at his own expense, and sang along with Frank Sinatra and the Andrews Sisters on the radio. He was so attentive to Eleanor, and so affectionate, gently caressing her neck or her shoulder and stealing kisses whenever she made a good play or won a hand of cards. They were all having fun. Hours passed and no one cared.

"Hey, let's make popcorn," Eleanor decided after Rick won another round.

"Good idea. I'll make it," Cynthia jumped up to plug in the hot plate, then halted. "Wait, I can't. The oleomargarine is down in the basement refrigerator."

"Can't we go get it?" Steve asked. "I'm not afraid."

Rick began making spooky, moaning noises, like a ghost. "Who's down there, Frankenstein?" he asked.

"We'll all go down together," Eleanor decided. "Come on."

They crept down to the basement, giggling and hushing each other. The blackout curtains hadn't been closed, so they didn't dare turn on a light. But when Cynthia opened the refrigerator door to get the margarine, it cast enough light for Rick and Steve to have a look around.

"Leave it open a minute," Rick said. "Let's see how many ghouls are down here." Cynthia watched nervously as they explored the basement, joking about seeing ghosts and daring each other to open one of the coffins. When Rick lifted a lid and found the coffin to be empty, he climbed inside, lying down on the satin lining with his hands folded and his eyes closed like a dead man.

"Don't, Rick! Come on, that's morbid," Eleanor said, but she was laughing along with everyone else. "Come on, get out of there," she urged.

Rick waited until she came over to nudge him, then suddenly sat up, shouting, "Boo!" Eleanor shrieked, then clamped her hand over her mouth.

"I'm getting out of here," Cynthia said. She closed the refrigerator and hurried up the stairs with the oleomargarine. Steve followed close behind her. The two of them had the popcorn cooked by the time Eleanor and Rick came back a few minutes later. Cynthia could tell by their flushed, happy faces that they had been kissing.

They all munched popcorn and laughed some more. None of them wanted the evening to end. Cynthia had forgotten her earlier misgivings and had lost all track of the time until she heard Doris and Lucille clomping up the steps.

"Hey, I smell popcorn!" Doris called.

"Quick! Hide!" Cynthia gasped. She jumped to her feet, pulling Steve with her, and shoved him into the closet. It wasn't big enough for both men, so Rick rolled onto his stomach and crawled under Eleanor's bed. Eleanor leaped on top of the bed and dove beneath the covers.

"Ouch! That's my head!" Rick grunted.

"Shh!" Cynthia hissed. She ran around in circles trying to hide the playing cards and the two extra water glasses.

"Knock, knock!" Lucille sang. She and Doris walked in the way they always did. "How's the patient? Up awfully late, aren't you?"

"Miserable," Eleanor moaned from under the covers. "I tried to go to sleep and couldn't." She coughed convincingly a few times.

"Why do you have your coat on, Cynthia?" Doris asked. Cynthia felt the blood rush to her face.

"I . . . um . . . it's warmer than my bathrobe." She breathed a sigh of relief when Doris changed the subject. The two neighbors rattled on and on about their evening at the USO, describing all the fellows they'd danced with.

"Your boyfriend was looking for you, Eleanor. Big-mouth Lucille spilled the beans and told him where you lived. I hope he doesn't come around and pester you."

"He said he wanted to send her a card," Lucille explained. "I didn't see the harm in telling him."

"I don't mind," Eleanor said. "Don't worry about it. The army keeps him much too busy to become a full-time pest."

Cynthia turned out all but one light, hoping their two neighbors would get the hint. They didn't. Lucille picked up the bowl of leftover popcorn and sat down on the sofa to share it with Doris.

"You're breaking the rules, you know," Doris said. "Mrs. Montgomery told us we weren't supposed to cook in our rooms."

"Making popcorn isn't considered cooking," Eleanor said. "It's no different than boiling water. Hey, I hate to be a spoilsport, but it's late, and I'd better get some rest or I'll never make it to work on Monday."

A few more minutes passed before they finally finished eating popcorn and left. Cynthia quietly locked the door behind them so they couldn't barge in again. When she turned around and looked at Eleanor, they both started to giggle. Eleanor leaned over to peer beneath the bed.

"They're gone. You can come out, now," she said. Rick rolled out from under the bed, sneezing. Eleanor brushed dust bunnies from his hair. Steve opened the closet door a crack and stuck his head out.

"Is it safe? Phew! It smells like mothballs in there. Another minute or two and I would have conked out." They were all laughing and whispering and shushing each other.

"You'd better go," Eleanor said. Rick pulled her into his arms.

"That really is a terrible cold you have, ma'am. Dr. Rick better give you a kiss to make it better." Cynthia saw the tender way he looked at Eleanor as he tucked a strand of hair behind her ear, and she wondered if she would ever meet a man who would love her that much. He and Eleanor kissed as if it was their last hour together on earth, and Cynthia and Steve turned away to give them a moment of privacy.

"Thanks for a fun evening," Steve whispered.

"We'll do it again sometime," Cynthia promised. "But probably not here. It's too nerve-wracking." They both snickered.

Rick finally tore himself away from Eleanor, and Cynthia herded the men down the pitch-black stairs, the wooden risers groaning and creaking as they went. She breathed a sigh of relief when the door was safely bolted behind them. When she tiptoed back to their room, Eleanor was sitting up in bed with tears streaming down her face.

"Are you falling in love with Rick?" Cynthia asked.

"I'm not 'falling,'" she said miserably. "I already fell . . . and landed hard." Eleanor swiped at her eyes, then blew her nose. "I never intended for this to happen, you know—it just did. I've never felt this way about anyone before. And neither has Rick."

Cynthia hung up her coat and switched off the light, then climbed into her own bed. "Didn't you tell me that all rich guys are liars?" she asked after she'd snuggled down under the covers.

"Rick is fed up with that phony life. That's why he defied his father and enlisted. Now that he's free from his father's shadow for the first time and making his own decisions, he doesn't want to go back to that country club life. He wants a real life, with kids who live at home instead of in fancy boarding schools and who go fishing with their dad on the weekends. Rick's father worked all the time, and he hardly even knows him. He plans to give the company to Rick so that he'll have to work hard all the time, too, and be miserable. That's not a life. Rick is going to chuck it all when the war is over and make it on his own. I respect him for that."

"What about all that stuff you said about GIs having a girl in every port?"

Eleanor laughed softly. "This is Rick's first assignment. He hasn't had time to collect a bevy of women."

"Didn't you say you wanted to marry a man who had something in common with you?"

"We have more in common than you think."

Cynthia waited. Eleanor never talked about herself or her family, except for her brother, Leonard. "My father was very wealthy, too," she finally said. "Very upper class. But he cared more about money than anything else—including Leonard and me and our mother."

Cynthia waited for more, but that was all the information that Eleanor was willing to disclose. She was silent for so long that Cynthia wondered if she had fallen asleep.

"Maybe I'm a fool for falling in love," she finally said, and Cynthia heard tears in her breaking voice. "But this is more than just physical attraction—although I'll admit that's part of it. We spend more time talking than we do kissing, believe it or not."

"What do you talk about?"

"Everything. What we want from life, how we're looking forward to really living when the war is over. The places we want to visit, the things we want to see. Rick is as excited about seeing the world as I am. I never met a guy like him before. Most guys just want to make piles of money and boss their wives around. As soon as the war is over, we're going to forget the past and start all over again, together." She paused for a moment. "I'll tell you a secret if you promise not to tell anyone."

"Of course, Ellie. I promise."

"Rick asked me to marry him. I told him yes."

"Oh, Eleanor! That's wonderful! I wish I could meet somebody special—rich or not."

"You will, Cynthia. You will. Probably when you least expect it."

Chapter

16

Cynthia gazed at her reflection in the darkened bus window, the laboring engine droning in her ears as the bus swayed down the now familiar route from Bensenville to Riverside. The rural road was deserted this late at night, and with blackout curtains shrouding the windows of any houses they passed, Cynthia felt as though she traveled beneath the sea. She could see Eleanor's reflection beside her own, gazing silently into the darkness, and she wondered what was wrong. Eleanor usually came alive at night, entertaining Cynthia and everyone else with her laughter and witty jokes as they rode back to Riverside after a dance or the movies. But Eleanor and Rick had both been subdued all evening, huddling together at one of the corner tables at the USO. They hadn't even gotten up to dance.

"Did you have a fight with Rick or something?" Cynthia asked her. "You've been awfully quiet all evening."

"No, we didn't have a fight," she said with a sigh. "But we're living on borrowed time."

"What do you mean?" Cynthia couldn't imagine their relationship ending. They seemed so deeply in love, so happy together.

Eleanor sighed again. "Rick finishes his training in two weeks. We'll have one more Saturday night together. He'll get a three-day furlough to go home and see his family, then he's being shipped out."

"Oh, Ellie. You poor girl." Cynthia turned to give her a hug. Eleanor usually seemed uncomfortable with such emotional displays, but she accepted Cynthia's embrace with a sniffle. They rode in silence for the remainder of the trip, then hurried through Riverside's deserted streets to the funeral home. Eleanor still seemed troubled when they reached their room.

"Cynthia. . . ? Can we talk?" she asked.

"Of course. I'm your best friend. You can tell me anything." Cynthia sat down on the sofa and gestured to the place beside her, but Eleanor remained standing, too upset to sit. She hesitated for a long moment, as if afraid of something.

"Rick wants us to be together on his last weekend," she finally said. "I don't know whether I should or not."

Cynthia stared at her, not comprehending. "Why wouldn't you want to be together?"

"Not *together*, like we are every weekend," Eleanor said with an irritated frown. "He wants to sleep with me before he ships off."

"Oh." Cynthia looked away, embarrassed by the subject matter—and by her own naïveté. "I think that's a bad idea," she finally said.

"I know, I know," Eleanor said as she paced across the rag rug in front of Cynthia. "I've been telling him no because of my—never mind. But I keep worrying that something terrible will happen to Rick and I'll never get another chance to be with him. I would regret it for the rest of my life."

"Listen, I know I'm pretty naïve," Cynthia said, choosing her words carefully, "and I'm not nearly as knowledgeable about these things as you are. But the girls in school always said that a boy wouldn't marry a girl who gave in to him. And what if you get pregnant?"

"I know, I know. But so many men are dying, and . . . and I may never see Rick again . . . and I want to know what it's like to be with him. I love him so much!" She bit her lip, trying to stop her tears.

"Everyone can see how much you love each other, Ellie, but it's still not a good idea. I know this sounds old-fashioned and all that, but the Bible says it's wrong to do it if you're not married."

Eleanor's shoulders slumped, and she sank down in the armchair as if the nervous energy that fueled her had abruptly discharged, like a pin-pricked balloon. "I know. That's the main reason why I've been saying no. I was brought up in the church, too." She must have seen Cynthia's surprise because she added, "Leonard stopped going to Mass when we were in high school, so I eventually stopped, too. But I do believe in right and wrong. And I know that there are always consequences when people break God's laws. I've seen it in real life." She paused, then added, "But I love Rick so much! I wish we could get married right now."

"You're both so young, Eleanor."

"I'm almost twenty. Rick has never been with a girl . . . that way. He knows he could die, and he wants to know what it's like. . . . And he wants it to be with me. I don't want to make him mad, Cynthia—not now, not right before he leaves."

"If he gets mad that's his problem. Besides, he's wrong to use anger to talk you into this. Stick to your principles. He'll respect you for it."

"You're right," Eleanor said with a sigh. "Thanks for your help." She braced her hands on the arms of the chair and stood. But she still looked preoccupied as she put on her pajamas and climbed into bed, and Cynthia couldn't help wondering what she was really thinking.

The following weekend, as Eleanor was preparing for her last Saturday night date with Rick, Cynthia decided to bring up the subject once again.

"Please don't do it, Eleanor," she urged. "It would be a mistake that you could never undo."

"I won't. I know you're right." Eleanor smiled, but it seemed forced. "Listen, don't wait for me at the bus station. Rick says he'll bring me home."

Cynthia worried about her friend all evening. She rode the bus back to

Riverside alone and was in her bathrobe, pacing the floor long after mid-night, when she finally heard Eleanor's key rattling in the downstairs door. A moment later Eleanor burst into the room, dancing with excitement. She grabbed Cynthia's hands and whirled her around in a circle saying, "Guess what? Guess what? Guess what?"

Cynthia was afraid to guess, worried that she had given in to Rick after all.

"Rick and I are getting married!"

"Married? After the war, you mean?"

"No! Next weekend. He has a three-day furlough before he ships off, so we're going to go before a justice of the peace and get married. Rick says we can renew our vows with a priest and get the blessing of the church when he comes home."

"Are you sure you want to do that? You've only known him a short time."

"I'm positive. If the war has taught us anything, it's that life is very short and time is precious. If something should happen—well, at least I'll know what it was like to be his wife. And Rick says it will get him through all the rough spots ahead if he knows he has a life with me to look forward to after the war."

"And what if you don't feel the same way about each other after the war?"

"We will! What a dumb thing to ask! I want to spend the rest of my life with Rick. I can't imagine living without him."

"Is he this certain, too? Are you sure it's not just a way for him to . . . you know?"

"No! For pete's sake, Cynthia! How could you think that of Rick?"

"I'm sorry. I've never been in love, so you'll have to excuse me. I don't know what you're going through."

Tears filled Eleanor's eyes. "It hurts so much whenever we're apart; it hurts to breathe and to eat and to sleep. . . . I feel like I'm only half of a person without him. But when we're together . . . oh, the world is such a wonderful place, and I feel like I'm bursting with life! I never imagined that falling in love would be this terrible and this wonderful, did you?"

"My parents never talked about love very much when I was growing up. They believed that people got married so they could work together and raise kids. I never saw much affection or anything between them."

Eleanor gazed into space as if she'd forgotten that Cynthia was there. "My mother told me once how much love hurts, but I didn't believe her. She was crazy about my father and would have licked his shoes clean for him. I never wanted to be so hung up on a man that I would lose myself that way. And now, here I am—completely lost! Oh, I don't think I could live without Rick—" She covered her face and wept.

Cynthia gathered her into her arms. "Hey, there's no time for tears. We've got a wedding to plan—one week from today, right? You'll need a marriage license and a dress and a place to honeymoon. . . . I'll be your maid of honor or your flower girl or your best man or whatever you want me to be. Just name it."

Eleanor laughed through her tears and hugged her in return. "Thanks, Cynthia. You're the best friend I ever had."

A week later, Cynthia witnessed Rick and Eleanor's vows as they stood before a justice of the peace in Bensenville. They looked deliriously happy as they gazed into each other's eyes and promised to love each other, for richer or for poorer, until death parted them. Three other couples waited in line behind them, and the grooms were all soldiers from Rick's military base, about to be shipped overseas.

Mr. Tomacek had grudgingly excused Eleanor from work on Monday and Tuesday—without pay, of course—so she could go on a brief honeymoon, then see her new husband off at the train station. When Cynthia returned home from work on Tuesday afternoon, Eleanor was already there. She wore an apron tied around her waist and a kerchief on her head, and the music of Glenn Miller blared from the radio as she turned the room upside down in a cleaning frenzy.

"Well, if it isn't Mrs. Richard Trent," Cynthia said as she set her empty lunch pail and thermos in the sink. "Married only three days and I see you've already become a busy little housewife."

Eleanor smiled as she bent to sweep a pile of dust into the dustpan. "Rick's train left this morning. I didn't know what else to do with myself."

"How's married life, Mrs. Trent? Is it as wonderful as you dreamed it would be?"

"It's heaven!" Eleanor said, laughing. "We barely left the hotel room for three whole days. Being with Rick is—" She couldn't finish. Eleanor's façade crumbled, and she sank to the floor in the pile of dust and wept.

In the following weeks, Eleanor kept her false front carefully in place in public, but Cynthia knew how thin and brittle her calm, poised veneer really was. Eleanor approached everything she did with a fevered intensity, as if trying to distract herself from thoughts of Rick. Her emotions rose or sank with the daily mail. Eleanor raced home every afternoon after work to see if Mrs. Montgomery had shoved a letter from Rick under their door, then sat at the desk every night, crying her heart out as she wrote back to him. Rick wrote to her nearly as often, and if she didn't find a letter from him one day, there likely would be two from him the next.

Eleanor's worry over her husband was a constant, simmering flame that fueled a restless energy. She attended Mass every day, offering endless prayers for him. She cut out maps of Europe and the Pacific islands from the newspaper and pinned them to the wall so she could follow the battles on the radio and in the news. She knew all of the generals' names and their divisions, charting their movements as if only her daily vigilance would keep Rick safe.

Cynthia worried as her friend grew increasingly nervous, and she worked hard to find distractions to help Eleanor relax. "Come to the movies in Bensenville with me," she begged. "There's a Mickey Rooney film playing—*The Human Comedy*." They went, but Cynthia had forgotten that they always showed a newsreel about the war before the main feature. Too late, she noticed Eleanor's pale face as she stared intently at the grainy images, as if searching for Rick among the many soldiers.

They donated blood at all the Red Cross blood drives. Cynthia taught

Eleanor how to knit, and they made scarves and mittens and socks to send overseas. But all the while she worked, Eleanor seemed to be marking off the days and hours and minutes like rows of knitting, waiting until the war would end and Rick would come home to her. She still looked like the same old Eleanor on the outside, but Cynthia saw the act for what it was. Inside, Eleanor was a tightly wound bundle of false brightness, trying to keep Rick safe and will him home again by sheer determination.

As winter changed to spring, then summer, Cynthia grew tired of it all. She was sick of following the news, sick of hearing about the ups and downs of war, sick of the devastation and death. Since Eleanor would no longer go to the USO dances with her, Cynthia decided to go by herself on Saturday nights. She had gained self-confidence and enjoyed playing the field and meeting all kinds of guys. She agreed to write letters to several of them, but none of these relationships became serious. Then, after a while, Cynthia no longer enjoyed the USO dances, either. As the war dragged on, the new recruits she met were younger and younger, and seeing their vitality and fresh-scrubbed eagerness depressed her. She knew what they would soon face.

Cynthia's life began to feel as though it had ground to a halt. Shortages of everything from food to shoes to new clothes made shopping a chore, not a pleasure. Eleanor wasn't interested in buying makeup or new clothes or shoes. She saved every spare cent of her paycheck, as if believing that Rick would be allowed to come home if only she saved enough.

Every day seemed the same to Cynthia, as if she were stuck in a monotonous film that had no ending. She wanted to get on with her life—to fall in love, get married, have children. And she was deathly tired of her factory job.

"This work is so boring and repetitious," she complained to Eleanor as they sat on the grass eating their lunch one warm summer day. "I can't imagine working here for the rest of my life, can you?"

"When I'm bored, I just think about how much I'm helping our troops," Eleanor replied. "I only wish I could do more."

Cynthia shook her head as she took another bite out of her bologna sandwich. "I have a hard time imagining that connecting hundreds of wires all day has anything to do with what's going on in the rest of the world."

Eleanor picked at the crust of her bread, tearing it into little pieces but not eating it. "Every time I solder a wire, I think of Rick. His life or one of his friends' lives might depend on that very gauge or bomb switch." Her fixation with Rick was starting to grate on Cynthia's nerves.

More than a year after Rick and Eleanor were married, the long-awaited D-day finally arrived. The Allied invasion of Nazi-occupied Europe finally began. Rick's squadron of paratroopers took part in the assault, as did most of the soldiers that Cynthia wrote to. Eleanor's brother, Leonard, was marching up Italy's boot with the Allies to liberate Rome.

Rick wrote from liberated Paris eleven weeks later. But his letters became less and less frequent once he began fighting in Europe, and Eleanor became more and more anxious and preoccupied. Cynthia worried about her.

One afternoon after Eleanor had volunteered to take their ration coupons to the store and stand in line for coffee and sugar, Cynthia spotted a tissue-thin V-mail letter from Rick lying open on the desk. She couldn't resist the urge to snoop.

Dear Eleanor,

It's a beautiful fall day and I have a few minutes to spare before we march, so I thought I would spend them visiting with you. We've had trouble getting our mail lately. I didn't get any letters from you for three days, then I got three all at once. Please keep them coming. They're a lifeline to me, reminding me that there is still a sane world out there and a woman who loves me.

I've told no one but you, darling—but I'm so afraid. No one who hasn't been through it can truly understand what this war is like, and there aren't enough words to describe it. It's days and days of boredom and waiting, then hours of sheer terror when you're certain that each second is your last. I've confessed and prayed and prepared to die so many times now that God is probably tired of hearing from me. But I'm still here, still miraculously unhurt. I know that when the war finally ends I'll never be the same.

I wish I could explain to my father that all of the things he values aren't what really matters. Life and love and the people God gives us are the most important things, not how much money we have, or how many possessions and titles and honors we accumulate. Your love is priceless to me, Eleanor, worth much more than my father's money. I'm tired of keeping our marriage a secret. I know we said we would wait until the war ends, but I've thought it all through and I've decided to write to my family and tell them about us. My dad will hit the roof, but I don't care. I'm sick of lying. He needs to know that I'm not coming home to the phony life he planned for me after the war.

We're hearing good news from—the censors had cut out the word, leaving a hole—that we have the enemy on the run. Maybe this war will be over soon. I want to come home so badly and hold you in my arms again. You're all I think about, and I'm so afraid that after surviving the war this long, I'll end up dying just when I'm close to coming home. I'm not afraid to die, but I want so badly to live—to share my life with you and grow old together. . . .

Cynthia dropped the letter on the desk when she heard Eleanor running up the stairs. "I got the sugar," she said, breathless from the climb, "but I don't know what good it will do us without any coffee to put it in. They ran out again."

"No coffee?" Cynthia repeated. "Honestly, I wish we didn't live in such a dinky little town. They're always running out of things . . ." Cynthia hardly knew what she was saying. Rick's words had upset her, and she knew they would have had a worse effect on Eleanor.

"The guy that runs the Valley Food Market is as crooked as all get out," Eleanor continued. "He sells all the coffee to his friends, whether they have ration stamps or not. But look what I did get—" She unwrapped a packet of white butcher paper to display two tiny pork chops. "Ta-da! Real meat, Cynthia."

"That poor pig must have died of malnutrition."

"Hey, don't look a gift-pig in the mouth—I waited in line for more than an hour for these."

"I know. And I'm grateful."

"I'm going to cook them up for us, too," Eleanor said as she dug through their small stash of cooking supplies. They kept all their pots and pans and spices hidden in the bottom drawer of their dresser so Mrs. Montgomery wouldn't find out that they were cooking in their room. "I told Rick that I was going to learn how to cook so I'd be an expert by the time he gets home. I thought I'd practice with these chops."

Cynthia heard the anxious determination in her friend's voice, as if learning to cook was the latest project that would guarantee Rick's safe return. But in reality, Eleanor was helpless; nothing she did—or failed to do—would change the course of the war or alter Rick's fate. And Cynthia was just as helpless. All she could do was try to keep up her friend's spirits and hope that the worst didn't happen to Rick.

"I don't know," Cynthia said, forcing a smile. "It'll be pretty hard to become a gourmet chef with only a hot plate to practice on."

"I cut out this recipe from the newspaper. It calls for a can of tomato soup. Open the windows," Eleanor said, gesturing to them with the frying pan, "so Mrs. Montgomery doesn't smell meat frying."

"Isn't Rick's family rich enough to afford a cook?" Cynthia asked as she tugged open the sash. Cool, fall air flooded the room.

"He's not going back to that life—I told you that."

"How is he going to make a living?"

"He has a college degree from Princeton, remember? We'll be fine."

"Have you talked about where you'll live and all those things?"

"We're going to live in 'Paradise, New York,' of course. As long as we have each other, any place will be heaven!"

The pork chops came out nearly as tough as shoe leather. Eleanor held up one of her worn out work shoes as they tried to gnaw the leathery meat. "We should have used the chops to patch our shoes instead of trying to eat them." Her laughter sounded too bright, her smile too phony. Cynthia thought of Rick's letter—how he was afraid he would die—and she knew that it was what Eleanor feared, as well.

Just when the Allies seemed to be winning in Europe, the news turned gloomy again. Hitler had gone on the offensive in what was being called the Battle of the Bulge. It raged from mid-December until the end of January in frigid, snowy weather. Rick's letters always arrived at least a week behind the news, and Cynthia feared that Eleanor would have a nervous breakdown as she waited to hear if he was among the more than 81,000 casualties in the long months of fighting.

"I don't know what I would do without Rick," she said over and over. "I don't know what I would do."

Rick came through the battle unscathed. Eleanor wept as she read his letter describing the allied victory. Everyone said that the European war had reached the turning point, and that the Nazi retreat had begun.

"I'm so tired of being brave," Eleanor said. "I want this all to end . . . but I'm so afraid . . ."

Cynthia could guess what she was afraid to say. "We're close to the end now," she soothed. "Rick made it through some tough battles, Ellie. He'll be okay."

The warm spring weather made everyone hopeful. Cynthia saw daffodils and crocuses as she and Eleanor walked to work, and robins singing in the trees outside their window. When three days passed without a letter from Rick, Cynthia helped Eleanor dream up excuses the troops were too far inland; the letters got put in the wrong mailbag; Rick was too busy to write.

A week passed. Then two. Neither of them could sleep. The workdays seemed endlessly long as they waited to hurry home and get the mail.

On Monday of the third week, Eleanor broke into a run as soon as the funeral home came into sight. She raced up the stairs far ahead of Cynthia. When Cynthia finally caught up to her on the third floor and saw Eleanor standing in their doorway holding a letter, she nearly collapsed with relief. Then she noticed the deathly pallor on Eleanor's face, and her heart speeded up.

"What's wrong?"

"This letter came for me. It isn't Rick's handwriting." Tears spilled down her face. "Y-you open it for me. I-I can't."

Cynthia was terrified for her friend. She tried to rationalize it away. "Wait a minute. It's probably not what you think, Eleanor. If something bad happened, the army would notify you. They always send a telegram to the wife—'We regret to inform you . . .' and all that. The telegram has one red star if he's wounded, two red stars if . . . And besides, they'd ask your priest or your minister to come if they had to deliver that kind of news."

Eleanor shook her head. "The army doesn't know we're married. Rick didn't list me as his wife."

"Why not?"

"He didn't want his parents to find out about us. He was afraid that his father would do something drastic to break us up. His father has a lot of connections with judges and politicians up in Albany. That's why Rick waited until the war was almost over to tell him the truth. . . ." She shoved the letter into Cynthia's hands. "Open it! Please! I can't!"

"Let's at least go in and sit down, okay?" She pulled Eleanor through the door and forced her to sit on the sofa. But Cynthia felt just as sick as Eleanor did as she ripped the envelope open with shaking hands and pulled out a folded letter. A second letter fell out from inside the first one, and she saw Rick's signature on it. So did Eleanor. She went very still.

"Oh, no. Please, God, no. . . ." Eleanor murmured.

Cynthia scanned the first letter. It was from one of Rick's army buddies. Rick had been killed in action. Cynthia closed her eyes as her vision blurred, unable to read the rest.

"Rick is dead, isn't he," Eleanor said.

Cynthia couldn't speak. She didn't want to say the words out loud, knowing that when she did, Rick's death would suddenly become horribly real.

"Rick told me about the pact he and all his buddies have," Eleanor said. "I know they all wrote good-bye letters to their loved ones, and their friends are supposed to mail them if anything happens to one of them. Rick had to send letters after three of his friends died. . . . This is my letter, isn't it."

Cynthia nodded.

"Oh, God!"

Cynthia pulled Eleanor into her arms, and they wept together for a long, long time.

"Why, God?" Eleanor raged. "Why did you have to take my Rick? All I ever wanted from you was for Rick to live! Why did you take him away from me? Why couldn't you let me be happy—just once?"

Cynthia sobbed as hard as Eleanor did, grieving for her friend, remembering Rick's handsome, smiling face and the way he looked at Eleanor, his eyes shining with love. It was so unfair.

At last Eleanor freed herself from Cynthia's embrace and wiped her eyes. "Read Rick's letter to me," she whispered.

"Are you sure?"

"Yes."

Cynthia swallowed. She could barely speak as tears choked her voice.

"Dear Eleanor,

If you're reading this letter then the worst has already happened. I'm in heaven where there's no more pain and no tears. How I longed to spend the rest of my life with you, making you happy every minute of every day—but God has decided otherwise.

My beautiful, sweet Eleanor, promise me that you won't grieve a long time. This war has caused enough suffering, and we've shed too many tears already. I could have died a hundred different ways back home, but at least my death counted for something over here. The world will be a better place, where you can raise your children and live in freedom. That's what you need to do, Ellie. You're a beautiful, wonderful woman, and I have no doubt at all that you'll find someone who loves you as much as I do—it's impossible to find someone who could ever love you more. Spend your life with him and be happy again. That's the best way to honor my memory. God is in control, and He knows what He's doing.

Our brief time together gave us a little taste of paradise, didn't it? And I know we'll meet each other in heaven someday and be together forever. Neither one of us will ever have to shed another tear. Until then, I'll love you in heaven even more than I did on earth. God bless you, my love.

I'll love you forever,
Rick"

Chapter

17

E leanor mourned a very long time, a widow at the age of twenty. She fell into such a deep depression, refusing to eat and losing so much weight, Cynthia feared she'd get sick. She often heard Eleanor pacing in the dark at night, sobbing quietly, unable to sleep.

"I don't want to live anymore," Eleanor would say when Cynthia tried to console her. "I miss Rick so much that I don't know how I'll live without him." Cynthia worried that she would end her own life just to be with him. Eleanor stopped going to Mass and would weep and rage at God, asking, "How could He allow this to happen? What kind of a God would allow innocent young men to die? Rick had his whole life ahead of him— our whole life. How could God be so cruel?"

"I think you should talk to your priest," Cynthia said. "I don't have any answers, but maybe he could help you get through this."

"I'll never walk through the door of a church again," Eleanor said. "I'm finished with God if this is the way He runs the world."

Cynthia didn't understand what God was doing, either. The world seemed to have gone insane while He looked the other way. She bit her tongue to keep from adding to Eleanor's rage by reminding her that she wasn't the only person mourning a loved one. What about the hundreds of thousands of soldiers who had perished worldwide? What about the demolished cities and the starving refugees and the millions of innocent Jewish men, women, and children who had died in concentration camps, as the latest news from liberated Europe was reporting? Yes, there were a lot of deaths to be explained, not just Rick's.

Once her initial shock and grief began to ebb, Cynthia felt desperate to return to her normal routine and help Eleanor resume her life, as well. But the simplest things would remind them both of Rick and send Eleanor spiraling downward into grief again. Cynthia had started to cook popcorn one night when the aroma suddenly reminded her of the night Rick had come up to their room, so alive and full of fun.

"Stop!" Eleanor said suddenly, as if remembering the same night. "Don't make popcorn!" Cynthia unplugged the hotplate and scraped the unpopped kernels into the trash. She scrubbed the pot with steel wool, as if trying to scrub away the memory of the four of them creeping down to the basement to get the margarine, laughing and joking. Rick had crawled into one of the caskets and pretended to be dead—and now he was. Cynthia closed her eyes, wishing it would turn out to be a joke, as it had been that night—wishing that Rick would spring back to life, calling, "Boo!" But Eleanor's handsome husband, Richard Trent, was dead.

Their room above the mortuary proved to be the worst possible place for Eleanor to live. Every time Montgomery's Funeral Home held a service for an area soldier, Eleanor would dress in black and go downstairs to weep as if she'd known the man. At first Cynthia thought that it was a good idea, and she hoped that Eleanor would finish mourning after one or two services. But attending wakes and funeral services soon became an obsession with her. It didn't matter if the deceased was a soldier or not—old or young, man or woman, an acquaintance or a stranger, Eleanor would sit in the back row and weep as if the casket held her beloved husband. Cynthia confronted her one night when Eleanor came back upstairs, her face ravaged with tears.

"Going to all these funerals isn't good for you, Ellie. You've got to stop."

"I can't. Not yet."

Neither one of them followed the news of the war any more. In April they were as shocked as the rest of the nation when they learned that President Roosevelt had died suddenly. The entire nation mourned along with Eleanor. But the nation's mourning turned to quiet joy three weeks later on VE day. The war in Europe was finally over. Eleanor didn't seem to notice.

Cynthia was tired of death and ready for a change. On her way home from work one afternoon, she saw a *For Rent* sign in one of the apartments above the Valley Food Market, and she went out after supper, alone, to have a look. The rooms cost more than their rent at the funeral home, but the apartment had a tiny kitchen with a stove and oven and their own bathroom. Cynthia signed the lease, then went home and gave Mrs. Montgomery their notice without telling Eleanor.

"We're moving out of here," she told Eleanor at the end of the month. "I rented an apartment above the Valley Food Market." Eleanor didn't react. She made no effort to pack. Her lethargy had become chronic, and she would lie in bed or on the sofa for hours, doing nothing. Cynthia packed all of Eleanor's belongings along with her own and paid William a few dollars to help them move. But even away from the funeral home, Eleanor's gloom didn't lift.

The summer weather turned hot, and their new apartment was stifling. "Let's go somewhere and do something," Cynthia suggested one sunny Saturday afternoon. "I'll pack a picnic lunch, and we'll go down to Bear Mountain."

"How can you even suggest a picnic?" Eleanor said angrily. "You have no idea how I feel."

Cynthia drew a deep breath, trying not to vent her own anger. "You're right, I don't know how you feel—I can't even imagine. But I feel like I'm walking on eggs around you, always trying not to upset you. It's so hard to see you suffering this way. I want to help you, to lift your spirits—*some-thing*! But I don't know what to do."

"There's nothing you can do. Nothing anyone can do."

Cynthia had to walk away. She took refuge in their tiny bathroom, attacking their bathtub with a can of Ajax cleanser. Eleanor made her so frustrated and angry at times. Cynthia was tired of living under a cloud of gloom, and she wanted Eleanor to snap out of it. But then Cynthia immediately felt guilty for her lack of patience. How would she feel if she'd lost the love of her life? There must be a way to help Eleanor through this, yet Eleanor refused to be helped. She was determined to mourn for the rest of her life. And Cynthia was sick of it. She longed to get away from her. But no . . . Eleanor was her dearest friend.

When the tub was clean, Cynthia dried her hands on a towel and went back into the living room to try again. "You need a new start, Eleanor. Rick is the one who died, not you. He would hate to see you this way."

Eleanor didn't reply.

"Please tell me what I can do to help you," Cynthia begged.

"You can leave me alone. Stop trying to cheer me up. Go out and have fun."

"How can I go out and leave you this way? You're my friend!"

"Because I'm telling you to go. That's the best way to help me—go away and leave me alone."

"Fine. I'm going, then." Cynthia was certain that it was the very worst thing to do, but she was tired of it all. She took the bus to Bensenville and wandered through the department stores, then went to the USO dance that night, alone. But the entire time she was there, she couldn't stop thinking about Eleanor—and feeling guilty for deserting her.

Eleanor wouldn't listen to the radio anymore. She hated the music, saying it reminded her of the USO dances where she'd met Rick. She would shut herself in the bedroom if Cynthia listened to *The Abbott and Costello Show* or *The Jack Benny Program* or *Dick Tracy*. Eleanor hated the news. Even though the Allies were clearly winning, she said it was too depressing to be reminded of all the men who were dying—every one of them a tragedy.

Cynthia bought the newspaper every day and read the good news aloud to Eleanor, avoiding the bad. When the United States dropped an atomic bomb on Hiroshima, Japan, in August, Cynthia couldn't comprehend it. The president explained that it would end the war swiftly and save thousands of American soldiers' lives, but the destruction was beyond imagining. Three days later, they bombed Nagasaki, and for the first time since leaving home, Cynthia went to tiny Park Street Church in Riverside to pray. On August 14, 1945, her prayers were answered when Japan surrendered. The long, terrible war was finally over.

And it was time for her life, and Eleanor's life, to start over. The war had been like a slow, sad song playing endlessly on a worn-out phonograph. It was time to lift the needle and take the record off; time to put on a new song, time to get up and dance again.

"I bought two round-trip train tickets to New York City," Cynthia told Eleanor. "We're going there tomorrow to celebrate VJ day." She had decided not to consult Eleanor ahead of time but simply inform her that they were going, the way Cynthia had when they'd moved out of the funeral home. Everyone in the factory had the day off from work.

"We finally have something to celebrate," she continued, "and I know Rick would want you to go. This victory is his. He helped earn it with his life." She had also made up her mind to stop avoiding Rick's name or anything that would remind Eleanor of his death. Maybe talking about him would help her to heal.

They took the bus to Bensenville early the next morning, August 15, 1945, then caught the train to New York City. Millions of people thronged Times Square, laughing, cheering, celebrating. The frenzied excitement filled Cynthia with energy and joy for the first time in months—maybe years—and she clung to Eleanor's hand, her heart bursting with happiness as she towed her through the crowd. The war was over! Life could go back to normal. Groups of strangers broke into spontaneous song, others danced in the street, sailors threw their hats into the air, car horns blared.

Cynthia was content just to wade through it all, feeling like part of the crowd, sharing in the joy of this hard-fought victory. Swept away by everything, she didn't think to ask Eleanor how she was faring until nearly three hours had passed. When she finally turned to her friend and saw the pained expression on her pale face, Cynthia was appalled. Thousands of jubilant soldiers and sailors and airmen jammed the streets, and Eleanor was scanning all of their faces as if searching for Rick's. It seemed she believed he'd become lost among them and if she just looked hard enough, long enough, she would find him. Rick should be here, laughing and alive and full of fun.

Coming here had been a mistake, Cynthia realized, as damaging to Eleanor as going to strangers' funerals. "Let's go home," she shouted above the deafening cheers. Eleanor simply nodded.

When they returned to work, Mr. Jackson gathered all the employees together on the factory floor to make an announcement. "Well, we won't be needing bomb switches and gauges anymore," he said jovially. "You girls did a mighty fine job of filling in for the men when you were needed—a mighty fine job. The good news is that you won't have to do men's work anymore. I know most of you gals will be plenty glad to get back to your homes and your families, right?"

The women broke into cheers and applause, and Cynthia joined them. She was tired of this monotonous job and ready for a change. But she stopped when she noticed that Eleanor wasn't cheering.

"There are going to be layoffs in the coming weeks," Mr. Jackson continued. "I'm giving you girls fair warning so you can make other arrangements. We're going to close down the factory for a short time so we can retool to make appliances. As I'm sure you girls know, consumer goods have been scarce since the war began. But now that our boys are coming home, there are going to be a lot of weddings. We're going to need a lot of toasters!"

The women cheered again, but Eleanor's face turned very pale at the mention of weddings. Cynthia groped for her hand and squeezed it. "People say such thoughtless things," she whispered.

Mr. Jackson finished his speech and dismissed everyone to begin working, but Eleanor stormed after him, following him into his cubicle.

"Mr. Jackson—wait."

Cynthia went after her, afraid of what her friend might say. It was obvious that his speech had infuriated Eleanor—and calling them "girls" had probably been the least of it.

"Mr. Jackson, I need this job. I don't want to be laid off. Not all of us have husbands to support us, you know."

"I know," he said with a smile. "But young girls as pretty as you two shouldn't have any trouble finding one."

Cynthia's mouth fell open in astonishment. When Eleanor took a menacing step toward Mr. Jackson, Cynthia was certain she would punch him in the nose.

"I *am* married, Mr. Jackson. My husband was killed over in Germany. I don't want another husband—what I want is to keep my job!"

"I-I'm sorry. I'm very sorry for your loss. . . . But I have orders to lay off all my temporary defense workers and make room for returning servicemen who need these jobs."

"I need this job, too!"

"I'm sorry. There's nothing I can do."

"Well, you won't have to lay me off, Mr. Jackson, because I quit!" Eleanor ripped off her identification badge and threw it on Mr. Jackson's littered desk. Then she pushed past Cynthia and strode from the building.

Cynthia didn't know what to do. She was afraid to leave Eleanor on her own, afraid of what she might do. But she knew that Eleanor would never accept consolation, anyway—not when she was this angry. The truth was, Cynthia didn't want to be around her. And she didn't want to quit working until she had to. She mumbled a vague apology to Mr. Jackson and went back to her workstation.

Cynthia spent all day rehearsing what she would say to Eleanor when she got home and planning what she would do with her own life after she was laid off. By the time the three o'clock whistle blew, Cynthia had her speech all prepared. She trudged up the steps to their second-floor apartment and found Eleanor lying in bed in her work clothes, staring at the ceiling. Cynthia drew a deep breath.

"The way that Mr. Jackson went about things today was really stupid and thoughtless," she began. "But I have a feeling we're going to hear a lot of thoughtless comments from people in the months to come, and you can't take it so personally, Ellie. People are sick of the war, sick of thinking about it and talking about it and living with it. There's a feeling of prosperity in the air, and everyone wants to forget about all the suffering and move ahead to something new. People want cars and houses and a normal life. . . . Eleanor, I know you're tired of hearing this from me, but you have to get on with your life, too. You and I came here to Riverside to start over three years ago. It was hard work, but we did it. And now we're going to have to do it again."

Eleanor didn't respond. Cynthia hadn't really expected her to. Most of Cynthia's speeches were met with silence or anger, and she found she preferred the silence. She kicked off her shoes and began changing out of her work clothes.

"I read in the paper about a secretarial course they're offering at the business college over in Bensenville," she continued as she undressed. "They teach typing and dictation and everything else you need to know to get a good secretarial job. The fall semester is just starting, and I've decided I'm going to sign up. Why don't you take it with me? If we start going to classes now, at night, we'll be well on our way by the time we get laid off. And they're bound to need plenty of secretaries down in New York City. We can find an apartment down there, and—"

"You can be a secretary if you want to. It's not for me."

Cynthia paused, bracing for all the usual arguments. "All right, then. You used to talk about going to college, remember? Isn't that what you've been saving your money for?"

"No," Eleanor said angrily. "I've been saving so Rick and I could start a new life together."

Cynthia sighed. "I know I've said this before, too, but Rick wouldn't want you to mourn like this. He'd want you to get on with your life. You used to want a career, remember?"

"Well, I don't feel like it anymore." Eleanor climbed out of bed and began changing out of her clothes.

Cynthia groped for words. She had rehearsed a much longer speech, but she was too discouraged to remember it all. She was getting nowhere. She watched as Eleanor combed her hair, then put on her hat with the black mesh veil—and suddenly she realized what Eleanor was doing. She was dressing in black to go to the funeral home again. Tears of anger and frustration filled Cynthia's eyes.

"What are you doing, Ellie? Come on—please! No more! It's morbid to keep going to funerals of people you don't even know. You've got to stop."

"I need to go to funerals," Eleanor said in a hollow voice. "I need to try to grasp the fact that he's really gone."

"But it isn't helping. Can't you see that? It's been months and months, you've gone to dozens of funerals, and you still haven't grasped it. You're still in mourning."

"That's because I know it isn't really him in the casket." She gave a strangled sob and sank down on the bed, weeping. Cynthia sat beside her, rocking her in her arms.

"You're too young to stop living, Ellie. You've got to figure out what it will take to get over this and do it."

"Maybe if I saw Rick's grave . . ."

"Then, do it, Ellie. For heaven's sake, go to Albany or wherever he's buried and put flowers on his grave. Then maybe you can get on with your life. You're only twenty-one years old."

"Will you come with me, Cynthia? Please?"

Cynthia remembered the confident, poised woman she'd met on their first day at the electronics plant—shaking hands with their new boss and telling him not to call them girls—and she wondered what had happened to that woman. Eleanor was begging for help like an insecure child. If this is what happened to a person when her heart was broken, then Cynthia didn't ever want to fall in love.

"Of course, Ellie. Of course I'll go with you. I'll pick up a bus schedule, we'll go to Albany next weekend, and we'll put flowers on Rick's grave."

Chapter

18

B y the time they reached Albany the following Saturday, Cynthia was
sorry she had agreed to come. Riding the bus had exhausted her. It
had stopped in every little town between Bensenville and Albany, crowding
dozens more people onboard, it seemed, than the bus could hold. Albany
was a good-sized city, and Cynthia didn't know how they would ever find
Rick's grave—or if he even had one here. It had occurred to her after
promising to come that thousands of servicemen had been buried overseas
near the battlefields where they had died. The task of finding Rick's grave
seemed insurmountable. But she would sail to Europe with Eleanor to see
it if it would help her get on with her life.

As she stood in the noisy bus station feeling hot and dazed, Cynthia
wondered where to begin. Eleanor clung to her arm, looking sad and lost.
The old Eleanor would have taken control, recruiting every porter, ticket
clerk, and security guard in sight to help her. They would be turning the
town upside down by now, as they helped her search for Rick's grave. But
that charming, confident woman had died along with Rick, leaving behind
a bewildered girl who gazed around the bustling station as if she'd just

awakened from a nightmare and didn't know what to do. Cynthia knew she would have to take the lead.

"There's a phone booth over there," she said, as if spotting a lifeboat. "Come on, we'll look up his father's name and see if there's a listing. Rick was Richard Trent, Jr., wasn't he?" She saw Eleanor wince and realized she had referred to Rick in the past tense.

"Actually, he's 'the third,'" Eleanor said. "Richard Trent III. I used to tell him he sounded like an English monarch."

They crowded into the phone booth, their breath fogging the glass as Cynthia dug in her purse for loose change. She could hardly believe their luck when the information operator gave her Mr. Trent's phone number and address. She scribbled down the information on a napkin. "Do you want to call him or should I?" she asked Eleanor.

"Neither one of us." Eleanor took the receiver from Cynthia's hand and hung it back in its cradle. "From the way Rick described his parents, they'll probably hang up on me. Let's just go over there. We'll ask one of his servants."

Cynthia went to the information booth and got directions. They had to take a city bus across town, then walk several blocks through an upper-class neighborhood until they found the right street. Cynthia's steps slowed as she counted off the house numbers. The sheer size of the homes shocked her. She walked slower and slower then halted at the end of a tree-lined driveway.

"That's Rick's house," Cynthia said in a hushed voice. She saw tears in Eleanor's eyes and wondered if maybe this hadn't been such a good idea. "We should have called first, Ellie. You don't go barging up to 'old-money' houses like these and pound on the door asking questions." She was about to suggest that they walk back to a drugstore and find a telephone when Eleanor gripped her arm.

"This is where Rick grew up. He was going to leave all of this for me."

Cynthia swallowed the lump in her throat and squeezed Eleanor's hand. "He loved you, Ellie. He really, truly loved you."

As she stood on the sidewalk, trying to decide what to do next, Cynthia heard a car engine start up somewhere behind the house. The motor revved a few times; then the car came into sight, backing slowly down the long drive. It was an older model sedan—new cars hadn't been made since the war began—and Cynthia suddenly decided to flag down the driver and ask if he could direct them. She had her arm raised halfway when she suddenly froze. The driver looked exactly like Rick!

Cynthia blinked, certain that she was imagining things. It must be Rick's brother—but Rick didn't have a brother! She couldn't believe her eyes. Then Eleanor saw him, too.

"*Rick . . .*" she whispered. Eleanor's knees buckled as if she'd seen a ghost, and she collapsed in a faint on the sidewalk. Cynthia bent to help her, then looked up again in time to see the driver clearly.

It was Rick Trent. He was alive! And he was a dirty, rotten liar.

"Rick!" Cynthia shouted. He hadn't noticed them as he'd backed into the street, and he was starting to drive away. "Rick, help me!" she shouted.

His eyes went wide when he saw who it was. The car screeched to a halt, then backed up.

Cynthia crouched down to cradle Eleanor's head, lifting it off the pavement. Rick got out of the car and came toward them, walking as if in slow motion. His face was as white as Eleanor's.

"What are you doing here?" he asked.

"What are *you* doing here, you monster? You're supposed to be dead! We came to find your grave!" She reached out with her free hand and started punching his legs. "How could you do this to her? How could you?" Rick backed away. Eleanor moaned as she started coming around.

"Is she okay?" Rick asked.

"Of course she's not okay! She thinks she saw a ghost. You're supposed to be dead!"

Eleanor's eyes fluttered open. She looked up and her eyes met his. "Is it really you?" she murmured. Rick nodded and squatted beside her. In the next instant Eleanor sat up and threw her arms around his neck, nearly knocking him backward with the force of her embrace. "Oh, Rick, you're alive! You're alive! I must be dreaming!"

"You're not. I—"

"The army made a terrible mistake! They told me you were dead! That's why I stopped writing to you. Rick! Oh, Rick!" She buried her face in his chest, hugging him, weeping.

Rick's eyes remained dry. Cynthia could tell by the look on his face that the army hadn't made a mistake. Rick had deliberately let Eleanor believe that he was dead. He'd deceived her. They were man and wife, and he'd taken the coward's way out and ditched her. Cynthia was angry enough to kill him.

"How could you do such a terrible thing?" she raged. "Eleanor is your *wife*! I watched you marry her! I heard you vow to spend the rest of your life with her!"

Rick glanced around nervously as a car drove past. "Shh . . . Not out here, Cynthia. Let's go inside."

They helped Eleanor to her feet, but she was so badly shaken she could barely walk. It took both of them to help her up the driveway to the front door of Rick's house. "Wait out here, Cynthia," he ordered. "Give us some time alone." His manner was as cocky and self-assured as on the night Cynthia first met him.

"Nothing doing, you creep! I'm not leaving Eleanor. You have no idea what she's been through since she learned you were dead. She nearly died of grief!"

"I'm sorry." He didn't sound sorry, he sounded angry. The apology wasn't for all the pain he'd caused Eleanor; he was sorry he'd gotten caught. He glared at Cynthia, then reluctantly led them into the living room.

"It's okay, Rick," Eleanor murmured as she leaned against him. "We've found each other again and that's all that matters."

He helped Eleanor sit down on the couch, then hurried away saying, "I'll get you some water."

Cynthia was only dimly aware of the magnificent room, decorated with antiques and fine oil paintings and oriental rugs. Classical music played softly in the background. The anger that pounded through her made the room seem unusually bright.

"Rick's alive. . . ." Eleanor whispered. "Oh, thank God! Thank God!"

He returned with a glass of water—and with a man who was an older version of himself, equally handsome, equally arrogant. Rick handed Eleanor the glass, and she took a tiny sip before setting it down. Her hands shook so badly she nearly dropped it.

"Eleanor, this is my father," Rick said.

She looked up at Rick and smiled. "Good. We'll tell him together, darling."

Cynthia's stomach made a sickening turn. Eleanor was in too much shock to read the cold, hard expression on Rick's face. She was imagining that they would confront his father with the truth about their marriage then walk out, arm in arm, to live the rest of their life together. But Cynthia knew that wasn't going to happen.

"You filthy, lying coward," she breathed.

"Stay out of this, Cynthia."

"You expect me to sit here and watch you kill her a second time? Never!"

"What's going on, Richard?" his father asked. "Who are these people?"

Eleanor had recovered enough to extend her hand to him, the confident, poised Eleanor that Cynthia remembered from their first day at the factory. "Hello, Mr. Trent. I'm glad we finally get to meet. I'm Rick's wife, Eleanor." Her pale face looked radiant, triumphant. Mr. Trent glared at Rick, then at Eleanor. Cynthia felt as if she might vomit, certain of what was to come.

"I know all about you, Miss Bartlett," Mr. Trent said. "What are you doing here?"

"The army made a terrible mistake. I was told that Rick had died during the war. I came to Albany to see his grave, and instead . . . I've found my husband again!" Tears filled her eyes as she smiled up at Rick. "It's like a dream or . . . or a miracle. Tell him, Rick. Tell him how we were married two years ago, before you were shipped overseas."

"I know all about your so-called marriage. My son is the one who made a mistake, Miss Bartlett, in the heat of the moment. Youthful passions often fly out of control in wartime when life seems uncertain. But the war is over now, and it's time for cooler heads to prevail. A lifetime decision such as a marriage should be made using logic and reason."

Cynthia's vision blurred as she saw where this conversation was leading. "You horrible, monstrous man!" she spat.

Eleanor seemed unruffled by his words. "You're wrong, Mr. Trent. Rick and I love each other. Our marriage vows were for a lifetime." She reached to take his limp hand as he stood over her. She seemed blind to the coldness in Rick's eyes, but Cynthia saw it. His allegiance was to his father, not Eleanor.

"Richard had the marriage annulled several months ago," Mr. Trent continued. "We tried to send you a copy, but it was returned without a forwarding address."

Eleanor shook her head. "Why would he have it annulled? We're man and wife. Don't let him do this to us, Rick. You were going to stand up to him, remember? Tell him the truth. Tell him that we love each other, that we're man and wife."

Rick said nothing. Cynthia hated him for the coward that he was.

"My son had the marriage annulled, Miss Bartlett, because you married him under false pretenses. You knew all about him and what he stood to inherit, but you lied to him about yourself. Had he known the truth about your family background, he never would have made such a foolish decision. Fortunately, our lawyer has convinced a judge that you are an unscrupulous woman who tricked Richard into a hasty marriage for his money."

"That's a lie!" Cynthia shouted.

Eleanor's face went from shock to disbelief as she turned to Rick. "Is that what you think, Rick?"

He didn't reply. He kept his gaze fixed on his father, allowing him to speak for him. The older man's voice raised in volume as he spoke each word with cold, bitter anger.

"We looked into your background—and your mother's—Miss Bartlett. The judge and the church authorities agreed that, since there was no child involved, the three-day marriage could be annulled."

Eleanor looked up at Rick. "You said you loved me," she said quietly. Her calm control frightened Cynthia more than tears or anger would have. "You told me you hated your father, hated the way he always manipulated you, like he's doing right now. Say something, Rick."

He cleared his throat. "You didn't tell me the truth about yourself, Eleanor."

"You never asked about my family or I would have. Besides, I never dreamed that it would matter to you. You said you loved me for who I was, the same way I loved you. We agreed that nothing else mattered."

"Well, it does matter. We're no longer married, Eleanor."

"Can you honestly stand there and tell me you never loved me?"

"I thought I did . . . at the time. But you never told me the truth about your parents, and—"

"What difference does it make? They have nothing to do with us or with the future we planned. We used to talk about values and what was really important in life, remember?"

"Family is important, too. My grandfather started this company. My father has worked hard to make sure he had something to pass along to me. I'm his only son. How can I throw that all away? Especially when you lied to me."

"This has nothing to do with my family, does it? It's about money. It's always about money. That's what you don't want to give up, isn't it? He threatened to cut you off if you stayed married to me."

Rick didn't reply. He didn't need to. His face spoke the truth. Cynthia glanced at Eleanor in alarm. She was slowly comprehending the terrible truth that the man she loved had betrayed her. The shock of it would probably devastate her more than his supposed death had. Eleanor's cool, calm facade began to slip as she struggled for composure. Cynthia could feel her body trembling uncontrollably. She took Eleanor's arm and pulled her to her feet. More than anything else, Eleanor would hate to break down in front of Rick and his father.

"Let's go, Eleanor. We were right all along—Rick Trent *is* dead. He must be, because he stinks just like a corpse!"

No one spoke as Cynthia helped Eleanor to the door, the classical music still tinkling pleasantly in the background. When Cynthia noticed Rick following them to his car at the end of the driveway, it took every ounce of restraint she possessed to keep from punching him.

"You no-good, rotten coward!" she shouted. "Oh! It's a good thing I don't curse or I'd tell you exactly what you are! How could you lie to her and let her think you were dead? You loved her, Rick. I know you did."

"I thought it would be kinder to let her think I died. She would mourn for a while but—"

"But she'd never find out what a louse you really are, right? She'd think you died loving her rather than discovering the truth that you threw her aside for your daddy's money."

"It's not that simple, Cynthia."

"What a cowardly thing to do! You don't deserve Eleanor. She's too good for scum like you!" Rick climbed into his car and slammed the door, peeling out of the driveway, tires squealing.

Neither woman spoke as Cynthia led Eleanor back through the quiet neighborhood to the city bus stop. It seemed to take forever to ride across town to the bus station in rush hour traffic. The next bus to Bensenville didn't leave for another two hours, and it would be well after midnight by the time they got home.

Cynthia didn't know what to say as they sat side by side on the hard wooden bench, surrounded by cigarette smoke and diesel fumes. But she had to try.

"Eleanor—"

"Don't say anything, Cynthia, please. I don't want to talk right now."

Eleanor's heart had broken in two when she'd learned that Rick had died, but at least she'd had an enemy to blame for his death, an enemy that ultimately had been beaten and destroyed. This was so much worse. This time her heart had been shattered beyond repair, and the damage had been deliberate. This time the enemy was the man she loved—and Cynthia feared that he had destroyed her.

A week after they returned to Riverside, the mailman delivered a thick, registered letter addressed to Eleanor Bartlett. As soon as Eleanor saw Rick's name on the return address, she handed it to Cynthia.

"Send it back. Whatever it is, I don't want it." She turned away and stood with her back to Cynthia, staring through the window. Tears blurred Cynthia's vision as she ripped open the envelope and pulled out an official-looking document, complete with the seal of New York State. The marriage between Eleanor Bartlett and Richard Trent III had been officially annulled. Included in the envelope was a pile of U.S. Government War Bonds—five thousand dollars worth—and a note from Rick.

> Eleanor,
>
> I never meant to hurt you. Please accept this money along with my sincere apologies, and use it to further your education.
>
> Rick

For a long moment, Cynthia was afraid to speak. "Rick sent the official paperwork and some money," she finally said.

"I don't want his guilt money. Send it back."

"I think you should keep it, Ellie. He owes you at least that much. You can use it to start all over again, and—"

"There's no such thing as starting over," Eleanor said in a hollow voice. "That's just a myth. We can never escape our past. It follows us wherever we go. All of the things our parents did, and their parents did before them—they follow us and we can't escape."

The despair in Eleanor's voice alarmed Cynthia. She recalled how Mr. Trent had used something from Eleanor's past as an excuse to annul their marriage, but Cynthia couldn't imagine any past so bad that it didn't deserve a second chance. Eleanor never talked about her family, and Cynthia wasn't about to pry, but she needed to convince Eleanor to keep the money. Rick owed her much, much more.

"Ellie, don't give Rick power over you to ruin your life this way. He's a cowardly liar who used any excuse he could dream up to get his hands on his father's money. You really *can* start all over again—I did. I got away from my small-town life, thanks to your help. You can start again, too."

Eleanor didn't respond. Cynthia exhaled and tried again.

"Look, Rick did a terrible thing to you, and I know that he hurt you very deeply. But take the money, Ellie. You can use it to go to college and have that career you always wanted. You deserve it."

Eleanor turned to face her, hollow-eyed, despondent. A dead woman. "No . . . I don't deserve anything."

Chapter

19

Cynthia studied her reflection in the bathroom mirror, pleased with what she saw. Her blond hair, pulled back in an elegant French twist, shone like white gold in the light. Her makeup was as fresh and flawless as a movie star's, and her new black cocktail dress was sure to turn heads—worth every penny she had spent on it.

She glanced at her watch. It was still too early to go downstairs and wait for her date. She had agreed to meet him in front of the Valley Food Market, unwilling to have him climb the rickety stairs to her apartment and see where she was living. It might spoil his image of her as a high-class woman.

Cynthia switched off the bathroom light and carried her high heels out to the living room. No sense putting them on until the last minute. She was searching for a notepad and a pencil to scribble a note to Eleanor when she heard footsteps slowly tromping up the stairs, then a key turning in the lock. She looked up in surprise when Eleanor came through the door.

"You're home early. I was just writing you a note."

"Yeah, the diner was slow tonight and I'm exhausted. I gave my tables to one of the other waitresses and came home." She sank down on the sofa as if her legs couldn't possibly hold her for another moment, then stretched out on her back. Cynthia was about to ask how she could be so tired after working only three hours on a slow night, but Eleanor spoke first.

"Where are you going all dressed up? I never saw that dress before."

"It's brand-new. How do I look?" She paced a few steps and made a slow turn, like a runway model.

"Like a million dollars. You've turned into a real class act, Cynthia. Although I can't imagine any man here in Riverside who's worthy of such an elegant-looking date. Who's the lucky guy?"

Cynthia hesitated, afraid to tell her. She hadn't discussed her social life with Eleanor since they'd argued over Eleanor's refusal to go out on dates. Eleanor had deliberately asked for the Friday and Saturday night shifts at the diner and was usually working when Cynthia went out and sleeping when she arrived home.

"He's just a guy I met at work," she said, glancing at her watch again.

"Come on ... Tell me all about him." Eleanor smiled, but it lacked warmth. "You're way overdressed for any of those jerks on the assembly line. Is it one of the salesmen?"

"No. . . . It's my boss."

"Your boss! Wow, that's news. I didn't know that bosses were allowed to date their secretaries."

"There's no law against it," Cynthia said, smiling shyly. She couldn't help smiling when she thought about Howard. "We've gone out for coffee and to the movies a few times, and we always have a lot of laughs. We talk about everything under the sun. But this is a step up, and I'm hoping it will be the turning point in our relationship. He's taking me to a dinner dance at his country club."

"Whoa! His *country club*?" Eleanor's smile vanished. "Are you out of your mind?"

"No—why?"

Eleanor pulled herself upright on the couch, frowning angrily. "Who is this guy? Tell me his name."

Cynthia was reluctant to reply. "His name is Howard—Howard Hayworth."

"Not the same Hayworths who just bought the electronics plant?"

"Well, sort of. The factory is owned by Howard's father. But what difference does it ma—"

"Cynthia! You didn't tell me you were working for the owner's son, much less dating him!"

"Why are you getting mad? You should be happy for me. Howard needed a secretary, and he picked me out of the typing pool. Now we're dating. What's the big deal?"

"You're so naïve! Can't you see that he's using you? Of course he picked you—you're gorgeous. But you'd be a fool to trust a spoiled rich boy. Run, Cynthia! Run before you get hurt."

"Not every rich man is another Rick Trent," she said quietly. "Can't you be happy for me?"

"I'll be very happy for you when you tell this guy to get lost. I'm warning you for your own good—ditch him before you get hurt."

"I knew I shouldn't have told you about him," Cynthia said angrily. "Just because you've stopped living, you think that everyone else should, too. You refused to go to business school with me, you gave up your dream to get an education and a career, and now you've stopped taking care of yourself. You dress sloppily, your hair is a mess, you work at a dead-end job. You seem to accept it as fact that you're no good, that you're not worthy of nice things or decent clothes. I know Rick did a terrible thing to you, but you've been depressed about it for much too long. I wish you would go back to the doctor, Ellie. Get some help!"

"For your information, it isn't just depression. I'm ill. The doctors aren't sure what it is yet, but I'm worn out all the time. I don't have the energy to go to school. And I don't feel like wasting my time and my money to get all dolled up just to impress a man. I'm trying to warn you for your own good not to trust this Hayworth creep, and you're jumping all over me! Thanks a lot!" She stumbled into the bedroom and slammed the door.

Cynthia knew that she should apologize, but there wasn't time. Besides, how dare Eleanor criticize Howard when she had never even met him? Cynthia put on her shoes and snatched up her purse, slamming the front door on her way out.

Cynthia was falling in love. Her night at the dinner dance with Howard was like a fairy tale: Cinderella waltzing with her handsome prince beneath glittering chandeliers, sipping champagne. The country club in Bensenville was the most elegant place Cynthia had ever been, the food exquisite, the orchestra sublime. And when Howard led her out onto the balcony beneath the stars and kissed her for the first time, she thought she had died and gone to heaven.

"You're so beautiful, Cynthia," he murmured in her ear. "How have I been lucky enough to find you?" She returned home from her date as if walking on air—and knew that she could never share one word of it with Eleanor.

On Monday the florist delivered a dozen red roses to their apartment. Tears filled Cynthia's eyes when she read the card: *I can't get you out of my mind—Howard.* But when Cynthia looked up, she saw Eleanor shaking her head, frowning.

"Please be happy for me, Ellie. I don't want this to come between us."

"How can I be happy when I know you're going to get hurt?"

"Howard isn't Rick Trent."

Eleanor exhaled angrily, then snatched up a letter from off the table. "Listen, my brother wants to come visit me. Is it okay if he stays with us for a few days?"

Cynthia didn't know why Eleanor had changed the subject, but she was grateful. "Of course! You don't even have to ask." Eleanor seemed to have a close relationship with her brother, and Cynthia hoped he could help lift her out of her depression.

"Promise me one thing, though," Eleanor said. "I don't want Leonard to know about Rick."

"You mean, you never told him you got married?"

Eleanor shook her head. "And I don't want you blabbing the news. Promise?"

"Don't you think it might help if you talked to your brother about—"

"No! You don't know Leonard like I do. He would kill Rick *and* his father. And as much as I'd like to see them both die a horrible death, I don't want Leonard to get the electric chair. Just . . . Please, don't tell him about any of it."

"I won't. But . . . you seem to be so close to Leonard—you wrote to him all during the war. Why didn't you ever tell him you were married?"

Eleanor shrugged. "I just didn't."

Cynthia took her roses into the kitchen to put them in water. She had lived with Eleanor for more than three years, and she still didn't understand her at all.

A week later Leonard arrived, and he wasn't alone. He brought along his war buddy, Donald Gallagher. The odd-looking, mismatched pair reminded Cynthia of Mutt and Jeff. Leonard was tall and thin and dark-haired—and so perpetually melancholy that Cynthia quickly gave up hope that he would cheer Eleanor's depression. Donald was the opposite: a short, sturdy, happy-go-lucky fellow with reddish-brown hair and freckles. He reminded Cynthia of the film star Mickey Rooney.

She was certain they wouldn't stay long once they saw how tiny the apartment was and how crowded it seemed with the four of them squeezed inside. There was no place for two extra people to sleep. But the two men quickly made themselves at home as if there was room to spare. Two days after they arrived, they hauled a mattress up the steps from who knows where, so Donald could sleep on the living room floor. Leonard slept on the sofa. Their bulging knapsacks and duffel bags overflowed all over the place, and they mooched three meals a day without ever offering to help cook or pay for the food. Neither man cleaned up after himself, leaving whiskers and shaving cream in the bathroom sink, wet towels on the floor, and beer bottles all over the place. Eleanor, who had once been the neater of the two roommates, didn't seem to notice.

By the end of the second week, Cynthia was ready to scream. She made meatloaf and mashed potatoes for supper one night, then took control of the conversation as soon as everyone was seated. "So, Donald, what are your plans now that the war is over?"

"The sky's the limit!" He grinned. "I want what everybody wants: a new house, a new car—the American Dream."

"That's great," she said. "How are you planning to go about it? I hear they're offering money to GIs who want to go to college. Have you thought about going back to school?"

"Nah, that's not for me. Leonard's the intellectual type, not me." He picked another slice of meatloaf off the platter with his fingers, then licked them.

"Donald and you have a lot in common, Cynthia," Eleanor said. "He grew up on a farm just like you did. And you're both chasing after the American Dream—except you're out to marry a rich man, right, Cynthia?"

Eleanor's tone had a nasty edge to it. Cynthia bit her tongue to keep from lashing back. First she had to get rid of these two bums, then she could try to repair her relationship with Eleanor. She pasted on a smile.

"Well, if you're looking to marry a rich woman, Donald, you'd better move out of Riverside. There aren't too many wealthy prospects around here."

Donald laughed. "My friend Leonard would never forgive me if I married a rich woman. He hates the upper class, right, Leonard?"

Leonard nodded and helped himself to the last of the mashed potatoes. Cynthia felt herself losing patience.

"So, will you both be looking for jobs around here, then?" she asked.

"I'm looking for investment opportunities," Donald said with a grin. "I won myself a nice little nest egg playing poker during the war, and I'm looking for opportunities to increase my winnings."

"Really? By playing poker?" She tried not to look skeptical.

"Even better. I know a guy who can put a bet on a horse at Belmont for me whenever I want. I'm just waiting for a sure thing." Cynthia had wondered why their apartment was knee-deep in newspapers. Evidently Donald had been following the horse races, waiting for a sure thing.

"Isn't offtrack betting illegal?" she asked.

"It's just a hobby of mine," he said with a shrug. "You need to lighten up, Cindy."

"Oh, don't ever call her *Cindy*," Eleanor said with mock horror. "It reminds her of the farm. She likes to be known as *Cynthia*. And she *always* plays by the rules. You would have thought I was breaking one of the Ten Commandments when I wanted to heat up a lousy can of soup in our old apartment. It took me weeks to convince her it wasn't a grave sin."

"Well, when she sees all the dough I'll be making at the track, she'll be convinced. How about you, sweetheart?" he said to Eleanor. "You have any money you'd like to invest? I can set you up with my bookie."

"Maybe . . ." Eleanor said, smiling slightly. "I'll let you know."

Cynthia thought of the five thousand dollars in war bonds that Rick had sent Eleanor and shuddered. As far as she knew, Eleanor hadn't sent them back. They were probably stuffed into one of her bureau drawers along with the annulment papers.

"How about you, Leonard?" Cynthia asked, refusing to give up. "What are your immediate plans?" He leaned back in his chair with a frown, making a steeple with his long fingers, as if about to give a serious lecture.

"America is heading in the wrong direction," he began. "Instead of embarking on a materialistic quest, we need to address the grievous inequities that have developed between the social classes. I have been studying Marxist theory, and I believe that it's time for America's proletariat to rise up and claim what is rightfully theirs. This nation was built on their sweat and labor, yet they haven't been allowed their fair share of the wealth, and . . ."

There was more, but Cynthia tuned it out. The situation was worse than she'd thought. She was hosting two deadbeats—one a gambler and the other a Communist—and neither of them seemed to have any concrete plans for their futures.

Eleanor loved her brother, and he was very good to her, but Donald Gallagher had attached himself to Leonard like a stamp to a letter, and Cynthia couldn't host one without the other. It was hard to tell someone like Donald to get lost because he was so naturally good-natured. He didn't have a mean bone in his body. But he was a professional leech, who had latched onto a good thing in Leonard Bartlett, and he knew enough to hang on to the smarter man's coattails.

It was also clear as time passed that Donald was falling for Eleanor. He would pick flowers for her out of backyard gardens and present them to her with his boyish grin. He took her to the racetrack on her day off and showed her a good time. And he followed her around like a lovesick puppy, telling her she had eyes like topaz and other silly stuff like that.

Eleanor seemed flattered by his adoration, as if she couldn't believe anyone would love her—as if Donald Gallagher was all that she deserved. And he was as unlike Rick Trent as any man could possibly be. Eleanor had always had a heart for pitiful bumpkins like Donald. Cynthia remembered how she'd danced with the homely, awkward GI the night she'd met Rick, telling Cynthia that she thought country boys were sweet. Eleanor couldn't be foolish enough to get involved with Donald, could she?

But between Cynthia's hectic days at work and her romantic evenings with Howard, she didn't have many opportunities to confront Eleanor about their long-term guests. Especially since the men were always underfoot whenever she did have time to talk.

Cynthia knew that she was falling deeper and deeper in love with Howard and he with her. She was tired of meeting him on the street in front of the Valley Food Market for their dates and wanted to invite him up to her apartment, but she didn't dare with the two loafers hanging around. It didn't look good to be sharing an apartment with two strange men. Besides, she was afraid they'd attack Howard for committing the unforgivable crime of being rich.

After three months had passed and the two freeloaders still showed no sign of leaving, Cynthia went to the diner one evening to talk with Eleanor. She chose a stool in Eleanor's station and ordered a root beer float, then asked, "Can we talk a minute?"

Eleanor filled a tall glass with root beer, plopped in two scoops of vanilla ice cream, stuck a straw into it and said, "Sure. What's up?" She looked like a boxer with his gloves raised.

"Look, there's no easy way to say this, so I'll just say it straight out—Leonard and Donald need to find their own place. It's been three months. We have no privacy, the place is a slum, and they're eating us out of house and home. It's time, Eleanor. They're nice guys—but it's time they went their own way."

"Where are they supposed to go without any money?"

Cynthia poked at the ice cream with her spoon. "Have they even looked for jobs?"

"What's that supposed to mean? Of course they've looked for jobs. It isn't easy to find work, you know. Why don't you ask your hotshot boyfriend to get them a job in his factory?"

The thought of Leonard and Donald crossing paths with Howard Hayworth gave Cynthia the shivers. She wanted them out of Riverside and out of her life, not working for her boyfriend's company. Leonard hadn't lifted Eleanor's spirits any more than Cynthia had all these months. In fact, his Communist ravings seemed to fuel Eleanor's hatred of rich people. Cynthia drew a long sip of root beer, weighing her options.

"If I help them get jobs at the plant, do you promise they'll get their own place?"

"Of course! What are you implying, Cynthia?"

"Nothing! I'm just feeling squashed that's all. It's making me irritable. I have to tiptoe around in my own kitchen every morning before work while they're snoring like two chainsaws. Some days I can't even get the front door open because Donald's mattress is blocking the way. I want my privacy back."

"Why don't you just admit that you don't like them?"

Cynthia pushed her glass away and stood. "I have nothing against either one of them," she said, gritting her teeth. "But even Saint Peter and Moses would get on my nerves if they slept in my living room for three months. I'll ask if there are any openings at the factory." She pulled a dollar out of her purse and slapped it onto the counter.

Cynthia hated asking Howard for a favor, but it paid off. A week after

Leonard and Donald were hired at Hayworth Electronics, they rented a run-down house across the river in a dumpy part of town. The house was for sale, but the owner allowed the two men to rent it with the understanding that they would vacate when a buyer came along. Cynthia couldn't imagine why anyone in their right mind would ever buy it, so it seemed like an answer to prayer—except that Leonard and Donald still hung around her apartment, mooching food all the time. She found herself wishing she could be rid of all of them, including gloomy Eleanor.

Cynthia was sitting at her desk one afternoon at work, typing a letter, when Howard buzzed her over the intercom. "Could I see you in my office for a moment, Miss Bartlett?" he asked.

"Of course, Mr. Hayworth." She couldn't suppress a smile. They addressed each other very formally at work and had never told anyone that they were dating, but Cynthia knew that anyone with a pair of eyes could see that they were in love. Howard called her into his office at least once a day so he could kiss her, and she would emerge with her lipstick smeared and her hair mussed. She figured that was why he was calling her now, and she pictured him waiting near the door to take her into his arms. But when she entered his office he was seated behind his desk, his expression serious. He motioned for her to sit down.

"Howard, what's wrong?"

"It's about your two friends . . . Bartlett and Gallagher." He fiddled with his fountain pen, twirling it between his fingers. "I'm sorry, sweetheart, but I'm going to have to fire them at the end of this week. They knew they'd be on probation for the first six months, then a decision would be made whether to hire them permanently or not. I wanted to give you a heads up—they're going to be fired."

"Oh, no," Cynthia groaned. She imagined them moving back into her apartment, camping in her tiny living room, and tears sprang to her eyes. Howard rushed around his desk to take her hands in his.

"I'm sorry, Cynthia, but it has to be done. I don't know how to tell you this, but someone has been stealing items out of the locker room, and all the evidence points to Gallagher. And he has been warned more than once about running his betting pools on factory property. He doesn't listen. Leonard Bartlett is a whole different kettle of fish. He's been creating havoc by trying to organize a worker's union among our employees. We think our workers get a very fair deal here, and the last thing we need is a union agitator stirring up a hornet's nest. . . . Sweetheart, please don't cry. I know they're your friends—"

"They're not my friends, Howard. That's not why I'm crying." She wiped her eyes, careful not to smear her mascara. "They're my roommate's friends, and this news will crush her. But I know you're right, they are troublemakers. And I'm glad you told me."

He pulled her to her feet and into his arms. "You have such a tender heart, Cynthia. I love you so much—" He kissed her before she could tell him that she loved him, too.

Cynthia had expected Eleanor to be upset by the news that Leonard and Donald had been fired, but she wasn't prepared for the bitterness of her fury. Long after midnight, after the two men had finally gone home, Eleanor still paced the floor, raging at the unfairness of it all. Cynthia knew that the real target of Eleanor's hatred was Rick Trent and his father, but it hurt her to hear so much venom being spewed at the man she loved—and at herself for loving him.

"I've had enough, Eleanor," she finally said. "Good night. I'm going to bed."

"How can you still love Howard Hayworth after what he did to two good, kindhearted men?"

"Listen, I didn't want to say anything in front of Donald, but the reason he got fired was because he's been stealing from people's lockers."

"That's a lie!"

"And he was warned to stop running his betting rings, but he wouldn't. That's why they let him go." She walked into their bedroom and began to undress, hoping that Eleanor would finally let the subject drop, hoping that she wouldn't need to hear the truth about Leonard, too. But Eleanor stalked into the room behind her, hands on her hips, unwilling to quit.

"You never liked Donald, right from the start, did you? And now you've poisoned everyone's attitude at work, too."

"That's not true. I never said one word about him or your brother to anyone at work—including Howard. You know that Donald Gallagher is a gambler, Eleanor. Why are you pointing the finger at everyone but Donald himself?"

"It's all a bunch of lies. Leonard doesn't gamble, and they fired him, too."

Cynthia sank down on the bed, too tired to fight. She knew that Eleanor would never believe the truth about why her brother was fired. And if Cynthia continued to defend Howard and criticize Donald and Leonard, it would probably mean the end of their friendship. But right now she was so weary of all of them and so tired of living with a bitter, depressed roommate and two worthless deadbeats that she didn't care what happened.

"Listen, Eleanor. They fired Leonard because he's been stirring up trouble trying to organize a labor union. Nobody wants to hear all that Communist stuff he spouts. We're a Christian nation, a democracy—"

"Where freedom of speech is still Leonard's right!"

"Not on factory property, it isn't. Why should the Hayworths keep an employee who's always badmouthing them?" She climbed into bed and pulled up the covers. "I don't want to fight about it anymore, Ellie. Good night."

"Maybe it's time we went our separate ways," Eleanor said. "It's obvious that Leonard and Donald aren't welcome here, so I don't feel welcome here, either."

"I never said they weren't welcome. You're my best friend; I don't have any argument with you."

"But you're going to keep dating your snobby rich boyfriend, even after what he did to my brother and his friend."

"They did it to themselves," Cynthia said with a sigh. "And yes, I'm in love with Howard. And he loves me."

"Then I'm moving out. I can't stand to watch that man destroy you the way Rick destroyed me."

"That isn't going to happen."

"I'm moving out first thing tomorrow."

Cynthia hoped Eleanor would see things differently in the morning and change her mind. But Eleanor was up early Saturday morning, packing her belongings. Leonard managed to borrow someone's car, and he and Donald helped her move into their rundown house across the river.

When the dust settled and the apartment was quiet, Cynthia felt free for the first time in months. She cleaned the apartment from top to bottom and invited Howard to dinner the following Saturday. Three months later, he proposed.

In a town as small as Riverside, it didn't take long for Cynthia to learn that Eleanor had cashed in a pile of war bonds to buy the little house across the river. Tongues wagged at the odd trio and their bohemian lifestyle. But Cynthia didn't care what the gossips said. Eleanor was still her best friend and she wanted her to stand up for her at her wedding. She walked across town one Sunday morning and knocked on Eleanor's door.

"What do you want?" Eleanor asked. She had opened the door only a crack and remained behind it, as if ready to slam it in Cynthia's face.

"I want to talk, Ellie. Won't you invite me in?"

"The place needs some work. It isn't fit for company." From what little that Cynthia could see through the crack, Eleanor's words were an understatement. Leonard and Donald always had been slobs, but not Eleanor. Cynthia remembered how Eleanor used to clean their apartment above the funeral home—dressed in an apron and kerchief, with Glenn Miller's music pouring from the radio—and she wanted to weep.

"What happened, Eleanor?" she murmured.

"What are you talking about?"

"What happened to us? To our friendship? We've been through so much together—we can't just throw it all away." But the drooping, bedraggled woman who stood before her was a stranger. The stylish, poised Eleanor who had changed Cynthia's life, who had laughed and loved and wept with her, had disappeared.

"You threw it away, Cynthia, for your rich boyfriend."

"Why are you making me choose between him and you? Look, I didn't come here to argue. I came to ask if you'd be my maid of honor—" She stopped when Eleanor started shaking her head. Her refusal hurt Cynthia more than anyone ever had, but she tried one last time. "Won't you at least think about it?"

"No. We have nothing in common, Cynthia. We have different values, different lifestyles. I don't want you coming around here anymore, and I'm sure Howard Hayworth doesn't want you hanging around with me, either."

Cynthia could no longer halt her tears. "Eleanor, why can't we still be friends?"

"Because I don't need your friendship, and you don't need mine. Goodbye, Cynthia. Have a nice life."

She closed the door.

Part
5

KATHLEEN AND JOELLE

2004

Chapter

20

"Can I get you more coffee?" Cynthia asked when she finished telling her story. "How about some more lemonade, Joelle?"

"No thanks," they said in unison.

Kathleen felt as though she'd been struck by a stun gun. She wondered if Eleanor's story had shocked Joelle as much as it had her. Kathleen finally understood why her mother had scorned riches all her life and hated rich people, but the full truth had been deeply disturbing. She remembered how her mother had argued against going to a "snooty" college. *"The boys you'll meet there would never marry someone from our background,"* she remembered her mother saying. *"At least at the community college there will be others like you."*

Kathleen was stunned but also deeply moved by this glimpse into her mother's past. She wished she had known years earlier how Eleanor had been so cruelly betrayed and heartbroken. The petty slights of Kathleen's own childhood seemed insignificant compared to the deep wounds her mother had suffered.

"I had Ron ten months after I married Howard," Cynthia continued, "and May Elizabeth was born two years later. Eleanor had you around the same time. I was so pleased when you and May became friends."

Kathleen struggled to recover her scattered thoughts, remembering why she had come. "Thank you so much for everything you did for me during those years, Mrs. Hayworth. I never would have come to church if it hadn't been for you."

Cynthia shook her head. "I wasn't much of a Christian when I lived with Eleanor. I wish I had been. It might have saved us all a lifetime of heartache. Eleanor's faith was stronger than my own during the war, but she turned against God when she thought He took Rick from her. Then after everything else that happened, she grew very bitter. I was just the opposite. I had no use for God when things were going well in my life. But I turned to Him when my dream of an ideal marriage turned to ashes. You know a little about that, I think."

Kathleen nodded, looking away as she remembered what she and May had unearthed with their clumsy sleuthing. Cynthia reached over to pat her knee.

"It's all right, you don't need to be embarrassed for me. That wasn't the first time Howard got caught cheating on me—or the last, I'm sorry to say. He started running around after Ron was born. Every time I found out and threatened to leave him he would promise to stop. And I wanted to believe him. The only thing that finally stopped him was a heart attack."

"I'm so sorry." Kathleen had always envied May Elizabeth's pampered life, unaware of the secrets that went on behind closed doors. And there had been secrets in her mother's life, too—something in Grandma Fiona's background that Mr. Trent had used to seek an annulment. Kathleen wondered what it had been, and if it explained why Eleanor never went to Deer Falls to visit her mother.

"God used all the difficult times in my life for good," Cynthia continued. "I've learned that He can redeem our painful circumstances if we let Him. The truth is, I probably never would have known the Lord if I'd been happily married. Howard may not have been faithful, but God has never forsaken me. I just wish I could have shared everything I learned with Eleanor. She felt so unloved for most of her life—especially after what Rick did to her. We both came to Riverside in 1942 because we wanted to change our lives and start all over again. But God is the only one who can bring lasting change and heal all our wounds. And Rick and his family wounded her . . . there's no doubt about it."

"He sounds like a real jerk!" Joelle said, surprising Kathleen with her vehemence. "Eleanor should be glad she didn't stay married to him."

"What ever happened to Rick after he ruined my mother's life?" Kathleen asked.

"Oh, he's still around," Cynthia said. "I hear his name in the news every now and then. His family is very powerful upstate, and Rick eventually got involved in politics. He served as a state senator or something for years and years, then he ran for the U.S. Congress back in the '70s and won. I don't recall if he's still in Congress or not."

Kathleen sat forward in her seat. "Rick's father had the marriage annulled because of something in Mom's background. Do you know what that was, Mrs. Hayworth?"

"No. She never did share that with me."

"So you don't know why my mother left home and came here? I know it was to get a job, but I think something must have happened between her and my grandmother because they never visited each other when I was young. I only met my grandmother once when I was growing up, and that was when my Uncle Leonard took me to see her."

"I don't know," Cynthia said. "I know there was bitterness there, and Eleanor swore she'd never go back. But she wouldn't tell me why. I can't even imagine how horrible it must have been for you, Kathleen, after your mother was murdered. I wanted to—"

Joelle nearly leaped from her chair. "Murdered!" she shouted. The little dog that had been sleeping peacefully on Cynthia's lap woke up and started to yap.

Cynthia gripped him tightly, her eyes brimming with tears of apology. "I'm so sorry! I didn't mean to give away any secrets. . . . Kathleen, I'm sorry."

Kathleen took a deep breath. "No, it's okay. I needed to tell Joelle, anyway." She glanced at her daughter and saw how shocked and angry she was.

"When? When were you going to tell me, Mom?" she demanded. "You never tell me anything."

"I wasn't trying to hide it from you, Joelle. It's just hard to find the words to say something like that out loud."

Their conversation felt awkward after that. Kathleen wondered if the tentative bond that had been woven between her and Joelle had snapped again. She said good-bye to Cynthia Hayworth, promising to keep in touch, both of them knowing they probably wouldn't.

After they were alone in the car, Kathleen felt the tension between her and Joelle even more vividly. She knew that she was closing up again, shutting out Joelle. And she knew she had to take the first step to repair the breach.

"I'm sorry, Joelle. I was going to tell you about my mother, honest I was. I-I just didn't know how."

"Was she really murdered?" Joelle asked softly.

"Yes. . . . It's not something that's easy for me to talk about. I'm so sorry."

Joelle nodded. "It's okay." She reached out to take Kathleen's hand, and Kathleen knew that Joelle was trying to give her the benefit of the doubt. She was grateful.

"Did they ever catch . . . you know . . . the person who did it?" Joelle asked. Her voice sounded shaky, as if she was struggling to comprehend such a violent end to Eleanor's tragic life. Kathleen remembered how she'd reeled in shock herself when Uncle Leonard had told her the terrible truth on the steps of her apartment building in Albany. She understood exactly how Joelle felt.

"Yeah, they caught him," Kathleen said with a sigh. "Uncle Leonard drove me home from Albany for the funeral, but I couldn't bring myself to stay and sit through the trial and all the rest of it. I didn't even read about the case in the newspaper. I just walked away and closed the door and never looked back. I worked as hard as I could to put myself through college and graduate school. Eventually I got a job in Maryland and married your father—and I just never went back. Believe it or not, this is the first time I've been home to Riverside since my mother was buried."

"Can we drive past the house where you used to live?" Joelle asked. Kathleen hesitated. "Is that where . . . where your mother was killed?"

Kathleen nodded.

"Never mind, we don't have to go see the house. It's probably too hard."

"No, it's okay, Joelle. I think it's something I need to do." She thought of how her mother had needed to go to Albany to see Rick's grave.

The town was so small that they could drive from Cynthia's wealthy side to Kathleen's poor side in a matter of minutes. She showed Joelle the elementary school, then drove down the hill three blocks, past the high school, and continued down Main Street.

"The stainless steel diner is long gone, but it used to be right there. And that's the funeral home across the street." She saw that it was part of a larger chain of mortuaries now. Farther along, the Valley Food Market had disappeared, replaced by a new brick bank building.

Kathleen slowed the car as they crossed the bridge, approaching the house where she had grown up. Evening was fading to night and fireflies winked in the bushes along the river. But enough light remained in the sky for her to clearly see her old house, lit up from within. The sight of it shocked Kathleen. Someone had completely renovated it: vinyl siding, a new roof, the front porch had been repaired, and there was a lawn instead of the littered patch of dirt she'd grown up with . . . and flowers!

"That's it?" Joelle asked. "It's cute."

"Yeah . . . it *is* cute," Kathleen said in surprise. She never would have believed it was the same house if it weren't for the fact that Uncle Leonard was sitting on the front porch in a rocking chair, smoking a cigar—a Cuban cigar, no doubt. He had to be in his eighties by now, but she would have recognized his mournful face and crane-like body anywhere. She pulled to a stop in front of the house before she could change her mind.

"That's Uncle Leonard on the porch," she told Joelle.

"No way! I want to meet him." Joelle had her door open before Kathleen turned off the ignition. She followed her daughter up the steps, her feet dragging.

"Kathleen! You haven't changed one bit," Uncle Leonard said as soon as he saw her. "I'd know you anywhere."

His voice sounded cheerful, but the frown never left his face. He didn't stand up. Kathleen saw a walker parked nearby and wondered if maybe he couldn't. Leonard reached for her hand and squeezed it briefly, but they didn't hug or kiss. They never had and probably never would.

"Annie told me you were going to make an appearance at your father's party tomorrow. I must admit I found the news rather surprising."

"I surprised myself by coming. Uncle Leonard, this is my daughter, Joelle."

"Hi," Joelle stepped closer, stopping beneath the porch light, and the cigar dropped from Leonard's mouth.

"Why, she's the very image of Fiona!"

"I am?" Joelle asked. She looked pleased. "Wasn't she my mom's grandmother?"

"Yes, my mother, Fiona Quinn," Uncle Leonard said. "You're the spitting image of her! Except you have Donald Gallagher's hair. Fiona was a breathtakingly beautiful woman. People used to say she looked like Greta Garbo."

"Who's that?" Joelle asked.

"A very famous movie star," Kathleen told her. They talked for a while, their conversation stiff at first. But as Kathleen shared the details of her life with her uncle, they both began to relax.

"I still can't get over how much your daughter resembles Fiona," he repeated.

"Uncle Leonard, didn't your mother have a family photo album way back when? I remember looking at it with Grandma Fiona when I was a kid."

She then remembered her uncle saying that he'd gotten rid of all of

Fiona's things, and she was sorry she'd asked. He surprised her when he said, "I imagine Fiona's album is around here someplace. Come on in."

It took him a minute to haul himself from the chair, but he finally made it to his feet and led the way inside with the help of his walker. The house was surprisingly neat, not exactly a candidate for *Better Homes and Gardens,* but not the slum it used to be, either. It even smelled nice. The books that had once lain stacked on the floor in every room now filled several tall bookshelves. Kathleen recognized her uncle's old girlfriend, Connie, seated in a recliner, watching TV.

"Why, Kathleen!" Connie squealed when she saw her. "Well, for goodness' sake! How are you?" She clicked off the TV and fought her way out of the recliner so she could pull Kathleen into her arms. Connie's fair hair had turned white over the years, and her plump figure had grown noticeably rounder, but she seemed as good-natured as ever. Kathleen wondered if Uncle Leonard had ever married her. She took Connie's hands in both of hers and was pleased to feel a wedding band on her left hand.

"And who is this with you?" Connie asked.

"This is my daughter, Joelle."

"Who does she remind me of?" Connie mused. "Well, never mind. Would you like a cold drink? I've got—"

"Where is that old photo album of my mother's?" Uncle Leonard interrupted.

"Why do you want that old thing? Let them sit down and visit, for goodness' sake. "

"Kathleen wants to see it. Her daughter looks remarkably like Fiona, doesn't she?"

"Why, yes! That's who she reminds me of. Except that Fiona was in her sixties when I met her, and Joelle is a beautiful young lady, for goodness' sake."

"Connie—the pictures," he said gruffly.

She smiled. "I'll be right back."

Connie returned with a huge cardboard box, which had probably been stored under the bed, judging by all the dust bunnies clinging to it. She set it in the middle of the living room floor and began pulling out yellowing scrapbooks, packages of photos, negatives held together with rubber bands, and envelopes full of newspaper clippings. The old black photograph album that Kathleen remembered was at the bottom.

"Is this it?" Connie asked. She turned her head to one side and sneezed. "Phew! Excuse me. Sometimes I think my old vacuum cleaner just pushes the dust around instead of picking it up. It's getting so hard for me to bend over anymore and clean like I used to—"

"Connie . . . Connie," Leonard said, interrupting again. "Kathleen didn't come to hear a litany of your cleaning woes."

Kathleen turned to him, ready to leap to Connie's defense, but the tender expression on his face as he spoke to his wife stopped her short. She had seen that expression on him once before, when he'd greeted his mother. Then another thought struck Kathleen: Maybe it had been there all along. Maybe she had never bothered to study her uncle very carefully years ago.

"Will you look through this with us, Uncle Leonard?" she asked, sitting down on the sofa beside him. She felt a wave of nostalgia as she smelled the familiar aroma of cigar smoke on his clothing. It was as much a part of him as his Communist rhetoric. Joelle plopped down on the other side of him as if she'd known him all her life.

Uncle Leonard began paging through the album, explaining each picture as if he had taken it himself just a few days ago. Kathleen had forgotten how intelligently and articulately he spoke—like a college professor delivering an important lecture. Too bad his intellect had been wasted on his useless Communist causes. She longed to ask him how he'd adjusted to the downfall of the Soviet Union and the end of his dream—or if he still held out hope for China and Cuba to bring about a Communist revival. But now was not the time.

Leonard paused when they came to a page of old black-and-white photos of Fiona. Joelle did look remarkably like her: the same oval face and porcelain complexion, the same dreamy, slanted eyes—"bedroom eyes" people used to call them. In one photo Fiona looked like Joelle dressed up as a flapper for Halloween, wearing a raccoon coat and slouch hat, posed by the running board of a vintage car.

"Fiona was a beautiful woman," Leonard said. "These were all taken after she moved to America, of course. She was much too poor to own a camera over in Ireland."

He turned another page, and Kathleen saw Fiona with her children, Leonard and Eleanor. Fiona looked much too young to be a mother. In these and all the other pictures, she'd struck a graceful pose, looking as seductive and glamorous as a movie star. In fact, the poses reminded Kathleen of ones she'd seen in old movie star magazines from the 1920s. Fiona also looked extremely well-to-do—the clothing and cars, the jewelry and furs, the nice furnishings in the background all painted a picture of wealth and luxury. She couldn't get over the fact that Uncle Leonard and her mother had grown up wealthy.

"Here we are after we left New York City and moved to Deer Falls," Leonard said, turning another page. "It was during the Great Depression, of course, so there are fewer photographs. This is Eleanor at the lake. She was a lifeguard during the summer months when she was in high school."

"A lifeguard . . ." Kathleen repeated incredulously. "I didn't even know she could swim."

"Oh yes. Your mother was as sleek and graceful as a seal in the water."

Kathleen thought of the Eleanor she had known, lying weak and lethargic on the sagging sofa, and she found it impossible to visualize her mother any other way. She recalled what Joelle had said earlier about learning her mother's story so she could understand her better, and for the first time that Kathleen could ever recall, she wanted to understand her. The picture that Cynthia Hayworth had painted of Eleanor seemed like a completely different woman than the mother Kathleen remembered. She ached to know who her mother had really been, why she had done all the things she'd done—and what had led to her murder.

Grandma Fiona's life was another mystery that Kathleen had never bothered to unlock. Who was this glamorous woman in the photographs who had lived and loved a generation earlier than Leonard and Eleanor?

What secret had Rick Trent used as an excuse to file for an annulment? Kathleen ached to know it all, and as much as she hated to admit it, she knew that Dr. Russo had been right. She needed to follow that broken strand of yarn backward to see where it led. If she understood her mother, maybe she could begin to understand herself.

"What was Grandma Fiona like?" she asked her uncle.

"She was a remarkable woman. Eleanor and I never, ever doubted that she loved us. She gave her life for us—in spirit, if not in fact."

"Uncle Leonard, do you know why my mother left home? And why she never visited grandma?"

"That's not a simple question to answer. I'd have to back up and tell you Fiona's story, first, because they are interconnected. My mother's maiden name was Quinn—Fiona Quinn. She left Ireland with her father when she was only eighteen years old and started life all over again here in America. . . ."

Part

6

F I O N A

1 9 1 9 — 1 9 3 0

Chapter
21

Fiona . . . Fiona, wait. . . ."

Fiona Quinn had just pegged the last bed sheet to the clothesline when she heard someone calling her name. She turned and saw Kevin Malloy hurrying up the lane toward her, tugging a donkey and a jaunting cart filled with hay. Fiona paused to watch him, admiring the easy stride of his long legs and the way his muscular body filled his clothes. Kevin was tall and sturdily built, thick-necked and thick-armed from his labors. He tethered the donkey to the clothespole and reached to pull Fiona into his arms.

"Not here, Kevin! Someone might see us." She twisted away, blushing as she glanced up at the rear of the manor house. Kevin grabbed her hand and led her behind the blackthorn hedge, where they could kiss in private. She loved the strength of his brawny arms, the eager, fumbling way he held her, kissed her.

"I shaved this morning," he said breathlessly when they finally pulled apart. "I was hoping I'd see you." Fiona ran her hand along his square jaw. His usual dark stubble was gone. He bent and brushed his lips against her neck, sending shivers through her. Fiona didn't want him to stop, but she didn't want to get into trouble with the housekeeper, either, for abandoning her work.

"That's all, Kevin," she said, gently pushing him away. "Tomorrow's my half-day. Meet me here at one o'clock, and we'll have all afternoon together."

His hand lingered on her shoulder. "Promise?"

"Of course. Who else would I be wanting to spend my half-day with?"

"You're so lovely, Fiona. Any man in County Meath would be only too happy to spend the afternoon with you, if you'd let him."

Fiona smiled at his praise. She wasn't used to being told she was lovely. "Well, I don't want to be with any other man, Kevin. Just you."

She smoothed her hair and straightened her apron, then glanced around as she ducked out from behind the hedge again. She hoped no one had seen them kissing. Kevin followed her back to the yard and picked up her empty laundry basket for her.

"Will your father be coming tomorrow to collect your pay?" he asked.

"Aye, he always does. Every Sunday. The money is still warm from the estate manager's hand when it goes straight into my father's. Why?"

"I can't wait any longer, Fiona. When he comes tomorrow, I'm going to ask him if I can marry you. I love you."

"Oh, Kevin . . ." Fiona didn't know when she'd ever felt happier—or more afraid. "I don't know . . ."

"Don't you want to marry me?"

"Of course I do! More than anything in the world! It's just that . . . well, I'm a bit frightened of my dad, you see. He fought in the Easter Rebellion."

"I don't care. I'm not afraid of Rory Quinn or any other man. You leave him to me."

She felt a swell of love at Kevin's courage. "All right," she said, smiling. "Tomorrow, then . . ."

Kevin nodded and backed away from her, his eyes holding hers as he untied the donkey. Then he waved and led the donkey up the lane toward the barn.

For the remainder of the day Fiona alternated between joy and dread, imagining the wonder of being married to Kevin Malloy, yet fearing her father's reaction to his proposal. Fiona was nearly eighteen and certainly old enough to marry. And most fathers with nine daughters to feed would be glad to be rid of the eldest. But Rory Quinn would not be at all happy at the loss of Fiona's wages.

Early the next morning, Fiona attended Mass at St. Brigid's with some of Wickham Hall's other servants. The parish priest had a beautiful tenor voice, and the sound of it always sent chills up Fiona's arms, even though she couldn't understand the Latin words. She had always loved going to Mass: inhaling the scent of incense, listening to the soft rustle of rosary beads, feeling the touch of holy water on her forehead, the taste of the wafer on her tongue. She had once considered taking holy vows, but her father hadn't allowed it. He'd obtained a job for her as a scrub maid at Wickham Hall, instead.

Each time Fiona attended Mass she would gaze at the crucifix above the altar until the sight of Jesus' agony would finally make her look away. He had suffered for her sake, the nuns had taught her—for her sins. She couldn't imagine why.

She returned to the manor as soon as Mass ended and hurried through her chores. At noon she collected her weekly pay from the estate manager and ran out to the yard to meet Kevin. He was waiting for her behind the blackthorn hedge, eager to sweep her into his arms and continue where they had left off yesterday.

"It seems like I've been waiting for days!" he complained.

"I know. Why is it that a half-day of work goes by so slowly and our half-day off flies by so fast?"

He answered her question with a long, bruising kiss, then held her at arms' length, studying her. "You look beautiful today, Fiona."

"I look exactly the same as I did yesterday," she teased, "only I'm not wearing an apron. And my clothes aren't soaking wet from work." Fiona had been a wash maid at Wickham Hall for three years, ever since finishing school at age fourteen. She spent her entire day scrubbing things—dishes, laundry, floors, vegetables—whatever needed to be scrubbed. It seemed as though her clothes were perpetually damp down the front, her hands red and chapped.

"I went to Mass this morning," she told Kevin between kisses. "I asked the Blessed Virgin to please let everything go well with my father today."

"Mm-hmm . . . I'm glad . . ."

She kissed Kevin for a few more minutes, then reluctantly pulled away. "Dad will be here any minute. We'd better watch for him." They ducked out from behind the hedge and slowly walked down the lane to meet him, hand in hand.

Fiona recognized her father by his short, wiry frame and stiff stride as soon as he rounded the bend in the road. He wore knee-high boots and a woolen cap that was too large for him and fell down over his forehead. He carried the scent of sheep with him wherever he went. She dropped Kevin's hand as they stood in the middle of the road, waiting for him.

"Let's have the money, girl. All of it." Rory Quinn held out his hand, palm up. She dropped the coins into it and watched him count them. He looked up at her and smiled when he'd finished. "Good girl."

"Dad, there's someone I'd like you to meet," she said. "This is Kevin Malloy. He works with me at Wickham Hall."

"How do you do, sir," Kevin said, sweeping off his cap. His dark brown hair was stiff with sweat and creased from his hatband.

Fiona watched her father study him from head to toe, and she saw Kevin as Rory must be seeing him: a big, square lad in laborer's clothes, with a chipped front tooth and dirt under his fingernails. His hands always looked dirty, even after he'd scrubbed them with strong soap. Fiona wanted to defend Kevin, to explain that he was hardworking and cheerful, never angry or moody like her father often was. Kevin reached to shake her father's hand, then rested his arm around Fiona's shoulders. Rory Quinn reacted immediately.

"Get your blooming hands off my daughter!"

Kevin dropped his arm and his face colored slightly, but then he bravely groped for Fiona's hand as if staking his claim.

"I-I love her, sir. We'd like to get married if it's all right with you."

"Well, it's *not* all right with me! You're nothing but a boot boy!"

"That's not true, sir. I work in the stables with the coachman, and—"

"And a stable boy is all you'll ever be. You'll surely never be getting ahead in life, that's for certain."

"I earn a good wage. I can provide for her—"

"My daughter deserves more than what you can provide, more than a dirt floor and a house full of hungry mouths to feed. Is that all you want, Fiona? To work hard and birth babies till the blooming day you die?"

"I love Kevin, Dad. We don't need much—"

Rory Quinn made a harsh sound to show his disgust. Kevin bravely took a step toward him.

"Begging your pardon, sir, but I'm learning how to manage Mr. Wickham's motorcar. I keep the engine running for him, and . . . and I can drive it, too. I'm quite handy at it. I make an honest living, I do."

"So do I—as a blooming sheepherder!" Rory stormed off toward the stable with Kevin and Fiona trailing after him.

"Where are you going, Dad? You can't—"

"Quiet, Fiona!" He found the head coachman, an older man named Barclay, and without a word of greeting or explanation, Rory gestured to Kevin. "This lad work for you?"

"Aye. What's he done?"

"He's taken a liking to my daughter, that's what, and I'll thank you to make sure he keeps his blooming hands off her from now on. I'll not have him taking liberties that aren't his to take."

"But he hasn't, Dad. Kevin wants to marry me."

"And I said no!" He spoke the words fiercely, his face inches from hers, then he turned to Mr. Barclay again. "Kindly keep the lad away from my daughter. Make sure his half-day isn't the same as hers from now on."

"Aye, I understand," Barclay said with a nod. "I'm a father m'self."

"Come on, Fiona." Rory gripped her arm and pulled her toward the estate's main gate. Mr. Barclay laid his hand on Kevin's shoulder as if warning him not to follow.

"Dad, no!" Fiona cried. "It's my only afternoon off."

"Don't I know that well enough? You're coming home with me, where I can keep my blooming eye on you." He glared over his shoulder at Kevin. "And don't you be getting any notions about running off with her, either. You'll both lose your places here, and then how will you make your way in the world?"

"Please don't make me go home," Fiona begged. "It's my first afternoon off in two weeks!"

"Yes, please, Mr. Quinn," Kevin begged as he hurried after them. "Give me a chance to prove to you—"

"You'll get no such chance from me. Maybe a life with you is all that my foolish daughter wants, but I want much more for her than that. Look at her—she's beautiful."

"Aye, I know she is, sir."

"Then you should know that I'll not be giving her away to the likes of you. Good day."

Fiona wept all the way as her father dragged her back to the tiny stone cottage in the village where she had grown up. "Look at this," he said when they reached the threshold. "You want to live like this all your life?" He made a sweeping gesture with his hand as if to include the cottage's dirt floor, the roof that needed thatching, the smoky interior, the overcrowded room, her squalling baby sister.

Fiona didn't understand his question. This was the only life she knew. If she could live here with Kevin, it would seem like a palace.

"Can't you see this isn't Wickham Hall?" he asked.

"Of course I can see that, Dad." The family Fiona worked for lived in unbelievable luxury. In fact, the manor house's scullery was bigger than this entire cottage. But Fiona had been born here. She saw no sense in envying what was out of her reach. Her father, on the other hand, had always aspired for more—not that he had any means of getting it that Fiona could see. Rory had gone off to Dublin to take part in the Easter Rebellion three years ago, hoping that the fight for independence would lead to a better life. It hadn't.

"You were lucky to get away without being arrested or killed," Mam had told him when the rebellion failed. "So much for finding a better life."

Smoke from the peat fire stung Fiona's eyes as she ducked inside the cottage. Mam sat at the table peeling potatoes for their dinner. "I'll do that," Fiona said, taking the pan of potatoes and peelings from her. It would be an easier task than trying to soothe her baby sister.

"Go along with all of you! Outside!" Rory shouted, chasing three of Fiona's younger sisters out the door. "Leave a man to think in peace."

All nine of the Quinn children were daughters, much to Rory's regret. "My girls are my pearls," he would tell the lads down at O'Connor's Pub. "I have a whole string of them—lovely to look at, a fine decoration hanging about your neck. But as far as a man's concerned, they're not worth a farthing for getting on in life."

He seemed deep in thought as he sat in his chair by the hearth. Fiona tackled the potatoes, still angry with him for ruining her afternoon with Kevin, but she was worried, too. Her father had the same expression on his face that he wore when he was planning something: his head lowered until his chin nearly touched his chest, his brows meeting in the middle as he stared at the floor. She wondered if he was thinking about her and Kevin. None of them spoke as Fiona diced the potatoes, then helped her mother chop cabbage to make the *colcannon*. There would be a bit of mutton in it today because it was the Lord's Day—and payday.

Rory Quinn seemed to cheer up a bit by the time dinner was cooked and he'd eaten his fill. Fiona hoped he would change his mind after thinking things through and allow her to marry Kevin, after all. When he'd drunk the last of his tea, he leaned back on the rear legs of his chair and drew a deep breath, as if about to make an important announcement.

"I've been thinking about America," he began. "Do you know the difference between Ireland and America, Fiona?"

She shook her head. Which road had her father's mind wandered down this time? How had he traveled from Kevin's marriage proposal to thoughts of America?

"In Ireland you can never be anything other than what your parents were. If your father's a boot boy, you're a boot boy. If your mum's a scullery maid, you're a scullery maid. But in America—aye, things are different in America. You can be born to a humble working family like ours and still grow up to be a blooming rich man and live in a grand big house like Wickham Hall." He brought his chair forward with a thump as if to emphasize his words. "That's why we're leaving here, Fiona. We're going to start all over again in America."

For a moment, she was too stunned to reply. "But I don't want to leave Kevin," she said.

Her mother was much more practical. She slid her chair back and stood, clearing away the plates and cutlery, saying, "And tell me, Rory Quinn, just how will you be affording to take all of us to America on a shepherd's pay?"

"Not all of us, dearie. It will just be Fiona and me, at first. Her lovely face will get us through all the right doors. And once we've made our way inside them, we'll send for the lot of you."

"Dad, no . . ." Fiona moaned. Mam rested her hand on Fiona's arm to quiet her.

"Isn't your cousin Darby Quinn in America?" Mam asked. "Isn't he just as poor as he ever was in Ireland, working in that foundry day and night? What's the difference, do you mind telling me, if we're poor over there or poor over here?"

"Ah, but Cousin Darby doesn't have a daughter as beautiful as Fiona—*that's* the difference." He reached for Fiona's five-year-old sister and pulled her onto his lap. "Come up with you, girl, and give your dad a kiss." Rory could be gentle and affectionate with his daughters, especially on payday or early into his pints. But they all knew to keep away when he started ranting about the English or after he'd spent a long evening at O'Connor's Pub.

"Are we really going to America, Dad?" Fiona's sister asked.

"Aye, that we are, my girl. Your sister Fiona and I will go first, then send for the lot of you. Mark my words, we're going to live in a blooming mansion someday."

At dusk, Rory walked Fiona back to Wickham Hall. Her half-day was over and she'd spent a mere ten minutes of it with Kevin. She wouldn't get another one for two long weeks. She glanced around at the bushes as they neared Wickham's gates, hoping to see Kevin waiting for her, but he was nowhere in sight.

"I mean it, Fiona," her father said. "We're off to America, just you and me."

Fiona felt her afternoon's worth of frustration and disappointment boiling over. "But I don't want to go to America, Dad. I love Kevin."

"I'll hear no more about that boy! You deserve better than the likes of him."

"There is no one better than him," she said stubbornly. Rory didn't seem to hear her.

"You're the key to my plan, girl. You'll make it possible for all of us to live like lords." He gestured to Wickham Hall, its stately windows glowing with light and warmth in the evening twilight. "You're my oldest—aye, and the prettiest, too. I knew you were special from the day you were born, arriving on St. Brigid's Day and coming out backwards the way you did. Why do you suppose it is that you're working here in the manor house when none of the other village girls are? I'll tell you why. It's because you're the loveliest one."

"I scrub for a living, Dad. That's hardly an honor."

"Isn't that what I'm trying to tell you? It doesn't have to be this way for you, scrubbing all your life. Not in America. Now, listen to me, girl. There's something I need you to be doing in the weeks before we leave. Watch your masters, carefully. Pay attention to how they walk and talk and act. Someday you're going to be the mistress of a grand big house like this one, so you'll be needing to know how to do it proper-like."

Fiona looked up at Wickham Hall. You could fit a dozen cottages like her father's inside the huge, two-story, gray-stone house—and that wasn't even counting the attic where Fiona and the other servants slept. The manor house had twelve-paned windows made of real glass to let in sunlight and air. The floors were polished wood, not dirt—Fiona had scrubbed them—and were covered with colorful Turkish rugs. She had also scrubbed the linens and coverlets from all the beds, unable to imagine the luxury of sleeping beneath such sheets. But even more than a home and fine furnishings, Fiona envied a life with servants, having others do all the menial tasks that she hated doing.

The idea of living in a mansion like Wickham Hall appealed to Fiona, and as she climbed the back stairs to her dormitory on the third floor, she was no longer content to live a life like her mother's in a tiny, smoky cottage. But as she dreamed that night of owning a mansion like this one, she saw herself and Kevin both living there in luxury.

Kevin called to Fiona from behind the blackthorn hedge a few days later as she stood on the rear stoop, shaking crumbs out of the dining room tablecloth. "Psst . . . Fiona . . . come here a minute . . ." She ducked out of sight and into his arms.

"Any chance your father will change his mind?" he asked after he'd kissed her thoroughly. She loved Kevin. But she shook her head, remembering the determination in her father's eyes.

"No. Just the opposite, in fact. Dad has other plans for me now. He says we're moving to America so we can have a grand house like this one." Kevin stared at her blankly. "I've been doing some thinking about it myself," she continued, "and our only hope is for you to come, too. You can get rich in America, and then Dad would let us get married." Fiona knew by Kevin's expression that she might as well have suggested that they move to the moon.

"I can't imagine living any other place but here," he said after a moment. "Ireland's so beautiful with the green hills and rich earth . . ."

"I'm sure they have green hills in America, too," she said impatiently.

"But this is our home, Fiona. Why would your father want to be leaving here and going to a place where we don't belong?" His unwillingness to imagine a better life for them frustrated her.

"Dad wants a better life than what we have. Don't you?"

He bent to kiss her neck, murmuring, "If I had you, Fiona, I would have everything I could dream of."

She saw the difference then between Kevin and her father, and she felt a small stab of disappointment. She knew there was a lot of Rory Quinn in her, and now that he had opened the door to the possibility of having more in life, she wanted all of it.

"You can have me *and* America," she told him. "You need to save all your money so you can come, too. We can be rich together."

"You're really going, then?"

"Dad says we are."

"And you want to go with him?"

She paused, biting her lip, and realized how very much she did want to go. "Yes. I really want to."

He looked down at his feet for a moment, then back up at her. "In that case, I'll have to move to America, too, because I can't live without you, Fiona."

Chapter 22

Fiona waited in the dormitory on the third floor until the other servants fell asleep, then slipped on her shoes and wrapped a shawl around her shoulders. She would ruin her reputation if she got caught sneaking out after bedtime—and maybe even lose her job—but she needed to feel Kevin's strong arms around her.

Her father had made Fiona come home with him on every half-day since Kevin had proposed three months ago. She'd scarcely seen Kevin since then, and they'd had few chances to kiss. But Kevin had come to her this afternoon as she stood outside beating the rugs on the clothesline and he'd begged her to sneak out tonight and meet him near the hedge.

All the lights in the house had been turned off for the night and the backyard was very dark and unfamiliar-looking. She took small steps, unsure of her footing, and nearly cried out when Kevin suddenly emerged from the shadows.

"Shh . . ." he whispered, his finger to his lips. "This way . . ." He took her hand and led her to where he'd spread a blanket and lit a candle for them on a pile of hay in the barn. She savored his kisses for a while, then gently pushed him away.

"Stop that for a minute, Kevin. We need to talk."

"What about?"

"My father is serious about moving to America. He's been saving all his money in an old tea box. I've watched him counting and recounting it every week. Mam says he's even skipping his pints down at the pub, so I know he's serious. Have you been saving your money?"

Kevin looked down at her hand as he caressed it gently between both of his. "It's hard to save much, Fiona. A man likes his pints after a long day."

"Ach! Don't you love me more than your stupid pints?"

"Of course I do! Let me show you how much . . ."

She allowed him to kiss her awhile longer, but as she felt them both being swept away, she suddenly grew frightened and drew back. "Stop, Kevin. We can't go any further."

"But I love you, Fiona."

"And I love you, too. But the sisters at the convent said it's a sin to go any further unless we're husband and wife."

"If we had a baby, your father would have to let us get married." Kevin tried to pull her close again, but she pushed him away.

"No, he'd send me to live with the nuns, and they'd take the baby away from me as soon as it's born. I've seen it happen to other girls." And as hard as it was for Fiona to leave him, she stood and wrapped her shawl around her shoulders again. "I need to go back inside now."

"Fiona, please stay. I love you." His eyes looked soft and pleading in the candlelight.

"If you really loved me you would save your money for America."

The following Sunday when Fiona's father came to fetch her, he seemed unusually chipper, even without his pints. She asked Mam about it when they were alone.

"It seems you and your father will be leaving for America soon," Mam said. "He has enough money now, but he didn't want to tell you for fear you'd run off with that lad of yours."

"Where on earth did he get the money?" Fiona asked. Her mother replied with a shrug.

Fiona's heart speeded up. She was going to America! She was really going! She gave a little dance of delight, twirling in a circle, then sank down on a chair. Fiona loved Kevin; she was sure she did. But in the months since her father had come up with his plan, she'd grown to love the idea of being rich even more. She wanted a home like Wickham Hall, and if Kevin didn't love her enough to follow her to America, then he didn't love her enough.

Fiona watched her mother wipe the crumbs from the table with a damp cloth and suddenly wondered how she felt about Rory's plan. "Mam, do you mind that Dad's taking me to America first and leaving you and the girls behind?"

"No, child, I don't mind." She rinsed the cloth in the pan of gray dishwater, then lifted the pan to toss the water out the back door. "It'll give me a break from birthing babies—and heaven knows I need the rest. Let the man chase his fancies and I'll chase mine."

Fiona looked at her mother curiously. Until her father began talking about being rich in America, Fiona had fancied nothing more than marrying Kevin Malloy and living in a little house like this one and raising Kevin's sweet babies. It certainly had never occurred to her to dream of more—let alone wonder if her mother had dreams.

"If you could have anything you wanted, Mam, what would you fancy?"

"Peace and quiet," she said with a sigh. "A chance to sit with my feet up once in a while and drink a cup of tea without anyone bothering me. I was never one to chase pipe dreams the way your father does."

"Is that all it is, Mam—a pipe dream? Will I never have that grand mansion he talks about?"

Her mother looked into Fiona's eyes, cupping her cheek in her rough hand. "I believe that you will, Fiona. Your dad believes in you—and so do I."

Later that evening, Rory walked back with Fiona to Wickham Hall as he did on all of her half-days. But as soon as he was out of sight, Kevin sprang from behind the blackthorn hedge where he'd been waiting. "Fiona . . ."

"Oh! You scared me half to death!"

"Sorry, love. I didn't think you'd ever come!" He bent to kiss her, but she pushed him away.

"Stop that for a minute, and listen to me. Dad finally has enough money for our passage. I hope you've been saving, too." She knew by his expression that he hadn't, and it made her angry. "Good-bye, Kevin Malloy." She strode toward the back steps.

"Fiona, wait! How soon is he leaving?"

"Any day now."

"I can't let you go!" He grabbed her arm, turning her around. "Please run away with me! Now—tonight!" She saw tears in his eyes and felt sorry for him.

"Ah, Kevin . . . I can't run away with you," she said, brushing his dark hair off his forehead.

"Why not?"

She didn't reply. Instead, she let him take her in his arms and hold her close, inhaling the scent of his shirt beneath her cheek. She loved him— but in her heart she knew that her father was right. If they ran away and got married, she'd end up just like her mother in a few years, longing for nothing more than a cup of tea and a few minutes' peace. She felt sad.

"You can write to me, Kevin," she said after a moment. "We're staying with Dad's cousin, Darby Quinn, in New York until we get settled. Here, I copied the address for you when Dad wasn't looking."

She pulled the crumpled paper from her apron pocket and handed it to him. Kevin unfolded it, staring at it as if it spelled his doom—but he was looking at it upside down. She turned the paper around for him and saw his cheeks flush, even in the darkness.

"I never learned to read and write, Fiona. I always had to work for a living. My family couldn't afford to send me to school at the Christian Brothers."

She felt a rush of love for sweet Kevin. Her eyes filled with tears as he held her in his arms. "I promise I'll follow you to America," he said. "Wait for me, Fiona. Please wait for me."

"I will." But Fiona knew that he'd never come. She would never see Kevin Malloy again. She wondered if anyone would ever love her as much as he did—and if she could ever learn to love someone else.

A few days later, Rory Quinn walked into Wickham Hall's scullery in the middle of the working day, towing Fiona's fourteen-year-old sister, Sheila, by the hand. "Come, girl. Get your things," he told Fiona. "We're leaving tomorrow. I've arranged for Sheila, here, to take over your job."

Excitement and sorrow tugged Fiona in opposite directions. She was leaving—right now—and never coming back. "I need to say good-bye to Kevin and—"

Rory shook his head. "Put him behind you, Fiona. You deserve a man ten times better than he is."

But Fiona didn't know how there could ever be a man as sweet and loving and dear as Kevin. She began to cry.

"Stop that, now," Rory said. "You'll make a mess of your face."

She wiped her eyes on her apron, then slipped it over her head and handed it to Sheila. "Come on, I'll get my belongings and show you where to put yours."

Sheila followed her upstairs to the third floor, gazing around at everything in awe on the way. "It's a grand big house, then, isn't it?" she murmured. "Do you really think we'll have one like it someday?"

"Aye, Dad says we will." Fiona dumped her sister's things out of the sack, then stuffed her own meager belongings inside in their place. "You'll do fine here," Fiona said as she hugged her sister good-bye. "And we'll be sending for you girls and Mam before you know it."

She gazed all around the grounds of Wickham Hall as she left with her father, searching for one last glimpse of Kevin. But the motorcar was gone, and Kevin was nowhere to be seen.

Fiona and her father left early the next morning in a misty rain. She heard the bells of St. Brigid's church tolling for the early Mass, but thick fog erased all the familiar sights of home from view. Even massive Wickham Hall had vanished in the clouds.

Fiona clung to her mother as they hugged for the last time, finding it harder to leave home than she'd imagined.

"We'll see you again, won't we, Mam?"

"Of course, child. Your father says you'll be sending for us in no time at all."

"And you can sit with your feet up and drink tea every day in America. We'll even have servants to fetch it for you."

"Aye . . ." Mam said, smiling faintly. "God go with you, Fiona." The words were meant to comfort her, but instead they made Fiona feel as if she was disappearing into a void with a God she couldn't see or feel.

A friend of Fiona's father took them to the nearest town in his jaunting cart, toting what little baggage they owned. From there they took the train to Dublin. Fiona had never seen the city before, and it looked enormous and overcrowded to her, with brick buildings several stories tall stuffed against each other. The narrow, cobbled streets were jammed with people, carriages, and motorcars, their wheels rumbling as they crossed the bridges over the Liffey River. Fiona saw British police everywhere—the Black and Tans, as they were called because of their mismatched uniforms. Barricades blocked many of the streets.

"Dublin is still a mess because of the conflict," her father told her. "I see they haven't accomplished much since I came here to fight." Fiona tried to imagine her father armed with a rifle, taking part in the uprising—and couldn't.

"Will the Black and Tans let us go to America?" she asked.

He gave a short laugh. "Oh, aye! They'll be more than glad to see two more Irish leave. They'd be happy to see every last one of us go. And tomorrow morning we will."

Fiona felt a sense of loss—and yet anticipation. Fear and sorrow and joy were all mixed together in a stew, and she couldn't sort them out. She also felt very much alone. She had her father, true, but Fiona had never quite learned to trust him.

"God go with you," her mother had said. Funny, but Fiona had always thought of God as living in St. Brigid's church, back home. Yet as she stood on the busy street corner in Dublin, feeling lost and frightened, she realized that God didn't just live in St. Brigid's church—He was everywhere. Mam's words reassured her, and Fiona whispered them to herself as a prayer as she prepared to bid good-bye to Ireland.

"God go with me . . . please . . ."

————————

They sailed on St. Brigid's Day, the day dedicated to the saint who was known for her kindness and for her miracles. It was Fiona's special day, too—February 1, her eighteenth birthday.

"Are you sure the boat won't sink, Dad?" she asked as she stared up at the huge ship. It lay anchored at the end of a long dock, with a boarding plank for the steerage passengers spanning the choppy gray water.

"What kind of a question is that?" he growled as he tugged their belongings down the pier.

"When I was in school, the sisters told us how a grand big ship sank and all the people died."

"There was a war on when the Lusitania sank. That war is over with."

"Not that ship, Dad. It was before the war, when I was nine or ten years old, I think. The nuns at school told us to pray because a big fancy ship full of rich people got stuck in the ice and sank. Thousands of people drowned. Will there be ice on the way to America?"

Rory glanced at her, shaking his head as they waited in line to board. "Fiona, lass—why don't you put that wild imagination of yours to good use planning our future instead of worrying about things that happened years ago."

Yes, she decided, she would think about her future. America was the land of promise, a place where she could live in luxury and ease. But first she had to cross the cold, wide ocean. It occurred to her that this journey might be a bit like dying: She would leave the known world and traverse the unknown—and end up in paradise! Yet if this was truly a trip to paradise, Fiona quickly discovered that her voyage must be purgatory.

Nothing Fiona had ever experienced prepared her for life onboard the steamship. Their allotted place in steerage was in an overcrowded, windowless hold packed with hundreds of bunk beds. Many of the families rigged curtains for privacy around the space they'd claimed, but she and her father hadn't thought of that ahead of time. The other steerage passengers came from a variety of foreign nations and languages, and the babble of voices added to the confusion and chaos. Most passengers had packed food from home for the journey, and the hold soon reeked of garlic and onions and strong, sour cheese. These families seemed even poorer than Fiona's, with dozens of shabby, howling children. Everyone stank of body odor and sweat. The moment Fiona entered the hold, she longed to turn around and flee outside into the fresh air and sunlight, but she knew she would have to get used to it. This would be her home for the next few weeks.

Once the ship was underway, Fiona spent as much time as she could outside on the steerage deck, even though the wintry air was raw and the tiny deck was nearly as crowded as their space below. Her father began disappearing for long stretches of time; she didn't know where, nor would he tell her why. Steerage passengers weren't allowed to roam the ship, but that's what he seemed to be doing, sneaking off at midday or during the supper hour, then scribbling on a wad of paper he carried in his vest pocket when he returned. Fiona glimpsed the pages over his shoulder one evening and saw incomprehensible lists of numbers.

A week after the ship sailed, Fiona was sitting outside on the steerage deck one afternoon when her father beckoned to her. "Come with me, Fiona. I want to show you something." He led her inside, then up a forbidden staircase to the deck where the lifeboats were secured. She could glimpse the first-class passengers strolling around on the upper deck.

"I don't think we're allowed up here," she said when she saw where he'd taken her.

"Be quiet, Fiona, and listen to me. Do you know the difference between those wealthy people and us?" he asked, tilting his head in their direction.

She could think of plenty of differences—they had lots of money, plentiful food, a life of ease and luxury . . . and smooth hands. Their hands weren't all cracked and red like hers were from scrubbing laundry. But she shook her head, knowing that Rory Quinn didn't really expect an answer.

"Clothes, Fiona. The only difference between them and us is the clothes they're wearing on their backs. You and I aren't dressed in fancy garb the way they are, that's all." He turned to her with a rare smile on his lips and gently smoothed her windblown hair from her face. "But if you were to put on a lovely gown like that lady's wearing over there, with your hair all done up like hers, you would stop the heart of every man on this ship. All we need are the right clothes."

She watched the rich passengers for a moment, strolling around in their finery and winter wraps. Several wore fur coats. Fiona shivered in her thin shawl and wondered how it would feel to be wrapped in fur.

"Will we buy fine clothes when we get to America, then?" she asked.

"I have a better plan." He bent his head close to hers and whispered, "I've been watching the fancy staterooms, you see—keeping track of all the people coming and going, and counting how many are sleeping in each one." He patted the vest pocket where he kept the wad of paper with its lists of numbers. "I've also been watching to see what time they go up on deck or to the dining room to eat, and how long they're away. I know exactly which rooms I'm going to tap. But I'll need your help."

"Tap? W-what are you talking about?" But Fiona was afraid that she knew the answer. He intended to steal from the rich passengers' staterooms, and he needed her help. She wondered if he had stolen the money for their passage to America, too.

"Believe me, girl, this wealthy lot has so many clothes they'll never miss the few piddling things we'll be borrowing."

"We'll be giving everything back, then?" she asked hopefully. The idea of borrowing sounded much better than stealing. Rory made a face, waving away her question without answering it. He led her down a staircase and into a forbidden hallway. It was spotlessly clean and smelled of fresh enamel paint.

"Now, I'll need you to wait in this passageway and keep watch while I slip inside that first room, you hear? Make noise for me if someone comes."

"Dad, no!"

"Shh. . . !" He clamped his hand over her mouth to quiet her. "Hush, girl, and do as you're told. I need you to create a diversion."

"H-how do I do that?"

"Use your charm and your beauty, Fiona. Flirt with the stewards and distract them. Tell them you're lost and can't find your way out. You can do it, girl."

"But people are sure to make a fuss when they discover that some of their things are missing. What if the stewards search our bags?"

"Don't worry yourself. I won't be taking so much from any one room that they'll even miss it—a tie from one, a shirt from another. Do you see?"

"The nuns said that stealing was—"

"Hush, lass. The nuns don't need to bother themselves about what clothes they'll be wearing, do they now?"

Fiona was certain from what she'd been taught in school that stealing was a sin. But another of God's commandments said that she had to honor her father and mother. What was a girl supposed to do when two of God's rules disagreed with each other that way?

"Let's go, lass," Rory said, nudging her down the hallway. "We have work to do."

Fiona did as she was told. The first day that she and her father worked together was the scariest, with Fiona jumping at every sound, her heart pounding so hard she was certain it would burst. When they finally returned to their bunks in steerage, Fiona lay down on hers and wept with relief. Each day after that, it became easier and easier for her to stroll down the deserted passageways, looking lost and bewildered while her father broke into the rich passengers' staterooms—especially when she saw the beautiful clothing and jewelry he picked out for her to wear.

Two or three times a passenger exited one of the other rooms while Fiona waited in the narrow hallway, and at first she thought she might faint. But experience soon taught her to smile prettily and say "Good day" as if she had every right to be there. Only once did a steward approach her, and Fiona did exactly as her father had instructed.

"Oh, I'm so glad to see you," she told the steward, speaking loudly enough for her father to hear. "I'm afraid I'm terribly lost. Could you please show me which passage to take?"

As the days passed and their loot accumulated, a rush of excitement replaced the fear Fiona once felt. Each time she entered one of the narrow corridors and smelled the scent of enamel paint, she would smile and feel the delicious thrill of danger. She felt closer to her father than she ever had, and they returned from their adventures each afternoon laughing with exhilaration from the risk they'd taken. They weren't even in America yet, and already Fiona's life was more interesting than it had ever been back home in Ireland. Even so, when Rory came to her one day and said, "We're done, girl. We have all the clothes we'll be needing," she felt relieved.

Her relief was short-lived. The next day the sun shone warmly for the first time in days, and all the decks—first-class as well as steerage—quickly filled with people. "Scrub your face and fix your hair," Rory told Fiona. "I want you to dress yourself in one of your new outfits."

"Won't someone recognize their own clothes?" she asked.

"Not if you pick something plain to wear—like that dark skirt and white blouse."

"But it's chilly up on deck. I'll freeze!"

Rory borrowed a beautifully embroidered shawl from a Bohemian woman they'd met in steerage and wrapped it around Fiona's shoulders. Even with the shawl, she couldn't stop shivering with fear.

"No, Dad. Please don't make me do this. I'm scared to death that we'll get caught."

Rory pushed her along, ignoring her protests. "There's nothing to it," he insisted. "Just walk up the stairs and onto the main deck as if you belonged there. Hold your head up high. Believe me, everyone will be looking at your beautiful face, not at your clothes. And nobody ever asks a lovely woman such as yourself to show them her first-class ticket, that's for certain."

"W-what will I do once I'm there?"

"Stroll around a bit, then come back. That's all. This is for practice, Fiona." She was afraid to ask what she was practicing for. She did as she was told, her knees trembling as she climbed the stairs.

The first person Fiona passed was a steward who bowed slightly in respect as she swept past. When she glanced over her shoulder at him she saw that he had turned around to gaze at her. When he saw she had caught him staring, he hurried off, his cheeks bright. Fiona gained courage, pleased with the effect she'd had on him. Next she passed an older gentleman who tipped his hat to her and said, "Good afternoon, miss." She smiled sweetly in return. At last she reached the ship's rail, where she paused, hanging on to it for dear life until she could stop shaking.

The salt air was warm, the sky clear, and the first-class deck was so wonderfully different from the overcrowded steerage deck down below that, like her father, Fiona suddenly knew that she wanted this life, not her old one. She drew a deep breath and released her grip on the rail, ready to take a leisurely stroll down the length of the deck and back again.

Fiona walked past people lounging in wicker deck chairs, their legs covered with warm rugs as stewards served them tea and scones. She longed to lounge there, too, but didn't dare. She kept walking, passing a nanny tending two small boys and then a group of men in overcoats, talking and smoking cigars. The gentlemen tipped their hats to her and said, "Good afternoon." She noticed that the women all wore hats or carried parasols to protect their skin from the sun. She must tell her father to steal a hat for her. The thought made her smile. She'd been horrified at his plan at first; now she was getting particular about what he stole.

Fiona walked down to the end of the deck as far as she could go, swaying her hips as if she had the entire day at her leisure, then she turned and ambled back. This time she savored the open admiration she saw on all the men's faces, the envy she saw on the women's. She was beautiful, well-dressed, and they accepted her as one of their own. She inhaled one last breath of sea air, licking the taste of salt from her bottom lip, then swept gracefully down the stairs to where her father was waiting for her.

"Well, lass?"

"I need a hat," she said. "All of the rich ladies are wearing them." She held back her smile for as long as she could, then added with a grin, "A slouch hat—made of felt. With a flower on it, if you please."

Rory Quinn laughed as he lifted Fiona off the ground and twirled her around. "That's my girl!"

Chapter

23

For the first several hours after landing at the immigration center on Ellis Island, Fiona suffered gut-wrenching distress. She would never reach American shores. They were so close—she could see New York City in the distance—but God would surely punish her and her father for stealing from the other passengers onboard the ship. She would be sent to prison . . . or, worse, sent home.

"What's the matter with you?" Rory growled as they waited in a long maze-like queue.

"My stomach hurts. I feel like I'm going to be sick."

"Well, get a hold of yourself, girl. If they think you're ill, they'll never let us in the country."

"I'm scared, Dad. What if they look in our bags and find all the things—"

"Hush! No one's going to be looking in our bags. They'll be looking to see if we're healthy—and you look green around the gills. Stand up straight! Smile at the man, understand?"

"Yes, Dad."

Fiona watched to see how her fellow steerage passengers fared as she waited her turn and saw that her father was right; the American officials weren't inspecting the baggage too closely. But the officers seemed ill-tempered and impatient as they dealt with the noisy mob of immigrants, pushing the uncomprehending masses to and fro the way sheep dogs herded sheep. Fiona felt sorry for the poor souls who didn't speak English. The cavernous hall had a high, vaulted ceiling and the volume of noise grew louder and louder as the frustrated officials began to shout as if it might finally help the foreigners understand. The American version of the English language sounded so different to Fiona that she had to listen carefully herself in order to understand what the Americans were saying.

When her turn finally came for the dreaded Immigration Service inspection, the official needed only to make sure that she and her father were healthy and that they had a sponsor and a bit of money to support themselves. No one searched their bags. A few hours after landing, Fiona stepped ashore in America at last.

The area around the dock where they landed looked as shabby and derelict as what they'd left behind in Ireland. A crowd of drivers waited with hired drays to transport their things, and Rory bargained with a scruffy-looking man for a ride on his wagon, pulled by a swaybacked horse. She and her father didn't have much in the way of belongings, but they would have quickly gotten lost in the enormous city without the driver's help. He took them to Cousin Darby's tenement on the Lower East Side, and as soon as Fiona glimpsed the neighborhood she wanted to go home. New York was bitterly cold, with mounds of dirty snow and slush piled along the streets. The tiny patches of sky that she glimpsed between buildings were gray and smoke-filled. She missed the trees and hedgerows and green hills of Ireland.

"This is awful, Dad!" She pulled her handkerchief from her pocket and covered her nose and mouth with it to block out the stench from the open sewers.

"We won't live this way for very long, lass. You'll see. We'll have our mansion in no time."

But of course it wasn't true. Even with stolen clothes Fiona and her father weren't welcomed into the fancy parlors of New York's upper class any more than they had been welcomed in Ireland. Cousin Darby and his family had ten children and lived in an overcrowded tenement that was as noisy and stench-filled as the steerage hold had been. For the first month, Fiona slept in a bed with three of her cousins and was bitten nearly to death every night by fleas. She had to wait in line for everything, from the shared outhouses to the community water spigot. Rats as big as hedgehogs skittered through the streets, and filthy, poorly clad children crammed the tenement hallways and stairwells and sidewalks, jostling each other, begging for food. This couldn't be America, the land of promise. Everyone seemed so beaten down, so hopeless. Fiona felt as though she'd boarded the wrong ship, landed at the wrong destination.

"This is worse than at home, Dad," she said as they walked the garbage-strewn streets near the East River, searching for work. "At least my bedroom at Wickham Hall was clean and I had three meals to eat every day."

"Give it time, lass. First things, first. Once we find jobs and a place of our own, things will be better." But even Rory seemed disheartened.

They searched for employment from dawn to dusk, following every lead, going into every factory and business that posted a *Help Wanted* sign out front. Fiona and her father had two advantages over most of the thousands of immigrants searching for work: they spoke English, and they were much better dressed, thanks to the clothing that Rory had stolen.

On the first Sunday after she arrived, Fiona went to Mass at the parish church to try to atone for what she'd done. Before partaking of the sacrament, she confessed her sin of helping her father steal clothing from the staterooms. She wept as she did her penance. Afterward Fiona felt so clean and light she could have floated up to the ceiling along with the incense and candle smoke. Her sins had been washed away, she was forgiven, loved.

But at what price? The parish church had a crucifix hanging above the altar like the one in St. Brigid's back home, and as Fiona listened to the story of Christ's passion—how He'd been scourged, mocked, beaten, crucified—the price of her forgiveness seemed much too high. Still, the priest had assured her that God had forgiven her sins. He had given her a brand-new start in life, and she was grateful.

Then Rory needed her help again.

"America is colder than I bargained for," he told her after a long day of walking the streets, searching for work. "We'll be needing warmer coats." She knew right away what he had in mind—they certainly had no money to buy coats.

"No, Dad. I don't want to steal anymore. If we get caught here in America, they'll send us to jail or deport us or—"

"Hush, Fiona. I'll hear no more of it. Come with me."

He led her to a street lined with shops, and as they strolled down the sidewalk, peering into the storefront windows, Rory acted as if he was the richest man in the world with money to spare. It was after dark, and the shops were all closed for the night, but the streets were still surprisingly busy. Fiona watched her father carefully, wondering what he was up to, and saw him eyeing the constable who was patrolling his beat farther down the block. As soon as the patrolman's back was turned, Rory pulled Fiona into a dark, narrow alley between buildings.

Cold, slushy snow soaked Fiona's shoes as she sloshed through the unseen puddles. She heard rats squealing in the shadows. A moment later they emerged near the rear entrance to a tailor shop. She was surprised at how quickly and easily her father jimmied open the door. He went straight to a rack of men's suits as if he had picked one out ahead of time, tossed the hanger aside, then balled the suit up and stuffed it beneath the front of his knitted vest. Next he chose a fancy wool velour coat with a shawl collar for Fiona.

"Put it on!" he ordered. "Over top of your other wrap."

Fiona obeyed, barely able to see what she was doing in the dark, certain that the policeman would burst through the door any moment. Her father grabbed a tweed overcoat for himself, buttoning it over his jacket and his protruding sweater, then snatched a felt cloche off one of the mannequins and tossed it to Fiona.

"Here's your new hat. Put it on." Barely a minute after breaking in, Rory pulled the door shut behind them again and headed back down the alley. "Take my arm," he ordered when they reached the street. "Walk slowly, look in the windows. We have all the time in the world."

Fiona tried to convince herself that she wasn't a thief—her Dad was. But she knew she didn't dare attend Mass, especially in her new coat and hat, unless she confessed. What if she got the same young priest she'd confessed to the last time? He had told her to go and sin no more.

On Sunday Fiona waited in an empty pew with her head bowed, watching the confessionals until she saw an older priest enter the booth. She quickly rose and stood in his line, rehearsing what she would say.

"Forgive me, Father, for I have sinned," she began. "I-I'm sometimes reluctant to obey my father. This week I . . . I argued with him when he gave me an order."

"You must always obey your father," the priest said with a sigh. He sounded bored. Fiona wondered if he perked up whenever someone confessed a more interesting sin. "The Lord commands us to honor our father and mother that our days may be long on this earth," the priest told her.

"Yes, Father. I-I will obey him from now on."

Fiona did her penance, but this time she didn't feel quite as clean as the last time she'd confessed. Nor did she float on air with the incense. The coat she was wearing seemed to weigh her down.

One month after she arrived, Fiona finally got a job working for a milliner. She had worn her new coat, and she knew by the way the manager, Mrs. Gurche, sized her up from head to toe that her pretty face and nicer-than-average clothing had won her the job.

Madame Deveau's hat shop was in one of the nicer parts of town, a few blocks from Central Park. The store occupied the first floor of the two-story brick building; the loft where the hats were made filled the second. Fiona had traipsed through dozens of factories in her search for work, most of them noisy, hot, dreary places that looked as though a single match would burn them to the ground. Madame Deveau's workshop was pleasant in comparison, an open, airy space filled with light from windows in the front and rear.

"If you work hard and learn the business," Mrs. Gurche assured Fiona, "you can work your way up—or I should say *down*—to a job as a salesgirl on the first floor."

Fiona nodded and said, "Thank you, ma'am," but becoming a salesgirl was never her dream. She thought of the high hopes she'd had when she'd left Ireland of living in a mansion in wealth and ease. She remembered her mother and sisters, who'd been left to fend for themselves in the smoky cottage. She fought back her tears.

"Is something wrong, Miss Quinn?"

"Not at all," Fiona said with her prettiest smile. "I'm . . . I'm grateful for such an opportunity."

They walked up the back stairs to the workshop, and Mrs. Gurche gave Fiona a leather work apron to slip over her clothes. The experienced hat makers sat at tables near the window, creating their masterpieces of high fashion. They were gifted professionals, and Fiona enjoyed watching them work, making all sorts of hats in the latest styles from Paris. Their wealthy clientele ordered berets and boaters and turbans and cloche hats—all made from silk, velvet, jacquard, and brocade and trimmed with sequins, coq feathers, ostrich plumes, pearls, and lace.

But Fiona's work was boring and tedious, requiring little skill. Her first tasks were sewing the designer's labels into the finished hats and "swirling" millinery ribbon with a steam iron before sewing it inside the crown as a sweatband. As time passed and she gained experience, Fiona learned how to fit the finished hats on balsa head blocks to steam out the wrinkles.

"Let it cool on the block for at least ten minutes," Mrs. Gurche cautioned, "or the hat will lose its shape."

Fiona became adept at using millinery needles and special thread to sew on all kinds of trimmings: bows, flowers, ostrich plumes, dyed coq feathers, pheasant tail, dyed goose and peacock feathers. She learned how to cut out patterns and how to operate a sewing machine to shirr the fabric. Fiona worked in the hat shop for ten hours a day—from six in the morning until four in the afternoon—six days a week. Some of the other girls she worked with told her where to get piecework to earn extra money sewing at night.

When Rory Quinn found a job as a dock worker loading freight, he and Fiona moved out of Cousin Darby's apartment, renting two rooms in a noisy tenement much like their cousin's, two blocks away. They still had no water or electricity and still used communal outhouses and water spigots. An iron stove heated the rooms and cooked their food. It wasn't the life Fiona had imagined.

"Do you regret leaving Ireland?" she asked her father one night. They sat on either side of the stove, eating the thin stew she had cooked. It consisted mostly of potatoes, with a watery broth and a few morsels of beef from a neck bone.

"Of course not," Rory said between bites. "Although I wish Darby had warned me before we left Ireland that every blooming pub in America has been shut down for good. A man needs a pint or two at the end of a long day's work."

Fiona didn't reply. She was glad that the sale of alcoholic beverages had been prohibited all over America. They could save more money if her dad wasn't wasting it on pints every night, and that meant they could send for Mam and the girls that much sooner. Fiona longed for them to come—not only because she missed her mother, but because she was growing exhausted from so much work. She had to rise early every morning to make breakfast for her and her father and pack their lunches before hurrying off to Madame Deveau's hat shop. Then, after working a ten-hour day, she had to shop for groceries on the way home, get the fire going in their apartment, and cook supper. After washing their dishes, she would wash their clothes, hanging them on lines strung across the apartment. The constantly dripping laundry made their rooms clammy and damp. When Fiona finished the wash, she did piecework by lamplight, sewing on buttons or doing hand-stitching to earn a few extra dollars. This left little time to take care of herself, bathing and washing her hair, before falling into bed for a few hours' sleep.

No, this wasn't the life Fiona had dreamed of. She worked harder in America than she ever had at Wickham Hall—and ate considerably less. She cried herself to sleep nearly every night, homesick for Ireland. She missed Kevin. Her father had made a terrible mistake.

"When do you think we'll be sending for Mam and the girls?" she asked as she spooned the last of the stew into her father's bowl.

"Not until we can afford a bigger place to live."

"But this isn't any smaller than our cottage back home. Sheila could get a job, too, and help—"

"We're better off on our own. Besides, I can't afford passage for your mam and sisters, yet. I'll hear no more about it."

Fiona stood, too frustrated to continue this conversation, and went to fetch water to rinse their dishes. Sure, her father was better off—he didn't have to do all of the household chores after working all day. As Fiona waited in line in the chilly spring air for her turn at the spigot, she made up her mind to find a way out of this neighborhood, this life—with or without her father.

She began to study the wealthy ladies who patronized the hat shop: how they dressed, how they walked and talked and wore their hair. Compared to them, Fiona looked like a frumpy immigrant. If she ever wanted to rise out of the slum, she would have to do more than wear stolen clothes; she would have to look and act like an American.

Fiona learned from the girls at work that the most beautiful and glamorous women in America were the film stars from Hollywood. She began saving a few cents from her pay every week so she could go to the movie matinees on Sunday afternoon. She studied everything the gorgeous starlets did: how they wore their hair and did their makeup, how they walked and dressed. Her favorites were Greta Garbo, Mary Pickford, and Gloria Swanson. She dreamed of marrying a man as handsome and dashing as Rudolph Valentino or Douglas Fairbanks.

Spring turned to summer, bringing warmer weather and longer days at last. Encouraged by the girls at work, Fiona went to Woolworth's one payday after work and splurged on makeup. Then she went to a beauty shop and had her long hair bobbed in the latest style.

"Oh, you look just like Greta Garbo!" the ladies in the salon insisted. Fiona smiled at her reflection in the mirror, pleased with the modern American girl she had become. She passed a department store on the way home, and when she saw the latest dress styles from Paris in the window, she went inside and spent $11.95 for a new dress made of silk georgette crepe and Spanish lace.

"I'd like to wear it home," she told the salesgirl. Her father couldn't make her return it if it was already worn. Even so, she worried about what he would say—especially when he learned that she'd spent most of her pay.

"What did you do?" he shouted as soon as he saw her. He appraised her from head to toe, scowling fiercely. Fiona forced herself to sound bold and carefree.

"I got my hair bobbed. Long hair is so old-fashioned."

"Your face looks different, too."

"I bought some makeup. All the fashionable women wear lipstick and rouge. And this dress is the latest style from Paris. Do you like it?"

"That's not a dress! It's indecent! It looks like you're wearing your blooming nightclothes! I can see your ankles!"

"It's the style, Dad. You told me to dress like a rich woman—well, this is the way they dress. Besides, I have very nice ankles."

"Well, I'll not have you spending all your money to look like a tart. Take everything back!"

Fiona felt her temper flare. "How am I supposed to meet any rich American men if I look like a dowdy, old-fashioned immigrant? I thought that's why we came to America—so I could marry a rich husband and live in a mansion. Instead, all I do is work and sleep and work some more. I'm sick of it! It's high time we got out of this horrible tenement."

She had never defied her father before, and the confrontation left her shaken. But much to her surprise, Rory backed down. "Well, you'd better change out of that dress before you fix dinner," he growled. "You don't want to ruin it." He said no more about her new look. Nor did he complain about all the money she'd spent.

He began buying the newspaper every day and spent a great deal of time reading it, tearing out certain articles, circling others in pencil. Fiona looked through his collection and saw that he was saving articles about all sorts of social events: ribbon-cuttings, gallery openings, charity events, and receptions.

"What is all this? What are you up to now, Dad?" she asked as she peered over his shoulder one night.

"I have a plan to get us out of this place." He looked up at her and smiled—the first smile she'd seen on his face in a long time. "Here, I want you to sit down and read today's news, Fiona. Find out what's going on in the world so you can discuss things intelligently, understand?"

"Discuss . . . with whom?"

He ignored her question. "For instance, did you know that they're going to be electing a new president this fall? Everyone who is a United States citizen gets to vote for the man they want—either Warren Harding or James Cox. And women can vote, too, for the first time. Can you imagine such a thing?"

"What about the Catholics? Do they get to vote?"

"Aye. Religion doesn't matter over here. No one cares which church you go to in America. Read this," he insisted, thumping the newspaper with his hand. "It tells about the most famous thoroughbred in America, Man O' War. And you need to know about the new League of Nations. Rich men talk about these things, and you need to know, too, so you can converse with them."

"What if they ask questions about me? What should I say?"

"Anything but the truth, that's for certain."

The thought of committing yet another sin made Fiona afraid. "I'm not a very good liar, Dad. The nuns said that the devil is the father of lies, and—"

"Enough about the nuns. That's superstitious nonsense. If someone asks questions about you, tell them you're visiting from Ireland—that much is true. Tell them your father has business here—they don't need to know what that business is. And don't forget to look at their left hand for a wedding ring. Most married men in America wear them."

Several evenings a week and on Sunday afternoons, Fiona and her father dressed in their best clothes and rode the subway to the nicer sections of New York where all the fancy social gatherings took place. She was very nervous at first as she watched Rory bluff his way into various events. But once inside, Fiona gradually gained confidence. No one questioned their presence or asked to see their invitation.

She studied the upper-class women as she strolled around art galleries or nibbled canapés at receptions and quickly learned to imitate their manners and bright laughter. But it was the men who fascinated her the most. They seemed so handsome compared to the working men on the Lower East Side, so elegant and well-mannered. She loved the way they treated women with kindness and attentiveness.

"You must put on some weight, Dad," she told him as they rode the subway home one evening, the car lurching from side to side as it sped down the darkened tunnel. "All the rich men are plump—and their skin isn't brown and leathery from the sun."

"Nothing I can do about that, lass. I work outside in all sorts of weather."

"And your shoes are a disgrace. I'm surprised no one noticed them and tossed you out in the street." She hated telling him that, knowing how he would go about getting a new pair, but she needed better shoes, as well. Two nights later they broke into a shoe repair shop, and each took a pair of shoes.

Besides bluffing their way into receptions and social events, Fiona and her father started lounging around the lobbies of fancy hotels. Businessmen who belonged to the Rotary Club or Kiwanis often gathered there to attend meetings, and occasionally one of them would smile at Fiona or tip his hat to her. On Sunday afternoons, she and her father strolled around Central Park or along Fifth Avenue. They looked in the windows of expensive stores and spent some of their precious money sipping tea in the fine coffee shops where the upper classes went. One Friday evening, as they passed an overcrowded coffee shop, Rory spotted a gentleman seated all alone reading a newspaper.

"Quick, Fiona. Go inside and ask if you could join him," he urged.

"Won't he think I'm brash?"

"Tell him you've been shopping all day, you're tired, there aren't any empty tables. Go on, girl. This is your golden opportunity." He practically shoved her through the door. Fiona went forward on shaking knees.

"Excuse me, would you mind if I sat here?" she asked the man. He lowered his newspaper and looked up at her in surprise. "There don't seem to be any empty tables," she explained, gesturing to the crowded shop. She flashed him her prettiest smile.

"Not at all." He scrambled to his feet and helped Fiona with her chair. "I'm nearly finished, in fact."

"Oh, please don't hurry on my account. I wouldn't mind some company. I would have waited for a free table, but I'm dying for a cup of tea."

"I'll get a waiter for you, Miss . . ."

"Quinn. Fiona Quinn. Thank you so much." She ordered a cup of tea and heard the gentleman say to put it on his tab. He folded his newspaper closed, and after the waiter brought Fiona's tea and refilled his coffee cup, the man settled back comfortably to chat. He was a nice-looking man in his early thirties, with wavy brown hair and a clean-shaven face.

"I noticed you have an accent. May I ask where you're from, Miss Quinn?"

"My father and I are visiting from Ireland. He has business here in the city." She had rehearsed the words so many times, waiting for this opportunity, that they no longer seemed like a lie. She remembered her goal. Her family was counting on her.

"And what do you think of our fair city?"

"It's wonderful! I've been shopping all afternoon—which is why I needed this tea."

"Are you shopping all alone?" he asked, regarding her with sympathy.

"I'm afraid so. My father is occupied with meetings and such. I'm afraid to venture too far from our hotel."

"What have you seen since coming to New York? Have you been to the theater or the symphony orchestra?"

"I'm afraid not. We've only just arrived. But I'd love to go sometime." She waited, hoping he would offer to take her. He didn't. "So what brings you here on a Friday evening?" she asked as the silence lengthened. "Do you work nearby?"

"I work for a law firm down on Wall Street, but I'm meeting my wife for dinner here in midtown in about an hour. I'm just killing time."

"I see." Fiona smiled, trying not to let her disappointment show. "That's an odd phrase, isn't it—'killing time'? Exactly how does one 'kill' time?"

"I guess it is a strange expression. I never thought much about it." He seemed very solemn and humorless, and she told herself it was just as well that he was married. She wanted a man who was charming as well as handsome and rich—and, she prayed, a man with a sense of humor.

She saw no sense in prolonging the conversation. Fiona finished her tea and thanked him again for allowing her to sit with him, then rejoined her father out on the sidewalk.

"Well?" he asked hopefully.

"He was married."

"Oh. That's too bad. For a while there, you looked like you were getting on."

"No, not really. But he did pay for my tea."

Neither of them spoke as they rode the subway back to their shabby apartment and colorless life. Fiona had never felt so discouraged. She wished they had enough money to return to Ireland. She could ask for her old job back at Wickham Hall, marry Kevin, have children. She remembered how much Kevin had loved her as she climbed the creaking stairs to their dingy rooms.

"We tried, lass," Rory said as he shrugged off his suit coat. "We'll try again another day."

"Pretending to be rich is a stupid idea, Dad. It's never going to work."

Her father ignored her pessimism. He sat down at the dilapidated table he'd disinterred from the dump and opened the newspaper to the entertainment pages.

"I've got it!" he said, looking up at her with a grin. "Next Friday night we'll try the theater."

Chapter 24

Fiona knew that she and her father had made a mistake as soon as they reached the theater district. They'd timed their arrival to coincide with intermission, so the ushers would no longer be checking tickets, but they hadn't taken into account that the people milling around in the lobby and streaming outside into the warm summer air would all be wearing formal evening clothes.

"We'd better leave," she told her father. "You don't have a tuxedo."

"Never mind about that. Just hold your head high and walk into the lobby. No one will care." She did as she was told, pushing past the people who were drifting outside to light up cigarettes and fat cigars. The lobby was crowded, as well, and she smelled the aroma of coffee.

"Now what?" she asked her father. He was glancing all around, taking everything in.

"Find a man who's alone. Like that gentleman over there." He tilted his head to one side, indicating where Fiona should look. A group of people had lined up to buy coffee at a kiosk off to her left, and standing all alone at the end of the line was a tall, elegant-looking man who appeared to be in his forties.

"He's too old," Fiona whispered. "Can't you pick someone younger?"

"Go on with you, girl! Just meet him before you decide. If you make a good impression, maybe he'll introduce you to a younger friend. Hurry up, now. He's still alone. "

Fiona mustered all her courage as she made her way over to the man, telling herself that this was just for practice. Several more patrons had joined the line behind him by the time she got there, and she wasn't sure what to do. It would be awkward to cut in line alongside him. But her father was watching; she felt she had no choice but to follow through.

"Excuse me, sir," she said, touching his arm to get his attention. "Is this the queue for coffee?"

He turned to face her. "Pardon? The . . . what?"

"The queue—or I suppose they call it a 'line' here in America."

"Oh, yes. Yes, we do call it a line. But don't go to the end of it," he said, glancing back at the lengthening line. "Please, allow me to buy you a cup."

"Thank you. That's very kind of you, Mr. . . ."

"Bartlett. Arthur Bartlett."

"Fiona Quinn," she said, smiling. "How do you do?"

"Fine, thank you." He smiled in return—a charming, lopsided smile that went all the way to his eyes. They were wide and expressive and a very deep shade of brown. "You have a lovely name, Fiona Quinn, and a lovely voice. Are you . . . English?"

"From Dublin, actually. I'm visiting America with my father."

He studied her with interest while they talked, stroking his neatly trimmed mustache as if petting a small animal. Fiona studied him, as well. Mr. Bartlett had a pleasant, oval-shaped face, and he wore his thin, light-brown hair combed back from his high forehead. His full, pouting lips and somber eyes gave him a mournful look—until his smile lit up his face. He had a nice voice, too, deep and resonant. But he was too old. Fiona wanted someone young and handsome.

"How many coffees would you like?" he asked. They had reached the front of the line.

"Just one—for me." She was surprised when he ordered only one for himself. She would have guessed that he was fetching coffee for his wife or theater companions. Surely an elegant, well-to-do gentleman like Mr. Bartlett wouldn't attend the theater alone. He paid for both coffees, then moved aside to the counter where the cream and sugar were served.

"How do you take yours?" he asked.

"A little of each, thank you." Fiona hated coffee and wondered how she would manage to choke it down. She watched his hands as he stirred in the cream and sugar; the ring finger on his left hand was bare.

"Did you come to the theater all alone?" Arthur asked as he turned from the serving table, carrying her coffee.

"No, actually, I came with my father. He's around here someplace, talking to friends." She looked around as if searching for him, then turned back to Arthur. "I don't see him right now."

"Well, since your father is missing momentarily, might I have the pleasure of joining you for coffee? I hate to think of such a lovely woman sitting all alone."

"I would like that very much." He chose one of the little tables that surrounded the coffee bar and held the chair for Fiona before taking a seat across from her—a true gentleman. She scrambled for something to say.

"Are you enjoying the show, Mr. Bartlett?"

"It's so-so," he said, waving his hand. "There's too much talking and not nearly enough action for my tastes. And the actors aren't very good, either. But what do you think?" Arthur leaned toward her, giving her his full attention.

"I haven't seen many plays to compare it to. And it's the first one I've seen here in New York."

"I take it you haven't been here very long. Are you enjoying the city?"

"Oh, yes—so far. I've been wanting to see some of the galleries and museums and attend some social events, but my father's business has kept him tied up much of the time."

"And you're left on your own?"

"I'm afraid so." She gave a little shrug and flipped her bobbed hair from her eyes, flirting shamelessly. She could see that he was smitten. She sat sideways in her chair with her legs crossed daintily, her exposed ankles where he could see them. His eyes wandered from her face to her figure and back again as if he were reading a map, memorizing her. She enjoyed the power she had over him, even if he was an older man.

"I've lived in New York all my life," he told her. "I would consider it a privilege if you would allow me to show you around the city. Shall I speak with your father and arrange it sometime?"

"That would be lovely, Mr. Bartlett."

They talked for a few more minutes before the house lights flickered. The show was about to resume—and just when she was finally getting somewhere with a man. Arthur stood and held her chair again.

"May I escort you back to your seat, Miss Quinn?"

For a moment, Fiona panicked. She had no seat. He would find out she was an imposter.

"I . . . um . . . I haven't been enjoying the play very much, either. Perhaps I'll leave. But thank you anyway."

"Then I would like to offer you and your father a ride to your hotel, if I may. It's not often that I get to meet such a charming woman. I really don't want to say good night."

She took a moment to consider his offer and couldn't see the harm in accepting a ride with him. "That would be very kind of you."

"Wonderful. If you'll excuse me for just a moment, I'll tell my friends I'm leaving. I'll be right back."

As soon as Mr. Bartlett was out of sight, Fiona hurried over to where her father was watching from a distance. "He wants to drive us home, Dad. What should I do?"

"Exactly as we planned. Tell him we're staying in the Chelsea Hotel and let him escort you as far as the lobby. Tell him you'd like to walk there—that it's a lovely night and all that. I'll follow you to keep an eye on him and meet you in the lobby. We'll go back to the tenement when he's gone."

"Right, Dad. Wish me luck." She turned to hurry away but he called her back.

"Did you find out if he's married?"

"He isn't wearing a ring."

"Ask him."

"Isn't that a rather rude question to ask someone I've just met?"

"He looks to be in his forties. I don't want to waste our time on him if he's married."

Fiona nodded and hurried back to wait for Mr. Bartlett, wondering how in the world she would find out if he was married. He broke into a wide smile, as if he couldn't help himself, as soon as he saw her waiting for him.

"There you are. I've managed to free myself," he said. "Did you find your father?"

"Yes, but he has decided to stay until the end of the show."

"Splendid. I have you all to myself, then." Arthur held the door for her and they walked outside. "I'll hail a cab."

"Wait . . . It's such a lovely evening, isn't it? Why don't we walk? My hotel isn't far."

"That's a wonderful idea. It will give us more time together." He offered his arm, and she held it the way society ladies did when walking with their escorts. Arthur was at least a foot taller than she was, and Fiona had to look up to talk to him. She liked the feeling.

"Did your friends mind you leaving, Mr. Bartlett?"

"Please, call me Arthur. And may I call you Fiona?"

"Yes, of course."

"No, my friends didn't mind my leaving at all. I was the odd man out anyway, since the others came with their wives."

"And you aren't married?" He hesitated for a moment, and Fiona saw him wince.

"I was at one time. I'm divorced." He looked down at her, his dark eyes sorrowful, and she thought she glimpsed pain in them. Her father would be glad to learn that he wasn't married, but she wondered if she dared pursue Arthur any further, knowing her church's position on divorce and remarriage.

"Divorce isn't allowed in my country," she told him. "Is it very common here in America?"

"No, not really. But our marriage was never a very happy one, I'm sorry to say. Our families arranged it when we were quite young—for social reasons, you understand. Love was never a factor. We both realized after only a few years that it was a mistake."

Fiona saw the sadness in his eyes and quickly changed the subject. They talked about New York City for the rest of the way, and after he escorted her inside the hotel, they stood in the lobby and talked some more.

"This has been so much more interesting than the play," Arthur said with a smile. "In fact, I still don't want to say good night."

"Me, either," she said, laughing.

"Then, shall we walk some more? I'll show you some more sights of New York on the way. . . . Or am I being too forward?"

"Not at all. I'd love to."

"Will your father mind?"

Fiona couldn't think what to do. "I . . . um . . . I'm not sure. He's still at the theater."

"Why don't you write him a note and leave it in his mailbox?"

"Yes . . . yes, of course." Arthur walked with her to the front desk and asked the clerk for paper and a pen. Fiona scribbled a vague message on it and folded it in half, then wrote a random room number on it, shielding it with her hand so Arthur wouldn't see it. She handed it to the desk clerk.

Arthur smiled and offered his arm again as he escorted her outside, and this time he rested his hand on top of hers. She felt the warmth of his touch all the way to her toes.

He walked with her around a couple of city blocks near the hotel, giving her a tour of the landmarks along the way, and she learned that he worked on Wall Street as an investment banker. Arthur was very charming and surprisingly funny. She began to forget that he was divorced and at least twenty years older than she was.

"Thank you for a wonderful evening, Arthur," she said when they reached the hotel once again.

"I still don't want to say good-bye," he said, sighing as he took her hand. "Would you have dinner with me tomorrow night?"

"I would like that very much."

"Good. Let's say . . . seven o'clock? And please tell your father that I haven't forgotten my manners. Perhaps I can meet him when I call for you tomorrow? It's only proper."

"Of course. Until tomorrow. . . ?"

"Until tomorrow." He gave her hand a gentle squeeze before releasing it.

Fiona and her father were waiting for Arthur in the hotel lobby when he called for her the following night. They had both worked a full day— Rory at the docks and Fiona at the hat shop—and they had barely made it to the hotel on time after racing home, bathing, and changing into their stolen clothes and shoes. Fiona still felt a little frazzled as she introduced her father to Arthur. When Arthur asked Rory to join them for dinner, he declined.

"No, thank you, Mr. Bartlett. I have business to attend to this evening. Perhaps another time?"

"I'll look forward to it." Arthur had a beautiful 1920 Packard, and he drove Fiona to a little restaurant away from all the crowds and Saturday night activity. She felt a little disappointed that he hadn't taken her some-place famous where the upper class dined, but the food was so delicious, the atmosphere so cozy and romantic, that she soon forgot her disappoint-ment. They sat across from each other at a diminutive table, and Arthur's long legs brushed against hers from time to time, sending a pleasant shiver through her. His eyes held hers as they talked, and she saw his admiration in them. He looked almost handsome as he stroked his mustache in the soft candlelight.

"Do you like to dance?" he asked as they finished their dessert. "I know a place we can go that has a wonderful band. And we can get a martini or a glass of wine there, if you'd like."

"I thought all the pubs in America were closed. My father's quite put out that he can't have a pint now and then."

"They are closed," Arthur said, laughing. "Officially, that is. But you can get a drink in just about any building on Fifty-second Street between Fifth and Sixth Avenues if you know where to go. They're called speakeasies, and there are thousands of them in New York."

"You mean, they're all breaking the law? How do they get away with it?"

"Bribery, my dear. Most officials will simply look the other way if you pay them enough—federal prohibition agents, the police, district attorneys, they're all on the take. Even the beat cop will turn his back when the beer is being delivered if you give him forty or fifty bucks."

"Really." She smiled. The idea of such widespread corruption made her feel a little better about her own wrongdoings.

"Sure. All the best clubs serve liquor on the sly. Club Gallant in Greenwich Village is one of the fanciest. I also have a membership card to Club New Yorker on Fifty-first Street. And you should see the elaborate system of alarm buttons they have at the Twenty-One Club. I was there one night when the place was raided, and it was amazing how quickly the whole place swung into action. They have trapdoors and secret compartments everywhere, and in a matter of moments, all traces of liquor had simply vanished."

Fiona leaned across the table toward him, resting her chin on her fist. "And here I thought everyone in America was a teetotaler."

"Hardly! Tell your father he can make an appointment with a doctor and ask for a prescription for alcohol for medicinal purposes. It's perfectly legal for a druggist to dispense gin or brandy and so forth if you have a prescription."

Fiona laughed with delight. "America certainly is an interesting place. I think I'd like to see one of these . . . What did you call them? A speaksoftly?"

"A speakeasy," he said, laughing with her. "All right, then. Let's go find one."

Arthur drove to an ordinary-looking brownstone in midtown, then led Fiona down a flight of stairs to the basement door. A peephole opened after they'd knocked, and Arthur gave his name. A moment later the door swung wide and Fiona heard music and laughter and the tinkle of glasses. It took a moment for her eyes to adjust to the dim light and see that the entire basement had been converted into a nightclub. The doorman led them to a small table for two in a cozy nook, and Arthur ordered them each a drink. Fiona sipped hers slowly as they talked. She had never drunk alcohol before, but she liked the pleasant, swirling feeling it gave her. The band music was so lively she couldn't help tapping her feet.

"Care to dance?" Arthur soon asked. Fiona had been watching the other couples. All she had to do was imitate them.

"I'd love to."

Arthur was a wonderful dancer, so smooth and graceful that she saw other people watching him with admiration. And she felt graceful herself as she floated around the dance floor in his arms. By the end of the evening she longed for Arthur to hold her closer, remembering how wonderful it felt when Kevin held her tightly in his arms. But Arthur was a gentleman, holding her chastely while they danced, kissing her lightly on the cheek when he said good-night to her at the hotel, the way she'd seen upper-class people saying farewell to each other.

"I had a marvelous time," she told him. It was the truth.

"I didn't show you much of New York, did I? We'll have to make another date for next Saturday night."

"I'd like that very much."

She was waiting for him in the lobby again a week later. Fiona watched as he strode through the door like he was the lord of the manor, looking all around for her.

"Fiona! There you are!" She loved the way his face lit up when he saw her. It made him look dashing and young. He took both of her hands in his and greeted her with a soft kiss on the cheek. He smelled wonderful.

His after-shave permeated his skin and his clothing, and the manly scent was as intoxicating to Fiona as the drink he had bought her at the speakeasy.

"I thought we would go sailing tonight," he said as they walked to his car.

"Sailing? At night?"

"Well, not exactly," he said with a grin. "I've made reservations for us on a ship that's anchored three miles offshore. There will be dining and dancing—and liquor is legal, of course, out in international waters."

"Don't tell me! Is this another way to skirt around the prohibition laws?"

"Of course—and a very lucrative one, too." His eyes sparkled as he glanced down at her. "There are hundreds of ships, in fact, anchored off the U.S. coast from Maine all the way to Florida."

He parked near the river, where a speedboat was waiting to ferry passengers to and from the ship. The air was cool on the ride out from the harbor, and Arthur wrapped his arm around Fiona's shoulders, cuddling her close to help her stay warm. The ship Arthur had chosen was magnificent, with mahogany paneling in the dining lounge, linen tablecloths, fine china, and crystal chandeliers. They dined on thick steaks and drank wine and gazed across the table at each other.

"You're the most beautiful woman I've ever met," Arthur murmured. She smiled, not knowing how to reply.

Later they danced until their feet ached. Fiona didn't need to drink much liquor in order to feel light and giddy; the lush music, the look in Arthur's eyes, and the feel of his arms around her were intoxicating enough. She couldn't imagine how she ever thought he was too old for her. He was so gentle and attentive, always impeccably dressed in bow tie and evening clothes. She loved the way he looked at her with his deep brown eyes and slow, sad smile; loved the warmth of his hand on her waist as they danced or on her back as he escorted her to her seat. He had smooth hands with long, elegant fingers and buffed nails. He held her hand as they sat at their table and sipped drinks, and sometimes he lifted her fingers to his lips and kissed them. But as he said good-night, he once again kissed her softly on the cheek, leaving Fiona longing for more.

When they had been dating for a month, Fiona finally got her wish. They had gone out to Arthur's favorite ship again, and after dining and dancing for hours, he led her up on deck beneath a starlit sky. As the glittering lights of New York City flickered in the distance, Arthur took her in his arms and kissed her properly for the first time—not the good-night pecks on the cheek he'd been giving her when they parted. Not the bruising, fumbling kisses that Kevin always gave her. This was a slow, wonderful kiss that left her breathless. He was a man in complete control, not simply taking something for himself, as Kevin had, but giving Fiona something in return—a man who knew how to really kiss a woman.

"I'm falling in love with you, Fiona," he whispered when they finally drew apart. He rested his palm on her cheek and brushed her lips with his thumb. Before she could reply, he pulled her close and kissed her again.

As summer turned to fall, Fiona noticed that Arthur never took her to the theater or the symphony or to other society events. He always chose dark, cozy, intimate places where they could cuddle at their table between dances. He never introduced Fiona to any friends or acquaintances. In fact, Arthur never seemed to run into anyone he knew, until one night, as he and Fiona were leaving a speakeasy on Fifty-second Street, a gentleman on his way into the club stopped him.

"Arthur! Where have you been lately? I haven't seen you in months." The man reached to shake Arthur's hand, and Fiona saw a look of surprise on his face when he noticed Fiona holding onto Arthur's arm. "Oh, hello . . ." he said to her.

For the space of a heartbeat, Arthur seemed embarrassed. He quickly recovered. "Phil, let me introduce you to my guest, Fiona Quinn, from Dublin. Her father is here in New York on business, and I've offered to show her around. Fiona, this is Phil Holmes."

"How do you do, Miss Quinn," he said, bowing slightly. "I trust Arthur is showing you the very best of our fair city?"

"Oh, yes. He's doing a marvelous job."

"You always get the plum jobs, Arthur." He nudged him in the ribs and winked. "Sorry, but I have to run. Will I see you and your wife at the mayor's reception next week?"

"Yes, of course."

"Good. Give Evelyn my regards."

"I will. Good night."

Mr. Holmes hurried off, leaving behind an awkward silence.

"Is Evelyn your ex-wife?" Fiona asked when they were outside in the street. Arthur nodded solemnly. "And are you really taking her to the mayor's party?"

"I'm afraid so," he sighed. "It's still my duty to escort her to these things. She knows the mayor and all those other society people. It's not the sort of event she would attend alone—you understand."

"I'm not sure I do. Mr. Holmes referred to her as your wife. Doesn't he know about your divorce?" Arthur stopped beside his car, gazing down at his feet, not at Fiona. He looked so uncomfortable that she decided to drop the subject, worried that she had upset him. "I'm sorry, Arthur. You don't owe me any explanations."

"Yes, I do, Fiona." He finally looked up at her, his face grave, his eyes sorrowful. "Our divorce isn't final yet."

"What?" Fiona leaned against the car fender to steady herself. She didn't want to believe that he had lied to her all this time. "Y-you mean you're still *married*?"

"Yes . . . I'm sorry."

Tears filled Fiona's eyes. She didn't want to cry, but she couldn't seem to stop them from falling. Arthur opened the passenger door, then rested his hand on her back, gently guiding her inside. "Please, let's sit in the car," he said. "I'd like to explain."

He walked around to the driver's side and slid behind the wheel, but he didn't start the engine. Fiona looked straight ahead through the windshield. The corner street lamp glistened through her tears.

"Everything else I told you about my marriage is true," Arthur said softly. "It's been over for years. I don't love Evelyn, and she doesn't love me. We agreed to divorce some time ago, but now she's stalling, arguing for more money. My lawyer is handling it. In the meantime, we occasionally attend social events together—to keep up appearances. For the children's sakes."

Fiona's breath caught in her throat as she turned to stare at him. "You never told me you had children." She felt as if she were onboard a ship in storm-tossed seas and had slipped off the deck into the cold, dark water.

Arthur drew a deep breath, as if he were about to plunge into the frigid water with her. "Yes, I have a son and a daughter. The breakup has been especially hard on them."

Fiona struggled to get it straight in her mind, to comprehend the truth. "You're a married man, then? And you're living with your wife, going places with her—and with me?"

He didn't answer right away. He reached to take both of her hands in his as he gazed at her. "I'm so sorry if I've misled you, Fiona. I wouldn't blame you for hating me. It was selfish of me not to tell you the truth right from the start. . . . But I was afraid you would have nothing to do with me if you knew—afraid you'd walk away from me that first evening and I'd never see you again. And I couldn't bear the thought of losing you. Can you ever forgive me?"

She didn't answer right away, shocked by the knowledge that she'd been involved with a married man all this time. "W-when will your divorce be final?" she finally asked.

"Any day." He released one of her hands and smoothed her hair off her forehead. "That's what my lawyer keeps telling me—any day. When I first started seeing you, I thought it would all be over with by now. It *should* be over. I never imagined that I'd have to continue misleading you this long. I'm so sorry, Fiona."

"Maybe . . . maybe we shouldn't see each other until it's final," she said, pulling her hand free. "Especially if you're still required to attend social events with her."

Arthur closed his eyes for a moment, as if her words had caused him great pain. "I understand," he murmured. "I don't know how I'll bear it, but I understand."

He started the engine and they drove back to the hotel in silence. Fiona felt torn between her conscience and her longing. She knew that what they'd done was wrong, and she felt deeply ashamed that she'd been involved with a married man all this time. But she couldn't bear the thought of never seeing Arthur again. Even now, all she could think about was kissing him, feeling his comforting arms around her, inhaling his rich scent. But that was wrong—so wrong. The sins of stealing and lying already stained her soul, and now she would have to add the sin of adultery to them. Arthur had a wife and children—two children.

He parked the car near the hotel but didn't move to get out. Finally he turned to her. "Please . . . tell me I haven't lost you forever. Will you let me call on you again when I'm free? Will you still be here?"

"Yes. Yes of course," she said eagerly. But she realized that she wouldn't be here. She didn't live in this hotel. She had lied to Arthur the same way he had lied to her. If she said good-bye to him tonight, he would have no way to get in touch with her after his divorce was final. He could hardly call on her at her tenement on the Lower East Side or pay her a visit in the workshop above Madame Deveau's hat shop. She saw tears in his eyes as he took her face in his hands and tilted it toward him.

"Let me memorize your beautiful face, Fiona. Until I see you again, it will be like living in darkness with no sunlight." He ran his hands through her hair, over her shoulders, down her arms. Then he pulled her close for a final, tender kiss. When he pulled away, a single tear rolled down his cheek. "I love you, Fiona. I don't want to lose you."

"I love you, too!" she cried as she flung herself into his arms. It was true. In the beginning he had been nothing more to her than a wealthy man who could give her a comfortable life. But now she was genuinely in love with Arthur Bartlett. She wasn't pretending.

"How long . . . until we can be together?" she asked as she buried her face against his neck.

"I don't know. I wish I did. I would marry you now, tonight, if I were free. I want to spend the rest of my life with you."

Against all her wishes, against all that she'd been taught about right and wrong, she had fallen in love with a married man. She couldn't help herself. And now she couldn't bear to be separated from him. In that moment, Fiona made up her mind.

"I don't want to be apart at all, Arthur—ever. Forget what I said, before. It doesn't matter if . . . if you aren't free yet."

"Oh, thank you, darling." He pulled her closer, and she heard his sigh of relief. "Can I see you next weekend, Fiona? Shall we go dancing? Please say yes."

"Yes, my darling, yes. Next weekend."

Chapter
25

H appy new year, Fiona!" Arthur pulled her close and kissed her, right in the middle of the dance floor. Fiona circled her arms around his neck to kiss him in return. All around them, people were blowing toy horns and noisemakers, tossing confetti into the air and kissing. A brand new year had just begun—1921—and Fiona felt as though her life was about to begin, as well. A year ago she had been a scrub maid in Ireland; now she was in love with the most wonderful man in the world. The fact that he was spending New Year's Eve with her and not with his wife meant that he loved her, too. He was telling the truth about his marriage being over.

They danced awhile longer before Arthur said, "All this noise and cigarette smoke are getting to me. Would you mind if we left and went someplace else?"

"Not at all." He fetched her coat, and they walked out into the snowy night, their arms wrapped around each other, their breath fogging the air in front of them.

They found Arthur's car, and Fiona sat inside with the motor running while Arthur brushed off the freshly fallen snow. She watched him work, realizing how very much she loved him. Fiona had once thought she loved Kevin Malloy, but this was so much better—like the difference between smelling an orange and eating one. Kevin never talked to Fiona about anything or took her anywhere. He couldn't even read or write. He smelled of sweat and horses, and his hands were chapped and rough, his fingernails dirty. How could she ever have thought that she loved him? She'd been glad a thousand times over that her father had stopped her from marrying him.

Arthur finished cleaning off the snow and climbed behind the wheel, turning to face her. "Fiona, I don't want to say good-night yet. But I'm tired of sitting in noisy clubs and smoky cafes. I was wondering if we might go to your hotel suite—but only if your father is there, of course—so we can talk where it's quiet." He caressed her cheek, sending warmth through her, even though his fingers were icy cold. She didn't want to leave him yet, either. But she and her father didn't have a room in the Chelsea Hotel. She didn't have to feign disappointment.

"I'm so sorry, Arthur, but it's impossible. My father will probably be asleep by now. I would hate to disturb him."

"Well, could I take you to my place, then? Please? Just for a little while longer. I don't want to end our evening yet. And it's too cold to sit in the car—you're shivering."

"Your place?" she repeated. The shivery feeling that tingled through her had nothing to do with the January air. She stalled for time as she tried to make up her mind. Arthur's dark eyes looked soft and pleading.

"I have an apartment here in Manhattan. It isn't far."

"All right . . . but I can't stay too late." She was already thinking ahead, knowing it would be difficult to make her way from the hotel to her tenement in the frigid weather. It was already past midnight.

Arthur drove carefully through the snowy streets, the wipers swishing rhythmically to keep the windshield clean. He parked near an apartment building on a quiet, tree-lined street, a few blocks from Central Park. The yellow brick building was six stories tall, U-shaped, with a garden courtyard in the middle and a uniformed doorman in the front lobby. Fiona felt a stab of disappointment. It was a very nice building—certainly nicer than the walk-up tenements in her neighborhood—but she'd expected Arthur to live in a mansion like Wickham Hall, with dozens of servants.

"Good evening, Mr. Bartlett . . . ma'am," the doorman said as he held the door for them.

"Good evening, Charles. How are you?"

"Just fine, Mr. Bartlett. Snowy night, isn't it?" Charles hurried across the lobby to open the elevator doors for them. "You have yourself a happy new year, now, Mr. Bartlett."

"Thank you. You, too." Arthur pushed the button for the fifth floor, and as soon as the doors closed, he pulled Fiona into his arms for a kiss. She'd never ridden on an elevator before, and she wasn't sure if the little wave of dizziness she felt was from the ride or from his impassioned kiss. He pulled away as the elevator coasted to a stop and the doors opened. He took her hand and led her down a carpeted hallway to his apartment door, taking a moment to fish his keys from his pocket and unlock it. The hallway was bright and clean, the carpeting thick and luxurious beneath her feet. It was so different from the noisy, smelly tenement hallways where Fiona lived that they might have landed on a different planet.

"Now, where were we?" Arthur said when they were inside. He reached to kiss her again, but Fiona backed away, a little frightened by what she might be getting herself into.

"It's very dark in here, Arthur."

"Of course. I'm sorry." He flipped a switch and a ceiling fixture in the foyer came on.

"You live here?" she asked, gazing around. The apartment was very neat and orderly, and the furniture looked brand-new, but she didn't see any of Arthur's personal belongings anywhere—there were no books or photographs or bedroom slippers lying around. The place didn't look lived-in. But compared to the grimy, rat-infested apartments where she lived, it was a palace.

"I live here part of the time." He moved ahead of her into the living room and switched on a lamp beside the couch. "I rent this apartment in the city so I have a place to sleep when I'm too tired to drive all the way home. Sometimes a meeting lasts too long or the theater runs late . . . or I drink too much," he added with a laugh, "and so I spend the night here." He moved around the room as he talked, switching on another lamp, shrugging off his coat. He helped Fiona remove her coat and hung them both in the front closet. "I have a home in Westchester, where I live most of the time. You understand that my wife and children are living there, too, until the divorce is final. I have an obligation to provide for them. Would you like a tour of the place?"

"Okay."

He held her hand as he led her around. The apartment was neat and spacious and clean—and smelled of Arthur's scent. The kitchen was very modern with an electric icebox and built-in cabinets. The tiled bathroom had a sink and a toilet and a claw-footed bathtub big enough for Fiona to luxuriate in. And she wouldn't even have to haul the hot water first—it came right out of the tap. There were radiators in every room, and the apartment was comfortably warm all over. Fiona thought of the two drafty rooms where she lived with her father, and Arthur's apartment began to seem like a mansion after all. Even Wickham Hall didn't have central heating or so many modern conveniences. She imagined living here with Arthur and tears came to her eyes.

"Well, what do you think of it?" he asked when they returned to the living room.

"It's lovely, Arthur . . . and so clean." She realized that it had been a stupid thing to say when he laughed out loud.

"I have Mrs. Murphy, my cleaning lady, to thank for that. Have a seat, Fiona." He went to the refrigerator and retrieved a bottle while she made herself comfortable on the sofa. "I've been saving this for a special occasion. Do you like champagne?"

"I've never tasted it."

"Then you must try some." He crossed to a bar in one corner of the living room and took out two glasses. His movements were smooth and elegant, and she loved watching everything he did. When the cork came free with a hollow pop, Arthur sat down on the sofa beside her to pour the champagne.

"To the most beautiful woman in New York City," he said, raising his glass for a toast. "To us—and to a new beginning in 1921." They touched glasses and kissed, then Fiona took a sip.

"It has bubbles!"

"Do you like it?"

"Yes, it's wonderful."

By the time she finished her first glass she felt relaxed and happier than she'd ever felt in her life. Arthur poured a second glass for each of them, then took off his tuxedo jacket and tossed it on a chair. He pulled off his bow tie and loosened his collar and cuffs.

"That's better," he sighed.

"I've never seen you without a jacket and tie," Fiona said, laughing. "You look very . . . content."

"May I turn off the lights for a minute? I want to show you something." He stood and switched them off, then pulled the drapes open. From where she sat on the sofa, Fiona could see the lights of New York sparkling like stars against the black sky, with the darker void of Central Park in the distance. Snow still sifted from the sky, making the scene into a fairyland.

"Oh, Arthur! What a beautiful view!" He crossed the room to sit beside her, and they gazed out of the window together, sipping champagne.

"I've fallen hopelessly in love with you, Fiona," he murmured as they finished their second glass.

"I love you, too. I wish we could stay here forever."

He set both of their glasses on the table and pulled Fiona close, kissing her until she was breathless.

"Wait!" he said, pulling away suddenly. "I just remembered. I have a New Year's present for you. Let me think . . . Where did I put it?" He searched his pockets, then stood and started opening and closing drawers to no avail. "Ah, I remember!" he said, laughing at himself. "I left it in here. Come on." He took her hand and pulled her to her feet, leading her into his bedroom. The room whirled and swayed as Fiona walked, and she knew she had drunk too much champagne.

"Sit down and close your eyes," he told her. She sat on the edge of the bed, sinking into its softness. The beautiful bedspread felt luxurious beneath her hand, and she knew that the mattress probably had fine linen sheets on it like the ones she used to scrub at Wickham Hall. There was artwork on the walls, and the headboard, nightstands, and dresser all matched, made with inlays of different kinds of wood. Arthur's scent was even more powerful in here. Fiona knew she would think of this room, this bed, and weep when she returned to her squalid mattress in the tenement.

"Close your eyes," Arthur said. Fiona obeyed, her head spinning when she did so. She heard him open a drawer in the nightstand, then close it. He took her hand and placed something in her palm. "You can look now."

She opened her eyes and saw a black leather jeweler's box, tied with a red ribbon. She pulled it off and opened the lid to see a beautiful golden ring with a star-sapphire stone.

"It's a promise ring, Fiona. Please accept it with a promise of my undying love." He pulled it out of the holder and slipped it onto her finger. "I love you, darling. Happy new year."

She threw her arms around his neck as her eyes filled with tears. "Oh, Arthur! I love you so much!" And she did—more than she ever imagined she would love anyone. "Arthur . . . Arthur . . ." she whispered as he covered her face with kisses.

Suddenly, it was as if a tidal wave of love and longing washed over her, and Fiona was lost in the deluge.

The dawning sun woke her up. Arthur hadn't closed the bedroom drapes. For a moment Fiona didn't know where she was. Then she saw Arthur asleep in the bed beside her, and she began to cry. What she recalled of last night had seemed wonderful at the time. But now that the champagne had worn off, she felt ashamed and embarrassed. She wondered if he had deliberately planned to seduce her this way, and if she had foolishly fallen into his trap. And she wondered if Arthur would still want her now that he'd had his way with her. She was eighteen years old and he was forty-two—and married. Fiona couldn't hold back a sob.

Arthur stirred, then woke up and pulled her close. "No . . . darling, no," he soothed. "Please don't cry."

"What have we done?" she wept.

"Fiona, you know in your heart that we were meant to be together this way. And we will be . . . forever."

She struggled to control her tears. This was America, not Ireland. They wouldn't lock her away with the nuns.

"I wish I could say I'm sorry," Arthur told her, "but I'm not. And you shouldn't be sorry, either. I love you, and I know you love me. You're wearing my promise to you on your finger. Soon, very soon, we'll be able to be together . . . always."

She nodded, unable to reply. Her emotions were a tangled mess of happiness and shame, fear and hope. She couldn't begin to unravel them all, especially with Arthur lying next to her, holding her.

"I need to go home. My father—" She stopped, afraid to finish. Rory Quinn would murder both of them. She began to cry again.

"Of course. I'll let you get dressed," Arthur said softly. He climbed out of bed and went into his dressing room next to the bathroom. Fiona couldn't stop crying as she hurriedly put on her clothes.

"I'm coming up to your hotel suite with you so I can speak to your father," Arthur said when he emerged from the dressing room in a suit and tie. "I'm worried that he'll be angry with you, and I want to explain to him that it was all my fault—that we lost track of the time."

"And it was snowing," she added numbly. But as they drove to the hotel, Fiona worried more about what excuse she could give Arthur than what she would say to her father. Rory wouldn't be at the hotel, of course. How could she explain his absence—so early in the morning on New Year's Day—to Arthur?

"I think I'd better talk to my father alone," she said when Arthur pulled his car to a stop in front. "Maybe it would be better if he didn't know I was with you all night."

"But I want to take full responsibility—"

"Let me talk to him first. I'll let you know what happened when I see you tonight." She gave him a quick good-bye kiss and hurried inside the hotel. As soon as Arthur's car was out of sight, Fiona took the subway home to her tenement. Rory was waiting for her, pacing the floor, furious.

"Where have you been all night? I've been frantic, girl!"

"I'm sorry. Arthur took me to see his apartment. We had a few drinks, and before we knew it, it was too late to wander the streets. He'd had too much champagne and the weather was bad. He thought he'd better not drive."

"Did that man seduce you? I'll demand that he marry you if he did!"

Fiona could never tell her father that he had. Rory would have every right to demand that Arthur marry her—but Arthur, of course, was already married. Fiona could never make her father understand that Arthur did love her, that he was going to marry her just as soon as he got his divorce.

"Of course he didn't seduce me," she lied. "Arthur is a gentleman. He slept on the sofa. I'm sorry if we worried you, Dad. In fact, Arthur begged for a chance to come and explain everything to you himself, but he couldn't very well do that now, could he? We don't really have a room at the hotel, and I could hardly bring him here."

"Don't be playing games with me, girl. You'll ruin all your chances for a decent life if you let him take advantage of you."

"He gave me a ring—an engagement ring." She held out her hand for him to see. Rory appraised it with a scowl.

"That isn't a diamond. I thought he was rich."

"Arthur doesn't do things the conventional way." She smiled, realizing even as she spoke the words that it was one of the things she loved about him. Arthur was very romantic, yet he hated the usual clichés of romance.

"When are you seeing him again?"

"Tonight." Fiona glanced around the dismal apartment, remembering the smooth feel of Arthur's bed linens; the clean, tiled bathroom and modern kitchen; the view of the city and Central Park. And she remembered how Arthur had looked at her with love shining in his eyes when he'd awakened beside her this morning.

"Excuse me, Dad. I need to use to the privy." She was going to burst into tears any moment if she had to spend one more minute in this apartment, smelling the stench of mildew and chamber pots and filth after spending the night at Arthur's.

But as she walked past the communal outhouses, disgusted by the run-down neighborhood, her tears fell fast. Even the layer of clean, white snow couldn't hide the ugliness. Fiona hesitated as she passed the parish church, wondering if she dared to go in. She knew she had sinned. She needed to beg God for forgiveness. But when she pictured Jesus impaled on the cross, dying in agony for her sins, she knew she could never ask such a sacrifice from Him yet again. Her sins had piled too high, the weight of them had grown much too heavy: thou shalt not steal, thou shalt not bear false witness, thou shalt not covet thy neighbor's house, honor thy father and mother . . . and now adultery. Nor could she compound those sins by lying to the priest again. The nuns had taught her that Satan was the father of lies.

"If you lie, you sin twice," the sisters had said. *"The thing you're lying about is usually a sin, and the lie doubles it!"*

Fiona hadn't sinned in ignorance but willfully. She didn't deserve Christ's forgiveness. She couldn't face the priest, the crucifix.

She cried as she walked, shivering in the cold January air. How could what she had shared with Arthur be so wrong, yet be so wonderful?

Rory insisted on coming to the hotel with Fiona when she went to meet Arthur for their date that night. Fiona was terrified. Her father was going to confront Arthur and scare him away. She didn't want to lose him. She held her breath as the men greeted one another, and it startled her to realize that her father and Arthur were about the same age. Except for the first night that she'd met Arthur, Fiona had never thought of him as old.

He was so vibrant, so exciting to be with. And her father looked a decade older from a lifetime of hard labor.

"May I buy you a cup of coffee, Mr. Quinn?" Arthur asked when he saw Rory.

"Aye, that would be fine." They went into the hotel coffee shop and sat in a booth. Arthur and Rory both ordered coffee, but Fiona was too sick with fear to order anything.

"I'd like to ask what your intentions are for my daughter," Rory said without preamble.

"Honorable, I assure you. I know there's an age difference between Fiona and me, and I'm sure that must concern you. But I've given her a ring as a pledge of my good intentions."

"You intend to marry her?"

"Yes, I do."

"Shall we set a date for the wedding, then? I'll have many arrangements to make. And the wedding must be soon, since my business may require us to return to Dublin shortly."

What a liar her father was. Fiona felt as though she might throw up any minute. She was terrified of being found out—both by her father and by Arthur. She wasn't sure which would be worse.

"Unfortunately, it's not possible to set a date, at the moment," Arthur said. "That's why I've been eager to speak with you. It would help if I knew how much longer your business will require you to stay in New York and when you might be returning to Dublin."

Rory took a sip of coffee before answering. Fiona knew he was stalling. "I'm not sure when I'm going back."

"What exactly is your business here, Mr. Quinn—if I might ask? I have many contacts in the financial world. Perhaps we could help you get settled here on a more permanent basis. If it's a question of financing, I would be pleased to offer a business loan to my future father-in-law."

Fiona could scarcely breathe, fearing disaster.

"Which bank would that be, then?" Rory asked, as if he did business with dozens of banks. Arthur told him the name. "Aye, that's a fine institution," Rory replied. "I appreciate the offer, Mr. Bartlett, but I have all the business I can handle, at the moment." He glanced at Fiona, then down at her sapphire ring. "Perhaps we should keep the date open for now."

"Thank you," Arthur said. "I assure you that Fiona and I will set a date as soon as we're able. I love your daughter, Mr. Quinn. I won't rest until she becomes my wife."

Her father finished his coffee and quickly excused himself, as if Arthur's probes into his business affairs had scared him off. Arthur had won this round. But Fiona couldn't stop trembling for an hour.

Chapter
26

At first Fiona promised herself that she wouldn't go to Arthur's apartment again, but she couldn't seem to stay away. They got into the habit of leaving the speakeasies early in the evening so they could spend a few hours at the apartment and Fiona could still return to the hotel at a decent hour. And each time she was with him, Fiona found it harder and harder to leave his bed. Her longing for Arthur grew greater each day. He was so tender, so loving. She wanted to remain in his arms forever. If only his wife would let him go.

Spring arrived, and the trees and flowers on the street where Arthur lived burst into bloom. Central Park, a few blocks away, seemed like paradise—so lush and green it reminded Fiona of Ireland. She hated returning to her apartment on the Lower East Side, but she was afraid to keep nagging Arthur by asking, "How much longer?"

As they lay in bed one Friday evening, listening to the rain beat against the window, Arthur turned to her and said, "Why don't you move in here with me, Fiona? If you lived here all the time, we wouldn't have to run back and forth anymore. Please?"

Fiona closed her eyes, imagining how wonderful it would be. She wouldn't have to go back out in the rain tonight and walk from the hotel to the subway after Arthur dropped her off. She wouldn't have to ride the train across town, then walk four more blocks from the station to her tenement and sleep on a mattress in a cold room with no plumbing or electricity.

"I wish I could stay," she said with a sigh. "If only your lawyer would hurry up with the divorce."

"I'm tired of waiting for it to be final, aren't you, Fiona? I want to start our new life together right now."

"I don't see how that's possible."

Arthur didn't know that she worked in a hat shop all day, six days a week. He didn't know that she daydreamed of the life they would have together as she fitted hats onto head blocks to steam them or as she cut hat patterns from brocade and felt. He didn't know that she had a mother and eight sisters in Ireland, waiting for her to earn enough money so they could come to America, too.

"Why not?" he asked. "What's stopping you from moving in?"

She thought of the parish church that she passed each day on her way to and from work—the church she could no longer go inside.

"For one thing, my father would disown me," she said, "and then how would I afford to live? I have no money of my own. I'm dependent on him for everything."

"Let me support you. I'll gladly pay for the apartment and give you a generous living allowance to spend any way you want. I already feel as though you're my wife. . . . You're my life, Fiona! The only thing standing in our way is a piece of paper with my ex-wife's signature on it."

"Do you think she'll sign it soon?"

"She'd probably sign it much sooner if she knew you were living here. And I'll marry you the moment she does, I promise you. But I don't want to lose you. I can see that your father is growing impatient with me. He wants to see you happily married, and I don't blame him. I'm so afraid a younger, more handsome man will come along and steal you away—a man who is free to marry you."

"I love you, Arthur. I don't want another man."

"Then, move in here. We can tell your father that we eloped—it'll be true, soon enough. I can only stay here one or two nights a week, anyway, and the rest of the time this place will be all yours."

"I don't understand. Why wouldn't you live here all the time?"

"My lawyer advised me not to. I need to maintain legal possession of my house in Westchester by living there. And there are always matters to discuss concerning the children and so on. Aren't you tired of staying in the hotel, Fiona? Wouldn't it be so much better for both of us if you lived here?"

She longed to say yes—but how could she? "I'll think about it," she promised. And she did—all the way home on the subway and as she walked though the dark, rainy streets. She had come to America to have a better life, but she certainly wasn't better off in the tenement. How wonderful it would be to quit her job and live in a modern apartment with electricity and plumbing. She could set aside part of the living allowance Arthur gave her to send home to Mam and the girls.

Fiona was still deep in thought as she climbed the steep stairs to her rooms. She heard a baby wailing somewhere on the first floor and two men arguing in a foreign language on the second. The hallways stank of onions and boiled cabbage. Arthur's apartment was warm and quiet and clean.

It would be wrong to live with Arthur if they weren't married. But he had said that he wouldn't really be living there; she would have the place all to herself most of the time. And she was already committing a sin by sleeping with him; at least she wouldn't have to come home to this place anymore. Arthur was going to marry her soon—he'd promised.

Rory was sound asleep, snoring loudly when Fiona let herself into the dark apartment. Why should she have to come back here every night to cook and clean and wash for him? What was he doing to make a better life for them in America? As far as Fiona could tell, nothing! She had done all the work of introducing herself to Arthur, flirting with him, getting him to fall in love with her. Now she had a chance at a better life, so why not take it? The fact that she truly loved Arthur was an added bonus. What more did she owe her father? After working in the hat shop for more than a year, she surely must have repaid him for her passage to America by now.

Fiona undressed in the dark and crawled into bed, but she couldn't sleep. Why should she continue living this way? No one could blame her for choosing a better life with the man she loved. If her father had an opportunity like this one, he would certainly take it.

After tossing in bed for several hours, wrestling with her thoughts and her conscience, Fiona finally reached a decision: This would be the last night she would ever spend in this bed and in this apartment. She fell asleep then, content with her choice.

The next morning, Fiona made breakfast for her father and went to work at Madame Deveau's hat shop for the last time. "I'm leaving to get married," she told her boss, Mrs. Gurche. "Today will be my last day here." The girls she worked with hugged and congratulated her when she showed them the ring Arthur had given her; she hadn't dared to wear it to work before.

Fiona collected her pay that afternoon and raced back to the tenement so she could pack her belongings before her father got home from work. She left him her entire week's pay from the hat shop and a note: *Arthur and I have eloped. I've quit my job and moved into his apartment. If you come by once a week, I'll give you money for Mam and the girls out of the living allowance Arthur gives me.* She wrote down his address.

Fiona had no regrets as she walked away and no second thoughts. She never once looked back.

Fiona was alone in Arthur's apartment a few days later when the doorman rang for her. "There's a gentleman down here to see you, ma'am. He says his name is Rory Quinn."

For a moment, Fiona couldn't think what to do. The truth was, she didn't want to see her father. She didn't want to be reminded of who she really was and where she'd come from. In the few short days that she'd lived here, Fiona already felt like a different woman—a wealthy woman who lived in a lovely, modern apartment and could afford to shop in expensive stores. Arthur was a very generous man. He'd not only given her spending money, he'd gone out and bought new clothes for her himself: a beaded cocktail dress and silk stockings and lingerie that felt as light and smooth as water against her skin.

"Ma'am? Are you still there?" Charles asked when she didn't reply.

"Yes—thank you, Charles. Tell him I'll be right down." The apartment would feel tainted, somehow, if she invited her father up.

"Hello, Dad," she said when she reached the lobby. She wanted the doorman to know who Rory was in case he told Arthur that a strange man had come calling. "Let's go for a walk, shall we?"

She was afraid, for a moment, that Rory would refuse and make a scene right there in the lobby in front of Charles. Fiona could tell by the high color in her father's cheeks that he was angry—and barely holding back his temper. She took his arm and led him outside before he could refuse.

"Isn't this a lovely neighborhood?" she asked as they walked. "And Central Park is only a few blocks away. The park is so beautiful this time of year, and—"

"I didn't come for a stroll in the park, Fiona." He stopped, pulling her to a halt beside him. Fiona glanced back at the apartment building, hoping the doorman wasn't watching.

"I'm sorry that we ran off and eloped without your permission, Dad, but—"

"Stop the lies, girl! I know the truth. I looked into the man's background. Arthur Bartlett is every bit as rich as he says he is—a Wall Street banker with investments everywhere. But he's *married*, Fiona. He's a married man with two children."

"I know," she said quietly. "I've known for some time. Arthur told me the truth months ago. But he's in the process of divorcing his wife, and we'll be married as soon as it's final. She'll probably be eager to sign the papers now that she knows I'm living here. I love Arthur, and he loves me."

"You're so naïve," Rory said in a trembling voice. "Now that he's moved you in here and made you his mistress he'll never divorce his wife."

"I'm not his mistress! Arthur *does* want to marry me. He says that I'm his real wife, not her." Rory closed his eyes for a moment, and when he opened them again Fiona saw tears in them.

" 'Tis my own fault for driving you to this—my own daughter. But this isn't the life I wanted for you, Fiona. I never meant for this to happen. Go get your things. You're leaving him and coming home with me."

"No!"

"You'll do as I say, do you hear?"

"I won't. I've done everything you've said, all along, but I won't anymore. You didn't get this lovely apartment for me—I got it myself. And now you expect me to just leave it all because *you* said so? You expect me to go back to work in some sweatshop again and live in rat-infested rooms with all the dirt and disease? Never! You're the one who taught me to want more in life than what Mam had—and I did everything you said. You can't expect me to go back to that now. I won't do it!"

"Arthur Bartlett deceived you. He pretended he wasn't married when all the time he was."

"And we deceived him, Dad. I pretended to be someone I wasn't. What's the difference? You can hardly cry 'unfair.'"

"What about your mother and sisters? You were supposed to marry well and help pay their way. Do you think he'll let them move in here with you?"

"I'm certain Arthur will help pay their way once we're married. Besides, I've been giving you my pay every week for almost a year. What happened to all the money we've earned? Why haven't you sent for Mam and the girls?"

"I'll not have you talking to me this way."

"And I'll not have you controlling my life for one more day. I've done everything you said—giving up Kevin Malloy, stealing onboard the ship, breaking into stores at night, and throwing myself at Arthur at the theater that first time. But not anymore, Dad. Without me to cook and wash for you, maybe you'll finally have a reason to send for Mam."

Rory stared at her, his mouth gaping. He seemed too stunned to speak. Fiona began slowly backing away from him toward the apartment.

"Arthur gives me a generous living allowance. If you come by each Friday, I'll leave an envelope of money for you with the doorman. Let me know when Mam and the others come from Ireland. I want to see them. . . . Good-bye, Dad."

Fiona turned and hurried inside, grateful that her father didn't follow her. She had escaped from him, but as she rode the elevator upstairs, she couldn't escape from his words. Was Rory right—was she being naïve? Was she simply Arthur's plaything—his beautiful bird in a golden cage? The apartment seemed small and confining as she paced around it, wondering if Arthur's wife was the one who was delaying the divorce . . . or if he was. Fiona was still upset when Arthur stopped in to see her later that night after work.

"Fiona, darling, what's wrong?" he asked as soon as he saw her. Fiona moved into his arms, immediately sorry for having doubted his love. Arthur was so loving, so sensitive that he could read her every mood even before she spoke a word.

"Nothing, Arthur—"

"But I can see that you've been crying. Come, sit down and tell me all about it." He led her to the sofa. Fiona felt safe and loved once again as she nestled in his arms. "What happened?" he asked gently.

"My father came to see me today. He . . . he knows we didn't elope. He knows you're still married, and he's very angry about it. I'm afraid he'll cause trouble for us."

"Don't worry about him, Fiona. We have each other, now." He began kissing her neck, his bristly mustache tickling her skin. "I've been thinking about you all day . . ." he murmured.

Fiona's earlier worries came rushing back. Was she being a fool? Was this the only reason Arthur came to see her? She didn't want to pressure him and scare him away, but she didn't want to be his mistress all her life, either.

"Didn't you hear what I said, Arthur? My father knows the truth about us, and he's furious. You have to do something! I'm afraid he'll try to marry me to another man or else take me back to Dublin with him."

Arthur stopped kissing her and sat back. His dark eyes lost their velvety softness, and there was a coldness in them that she had never seen before.

"He can hardly afford to take you back to Ireland on a dock worker's pay, can he?"

Fiona stared at Arthur, horrified. "How long have you known?" she whispered.

"New York only seems like a big city, darling. In fact, it's not. Everyone knows everyone else among high society. And that's true in the business world, as well. No one has ever done business with Rory Quinn—except on the loading docks."

"You knew all along that I was an impostor?"

"It didn't matter to me, Fiona."

She struggled out of his arms and leaned back against the sofa, feeling as if she might faint. What had she done? Why had she let this man ruin her life? The nuns were right, after all—one small sin leads to bigger and bigger ones, until you can never escape from the mess you've made.

"My father was right," she wept. "You were just using me!"

"Oh no, you're wrong, Fiona. I fell in love with you long before I learned who you were or where you came from. By then I didn't care."

She heard the emotion in his unsteady voice, and when he took her face in his hands and made her look at him again, she saw the love shining in his eyes.

"The most beautiful woman I'd ever seen walked up to me at the theater one night, and I was captivated. Then I got to know you, and you were as fascinating and as enchanting as you were beautiful. I was so lonely, Fiona. My marriage has been over for years, and there were times when I thought I would never be happy again. Then you showed an interest in me, and I could scarcely believe it. You could have married any man in New York—handsome men, younger men half my age. But you looked at me as if I were handsome—"

"But, Arthur, you are handsome."

He pulled her to himself, clutching her tightly. She felt his tears on her neck. "See, my darling?" he murmured. "How could I resist falling in love with you?"

He stayed all night for the first time since she'd moved into the apartment. This time it felt wonderful to wake up beside him. She felt like Mrs. Arthur Bartlett. She made breakfast for him in the morning before he left for work, and he kissed her good-bye as if he didn't want to leave her.

"Meet me for lunch, Fiona. There's a place down by my office, just off Wall Street. Shall we say, twelve-thirty? Charles will call a cab for you." He gave her the address and money for cab fare, then kissed her good-bye again. "I don't know how I'll ever wait until twelve-thirty," he said with his sad, lopsided smile.

Fiona floated on air all morning. Her father was wrong. Arthur truly loved her.

Chapter 27

Fiona stepped from the hired cab, her arms loaded with packages from her day of shopping. Charles hurried out front to help her.

"Let me get those for you, ma'am."

She smiled and thanked him, but she couldn't quite meet his gaze. She'd noticed that Charles always called her ma'am, not Mrs. Bartlett or even Miss Quinn. She heard him addressing all the other residents by name, and she wondered what he thought of her. He must know that she and Arthur weren't married.

"Oh, and ma'am?" Charles said before opening the elevator door for her, "Mr. Quinn left something for you when he came to pick up his envelope today."

He set down Fiona's packages and retrieved an envelope from behind his counter. She glanced at it and saw that it was the same envelope she had given her father a week ago, his name printed on the front in her handwriting, the seal opened. She avoided looking inside until Charles finished carrying her packages into the apartment for her and she'd closed the door behind him.

Her father had sent her a newspaper clipping, torn from the society pages. It told about a political fund-raising dinner held the previous week. But it was the photograph, not the article, that caught Fiona's attention. Arthur had his arm draped protectively around a woman's shoulders, pulling her close the way he always did with Fiona. It was an affectionate gesture that Fiona loved; it made her feel as if Arthur was claiming her for his own and saying to the world "Hands off—she's mine." According to the caption, the woman was Mrs. Arthur Bartlett.

Fiona felt a chill of fear as she took the picture over to the window to study it. Even in blurred, black-and-white newsprint, she could see that Evelyn Bartlett was a striking woman, with fair skin and dark hair and a radiant smile. Arthur was looking down at his wife, not at the camera, but Fiona knew by the expression on his face that if she could see his eyes, they would be soft and warm and filled with love.

She crumpled the picture into a ball and tossed it into the trash, refusing to torture herself with it. Nor would she mention it to Arthur. The dinner had taken place last Saturday—the night he had told Fiona that he couldn't see her. But he had made it up to her by spending all day Sunday with her. Arthur loved her, not his wife. The dinner had been a social obligation he couldn't squeeze out of.

A week later Rory sent two articles. The first one reported on a group of society women attending a lecture. He had underlined the words *Evelyn Bartlett, the cultural society's president, is the wife of banking mogul Arthur Bartlett*. The second article told about the opening of a new play: *Present at the theater's grand opening last night were financier Arthur Bartlett and his wife, Evelyn.*

Rory sent more articles the following week and the week after that. Fiona quickly recognized a pattern: The society events were always on evenings that Arthur hadn't been able to come to the apartment. But many of them had taken place on the same day he'd visited her for an afternoon tryst. She felt a stab of jealousy at the thought that he'd been with his wife after assuring Fiona of his love that afternoon. Now that she'd seen a picture of Evelyn Bartlett, she couldn't get the image of her and Arthur out of her mind.

Fiona promised herself she wouldn't read the articles anymore. She vowed to throw away the envelopes without even looking inside them. But each time something would compel her to read about the man she loved, to learn more about the double life he was living.

One hot summer day, Fiona pulled an article from Rory's envelope and read the words, *Mr. and Mrs. Arthur Bartlett hosted a dinner at their home on July first in honor of their twentieth wedding anniversary*. She ran into the bathroom and vomited. Why would Arthur agree to an anniversary celebration if he and Evelyn were fighting a bitter divorce?

Fiona couldn't stop crying. Her nausea lasted all day, and she was grateful that Arthur didn't come to see her that evening. But as she cried herself to sleep, Fiona wondered where he and Evelyn were that night and what news she would read about them in the next batch of articles.

Fiona was still sick in bed when Mrs. Murphy came to clean the apartment the following morning. "You poor dear," she soothed. "Shall I make you a cup of tea to settle your stomach?"

"I'll try one . . . but to tell you the truth, Mrs. Murphy, the thought of eating or drinking anything makes me feel sick."

Mrs. Murphy paused in the doorway as if considering something. When she turned to speak, Fiona saw the look of concern on her face. "I know that it's none of my business, dear, but are you sure it's just the flu?"

"What else would it be?"

Mrs. Murphy regarded her steadily. "Well . . . might your monthly curse be a wee bit late, too?"

Fiona felt the rush of heat to her cheeks. She suddenly knew what Mrs. Murphy meant—and she also knew that she was right. Fiona's cycle was more than a week late. But how could she be pregnant? Arthur always assured her he was taking care so that wouldn't happen.

Mrs. Murphy must have seen the certain knowledge on Fiona's face because she stepped back into the room and sat down on the edge of the bed. "I've known some girls who've had the same trouble that you're having, dear. I can give you the name of the doctor they went to see. Mr. Bartlett doesn't ever have to know about it."

Fiona went numb with disbelief. She was pregnant with Arthur's child. He was married to Evelyn, not to her. And the cleaning lady surely knew that she was living here in this apartment as his mistress. Mrs. Murphy was counseling her to have an abortion. Fiona felt too dazed to be shocked by the offer. "I-I'll let you know," she mumbled.

"Don't wait too long, dear. The sooner you take care of things the better." She patted Fiona's hand and left to fix the tea.

Fiona had all day to pull herself together and decide what to do before Arthur arrived. In the end, she realized that she had no other choice except to tell him. Her father would never take her back with a baby on the way, and she had no way to support a child on her own. She wouldn't even consider Mrs. Murphy's proposal and kill her baby before it was born. She clung to the hope that Arthur would finally leave his wife when he learned the news and marry her. But the idea of telling him terrified her. What if he left her instead?

She waited until he was lying contentedly in her arms before bringing it up. "I have something to tell you, darling," she began. "We . . . I . . . I think I'm going to have a baby."

Arthur grew very still. "How certain are you?"

"I-I haven't been to a doctor, but . . . I'm fairly certain."

Arthur swore softly, and Fiona began to cry.

"No, darling, don't cry," he soothed. "I'm sorry. I didn't mean to swear. I'm angry with myself, not you."

"But what are we going to do? We have a baby on the way, and we aren't married."

"I'll take care of you and the baby. It doesn't change the way I feel about you."

"But things have to change, Arthur. I don't want to have a baby out of wedlock. We have to get married!" She felt him move away slightly, his high forehead furrowed. She had never made demands of him before, and she was sorry that she had to make them now. But the deep fear she felt—

for herself and for her child—had driven her to do it.

"You know I want to marry you, Fiona. You're wearing my ring."

"Will you tell your wife about the baby? Will she divorce you now?"

"Perhaps." Fiona felt him pull away a little more. "Don't worry about it, darling. I'll take care of everything."

"But if we're not married, our child won't have a name. He'll be a—"

"He'll be my child," Arthur said, covering her lips with his fingers. "He'll have my name. And so will you, darling. So will you."

"When? When can we get married?" He didn't answer. Fiona was tired of asking. "Do you know what I've become, Arthur? Do you know what people think of me? My father warned me that you were just using me as your mistress, and now—"

"No! It isn't true!" he said, clutching her tightly. "That's not what you are, Fiona—you're my salvation. I hated my life before I met you, hated going home from work to that cold, empty house. I felt so trapped. There were times when I thought I would never be happy again, times when I just wanted to stop living and end it all. Then I met you, and you gave me a new life with love and companionship and tenderness—all the things I'd been missing for so long. You're *already* my wife, not Evelyn. Can't you see that?"

"Then why do you take her to theater openings and social events instead of me?"

"I told you, Fiona. I have to keep up appearances—"

"I know all about the anniversary party you and Evelyn had. Twenty years! How can you celebrate a marriage that's over?"

He released her and lay on his back, staring up at the ceiling. "That was Evelyn's idea, not mine. She wants to make sure our son gets into a good prep school next fall, and that won't happen if there's a scandalous divorce. I don't know how to convince you that it's over between Evelyn and me. I go to Westchester because I have to—but I come here because I want to. This is my home, Fiona." He turned to her again and took her gently into his arms.

"Maybe, deep inside, I wanted a child of our love. I'm not sorry about the baby. This is the family I've longed for, right here in this apartment. The child is ours. How can I help but love him when I already love his mother so much? Fiona, what's wrong?" he asked when she began to cry again.

"Nothing—I'm happy, that's all. Happy that you want our baby." He smiled and used a corner of the sheet to dry her tears. "But where will we put the baby, Arthur? There's only one bedroom."

He laughed. "That's easily fixed. I'll tell the landlord we need a bigger apartment—two bedrooms, maybe even three. We'll move as soon as one becomes available."

"I love you, Arthur," she said, kissing him again. "You're the most wonderful man in the world."

The next time Fiona left money for her father, she added a note to it: *Don't send any more clippings. I won't read them.* The newspaper articles—and Fiona's anxious jealousy—quickly stopped.

By the end of October, Fiona's pregnancy was already starting to show on her slender body. When she returned home from her appointment at the beauty salon one afternoon, she was surprised to find her father standing on the sidewalk outside her building, waiting to see her. She tried to draw the edges of her jacket around her so he wouldn't notice, but she saw the recognition in his eyes right away.

"You're pregnant?" he asked without a word of greeting.

"What do you want now, Dad?"

"Answer my question, girl. Is that man finally going to marry you now that he has you in a family way?"

"Of course. Arthur loves me—and our baby."

"That isn't love," Rory said, shaking his head. "Love is something you can *see*, Fiona. It's not just useless promises and meaningless words."

"Do you *see* this lovely apartment? Have you *seen* the money he gives me every week, the clothes he buys for me?"

"Those things are for his own sake, not yours. He wants to keep you for himself, and the fancy apartment and the money he gives you ease his guilt. He's so rich he never misses one cent of it. But what is he willing to do for *you*, to sacrifice for *you*, eh? Nothing! He would lose his good name and his fine reputation if he divorced his society wife and married his poor, immigrant mistress—and he certainly isn't willing to sacrifice that. No, Fiona, don't you ever believe that the man loves you just because he *says* so. Make him *show* his love by giving something up for you. *Sacrifice* shows love, not empty words and lies. If he loved you he would marry you, no matter the cost to himself. He would make this child legitimate."

"Arthur promised me that he would," she began.

Rory gave a short laugh, echoing the doubt that Fiona herself was starting to feel. "The man is cheating on his wife, girl. If he ever does divorce her and marry you, don't you suppose he'll find another mistress to replace you? Once a cheater, always a cheater."

"No. He loves me, Dad. He's going to marry me."

Rory gripped her shoulders, his face inches from hers. "He *never* will, Fiona. Never! Leave him and come home with me."

"I can't leave him now. Who will take care of my baby and me? I don't want my child to grow up in that horrible tenement, to walk the streets in rags, begging like all the other urchins. Is that the life you want for me, Dad?" He released her, and she saw the look of pain in his eyes. His shoulders sagged.

"We've made a mess of things, Fiona. A blooming mess of things."

Aye, we have at that, she thought. But she didn't say the words aloud, afraid to let her father see her doubt and her fear. "Did you come to see me for a reason, Dad?" she finally asked.

"I've missed you, girl," he said hoarsely. "I came to see how you were doing and . . ." He gestured to her growing belly. "And now I see."

"When are Mam and the girls coming?" she asked.

Rory shook his head.

"Good-bye, then, Dad. I have to go. Arthur will be home soon."

She hurried inside with Rory's speech about sacrifice still echoing in her mind. The word reminded her of Christ's sacrifice, and as she thought of Him impaled on the cross, tears came to her eyes. Fiona was so sorry that her sins had made Jesus suffer, but there was no way out for her now.

All she ever wanted was a mansion and servants and a wealthy husband. But she had wanted the wrong things and had gotten them the wrong way. After living with a married man and bearing his child, Fiona's life would be ruined as far as marrying a respectable man was concerned. Even Kevin Malloy wouldn't marry her now. But she had no way out. She had even stopped nagging Arthur about the divorce, knowing that if she made him angry, he might simply walk away and never come back, leaving her and the baby with nothing. She didn't want to go back to the tenement. She couldn't do that to her child. She had to stay with Arthur, continue her sinful lifestyle. She had to make this sacrifice for her child.

Fiona tried to put on a happy face whenever Arthur came, but the pregnancy made her emotional, and she couldn't always control her tears. One of those times was when Arthur suggested they stay home in the evening instead of going out dancing together. She knew he couldn't risk being seen with her in her condition, but she couldn't hide her disappointment. When he left, she felt as though she had let him down.

"I have a surprise for you, darling," Arthur said when he arrived the following weekend. He left the apartment door open a crack and hurried inside to lead Fiona to the door. Then he stood behind her, covering her eyes with his hands. "Okay—bring it in, Charles."

Fiona heard thumping and grunting as Charles wrestled something through the front door. Wheels squeaked as they rolled across the hardwood floors. "Ta-da!" Arthur sang as he removed his hands from her eyes. Fiona stood blinking at a tall mahogany cabinet with a coffin-like lid and two lower doors. "It's a phonograph, darling," Arthur said with a proud grin. He fished money from his pocket to tip Charles, then sent him on his way.

"Now we can still dance the night away, and—" He didn't get to finish. Fiona threw her arms around his neck and cut off his words with her kisses.

"I love you so much, Arthur!"

"And I love you. Here, I'll show you how the phonograph works. . . . You lift this lid, and . . . see? There's the turntable where the recordings go. They're stored down here," he said, bending to open the lower doors. "I bought thirty recordings that I thought you might like, but you can pick out some more later on. The crank goes in the side, like this, and you wind it five or six times—" It made a grinding noise as Arthur wound it. "Don't wind it too much or even the waltzes will sound like the nickelodeon. Then you lower the needle, like this, and . . . ta-da!"

"May I have this dance?" he asked as the music began to play. Fiona floated in his arms, loving him more than she ever thought possible.

But even with music to listen to, she sometimes felt claustrophobic in the apartment. She grew tired of shopping, and with Mrs. Murphy to clean and do the laundry and shop for groceries and cook, there was little for Fiona to do. It was the life she'd once thought she'd wanted, complete with a servant to do all the work, but she often felt lonely and bored, especially when Arthur didn't visit for four or five days. She reminded herself not to nag or complain when he did visit though, remembering that she had no hold on him except her love.

Arthur brought home a radio soon after the phonograph, and it did bring Fiona a measure of companionship on the days and nights when he wasn't there.

Then he had another surprise for her one Friday evening—a new suitcase.

"I know you've been feeling a little cooped up," he said. "So pack some warm clothes, darling. We're going on a little trip."

Fiona was ecstatic. She hadn't been out of New York City since arriving with her father on the ship nearly two years ago. She quickly packed the new bag, and they drove to a little resort town in the Pocono Mountains called Deer Falls. They spent the weekend in a rustic log cabin on a lake, where the air smelled of pine and the moss and needles felt as soft as carpeting beneath her feet. On Saturday Arthur rented a boat and rowed her out on the mirror-like water. They watched a flock of geese flying south overhead, and she trailed her fingers through the cool, clear water.

"It's so peaceful and quiet here," she said softly, hating to disturb the tranquil day. "It reminds me of home."

"Ireland, you mean?"

She nodded. "It's very green there, with beautiful mountains and rolling countryside, much like this."

"Do you miss it, darling?"

"Never—when I'm with you." She drew a deep breath, inhaling the rich scent of earth and pine. "I could live up here with you forever, Arthur." He gave a slow, sad smile.

"My wife always hated it up here. She complained about the bugs and said there was nothing to do."

"I can think of plenty to do," she said softly. Arthur lifted the oars and rowed them back to shore.

Later, they sat beside the lake wrapped in a blanket, enjoying the warm sunshine. That night they built a fire in the stone fireplace to warm the cabin. From the front porch, they had a view of a million stars.

"Do we have to go back?" she asked as Arthur began to pack on Sunday afternoon. "Can't we just live here like two hermits? Our baby could grow up in the fresh air and swim in the lake all day until he was as brown as a trout."

"I'm afraid we can't," Arthur said sadly. "But I promise I'll bring you back as often as I can."

They returned to Deer Falls for a weekend in December, when the woods were white with snow and deer came to the clearing behind the cabin. Arthur brought her back again in February for her twentieth birthday. But March, when their baby would be born, was drawing close, and Fiona was still distressed because she and Arthur weren't married; her child would be illegitimate. She was running out of ways to ask him about his divorce.

"What's going to happen next month, when the baby comes?" she asked as they drove home from Deer Falls after her birthday.

"I've made all the arrangements for your confinement at a maternity hospital over on Amsterdam Avenue. If I'm not around, Charles will call a cab for you, and—"

"Can't I call you? Can't you come and drive me to the hospital?"

He glanced at her before turning his attention back to the road, and the cool look in his eyes chilled her. "That would be very awkward, Fiona. You know you can't call me at work, and it would be out of the question to call me at home."

"I see." It unnerved her that he'd referred to his house in Westchester as "home."

"I've already registered you at the hospital under my name."

"What should I tell them my name is?"

"Fiona Bartlett, of course. That *will* be your name, darling. Soon."

She sighed as he reached to squeeze her knee; she was trying hard not to calculate how long he had been telling her "soon." For the first time, Fiona realized that she might have to endure her child's birth alone. Arthur came and went sporadically, rarely telling Fiona his plans and seldom staying overnight. His visits had become even less frequent as she'd grown larger and more ungainly, and at times she wondered if he'd taken another mistress in her place.

"Don't be frightened, darling," he said, misunderstanding the worried look that Fiona knew must be on her face. "It's a very modern hospital with the best of everything. You'll be in good hands."

"I just wish . . ." She swallowed, wondering if she dared to say aloud what she was thinking.

"You wish what, darling?" he prompted.

"I wish that I didn't have to go through this alone—that I had my Mam or . . . or someone with me."

"Doesn't a baby usually take hours and hours to be born?" he asked, frowning. "I wouldn't be much good to you, pacing in the waiting room all that time."

"No, I suppose not."

It turned out that Fiona was alone on the morning that her labor pains started. She waited until they were ten minutes apart as the doctor had instructed, then asked Charles to call for a taxi.

"I'll be sure to tell Mr. Bartlett where you are, ma'am," he promised as he tucked her and her suitcase into the cab. "I hope everything goes okay for you." She nodded, too tearful to speak.

Her son was born on St. Patrick's Day, March 17, 1922. His hair was very dark, and he had Arthur's long, narrow face and soulful eyes. She loved him fiercely from the first moment she held him in her arms, and knew she would gladly die before she ever let any harm come to him.

"He's a beautiful little boy, ma'am," the nurses told her. "What name should we put on the birth certificate?"

It seemed an odd way to ask what she'd decided to name him. Fiona wondered if they knew the truth about her. The nurses called her ma'am or Fiona, not Mrs. Bartlett—and the baby's father wasn't pacing the waiting room floor with all the others.

"We haven't decided on a name, yet," she replied. "I'll let you know."

Arthur finally arrived the next day, begging Fiona to forgive him for not coming sooner. He showered her and the baby with gifts and flowers.

"How did you get all of this into your car?" she asked.

"It was a tight fit," he said, laughing. "Good thing we moved to a larger apartment last fall."

"Yes, it is." Fiona bit her tongue, determined not to comment on the fact that she lived alone in the apartment most of the time. "Have you seen the baby, Arthur? Isn't he beautiful?"

"I peeked in the nursery window," he said, stroking his mustache. "I daresay he doesn't look too appealing just yet. But you look more beautiful than ever, darling. Radiant, in fact. It will be wonderful to be able to get my arms around you again."

"Yes . . . Arthur . . . we've never talked about names. I was wondering if we could call him Patrick since he was born on St. Patrick's Day."

"No, that's too Irish—no offense, darling. I've always liked the name Leonard."

"Could Patrick be his middle name?"

"If you'd like. Leonard Bartlett. It has a nice ring to it, don't you think?"

She nodded bravely, fighting tears at the thought that her child's name was Bartlett and hers wasn't. "Thank you for giving him your name, Arthur."

"He's my son—of course he'll have my name. And I'll always provide for him, Fiona—for you and for him."

"Will . . . will your wife divorce you now that we have a child?" She was so afraid to push, so afraid she would anger him and he'd abandon her. It would be very easy for him to do. She longed for security, especially for her son. "I hate it that he's . . . illegitimate," she said when Arthur didn't reply. "I want to make things right before he's old enough to know about . . . us."

"I want that, too—believe me, I do. But Evelyn has asked to postpone the divorce until our daughter has her coming-out party. It will be very difficult for Ruth to meet a suitable husband if her parents are divorced."

"Yes, I understand." But Fiona knew that the stigma of illegitimacy was even worse than the stigma of divorce, and she longed to fight for her child's rights as hard as Evelyn was fighting for hers.

"The nurses tell me that you can come home in a week," Arthur said, kissing her forehead. "I'll be back to take you and the baby home as soon as I'm done at the office that day."

"I won't see you until then?"

"I hate hospitals," he said, making a face. He slowly edged toward the door. "But I'll make it up to you, Fiona, I promise. When you get home, I'll come to the apartment every night until you're sick of me."

Chapter 28

Two years later Fiona gave birth to Arthur's daughter in the same maternity hospital where Leonard had been born. Once again, she took a taxi there and endured her labor and delivery alone. She was holding her two-day-old daughter in her arms, studying her perfect face and tiny hands, when she looked up and saw Arthur standing in the doorway with a bouquet of roses in his hand, watching her.

"Oh. How long have you been there?" she asked in surprise. She hadn't put on her makeup yet, and she hoped she looked presentable. She ran her free hand through her hair to untangle it.

"No, don't," he said, striding toward her with a smile. "I love your hair when it's all tousled that way." She smelled his after-shave mingled with the rich scent of the roses as he bent to kiss her. He laid the flowers on her nightstand, then sat down in the chair beside the bed, never taking his eyes off her. "You look beautiful, Fiona. These roses will wilt from envy if they have to be in the same room with you."

She felt tears filling her eyes, not because of the loving way Arthur was gazing at her, but because he never so much as glanced at their daughter.

He never showed interest in two-year-old Leonard, either, and whenever Arthur came to the apartment it was clearly to see her. It would probably be the same with this child.

"Thank you for the flowers," she said, hoping he'd mistake her tears for joy. "Did they tell you we had a daughter?" She lifted the baby higher in her arms and pulled back the receiving blanket so he could see her face. Arthur looked at her for mere seconds, then back at Fiona.

"When can you come home, darling?"

"The doctor said Friday. He wanted to sign the birth certificate today, but I didn't know what you wanted to name her. I didn't know when I would see you—" she paused to wipe away the tear that had rolled down her cheek—"so I was going to call her Brigid."

Arthur shook his head, making a face. Fiona hoped he wouldn't say "too Irish," like he had the last time. She wiped another tear. Nothing had changed since Leonard had been born. Arthur had promised two years ago that they would be married "soon," that Fiona's name would be Bartlett like her child's. Instead, her name was still Fiona Quinn, and the only thing that had changed was that she'd had a second illegitimate baby.

"Why are you crying?" he asked softly.

"B-because our daughter doesn't have a name . . . and neither do I." Arthur pulled his chair closer and took Fiona's hand in his.

"How about Eleanor? Do you like that name? Eleanor Bartlett?"

"What about m-me?"

"Don't you have a happy life with me? Don't I give you more than enough money to meet all your needs?"

"You've always been very generous, but—"

"You know the live-in nurse I hired to take care of Leonard while you're in the hospital? I'm going to ask her to stay on for a few months to help you with the baby when you come home."

"Thank you. But, Arthur. . . ?" She sniffed back another tear. "When is Evelyn going to give you a divorce?" He looked startled, as if Fiona had brought his wife into the room by referring to her by name.

"Fiona, our time together is always so short. Why do you make things difficult by pressuring me?"

She heard the hint of warning in his voice and wondered if she'd pushed too hard. She wanted to stop living in sin, to gain self-respect for herself and a future for her children. But she decided to appeal to his vanity, instead.

"I'm tired of sharing you," she said. "I want you all to myself."

Arthur smiled, and his dark, sad eyes looked hopeful. "Every day I'm amazed that a woman as young and as beautiful as you would love me. You know that I want to make you my wife. But Evelyn has money of her own—family money. She's willing to give a great deal of it to her lawyers in order to fight the divorce. I'm sorry."

Fiona nodded, but she didn't really believe him. Not anymore. Nor was she sure that she could continue loving a man who continued to lie to her. She wished she could find a way out of her predicament, but as she looked down at her fragile, helpless daughter—Eleanor, he'd named her—Fiona knew that she would stay with Arthur whether he ever married her or not, for her children's sakes.

They became her life, filling the lonely hours when Arthur was away and giving her a fuller measure of love than she'd ever dreamed of knowing. She spent hours playing with them and teaching them things, taking them on walks to the park, proudly pushing little Eleanor in her pram.

The doorman was helping Fiona maneuver the carriage through the front door one sunny morning when he suddenly said, "Oh, by the way, ma'am. Mr. Quinn never picked up the envelope you left for him yesterday. What would you like me to do with it?"

She felt a prickle of worry. It wasn't like her father to be late retrieving his money. When they'd lived in Ireland, he'd always arrived at Wickham Hall promptly on payday to collect Fiona's wages. And he'd never missed one of her paydays since.

"Hold on to it for another day or two," she told Charles. "Something must have delayed my father, but I'm certain he'll come for it soon."

Two days later, Charles showed her the envelope again. "He still hasn't come, ma'am. You still want me to hold on to it?"

"No . . . I guess not." Fiona took the envelope back, wondering what had happened to him. Was her father sick? This wasn't like him at all.

"If he comes," she told the doorman, "please ring for me right away."

Rory didn't come the following week, either. By the time he missed the third pay envelope, she was deeply worried. She left the children with their cleaning lady and rode the subway to his apartment on the Lower East Side to look for him. Fiona hadn't returned to the neighborhood since before Leonard was born more than two years ago, but the narrow, crowded streets and ramshackle buildings looked unchanged. She saw the same filth and despair, the same hopeless stares on the immigrants' faces. Gratitude flooded through her at having escaped from this life.

She found the building where Rory lived and climbed the steep stairs to his apartment. A woman opened the door a crack when Fiona knocked, peering out at her suspiciously. She had a red-faced baby in her arms, and Fiona saw a ragged toddler clinging to her skirts. They could have been Fiona's children. She whispered a prayer of thanks that Leonard and Eleanor were well-fed and warm and safe.

"I'm looking for Mr. Quinn—Rory Quinn. Is he here?"

The woman spoke very little English, but she finally made Fiona understand that he didn't live there anymore; the landlord had rented the apartment to her family two weeks ago. Fiona knocked on several neighboring doors, shouting, at times to try to make herself understood, but no one seemed to know Rory Quinn or what had become of him. Fiona practically ran the two blocks to Cousin Darby's apartment, her fear for her father barely contained. Thankfully, Darby still lived in the same squalid rooms.

"Fiona, come in, come in. I've been hoping you would—"

"I'm looking for my father. Do you know where he is?" Cousin Darby's expression changed. He looked so somber that she immediately felt alarmed. "What's wrong, Darby? Did something happen? Just tell me!"

He rested his hand on her shoulder. "I didn't know how to reach you, lass. I didn't know where you were living." He paused, unable to speak. "I'm sorry, Fiona. Your father has passed away."

Her heart lurched. It couldn't be true. She didn't want to believe that Rory was dead, but she saw the truth of it in Darby's eyes. She felt as if all the blood had suddenly drained from her body.

"How?" she whispered.

" 'Twas an accident at work. There was a loading crane—" He stopped. "Sit down, girl. You look as pale as a ghost. I'll get you some water." He ladled a cupful from a bucket, but Fiona's hands trembled so badly she could barely lift the cup to her lips. She was too shocked to weep. She knew that would come later.

"Perhaps it's best if you don't know all the details," Darby said gently. "But it was quick—he didn't suffer, thank the Lord. I went through his apartment, and I have all his things if you want them. There wasn't much."

"Keep them," she said. "Or give them to a family who needs them." She drew a deep breath to compose herself. "Dad was saving money so my mother and sisters could come over. Did you find any of it?"

"Nay, there was no money." Darby turned to rummage through a burlap sack that was lying with several others in a corner of the room, and he pulled out Rory's well-worn wallet. He opened it to show her a couple of dollars. "This was all he had on him. He must have been sending the rest home week by week." He handed her the wallet. She stared at it, unable to comprehend what she saw.

"Are . . . are you sure this is all there was?"

"I'm sorry, Fiona."

What had happened to all the money that she'd given Rory over the years? Had someone stolen it? Had he spent it all on himself? Maybe Darby was right and Rory had been sending it home all along. Whatever the truth was, she realized that Mam and the girls were her responsibility now—along with Leonard and Eleanor.

"I don't understand why he never sent for them, Darby. There should have been enough money by now. Dad and I came to America more than four years ago. I've been giving him money all along. I don't understand why the others never came over."

"Neither do I. Your father didn't confide in me, lass."

Grief began to well up inside Fiona on the way back to her apartment. She sat on the swaying subway car, remembering the closeness she'd shared with her father onboard the ship, the rush of excitement they'd felt each time they'd gotten away with yet another theft. He had chosen Arthur for her mark that night at the theater; she never would have looked twice at him, thinking him too old. If not for Rory, she would have missed meeting Arthur and having two beautiful children.

She wished now that she hadn't argued with her father that last time. She wished she had gone downstairs to meet him in the lobby once in a while instead of refusing to see him, instead of coldly leaving an envelope of money for him with the doorman. She could have gone for a walk in the park with him and let Leonard and little Eleanor meet their grandfather. Now it was too late.

Why had he never sent for Mam and the girls? Fiona couldn't understand it. But she would make it up to them, somehow. She would find out how much it cost for nine tickets to America. She would begin looking for a place where they could live. She couldn't ask Arthur to support them, but maybe he could help the older girls find jobs as maids or nannies with one of his wealthy friends. Or maybe they could work for her.

Fiona wept as she composed a letter to her mother, telling her about Rory's death. She promised Mam that she would send nine tickets for her and the girls as soon as she was able. She gave Mam her apartment address and begged her to write back soon. Then Fiona waited, watching for the mail every day.

A month passed and no reply came. She wrote again, worried that her letter had become lost in the mail. She sent another letter, and another, but it was as if they were sinking to the bottom of the vast ocean that stood between New York and Ireland. Desperate, Fiona sent a letter to her sister Sheila in care of Wickham Hall. Again, there was no reply. Finally, Fiona wrote to the parish priest at St. Brigid's church. His reply came nearly four months after Rory's death.

Dear Miss Quinn,

I am sorry to say that your mother and sisters are no longer living in this parish. Things went hard for your family after your father abandoned them, and a typhus epidemic took your mother and the three youngest girls. The two oldest girls have married and have homes of their own now. Your three remaining sisters had to be sent to the convent since no one was able to care for them. God willing, the nuns have found places for them by now.

I am sorry to be the bearer of such sad news, but I hope you'll find comfort in the love and will of our Lord and Savior.

Their father had *abandoned* his family? Fiona read the letter over and over, unable to grasp it. Rory had *never* contacted them after leaving Ireland? He'd sent no money at all to support them? Fiona couldn't believe it. The priest must be mistaken. He must have confused Fiona's family with a different one. She had given Rory money every week for four years, first from her job at the hat shop, then from the allowance Arthur gave her. Had someone stolen it from the mail before it reached Ireland?

Whether it was true or not that Rory had abandoned his family, one fact remained: They were gone. Fiona had lost all of them. Her mother and father and three sisters were dead and her remaining siblings scattered. Meanwhile she had lived in luxury. God would surely punish Fiona for her sins.

Leonard and Eleanor were the only family she had in the world. And if Arthur ever abandoned them, they would be as destitute as Mam and the girls had been. He'd been promising to marry Fiona for years, and she'd never doubted him, believing that they would be a family some day. But Fiona had finally understood the truth after Eleanor had been born. Rory had been right; Arthur would never marry her. And if she continued to pressure him, he might get angry and leave. She would lose everything she had.

"We've made a mess of things, Fiona," her father had once told her. *"A blooming mess of things."*

Yes, Fiona thought. *Yes, we have.*

Chapter 29

NEW YORK CITY — 1929

Fiona first noticed a change in Arthur in the fall of 1929. He seemed increasingly preoccupied whenever he came to visit her, and his visits became sporadic and infrequent. He no longer took Fiona dancing or to the speakeasies, seeming to want nothing more than an hour of comfort in her arms, and then he was gone again. She also noticed that he drank a great deal more than ever before. She wondered if he was growing tired of her now that she was twenty-seven years old, or if Arthur had decided to make some changes in his life at the age of fifty-one.

Fiona had long feared the day when Arthur would stop loving her, and she'd tried to prepare for it. She had shopped conservatively for the past five years, saving every extra dollar in a hatbox on a shelf in her bedroom closet. She had learned to drive an automobile and often borrowed Arthur's Cadillac to save money on cab fare, using the spare set of keys he'd given her. Eleanor was only five years old, too young to leave alone, too young for school—what would happen to her if Fiona had to find a job? She had to keep Arthur interested in her for at least one more year.

By late October, Arthur had become so distracted, his behavior so erratic, that Fiona began to feel desperate. She dug into the savings in her hatbox and splurged on a new hairdo and a flashy new dress. But Arthur went straight to the bar the moment he came through her door.

"Don't you love me anymore?" she asked as she watched him fill a tumbler with scotch.

He looked up at her in astonishment. "What. . . ?"

"Something's wrong, Arthur, I know it is. You haven't been yourself for weeks—and you're losing weight, I can see it. Are you . . . are you ill?" He lifted the glass and took a large swallow before answering.

"I'm fine, Fiona. If I've been . . . distant . . . it has nothing to do with you."

She waited until he took another swallow, then she crossed the room and drew him into her arms, resting her head against his chest. "Can't you tell me what's wrong, darling? Maybe I could help."

He gave a humorless laugh. "No one can help me, Fiona. I'm living a nightmare."

"Does it have something to do with finances? They've had articles about the stock trade in all the newspapers, but I don't really understand them." Arthur took another gulp of scotch and set down the tumbler. He took Fiona's face in his hands, and his eyes met hers for the first time since he'd come in. She saw his love for her, but also his deep distress.

"You shouldn't have to worry about financial matters. They're not your concern—they're mine." He kissed her briefly, then pulled free of her arms to pace the living room floor, sipping more scotch as he talked. "The New York Stock Exchange had another day of panic selling today. The floor was in chaos. Shares in Union Cigar fell from one hundred dollars to four dollars a share in one day—and that's just one example. Other companies' stocks are falling by the dozens, too, and they can't repay the loans we've given them. Our investors purchased stocks on margin, and now they're losing their shirts—owing more than the stocks are worth. It's turning into a disaster. Our bank is bleeding to death, and I can't stop the hemorrhage."

Fiona saw his fear and it multiplied her own. "What's going to happen?" she asked in a hushed voice. He drained the last of his drink and poured another, his hands unsteady.

"I don't know. I just don't know."

"Is there anything I can do for you, Arthur?"

He gazed down at her, and his dark eyes had never looked more sorrowful. "I love you, Fiona. I—"

She waited for him to finish, but he didn't. "I love you, too," she finally said, moving into his arms again. He rested his cheek on her hair, and she heard him sigh. It seemed more a sigh of resignation than contentment.

"My car is parked downstairs," he said softly. "I think you should drive up to the Poconos, spend a week there. It's beautiful in the fall. There might still be some leaves left on the trees."

Fiona looked up at him to see if he was serious. "We can leave first thing tomorrow, if you'd like," she said. "I'll ask Mrs. Murphy to watch the children."

Arthur shook his head. "You go, darling. Just you and the children. I know you've been wanting to take them up to see the cabin and the lake."

"But I don't want to go without you. Besides, Leonard has school."

Arthur smiled sadly. "He's a bright boy. He can miss a day or two."

Fiona gripped him tighter. This was so unlike Arthur. She was worried sick. "I'm not going anywhere without you," she told him. "I'm going to stay right here so you'll always have a place to come and someone to love you when you're upset. I want to be with you to help you."

"I don't think anyone can help me," he murmured.

He left a little while later after finishing the bottle of scotch. His steps were unsteady as he walked to the elevator. He didn't come the next day or the next. Fiona listened to the news reports on the radio and bought newspapers every day, trying to understand what was happening in the financial world and how it might affect Arthur. On Tuesday, the stock market plummeted so drastically that the newsmen dubbed it Black Tuesday. Fiona felt frantic. She had no idea how to get in touch with him; he had always come to her.

As she walked Leonard to school a few days later, Fiona made up her mind to try to find Arthur. She'd met him for lunch once, and he'd shown her the building on Wall Street where he worked. As soon as she and Eleanor returned to the apartment lobby, she asked Charles to call a taxi for her. She was much too upset to try to drive Arthur's big Cadillac Phaeton in the busy downtown traffic.

"Where are we going, Mommy?" Eleanor asked as they climbed into the back of the cab.

"To visit your father. Maybe he'll take us to lunch. Wouldn't that be nice?" When Fiona gave the driver the Wall Street address, he turned all the way around in his seat to stare at her in surprise.

"Are you nuts, lady? It's a madhouse down there. Don't you listen to the news?"

"Of course I do. Take us as close as you can, please."

Traffic on Broadway ground to a halt, well north of Wall Street. Fiona paid the cabby his fare and climbed out, clinging tightly to Eleanor's hand as they walked the rest of the way to the office building where Arthur worked. Not only cars but thousands of pedestrians jammed the streets, bringing traffic to a standstill all over the financial district. The normally sedate streets were in chaos. Angry patrons mobbed the banks to try to retrieve their money. Police shouted in frustration as they tried to maintain some semblance of order. All of the men looked angry, worried, desperate. *Poor Arthur.*

Fiona felt battered by the time she reached the main doors of his office building. Eleanor looked frightened by all the shouting and shoving. But even if Fiona had wanted to go inside and look for Arthur, she wouldn't have been able to; a cordon of police blocked the doors. She would have to wait and watch for Arthur to come out. It would be lunchtime soon.

She stood on the steps and peered down the curving street as far as she could see. It resembled a canyon of brick and cement and glass, and she felt as though it might crumble down on top of her. All around her, the anger and confusion and chaos grew worse by the hour. She didn't know what to do.

"Mommy, my feet hurt. Can I sit down?" Eleanor asked after a while.

"No, darling. The steps are filthy. You'll get your lovely coat all dirty." And Fiona also feared that if the crowd suddenly rushed this bank building the way they were mobbing so many others, little Eleanor would be crushed in seconds.

"We'll wait just a few more minutes. Your father should be leaving for lunch soon, and we can eat with him. Won't that be fun?" But the longer she waited, the more certain Fiona became that Arthur was truly living a nightmare, just as he'd said. He wouldn't risk coming out into this angry crowd for lunch, nor would he want to see Fiona and Eleanor.

"Mommy I'm hungry," Eleanor whined, tugging Fiona's coat. "When are we going to eat?" Fiona looked at her watch—it was after one-thirty, and still there was no sign of Arthur.

"I'll buy you a candy bar. Would you like that?" She glanced into the building's lobby one last time, then made her way back through the throng to a newsstand she remembered passing on the corner. She heard the hawker shouting out the headlines as they approached.

"Extra! Extra! Read all about the chaos on Wall Street."

Fiona boosted Eleanor up so she could pick out a chocolate bar. She wondered why anyone would need to purchase a newspaper telling about the chaos on Wall Street when the newsstand itself stood right in the middle of it all.

"Extra! Another stock market suicide!" the hawker yelled.

Fiona set Eleanor down again after she'd made her choice and dug into her purse for change.

"That's Daddy," she heard Eleanor say.

"What, darling? Where?"

Eleanor pointed to the newspaper lying on top of a large stack beside her. Under the word *Suicide* was a picture of Arthur. Fiona felt her knees give way as if someone had kicked her feet out from under her. She collapsed onto the sidewalk.

The next thing she knew, she was lying on the cold cement, dizzy and nauseated. Eleanor stood over her, crying loudly. Fiona could hear car horns honking in the distance and people shouting. Her head hurt from striking it on the pavement. A uniformed patrolman bent over her.

"Ma'am? Ma'am, are you all right?"

"I-I don't know." She couldn't remember what had happened.

"Everybody stand back," someone shouted. "Give the lady some air. Come on, stand back."

"Shall I call a cab or an ambulance?" the patrolman asked.

"A cab. I have to go home. Leonard will be home from school soon." And she must make herself pretty in case Arthur . . .

"Read all about it," the newsboy shouted nearby. "Another stock market suicide."

Fiona let out a sob. It couldn't be true. She sat up and snatched a paper from the top of the stack. She saw Arthur's picture again, prominently displayed. Then Eleanor blocked him from sight as she fell into Fiona's arms, weeping with fear. "Mommy . . . mommy!"

"It's all right, darling. Everything is going to be all right," she soothed. But it was a lie. The world had just come to an end, and she didn't know what to do.

The patrolman helped her up, then walked her down to the corner and hailed a cab for her. She felt grubby and disheveled and stunned. She'd torn her stockings on the rough pavement, and her coat was dirty, one sleeve ripped. She glimpsed her reflection in the taxi's window and realized that she had blood on her forehead. Her hands trembled as she pulled a handkerchief from her purse and tried to wipe off the blood.

The doorman rushed out to help Fiona when he saw her struggling out of the cab. "Are you okay, ma'am? What happened?"

"She fell down," Eleanor told him. "Mommy fell down."

"Here, let me help you," Charles said. Fiona leaned against him gratefully as he led her into the building and up the elevator, and then he helped her unlock her apartment door. "Are you okay?" he asked again. "Shall I call a doctor?"

She shook her head. What she wanted was for Charles to hold her tightly and tell her that the newspaper had made a mistake; it was the wrong photograph, the wrong person. But Charles hurried back downstairs to tend his door as soon as she was inside.

Arthur is dead, she told herself over and over, struggling to believe it. *Arthur is dead.* She couldn't stop trembling. She had a good supply of alcohol that Arthur kept in the apartment and she was tempted to start drinking it, numbing herself so she wouldn't feel grief or pain or fear. But she had to remain strong for her children. She couldn't fall apart. She had to think what to do.

She still gripped the crumpled newspaper in one hand, and she finally summoned the courage to open it and look at it again. Maybe she had misunderstood. Maybe Arthur's photo was on the front page for another reason.

She only needed to read the first line of the article to learn the truth: *Investment banker Arthur Bartlett died last night in his Wall Street office in an apparent suicide, the latest in a series of suicides following the stock market crash earlier this week . . .* She dropped the paper onto the floor.

Fiona's first reaction was fear. She had two children to support, and Arthur was dead. He hadn't abandoned her for another woman, as she'd long feared, but had taken his own life. What would happen to her and the children? How would they live? Had he left any provision at all for them in his will? But no, he couldn't have—Arthur had gone bankrupt. The fact that Fiona had ruined her own life by becoming involved with a married man was bad enough. But she had ruined her children's lives, too. Arthur was dead. How would she live without him? How could she?

In an instant her fear vanished, swallowed by grief. Arthur would never walk through the door again, never take her into his arms, smiling his lopsided smile. She would never see his love for her reflected in his sad, dark eyes; never sit on the cabin porch with him in Deer Falls counting the stars; never lie beside him at night.

Fiona wept and wept. Eleanor climbed onto her lap looking bewildered and afraid. "Don't cry, Mommy," she said over and over. "Don't cry." They were both weeping when Leonard came home from school.

"What's wrong?" he asked in alarm. Fiona saw the fear in his eyes as he gazed at her disheveled clothing and bloodied forehead. "Are you hurt,

Mommy?" He was only seven years old, too young to be her strength and support, but she saw his willingness to try, and it touched her.

"I'm all right, Leonard. It's just a scratch. Come here." She reached to pull him close to her, and all three of them huddled together on the couch as she told him the truth. "Your father died, darling. Do you understand what that means?" He shook his head. Fiona wasn't sure she understood it, either. She didn't want to understand. But in telling her children, the painful reality gripped her heart at last.

"It means . . . it means that he'll never come back to us. We'll never see him again. He's gone . . . forever."

"Can we find a new daddy?" Eleanor asked in a shaky voice. Fiona couldn't reply. She hugged her children closer, weeping until all her tears were gone.

She slept on the couch that first night, knowing she would never find rest in the bed they'd once shared. She didn't change out of her clothes, unable to go into the closet where Arthur's spare shirts were hanging. When she opened the medicine cabinet above the bathroom sink to get headache powders the next morning, she saw the razor and toothbrush Arthur kept in the apartment, and his favorite tooth powder. She began to tremble, not with grief but with anger.

Death hadn't taken him—he'd embraced it himself. He was a coward. The newspapers said that a lot of men had lost everything they had, yet only a few had resorted to suicide. She still would have loved him even if all his money was gone, but he hadn't given Fiona that choice. He'd ruined her life by never making an honest woman of her, and now he'd ruined their children's lives with the terrible legacies of bankruptcy and suicide. Arthur had abandoned them, just as Rory had abandoned Fiona's mother and sisters. What would they do now?

Fiona could barely function as her emotions spiraled downward in an endless cycle of anger and fear and grief. *How could you leave us, Arthur? How could you?* she asked over and over. Charles voiced his sorrow every time Fiona went in or out—which wasn't often. "I'm just so sorry about

Mr. Bartlett, ma'am. He was a decent man." She didn't know how to respond.

When Mrs. Murphy arrived on cleaning day, she had tears in her eyes. "I read in the papers about Mr. Bartlett, ma'am. I'm so sorry. He was always very kind to me." Fiona stared at her woodenly, her arms tightly crossed to keep Mrs. Murphy from embracing her. Fiona knew she would lose the slender grip on her composure if anyone hugged her.

"I can't pay you, Mrs. Murphy," she said coldly. "You may as well go home."

"But . . . I need this job. I don't know how I'll find work—"

"And I don't know how the children and I are going to live!" she shouted. Mrs. Murphy was immediately contrite.

"I'm sorry, ma'am. I'm . . . I'm so sorry."

Fiona looked away. "I know. And I'm sorry for yelling." Neither of them knew what else to say.

"Well . . . good-bye, then," Mrs. Murphy said. She bent to embrace Eleanor, who was waiting for a hug. "Good luck to you." She quietly closed the door behind her.

Fiona lived in a haze for a month, somehow managing to send Leonard to school each morning, fixing haphazard meals for the children, eating very little herself. She knew she couldn't succumb to grief forever; she would have to let it go soon and decide how she would make a living for herself and the children. But she couldn't seem to muster the energy or the courage to move on.

Then the landlord knocked on her door on a cold, gray day near the end of November. "I'm very sorry about Mr. Bartlett, ma'am. I read about him in the paper."

Fiona nodded mutely. Everybody had read about it. Everybody in the world, it seemed, knew that her children's father, the man she loved, had put a gun to his head and killed himself after going bankrupt. The landlord exhaled and looked down at the floor, as if what he was about to say was very difficult.

"I'm sorry to trouble you at a time like this, ma'am . . . but I'll be needing the rent payment on the first of December. I let last month's rent go by because your—because Mr. Bartlett paid me the first and last months in advance. But December's is due, you see. I wouldn't bother you if I could help it. Mr. Bartlett was a real good man."

"Can you give me a week?" she asked hoarsely.

"Sure, sure. But then you have to pay me or . . . or move out, okay? Please don't make me throw you out in the street. I'd really hate to do that to you, with the children and all."

"Come back in a week," she said, closing the door.

Chapter
30

Fiona counted the money in her hatbox and realized that it would disappear in six months if she used it to pay the rent. She gathered up all the jewelry Arthur had given her over the years and stuffed it into her purse, remembering a pawnshop she'd passed on one of their trips to the park. But as soon as she rounded the corner, holding Eleanor's hand, she saw long lines of desperate, well-to-do customers overflowing the pawnshop doors and spilling out into the street. She pushed closer and heard the owner shouting, "That's all I can give you! It doesn't matter what it's worth, there aren't any buyers!" Fiona clutched her purse tightly and walked home again, wondering where she could go, what she should do.

Her last hours with Arthur had played endlessly in her mind for the past few weeks like a well-worn phonograph record: how he'd paced the floor, sipping scotch; how he'd rested his cheek against her hair as they'd held on to each other; how he'd gazed at her with sorrowful eyes and said, *"I love you, Fiona."* But as she walked home from the pawnshop, feeling distraught, she recalled what else he had said—and how unlike Arthur it had seemed at the time: *"My car is parked downstairs. I think you should drive up to the Poconos. . . . Just you and the children."*

Did he know, then, what he would do? Had he deliberately reminded her of a secluded place where she and the children could find refuge? Fiona suddenly decided to drive to Deer Falls—if for no other reason than that Arthur had wanted her to go. She made sandwiches and threw some clothes into a suitcase for each of them, along with the children's favorite books and toys. As soon as Leonard arrived home from school, she bundled everyone into the car.

By the time they reached Arthur's cabin in Deer Falls, they were all exhausted. Fiona had never driven that far in her life, and her arms ached from wrestling with the huge car's steering wheel. Eleanor, who was used to the city's bright lights, was terrified of the murky woods. Neither child had ever been out of the city before, and both were much too frightened to go near the frigid lake. Neither of them wanted to use the outhouse.

"I want to go home," Eleanor bawled. Fiona rocked her in her arms, too tired to explain that "home" wouldn't be theirs much longer.

"So do I, darling," she murmured. But where was home? They couldn't stay here. The cabin was too small for the three of them and too rustic to live in for very long. What would they do when her money ran out?

Fiona built a fire, feeding it with wood Leonard hauled from the stack outside. But in spite of their hard work, the cabin still felt cold and damp. They ate their sandwiches by lantern light. The cabin had only one bed, so they all huddled in it together that night. The children finally slept, but Fiona didn't.

For a long time she replayed all the memories of her visits here with Arthur, remembering how safe and contented she'd felt as she lay in the bed beside him, listening to the forest sounds outside. But the reality of her current predicament kept crowding out those memories, along with the conviction that God was finally punishing her for her sins. *Punish me, then,* she prayed, *not my children.*

"I want to go home, Mommy," Eleanor wept as soon as she awoke. Fiona packed the car to return to New York. But foremost in her mind was the thought that only a few days remained until they would be evicted from their apartment.

She drove slowly through the town of Deer Falls, remembering how peaceful and quaint it had seemed when she'd visited here with Arthur. If only she and the children could settle in a place like this, a place where they could be anonymous, where her past would be forgotten. Halfway down Main Street, Fiona noticed a vacant shop with a *For Rent* sign hanging in the window. On impulse, she pulled the Cadillac to a halt beside the curb in front of it. The apartment on the second floor had a *For Rent* sign in it, as well.

"Why are we stopping here, Mommy?" Leonard asked. "Who lives here?"

"Nobody darling," she said. "We're just going to take a peek inside, all right?"

The children followed hesitantly as she got out of the car and pressed her forehead to the glass, peering into the store's front window. An idea was already starting to form in Fiona's mind. She could make this store into a hat shop using the money she had saved. Maybe she could sell thread and notions and dry goods, too.

She led the children around to the back of the building, and they climbed a set of wooden stairs to a small porch on the second floor. The apartment looked uninhabited, so Fiona peered inside those windows, too. She glimpsed a small kitchen and several other rooms beyond.

"How would you like to live here?" she asked, turning to Eleanor and Leonard.

"I want to live in our own apartment," Eleanor said, pouting. "Can we go home now?"

"I have to go to school," Leonard added. His eyes were as wide and sad as Arthur's had been but a much lighter shade of brown.

"Listen, my darlings," she began, crouching beside them. "We can't stay in our apartment anymore. Your father is dead, and—" Grief choked off her words. It was a moment before she could finish. "And we have to find another place to live." They gazed up at her, their eyes mirroring her own sorrow. She knew they didn't mourn for their father—he'd been a stranger to them—but they instinctively felt her sadness, and perhaps some of her fear.

"I think this would be a really grand place for us to live," she said. "Let's just go and see how much it costs, okay? Maybe it's all a pipe dream after all."

The *For Rent* sign listed the name of a local real estate agency where she could get more information. Fiona loaded the kids into the car again and drove the few short blocks to the address. Inside, an older woman with graying hair sat behind a counter talking to a portly man with shiny, black hair and a dapper three-piece suit. He appeared to be younger than Arthur by at least ten years, olive-skinned, foreign-looking. Fiona had seen a lot of immigrants when she lived on the Lower East Side, and she guessed that he might be Italian. He looked up when Fiona entered, and she saw his eyes travel over her from head to toe as if undressing her in his mind. The smile he gave her when he reached her face again made her uneasy.

"May I help you?" the woman asked.

"I'm interested in the shop and apartment for lease on Main Street. Could you please tell me what the monthly rent might be?"

"I'd be glad to help you," the man said. He stepped forward, extending his hand. "Lorenzo Messina. I happen to own the place." He held on to Fiona's hand a moment longer than necessary. Her uneasiness grew.

"My name is Fiona—" She started to say Quinn, then changed her mind. "Bartlett. Fiona Bartlett. These are my children, Leonard and Eleanor."

"Just three of you will be renting?" He was a handsome man in spite of the extra weight he carried on his medium frame. She could tell by his swaggering self-confidence that he was probably used to having women swoon over his good looks.

"Yes, just the three of us. I'm a widow. My husband, Arthur, passed away recently."

"Sorry to hear that, Mrs. Bartlett. Come on, I can show you around the place—you'll probably want to have a look inside before you decide."

He rested his hand on her back to guide her out, and she shivered involuntarily, missing Arthur's warm, loving touch.

"Well, perhaps you should tell me how much you're asking first, so I don't waste your time, Mr. Messina."

"Don't you worry about that just yet," he said with a grin. "Let's take a look-see, okay? I'm willing to negotiate."

"All right . . . Thank you." She tried to push aside her growing unease as she followed his car back to Main Street, telling herself it was just her own inexperience with men that made her uncomfortable, along with the rawness of her grief.

Mr. Messina unlocked the front door and took Fiona on a tour through the store. As soon as she saw the place, she immediately began planning how she could make it into a hat shop. There was an oak counter and glass-fronted cases where she could display her designs, and a small work area in the rear where she could view the front door while she cut and sewed her creations.

"What kind of a shop are you thinking of starting?" he asked as she looked around.

"A millinery shop—I make hats." She saw a peculiar expression cross his face before he disguised it behind one of his dazzling smiles.

"Good for you. Deer Falls doesn't have one of those. You'll have a corner on the market."

He was being polite and pleasant to her, but something about him seemed wrong. He acted too citified for a small town like Deer Falls, his clothing and air of sophistication out of place here. "Have you lived in Deer Falls all your life, Mr. Messina?" she asked.

"Oh, I don't live here year 'round," he said, laughing. "I have several business interests here, and a vacation place I come to. You were lucky to catch me in the office today. Most of my business enterprises are based in Philadelphia. Where are you from?"

"Manhattan . . . well, Ireland originally."

"I thought so from your accent. You have a nice voice. Come on, I'll show you upstairs." He led her up a back staircase to the apartment. It was much smaller than Fiona's apartment in New York—the children would have to share a bedroom—but it had electricity and modern plumbing and plenty of light streaming through the tall, second-story windows. Fiona was certain that she could make it cozy and pleasant for the three of them.

"How much?" she asked, dreading his answer. The price he named was so cheap that she wondered if there were strings attached.

"You look surprised," he said when she didn't respond.

"I guess I'm used to city prices, Mr. Messina."

"Please, call me Lorenzo. Do we have a deal, Mrs. Bartlett . . . Fiona?"

She scrambled to think things through. She had enough money in her hatbox for almost a year's rent—but they would have to live on that money, too, until the shop began to earn a profit. And she would have to buy equipment and supplies. But this opportunity offered her a brand-new start, a way to support her family and, hopefully, a chance to redeem her mistakes.

"Yes, thank you," she said, extending her hand to shake his. "We have a deal." Once again, he held it a moment longer than he needed to.

"Good," he said with a broad grin. "Would you have dinner with me tonight?" She tried to disguise her surprise—and disgust. Lorenzo Messina wore a wedding ring on his stout, left-hand finger. And like Arthur, he'd managed to completely ignore her two children the entire time.

"I'm still in mourning, Mr. Messina. My husband died only a month ago."

"I'm sorry. Another time, then. We'll celebrate your grand opening." He made it a statement, not a question. "Come back to the office, okay? And you can sign the lease."

Fiona made more plans as she drove back to New York that afternoon. She would move all of their furnishings to Deer Falls, hoping it would help the children adjust to their new life sooner if they were surrounded by familiar things from home. Besides, she knew before asking that she'd get next to nothing for Arthur's furniture from a pawnbroker.

"The children and I have to move away, " she told Charles. "Do you happen to know anyone with a truck who might be willing to transport my furnishings for a reasonable price?"

"I think I might, ma'am—though I'll be sorry to see you and the kids leave. Let me talk to my friend and I'll get back to you."

Fiona drove Arthur's huge car to the garment district where Madame Deveau's hat shop had been. With so many businesses closing, she was able to buy a few of the things she would need to start her own business, such as a millinery steamer and a sewing machine and several balsa-wood head blocks. She also bought a dressmaker's measuring tape, a millinery ruler and French curve, dressmaker's chalk, pattern paper, and millinery ribbon.

Fiona moved into the apartment in Deer Falls without fanfare three days later, resigned to live in genteel poverty. She had cried along with Leonard and Eleanor when they left their Manhattan apartment, walking through the empty, echoing rooms one last time. How could she miss Arthur so desperately yet hate him so fiercely for deserting them? To take her mind off him, she immediately set to work sorting through the clutter of boxes and furniture in their new apartment, trying to make a home for all of them. The children moped and whined for days. Every time they climbed the wooden stairs to the second floor, they talked about the elevator "back home" and their friend Charles. They begged to go back. Exhausted and grieving, Fiona finally lost her temper.

"We can't go back!" she shouted. "This is our home now, and the sooner you get used to it the better off you'll be! I wish that nothing had ever changed, too, but we can't always have what we want in life!"

Eleanor and Leonard stared up at her tearfully, stunned that she had yelled at them. Fiona immediately regretted her outburst. She saw glimpses of Arthur in their features and mannerisms, and the pain of losing him suddenly felt so immense she didn't know how she would ever go on. She dropped to her knees and pulled her children into her arms, crying with them.

"It's okay," she assured them. "We're going to be okay." She wished she could believe it.

When Fiona finally dried her tears, she determined never to shed another one. The fastest way to move forward was never to look back. On Monday she enrolled Leonard in the local school. To anyone who asked, she was Mrs. Arthur Bartlett, recently widowed. Fiona worked night and day, harder than she'd worked when she and her father first arrived in America nine years ago. Downstairs in the hat shop, she functioned as the designer, laborer, and saleswoman all rolled into one. And when the workday ended and she went upstairs, she worked as cook, laundress, and housemaid, besides mothering her children. When the housework was finished and the children in bed, Fiona stayed up late every night making more hats. They couldn't afford to buy a lot of clothes, but what they had would always be good quality. They would never be wealthy again, but Fiona wanted Eleanor and Leonard to be accepted as middle class, not as impoverished immigrants.

The store didn't celebrate the grand opening that Lorenzo Messina had talked about. Fiona simply placed the finished hats in the display cases and store windows one December morning and turned the sign that hung on the door around to the *Open* side. She had fashioned boater-style hats made of straw braid and trimmed with veiling; berets made of red satin, plain linen, and silk; turbans made of velvet and crepe de Chine silk; brocade pillbox hats trimmed with pearls; and cloches made of brocades and tweeds. The townspeople paraded past the shop all week, gazing in the windows. A few came inside and studied the price tags. No one bought a hat. Fiona tried not to sink into despair.

Two days before Christmas, Fiona heard the bell on the door jangle and looked up to see Lorenzo Messina strut into the shop. She abandoned the hat she was steaming and hurried to the front of the shop to wait on him. "Good morning, Mr. Messina. May I help you with something?" He wore a broad smile on his handsome face as he gazed around.

"Well! This is quite a shop you have here, Mrs. Bartlett."

"Thank you." He took another moment to stroll around inspecting the hats then walked over to her, standing uncomfortably close. She could smell the aroma of cigars on his overcoat.

"How long have you been open now?"

"About two weeks."

"Good, good. . . . And how's business?"

Emotion suddenly choked Fiona's throat, and it was a moment before she could reply. "I-I haven't sold anything yet."

His smile faded to a look of sympathy, and he draped his arm around her shoulder. "Don't be discouraged, Fiona. It just so happens that I'm here to do a little Christmas shopping. I'd be honored to be your first customer."

"Thank you. What can I show you, Mr. Messina?" She wriggled free and gestured to the display case.

"Now, stop right there," he said, planting his hand on her shoulder again. "I told you to call me Lorenzo, remember?" She nodded and tried to return his smile, wishing there was a way to escape his grip. "I need to buy . . . let's see . . . eight hats, altogether. I have a very big family—lots of aunts and sisters and cousins." She noticed that he hadn't mentioned his wife.

"Do you know their hat sizes?"

"No, I can't say that I do," he said, laughing. "How do you tell something like that?"

"Well . . . usually I would measure their heads—front to back, ear to ear, and around the top. I don't suppose they could come in to be measured, could they?"

"That would spoil the Christmas surprise. Why don't you just pick out eight of your best ones for me, okay? If they don't fit, I'll just have to come back and exchange them sometime."

"Yes, of course." She chose her best designs and carefully wrapped them in tissue paper for him—commercial hatboxes were too expensive for her to hand out. She battled ridiculous tears as Lorenzo paid the asking price and added a generous tip. He must have noticed.

"Don't be discouraged, Fiona. Business in Deer Falls is always slow in the wintertime. Just you wait, though. This place will be swinging, come summertime. You won't be able to keep up."

But those were the only hats Fiona sold all winter. In the spring, one of Deer Falls' wealthiest matrons bought a new Easter bonnet from Fiona's shop, and three more ladies quickly followed suit in an attempt to outdo her. After that brief spurt of sales, however, business was nonexistent. It was the same all over the country. The newspapers called it the worst economic slump in United States history, and they printed photographs of shantytowns and of out-of-work men waiting in long lines for a bowl of soup. Too late, Fiona realized that she never should have squandered her money on a hat shop. Hats were a luxury that most women abandoned in hard times. She needed to find another way to support her family—but with millions of men out of work, how could she ever expect to find a job?

Fiona had just added up her remaining money one morning in April, trying to calculate how much longer it would last, when Lorenzo Messina strode into her shop.

"Fiona!" he said with a broad grin. "How's business?"

She drew a deep breath to steady herself. "Not so good. I-I think I may have to close—"

"Baloney! I'm here on a buying spree, as a matter of fact. Your hats were very popular with the ladies in my family. They're asking for Easter bonnets now."

"That's great—you may take your pick," she said, gesturing to the shelves. "But . . . but could we discuss the rent when you're finished? I'm wondering if my children and I could continue renting the apartment without the shop—and what that rent would be."

"Fiona . . . Fiona," he said, his expression sad. "It hurts me to see you so discouraged. Let me treat you to dinner tonight, and we can talk everything through, okay?"

"I'm a widow—" she began, but he cut her off.

"This isn't a date! It's a business meeting, okay? Now, wrap up eight more hats for me, and I'll pick them up when I come for you at seven-thirty." He turned toward the door, not giving her a choice.

"Lorenzo, wait! I can't leave my children—"

"I'll send over my assistant from the real estate office to watch them. You know Isabel Watson, don't you? And dress up, Fiona. I'm taking you to Sanderson's for steaks. Ever been there?" She nodded. She and Arthur had often eaten there when they'd visited Deer Falls. "Good. See you at seven-thirty."

Fiona tried to convince herself that Lorenzo was simply being kind, that he'd invited her out to discuss business, as he'd said. But a wiser part of her whispered the truth of what he really wanted. She didn't know what to do. Her money would soon run out. She had no way to make a living, and she had two children to support. As Fiona tucked them into bed that night, leaving them with a sitter for the first time since Arthur had died, she vowed to do whatever she had to for their sakes.

Business was also very slow at Sanderson's Steak House that night. She and Lorenzo were the only customers. Even so, the owner seated them at a cozy table for two in a secluded corner. Determined to discuss business, Fiona brought up the topic as soon as they'd placed their orders.

"I don't know how much longer I can stay in business, Lorenzo. The newspapers say we're in an economic depression. I've sold a grand total of four hats, not counting your orders, and I don't think very many ladies will be buying them in the months to come."

"How about if I went into partnership with you? The ladies in my family loved your hats. I'll bet you could sell them by the dozens down in Philadelphia."

"Thank you, but I really don't want to move again. My children have finally adjusted to Deer Falls, and—"

"Who said anything about moving? You keep making your pretty little hats right here in Deer Falls, and I'll use my contacts down in Philly to sell them. What do you say?"

Fiona knew without asking that there would be a price to pay for such a favor. She longed to flee from this man and run home to her children, but how would they live? She was at his mercy—and they both knew it.

The waiter appeared with their soup course, sparing her from responding to his offer. Surprisingly, the waiter also produced a contraband bottle of red wine. She saw Lorenzo slip the man a few dollars, then he took the opened bottle from him and filled their glasses himself.

"I wouldn't want the fella to get into trouble on account of us," he said with a wink.

The interruption allowed Fiona to avoid Lorenzo's proposition. As soon as he'd finished pouring and had offered a brief toast, she asked her own question, instead. "What I'd really like to know is how much would you charge me to rent only the apartment?" She was fingering the stem of her wineglass, and he leaned forward, reaching across the table to cover her hand with his plump one.

"Nothing."

"Lorenzo, please—"

"I can see that you're a woman of wealth and privilege who has fallen on hard times, and I'd hate to see you reduced to poverty. I'd like to help support you and your children. Allow them to continue with a measure of the luxuries you're all accustomed to."

Her stomach made a slow, sickening turn. "And in return. . . ?"

"I want nothing more than your companionship. The pleasure of your company—and perhaps your affection—whenever I'm in town. You're a very desirable woman—"

"I'm still in mourning for my husband," she said angrily. She tried to pull her hand free but his grip tightened.

"Let's not pretend, Fiona—or is it Evelyn? I could have sworn that Arthur Bartlett's wife was named Evelyn . . . or am I mistaken? And wasn't his son named Russell, his daughter, Ruth?" Fiona closed her eyes in shame. Lorenzo finally released her hand.

"If you already knew the truth about me," she said when she was able to speak, "why did you play all of these games?"

"In my line of business, the only way to survive is by being ruthless. I guess I've been a thug for such a long time that I sometimes forget my manners. But you are a beautiful, charming woman in distress, Fiona, and I really would like to help you."

"I loved Arthur," she said in a trembling voice, "in spite of what you must think of me."

"I believe you. And I know I can't expect you to fall in love with a crude hoodlum like me. But I hope you'll at least give my offer consideration. I really can sell your hats down in Philadelphia—as fast as you can make them."

"And in return. . . ?" she asked again, brushing away a tear. This was surely God's punishment for becoming Arthur's mistress.

"Have dinner with me from time to time when I'm visiting from the city. I'd love for you to come out and see my summer place, too. It has a beautiful view of the lake."

"Won't your wife mind?" she asked bitterly.

"She overlooks my faults. I'm a very wealthy man, Fiona. My investments weren't in stocks or . . . how shall I say . . . legitimate businesses. There are certain things people will always want, even in an economic depression. Liquor, for example. Prohibition has caused hardships for some people but golden opportunities for others."

Once again the waiter interrupted, bringing their salad course. Fiona had a moment to compose herself and her thoughts. She hated the idea of what Lorenzo was proposing, and even though it might be the only way she could support her family, she made up her mind to resist as long as she possibly could.

"Thank you for your kind offer, Lorenzo. But I think I'll try to keep my shop open for a few more months. Who knows, maybe trade will pick up during the summer. If not . . . I might be willing to discuss your offer again in the fall."

His smile was cold. "If that's what you want, Fiona."

For the next few months she did whatever she could to economize, but sales during the summer months were still very slow. Fiona wished she could pray. She often walked past the quaint, white clapboard church a few blocks from her shop and wished she could go inside. She remembered the beauty and serenity of St. Brigid's church, how light and clean she felt after confessing. She longed for the peace of knowing that her sins were forgiven. But even if she could bring herself to confess everything to the parish priest, she was certain that God would never forgive her for living with a married man and having two illegitimate children.

It was too late for her to turn to God—but maybe it wasn't too late for her children. Maybe, in spite of her own mistakes, she could still raise Leonard and Eleanor to know right from wrong. As fall approached and it seemed inevitable that she would have to accept Lorenzo's help, she took her children to see the parish priest. Father Joseph was young—probably no older than she was—and he had a kind face.

"My late husband would have wanted our children to attend Mass and be raised in the church," she told him.

"What about you, Mrs. Bartlett?"

She couldn't meet his gaze. "Please don't ask questions that I can't answer," she said softly. "Leonard is eight years old—may I bring him to catechism classes this fall? And Eleanor, too, when she's old enough?"

"Of course, Mrs. Bartlett. We'd be pleased to have them. . . . And you, too, if you change your mind," he added softly.

Fiona shook her head.

Part
7

KATHLEEN AND JOELLE

2004

Chapter
31

B y the time Uncle Leonard finished telling his story, he seemed exhausted. He looked every one of his eighty-two years.

"Do you remember much about your father?" Kathleen asked him gently. "You must have been . . . what . . . seven years old when he died?"

"All of my memories of him are sketchy. My father would say hello to me or ask me about school, but I might have been a stranger—not his son—someone he needed to make polite conversation with. He would give me only a moment of his attention, a few spare words of praise; then his focus always returned to my mother. It was very obvious that he adored her, and he squandered any tenderness he possessed on her. He never offered Eleanor or me any physical affection, never took us onto his lap or carried us in his arms. I don't ever recall kissing him. He would converse with us for a minute or two, then he'd send us to our rooms so he and Mother could be alone." Leonard gazed into the distance for a long moment, and his face looked gray and lifeless in the dim light.

"Sometimes I would sneak into the hallway," he continued, "and peek out at them if they stayed in the living room. I'd see them on the couch together or mixing drinks at the bar or kissing. Once my father caught me spying, and he was so furious with me that I never did it again.

"Some weekends he would take Mother dancing, and he'd hire a baby-sitter to stay with us. I remember waking up one night just after they'd returned home, and they sounded so happy, laughing like two children and dancing in their stockinged feet to phonograph music. I wished I could go into the living room and dance along with them. I realized when I was older that they had probably been drinking." He drew a deep breath and let it out with a long sigh.

"What I remember most about my father is that he loved my mother and barely tolerated Eleanor and me. Fiona was the prize he sought in the box of cereal; we were just so many cornflakes that had to be dug through in order to reach that prize."

"I'm so sorry, Uncle Leonard," Kathleen murmured. It was little wonder that he'd never wanted children of his own, or that he'd never shown affection to her and the others as they were growing up. She knew that he and Connie had moved into this house to take care of Kathleen's siblings after her mother died, and she realized for the first time how challenging that must have been for both of them. Poke had been fourteen years old at the time, JT had been twelve, and Annie, ten. If Leonard and Connie hadn't offered to help, the kids would have ended up in foster care.

"Here, Kathleen. You should have this," Connie said, hefting the cardboard box filled with photo albums and other mementos.

"No, I can't take it. . . . What about Annie and the boys?"

"You're the oldest. I'll leave it up to you to divide it all up if you want to, but it should stay in the family. You can sort through it better than I can, for goodness' sake. Besides, I already made albums for Annie and the boys over the years, with pictures and clippings about their sports events and graduations and so on."

"She's the sentimental one," Leonard said with a faint smile. "You should see the way she cuts up the newspaper. Looks like Swiss cheese when she's finished with it. Of course, most of the capitalistic swill that sells for 'news' isn't worth reading in the first place."

"I still save everything," Connie admitted. "Only now I'm usually cutting out articles about one of their children. Although I did cut out an article about your brother just the other day."

Kathleen cringed, remembering how Mrs. Hayworth had also mentioned reading a newspaper article. "Which one of my brothers? What did he do now?" she asked, although she wasn't sure she wanted to know the truth.

"Well, this latest one was about Donald—nobody calls him Poke anymore. But JT has been written up a couple of times, too."

"I can well imagine," Kathleen mumbled. She watched with dread as Connie rummaged around on the overflowing end table beside her recliner, searching for the clipping. Kathleen had warned Joelle what her uncles had been like as children, but it still embarrassed her to have her daughter see more recent proof of their crimes.

"Here it is!" Connie sang, waving the clipping like a flag. She presented it to Kathleen; Joelle leaned close to read it along with her. It said *Riverside Chamber of Commerce Elects New President.*

Kathleen stared at the headline for a long moment, unable to comprehend the words, certain that Connie had given her the wrong article. Kathleen fished her reading glasses out of her purse so she could read the small print.

> Local businessman Donald L. Gallagher, 50, has been named President of the Riverside Chamber of Commerce, a spokesman announced. Gallagher, a lifelong resident of the village, is the owner of Gallagher's TV and Appliances, Sales and Service, a well-known sales and repair emporium. . . .

There was more, but Kathleen burst out laughing and couldn't continue. She handed the article to Joelle, and a moment later she was laughing out loud, too.

"What's so funny?" Uncle Leonard asked.

"It's so ironic!" she managed to sputter. "Don't you remember how awful our TV set was when Poke and I were growing up? And now he *repairs* televisions?"

"Well . . . I suppose so. But I still don't see—"

"And when I left home, Poke and JT were full-fledged juvenile delinquents, banished from every store in the Riverside Chamber of Commerce. I thought for sure that Poke would be in jail by now. But this is much worse! Uncle Leonard, he's a *capitalist!*"

Kathleen started laughing all over again. Suddenly she felt Uncle Leonard begin to tremble, and for a horrible moment she feared that she had offended him, that he was about to suffer a stroke or a coronary. Instead he let out a bark of laughter—the first Kathleen ever remembered hearing from him—as he joined her and Joelle.

"Why are you all laughing at poor Donald?" Connie asked. She pulled the newspaper article out of Joelle's limp hands as if she was sorry she had ever produced it. "I'll have you know he's every bit as respected as JT is."

"I'm sorry . . ." Kathleen sniffed as she tried to regain control. "Um . . . what is JT doing these days?"

"He's a history teacher at Riverside High School," Connie said with obvious pride.

Once again, Kathleen dissolved into laughter.

"He was named Teacher of the Year in 2002," Connie added, raising her voice to be heard. "Well, for goodness' sake. I just don't see why that's so funny."

Kathleen pulled out a tissue and wiped her eyes. "Maybe you don't know it, Connie, but JT once held the village record as the youngest student ever to be suspended from school. He was in kindergarten!"

Connie smiled uncertainly. "Well, he's changed since then, for goodness' sake. We're real proud of him now."

"You have every right to be," Kathleen said, meaning it. "Transforming my brothers into respectable citizens should qualify you and Uncle Leonard for sainthood."

Kathleen could see how exhausted her uncle was, and a few minutes later they said good-bye. Joelle stuffed the carton Connie had given them into the backseat, and they headed back to their hotel in Bensenville. The road was hilly and very dark, the trees forming an archway that blocked out the moon. Kathleen had to use her high beams and stay alert for deer. She was thinking about all the times that Eleanor and Cynthia must have traveled this route by bus during the war when Joelle interrupted her thoughts.

"Mom, what Grandma Fiona did . . . how she lived . . . Was that really unforgivable? I mean, I know she went to a different church than we do, but wouldn't God have forgiven her if she'd asked? Even though she did it more than once?"

"Yes, of course He would have. We're not supposed to misuse God's grace by sinning deliberately, but if we're really sorry for what we've done, and if we ask for forgiveness . . ." She trailed off, wondering if Joelle was asking about Fiona or herself. Her mother's intuition suddenly told Kathleen that the incident at the mall last month hadn't been the first time that Joelle had shoplifted—only the first time that she'd been caught.

"I feel so sorry for Grandma Fiona," Joelle said with a sniff, and Kathleen heard the tears in her voice.

"I do, too," she murmured. "But you know . . . I just remembered something else that happened that one time I met Grandma Fiona during the Cuban missile crisis." She gazed down the darkened road for a long moment, as the memory crystallized.

"Grandma Fiona was looking for another record to put on the phonograph, and I suddenly said, 'I know a song. Want to hear it?' At home, I never shared any of the songs we sang in Sunday School—nobody wanted to hear them anyway. But Fiona seemed to love music so much, and . . . and she looked up at me and said, 'Yes, darling. I would love to hear it.' And so I sang 'Jesus Loves Me' to her.

"She listened intently, and when I finished she asked, 'Did they teach you that in church?' I nodded. 'Do you go to Mass, then?' she asked hopefully. I told her that I went to a Protestant church. 'That's fine, too,' she said, and she forgot all about putting another record on the phonograph as she sat down beside me again and pulled me close.

"'I used to go to church when I was a little girl in Ireland. And I used to look up at the crucifix and believe just what you sang—that Jesus loved me. I could see how much He did. Go ahead, sing it again, dearie.'

"I sang the second verse: 'Jesus loves me, He who died, Heaven's gate to open wide. He will wash away my sin and let each child of His come in. Yes, Jesus loves me . . .'

"'It's easy to say those words: *I love you*,' Fiona told me when I'd finished. 'I've heard them many times, and you will, too, because you're a pretty girl, Kathleen. But do you know how you can tell if someone is telling the truth?' I shrugged and shook my head. 'Never listen to his words, dearie. Words are cheap. Nay, look at what he's willing to give up for you. Make him show you how much he loves you.'

"'Jesus loves you this much,' I told her, stretching out my hands the way Jesus had on the cross. 'He died for us.'

"She stared into the distance as if searching her memory. 'When I was a girl in Ireland they had a crucifix in the front of the church. Every time I went to Mass, I always had to look up at Jesus dying in agony. He was always nailed up there, suffering. I hated to think that He had suffered for me.' She seemed so sad that I wanted to cheer her up.

"'I know a Bible verse. Want to hear it? "God so loved the world—" Wait, we're supposed to put our name in there. *"God so loved Grandma Fiona that He gave His only begotten Son, that whosoever believeth in Him should not perish, but have everlasting life."* '

"'And you believe that?' she asked. Her eyes were watery, but I couldn't tell if it was from tears or her age.

"'The minister said that even if you were the only person who needed to be forgiven, Jesus still would have died for you.'

"'Sing your song again, dearie,' she said in a hushed voice. And I started all over again: 'Jesus loves me . . .' but I had to stop by the end of the first chorus. Grandma had tears running down her face. 'Don't cry, Grandma Fiona,' I begged. She hugged me tightly. Her body felt frail, her skin as soft as flannel, but she hugged me with surprising strength.

"'You'll know love is real,' she told me, 'by what someone is willing to sacrifice for you.'"

Kathleen drove in silence for a few moments, the road a blur through her tears.

"Do you think Grandma Fiona believed you?" Joelle asked softly. "Do you think she asked God to forgive her before she died?"

"I would like to think so. No one should ever have to live with such guilt when Christ's forgiveness and love are available."

Joelle carried the cardboard storage carton into their room when they reached the hotel and set it on the dresser. "When are we going to meet your father?" she asked as she flopped down on her bed.

"He'll be arriving home tomorrow."

"Arriving *home*? Where is he?"

Kathleen hesitated—too long. Joelle sat up. "What's wrong? Where is he? In jail again?"

"I don't know how to tell you this," Kathleen began. In many ways Joelle was still very unworldly. Kathleen hated to be the one to shatter her innocence—especially with the horrible truth about her own family.

"How to tell me *what*?" Joelle said impatiently. "What's the big mystery?"

"My father is being paroled from prison up in Attica. That's what this party is for. It's to celebrate his parole."

She saw surprise and shock in Joelle's eyes, and something else—pity. Kathleen hated pity most of all. It never failed to make her feel ashamed. And she dreaded the next question Joelle would ask even more.

"What did he do? Rob a bank or something?"

Kathleen tried to draw a deep breath and couldn't. "No. He was convicted of . . . of murdering my mother thirty-five years ago."

"No . . ." she said in a tiny voice. "Oh, Mom!" Joelle's eyes filled with tears, and she rushed into Kathleen's arms for a rare hug. It wasn't offered in pity, but in empathy and love. She was feeling all of the emotions that Kathleen felt and reaching out to her.

"Mom . . . Mom . . . I'm so sorry."

Kathleen was crying, too. "Sorry for what, honey? It's not your fault."

"For talking you into coming here, for making you dredge all this up." She paused, and her arms tightened around Kathleen. "And for . . . for stealing the lipstick. I didn't know, Mom. I didn't know how awful that would be for you."

"I never wanted you to know how terrible my childhood was. I hid the truth from everyone. I was so afraid no one could love me or respect me if they knew. One of the worst moments in my life was when I decided to tell your father the truth before we were married."

"But he loved you anyway, Mom—and so do I."

Kathleen hugged Joelle again. Dr. Russo had been right; by holding back the truth from her daughter she had withheld part of herself, seeming cold and distant to Joelle. It was the same mistake her own mother had made, never sharing the truth about how difficult her life had been. Maybe it would have helped Kathleen understand her own mother better if she had known.

Suddenly Joelle pulled free. "Wait a minute! Why is your sister throwing a party for him if he *killed* your mother? And why is Uncle Leonard going? Isn't he her brother?"

"You have to understand that my father always claimed he was innocent. Annie and Uncle Leonard and the boys always believed that Daddy was telling the truth, even after he was convicted and sentenced."

"But you think he did it? Is that why you never wanted to come back here?"

Kathleen sank down on the bed, rubbing her eyes. "To tell you the truth, I walked away so I wouldn't have to think about it. I felt so confused and betrayed. I never wanted to believe that my father had killed her, but I had no choice, especially after a jury found him guilty. I felt like I was being disloyal to my mother if I believed him. And I felt ashamed of myself because my last words to her had been angry ones. I never had a chance to tell her I was sorry. Or that I loved her. I always thought that there would be time to reconcile, and that she'd always be here. After she died I realized that I could never go back and make it right—and it was the most terrible feeling in the world. It seemed like I should hate my father for killing her and robbing me of that second chance. I had to blame someone."

Joelle sank down on the bed across from her. Kathleen could tell that she was still trying to absorb the shocking truth. "I've never met a real-live criminal before," she murmured.

"Well, he's not a mobster like Lorenzo Messina," Kathleen said, trying to lighten the tension. "But you can stay here at the hotel tomorrow, if you want. I'm only going to stay at the party for an hour or so. I'll make my peace with him and all the others; then you and I can go home and get on with our lives."

"Are you scared—you know—to be with him? I mean, what if he really is a murderer?"

The word "murderer" conjured up images in Kathleen's mind of all the criminals she'd seen portrayed in movies: tough, bitter men with knives in their boots and tattoos on their arms, spewing curses, ready to slit someone's throat. It shocked her to realize that her father had been a convicted murderer in Attica prison for thirty-five years. But then the images dissolved, and Kathleen thought of her father as she'd known him: laughing, happy-go-lucky, lifting her up in his freckled arms, playing with her and the boys. She couldn't recall him losing his temper or spanking them—even when they deserved it, even when he'd been drinking. And he'd always treated Eleanor with tenderness and love.

No, she couldn't imagine Donald Gallagher as a cold-blooded killer. And that's what had always made the murder too horrible to contemplate: to think she had known him, and to find out that she hadn't.

Joelle was waiting for an answer.

"No. I'm not afraid of him," Kathleen said.

"Then I'm not, either. I'll go with you, Mom. . . . But we'd better hide all the knives, just in case—right?"

Kathleen laughed and cried at the same time. Joelle was trying so hard to make it easier for her, to let her know that they were in this together, and that touched Kathleen. She pulled Joelle into her arms.

"Yeah. We'll make sure Uncle Leonard cuts the cake."

Being the night owl that she was, Joelle seemed hours away from falling asleep. She flipped on the TV, then started sifting through the items in the cardboard box. For once Kathleen felt wide awake, as well, and she sat down in the hotel chair with Fiona's album to take a closer look. She found several pictures of Arthur Bartlett, and it solved a life-long mystery for Kathleen as she stared at his wide, dark eyes. They were her own eyes, as warm as pools of melting chocolate, even in a black-and-white photograph. Her mother and Uncle Leonard had hazel eyes, her father, sparkling blue ones. She'd wondered as she'd studied genetics in college where her own dark brown ones had come from. Kathleen's husband had often told her that he'd fallen in love with her because of her eyes—not just the color but the sad expression in them. And here they were on Arthur Bartlett, of all people.

She couldn't help holding him in contempt for seducing her eighteen-year-old grandmother, then lying to Fiona all those years with promises of marriage. He'd been a selfish man, wanting both Fiona and his high-society life. And he'd been a coward, abandoning them all by committing suicide.

Kathleen dug deeper into the carton and found a scrapbook filled with mementos from her mother's high school years. There were pictures of Eleanor in a bathing suit, posing on the beach with her girlfriends, and a picture of Leonard in a graduation gown and several of him in his army uniform. And there were all the usual program bills from school plays and concerts and dances. Eleanor had lived an active social life in high school and had been both pretty and popular.

Kathleen paged through the book, viewing Eleanor's life as she would a stranger's. Then, tucked in the back of the scrapbook, Kathleen found a collection of yellowed newspaper articles. She carefully unfolded and skimmed through them—advertisements and critical reviews for several Broadway shows in New York City. The reviews were from 1939 and 1940. At first Kathleen couldn't understand why her grandmother had kept them. Then she read them more carefully and found one common element: the name Russell Bartlett. Arthur Bartlett's legitimate son had once produced and directed Broadway shows and plays in New York City.

"Mom, look!" Joelle said, interrupting Kathleen's reading.

"What did you find?"

"This manila envelope is full of newspaper clippings about your father's murder trial."

Kathleen grimaced. Part of her wanted to throw the entire contents into the trash. She knew none of the lurid details of her mother's death, and she wanted to keep it that way. But if she was going to face her father tomorrow for the first time in thirty-five years, perhaps it was time that she learned the truth. Joelle seemed to notice her hesitation.

"If you don't want me to read them, I won't," she said, holding out the envelope to Kathleen. "But aren't you curious, Mom?"

"Yeah, I guess I am. We'll read them together." She climbed onto the bed with Joelle and pulled out the envelope's contents. Connie had been very meticulous, numbering the articles chronologically from the time the murder was first reported until the judge handed down her father's sentence. Read in order, they told Kathleen the entire story:

Riverside's town constable had responded to an anonymous phone call and found Eleanor Gallagher lying dead on her kitchen floor. Her husband, Donald, was found with her, holding her in his arms, weeping, covered with her blood. Someone had stabbed Eleanor in the heart with her own kitchen knife. It had happened less than a half hour before the constable's arrival. The crime lab found Donald's fingerprints on the murder weapon—put there, he claimed, when he'd instinctively yanked it from her body.

State police searched the house and found a packet of love letters from another man in her purse, written during the war. With them was a marriage license issued in 1943 to Eleanor and the same man. Her purse also contained an envelope with three thousand dollars in cash, two unused train tickets to New York City, and two tickets to an off-Broadway play.

The prosecuting attorney alleged that Donald Gallagher's motive had been jealousy; that he'd been upset to learn about Eleanor's first marriage.

The cash and unused tickets pointed to the possibility that Eleanor either planned to leave her husband or was having an elicit love affair. Donald Gallagher had a prison record for theft and was a convicted con-artist. He had no alibi for the time of his wife's death.

Reading the facts, Kathleen understood how a jury would interpret the evidence and condemn her father. He had opportunity and seemed to have a motive. But it didn't fit with what Kathleen knew about her father. He might have been a thief, but he wasn't a murderer. He never even lost his temper.

Nor could she picture her mother leaving him for another man. Eleanor didn't have enough self-esteem—or energy—to have an affair. She couldn't even care for her own children, much less run off with another man. Donald had been her life. That's why she kept welcoming him back each time he got paroled.

So why had she saved the letters from Rick all those years? And why would she take the train to New York to see a play when she barely had the strength to get dressed in the morning or leave the house? And most mysterious of all, where had the three thousand dollars come from?

"Let's go to bed," she told Joelle. "I'm too tired to think. We can sort through all this another time."

But Kathleen didn't sleep. She tossed in bed, watching the numerals on the digital clock change, thinking about her mother. She rose and opened the blinds a crack so she could see Joelle's face better in the moon-light, and she thought about how much she resembled beautiful, tragic Fiona Quinn. Kathleen still couldn't sleep. She finally went into the bath-room and turned on the light to reread all of the newspaper articles, trying to figure everything out. Nothing made sense.

In the morning, her eyes felt swollen and bleary. She ordered breakfast from room service, even though a bagel, juice, and coffee cost nine dollars. Kathleen let Joelle sleep as long as she wanted, but she was awake well before they needed to leave for the party.

Kathleen felt numb as they drove from Bensenville to Riverside. As soon as the car pulled to a halt in front of their old house, Annie hurried outside to greet her. "Kathy, Kathy!" she wept. "I'm so glad you decided to come! Oh, it's so good to see you!" Kathleen looked at her sister's tear-stained face and smiled. At forty-six she was a pretty, plumpish woman with fair hair and a round, cheerful face.

"You look the same as I remember, Annie—tears and all. You always were a crybaby." They laughed and hugged again. Kathleen introduced her to Joelle, who had also climbed from the car.

"Hi, Aunt Annie," she said shyly. Annie hurried around the car to hug her, too.

Kathleen recognized JT, who had ambled out to the front porch, as soon as she saw him. He was as thin and wiry as he'd always been, with the same mischievous grin and dark, spiky hair that never stayed in place. He and Poke had tormented her endlessly when they were growing up, but she felt an uncharacteristic burst of love for him as they hugged for the first time that she could ever recall.

"How are you, JT? It's been much too long!"

"Good. I'm good. It has been a long time, hasn't it?" He cleared his throat. "Who'd you bring with you?"

"This is my daughter, Joelle."

"Well, come on in," JT said, holding the door open, "and meet the rest of the gang."

Kathleen met Annie's husband and Poke and JT's wives and all of their children for the very first time. With all the excitement and laughter, she couldn't even begin to remember everyone's name. Joelle made fast friends with two of her cousins, and they quickly lured her away from the adults. Kathleen could only hope that they weren't as mischievous as their fathers had been.

"Stay away from trains," she called as the screen door slammed behind them. JT laughed out loud. "Where's Poke?" Kathleen asked, looking all around.

"He drove up to Attica to get Dad," JT said. "They should be here in a little while."

"And you'd better not call him Poke to his face unless you want a fat lip," Annie added.

Kathleen's initial nervousness began to fade as they sat around visiting, catching up on each others' lives. She learned that Annie worked as a pediatric nurse in the Bensenville Community Hospital, and her husband sold cars. JT's wife was a teacher at Riverside High School like JT, and Poke's wife worked as the office manager and bookkeeper for his TV and appliance business. Poke's oldest son, Ryan, was married and had a one-year-old daughter.

"So you all ended up getting a higher education," Kathleen said in amazement.

"Don't act so surprised." JT's wry grin reminded her painfully of their father's. "Did you think we weren't as smart as you are?"

"You were busy being hoodlums when I left home," she replied. "How on earth could you afford college?"

"Poke got drafted and wound up in Vietnam—did you know that?" Kathleen shook her head. "Anyway, the GI Bill paid for his education after he came home. Uncle Leonard and Aunt Connie helped Annie and me." JT glanced at their uncle, and Kathleen saw gratitude and love in his gaze.

Eventually Annie, Connie, and the other women retreated to the kitchen to finish all the food preparations. "Can I help?" Kathleen asked.

"No, you sit tight and visit, for goodness' sake," Connie insisted. "But I could use JT's help getting the barbecue grill going. I've got a beef brisket that's going to take a while." Annie's husband wandered off with JT, and Kathleen sat down on the sofa to visit with Uncle Leonard. Joelle returned with a can of soda and sat down beside them.

Kathleen struggled for words, wanting to tell her uncle how grateful she was for the way he'd raised Annie and the boys, taking on a daunting, thankless job—but she didn't know what to say or how to begin. Besides, he would probably act gruff and try to shrug off her compliments if she did.

"I've been thinking about Grandma Fiona all night," she said instead. "Thank you for sharing her story. How . . . how did she die?" She was a little afraid to ask, knowing what she did about Fiona's life and remembering how Arthur had died.

"She had a coronary," he replied. "I guess she'd been having angina pains for a few years before that, but she must have developed a blockage. She called the parish priest one morning and said, 'You'd better come over. I don't feel well.' By the time he arrived she was dead, still sitting on the sofa with the phone in her hand. The doctor said she'd had a massive heart attack and was probably gone in seconds."

"Did you say she called the *priest?*" Kathleen asked in surprise.

"Yes. I was surprised, too. I'd never known Mother to go to Mass—even though she made sure we went when we were children. Father Joe was the one who called me, and when I went up to Deer Falls, he told me that she had returned to church within the last few months—almost as if she'd known that her time wasn't long. He said she'd made her peace with God."

Kathleen covered her mouth to hold back her tears, but she couldn't stop them.

"What's wrong?" Leonard asked.

"Nothing . . . I'm just so glad she found forgiveness. I loved Grandma Fiona. I only met her once—but I loved her."

Leonard cleared his throat. He looked as if he might cry, too, and didn't want to. "I have the star sapphire ring my father gave her, if you want it. It's one of the only things of hers that I kept."

"I would love to have it," she whispered.

He cleared his throat again. "I'll go ask Connie what she did with it." Kathleen watched him struggle to his feet and maneuver his walker, but she didn't try to help him. He needed an excuse to hide his own emotion, and she gave it to him.

The ring was beautiful—set in a style from the 1920s with a perfect star sapphire stone. It was too small for Kathleen's ring finger so she handed it to Joelle. It fit her finger perfectly. She held out her slender hand to admire it.

"She should have it," Uncle Leonard said hoarsely. "It suits her."

"Thank you," Joelle murmured. "I'll always treasure it."

He nodded, and his mournful face came very close to a smile as he dropped onto the sofa again with a sigh.

"Uncle Leonard, tell me about my mother," Kathleen said. "You finished Grandma Fiona's story last night, but you never said why Mom left home and came here—and why she never went back to Deer Falls."

"I wasn't home when Eleanor moved away from Deer Falls. I'd joined the army after high school in 1940. I only know the parts of the story that she told me in her letters—and the parts that she was willing to talk about when I came back. There are things about Eleanor that we may never know. . . ."

Part

8

FIONA AND ELEANOR

1936 — 1941

Chapter

32

Leonard grimaced as he tried to squeeze one last drop of glue from the bottle. It was no use. The glue was finished and his eighth-grade history project wasn't. It was due tomorrow, and the stores were all closed on Sunday.

"Drat!" he said, tossing down the empty bottle. It was as close as he dared come to saying a bad word. If his mother heard him swear, she would wash out his mouth with soap and make him go to confession.

"There must be more glue around here someplace," he mumbled as he rummaged through their apartment. His mother had gone to pick up Eleanor from a friend's house and would be back soon, but Leonard didn't want to wait. He wanted to finish his project. Maybe his mother kept some glue downstairs in her hat shop.

Leonard thundered down the stairs with the grace of a newborn calf. His awkward legs seemed to be growing faster than he could adjust to them. He opened one drawer after another in her work desk, trying not to mess up the contents too much, but he didn't find any glue. He yanked open the last drawer, lifting out a wad of fabric scraps—then he froze. On the bottom of the drawer was a folded, yellowing newspaper with a photograph of a man he recognized—his father. Leonard sank onto a chair and unfolded the newspaper to read it.

The story stunned him. He'd known that his father had died seven years ago, but not that he had committed suicide. And not that he'd been a wealthy investment banker who'd lost everything in the stock market crash. Leonard read the article all the way through. There were things in it that didn't make any sense at all, but the man in the picture was definitely his father. Leonard recognized him, even though his father had never really lived in the apartment with them—not the way other fathers lived with their families. He seemed to visit for only a few hours during the week, and once in a while he'd stay overnight on a weekend.

Leonard forgot all about the glue as he read the article through a second time. Then he read all of the other articles on the front page. He never heard his mother and sister arrive home, and was oblivious to any sounds from upstairs until his mother called down to him.

"Leonard? Are you down there? You need to come up and clear your schoolwork off the table so we can eat supper." He didn't reply. He couldn't make sense of what he'd just read, let alone mesh it with what he'd thought had been true these past seven years.

"Leonard?" she called again. "What are you doing down there?"

"Reading!" he yelled angrily. "Reading a bunch of lies about my—" A sob choked off his words. He couldn't finish. He felt the shame of what his father had done as if it were his own action. He heard his mother's soft steps descending the stairs, and when he looked up at her, he felt inexplicably angry with her.

"What's wrong?" she asked when she saw him. He held up the newspaper, unable to speak. His mother crossed to the desk and yanked it from his hand. "You had no right! What did you think you were doing, snooping through my things?"

"Is it true? Did my father really put a gun to his head and kill himself?" Fiona exhaled. She closed her eyes and nodded.

"What about all the other things the newspaper said? Why is everything all wrong? It says that his wife's name is Evelyn. And that my name is Russell and Eleanor's name is . . . I don't remember, but it was wrong. And it said that we lived in Westchester, but we didn't. Is this really my father or isn't it?"

Fiona took a step backward and leaned against the cutting table, her eyes still closed, her head lowered. Leonard saw that she was crying and then realized that he was, too.

"Arthur Bartlett was really your father," she said after a long moment. "He committed suicide seven years ago. That's why we moved up here to Deer Falls. I wanted to give you and Eleanor a fresh start in a place where nobody knew us."

"And those other things . . . those wrong names . . . did the newspaper make a mistake?" He wished his mother would laugh and say yes, of course they'd gotten it all wrong. Learning that his father had killed himself had been horrifying enough.

But somehow Leonard knew that she wasn't going to say that. His father had never lived with them; he'd never acted like a real father in any sense. "Please don't lie to me," he begged when she didn't reply.

Fiona looked up at him, meeting his gaze. "I wasn't his wife," she said through her tears. "I was his mistress. I should have known better than to let him do that to me, but I didn't. I was eighteen years old, dirt poor, living in a stinking tenement, and working in a sweatshop. I wanted all of the fine things he offered me. Your father promised to marry me, and I was fool enough to believe him. I loved him. God help me, I still do."

"Mommy?" Eleanor called down the stairs. "Are we ever going to eat?"

"I never wanted you children to know about this," Fiona said, wiping her tears with her apron. "Please don't tell your sister." She handed the newspaper back to Leonard and left him sitting alone in the now darkened store, devastated.

After that terrible day, Leonard became aware of other things he'd never noticed before. It was as if his mother had finished reading a book of fairy tales to him and had closed the cover, dissolving the fantasy and plunging him into the real world where there were no happy endings. He noticed how differently the coal miners lived compared to the mine bosses. He saw the shantytowns along the railroad tracks housing destitute men, women, and children, while the summer cottages that belonged to wealthy Philadelphians and New Yorkers stood vacant most of the year. He became aware of how differently his teachers treated students from impoverished families. It shouldn't be that way! It wasn't fair!

The knowledge that a man like Arthur Bartlett was able to take advantage of a girl like Fiona Quinn, simply because he was wealthy and she was a poor immigrant, fueled in Leonard a deep hatred toward the rich and powerful, and a new empathy for the workingman and his struggles. His mother's story exemplified the way all rich men abused and misused the poor—and there was nothing the poor could do about it. They had no way to break free.

Reading the daily newspapers inflamed Leonard's sense of injury and his passion for justice. He started buying as many as three papers a day, spreading them out on the dining room table at night, growing angrier and angrier as he sat hunched over them, reading. In the early months of 1937, when the new United Auto Workers' Union staged a sit-down strike, closing a General Motors plant in Michigan, Leonard cheered. When the strike escalated into a riot, he wanted to hitchhike to Michigan and join in the struggle. He followed the news religiously for the next month as the strike spread to GM plants in other states and production stopped. In the end, management caved in to the workingmen's demands. Labor unions gained new power to represent the weak against the strong, and Leonard felt as though he had personally triumphed over men like his father. Three months later, ten people died at a Republic Steel rally in Chicago, and as the union movement gained momentum and strength, Leonard knew he had found his life's purpose. He could fight against injustice; he could help right society's wrongs.

He became interested in socialism, then in Communism and its promise to eliminate the class system and give power to society's poorest members. When he was a senior in high school he started reading Karl Marx. That was the year that Britain and France declared war on Germany, and

World War II began. And it was also the year he found his half-brother, Russell Bartlett.

It happened by accident. Leonard had been pouring through a stack of newspapers, reading everything he could about Joseph Stalin's Red Army marching into eastern Poland, when he stumbled upon the New York society pages. The name Bartlett at the top of a wedding announcement leapt out at him. He paused to read it more carefully and discovered that his father's wife, Evelyn, had remarried. That news didn't interest him much, but the announcement also mentioned her son, Russell Bartlett, who was a Broadway actor and director.

Leonard began carefully reading the entertainment pages after that, keeping track of any advertisement, review, or feature story that mentioned Russell Bartlett. He had collected a good-sized stack of articles when Eleanor stumbled upon them, hidden under his bed, while cleaning.

"What are all these, Leonard?" she asked, waving the dusty pile.

"Nothing. They're nothing. Give them here."

She laughed, as if amused by his anxiety. "Too late—I already read them. I never knew you were interested in the theater."

"Give them back, Eleanor. I'm not in the mood for your stupid games. Those are none of your business."

"Well, I think they are my business," she said, turning snippy. "I saw our name on all of them. That's why you cut them out, isn't it? This Bartlett guy is a relative of ours, isn't he?"

A trickle of fear ran down Leonard's neck. She was uncomfortably close to the truth—a truth their mother wanted kept hidden. Leonard didn't blame his mother for not telling Eleanor. He had been devastated by what he'd learned, and the knowledge had altered his feelings toward his mother irreparably.

"He's an uncle of ours on Father's side," Leonard lied. "I thought I might look him up if I ever went down to New York. Now, give them back to me."

"Here!" She tossed them in the air, and they fluttered to the floor like falling leaves. "It gripes my middle kidney the way *some* people don't even say *please!*"

Two days after graduating from high school, Leonard was sitting at the table reading the newspaper when his mother came upstairs from the store with an envelope in her hand.

"Here. Mr. Messina bought you this graduation card," she said, handing it to him. "He's downstairs if you want to come down and thank him."

Leonard mumbled a vague reply. He didn't even want to open the envelope, much less talk to that pompous man. The landlord had been a shadowy presence in his mother's life ever since they'd moved to Deer Falls, and Leonard had never trusted him. No one really knew what all his so-called businesses were or how he'd earned all his money. The fact that he was rich was reason enough for Leonard to hate him.

He left the unopened envelope lying on the table until he finished the article he'd been reading. When he finally ripped it open, and a fifty dollar bill fluttered out, he was furious. It seemed like a slap in the face for Messina to swagger into the store, doling out charity to his poor tenant's son. Leonard stuffed the money and the card back into the envelope and went downstairs, not to thank him but to give it back.

His mother sat at her worktable with a half-finished hat in front of her. Messina stood close to her—too close—wearing one of his expensive suits. His dark hair was slicked back and shiny with pomade. For some reason, Leonard halted halfway down the stairs, watching them. He saw their landlord cup his mother's face in his fleshy hand and bend to kiss her. It wasn't a chaste kiss on the cheek, but a long, possessive one, his greedy lips pressed against hers.

Leonard would have cried out, but he couldn't draw a breath. He couldn't even move. He watched helplessly as Messina gave his mother a parting caress and left the store.

When his strength finally returned, Leonard didn't know whether to go back upstairs or to confront his mother. He felt rage billowing inside him, needing release, so he descended the stairs and threw the envelope on the table in front of her.

"Here. I don't want this," he said bitterly. "You can give it back to him the next time you see him."

"What's wrong with you? What did Mr. Messina ever do to you that you would treat him so rudely?"

"He's the same as all the other wealthy pigs! They make themselves rich on the backs of the poor. What I want to know is why you're so nice to him?"

"These are hard times. If Mr. Messina didn't take my hats to Philadelphia to sell, we'd never be able to make ends meet."

"Yeah? And how much profit does he keep from all your hard work? He's using you, Mom. Don't try to tell me he's just being nice. Tell him to get lost."

"Sure, and then how would we live? You read the papers, you know there's an economic depression in this country."

"We're doing all right. You're making a living from the store."

"You think I can make a living and support two children selling hats in Deer Falls? Think about it, Leonard."

But he didn't want to think about it. He didn't want to add up all the things that she was telling him and the things he had seen. Helpless frustration welled up inside him, boiling over. "I saw him kiss you, Mom!" She looked startled for a moment, then embarrassed, then resigned.

"Aye," she said quietly. "And I kissed him in return."

"He's a married man! A fat, filthy pig! How could you have feelings for him?"

"I don't!" she said sharply. "I hate him as much as you do—maybe more."

"Oh, no . . ." Leonard groaned. He shook his head as if he could shake off the truth as he realized what his mother was saying. "Don't tell me . . . you're not . . ."

"I do it for you and Eleanor. It's the only way we can get by. I have no other choice."

"NO!" he shouted, covering his ears. "It isn't true!" She stood and pulled his hands away, gripping his wrists, forcing him to listen. She was angrier than Leonard had ever seen her, her beautiful face pale with fury.

"If you want to take up a cause, Leonard, why don't you fight for all the women who have no husbands to take care of them, women who have no way to support themselves or their children. Women who can only get low-paying jobs in sweatshops or as maids and waitresses, jobs that don't pay enough to support a family. Go ahead, get angry, Leonard—but get angry at a world that gives women like me no other choice but to let men like your father and Lorenzo Messina take advantage of us."

She released him and sank onto her chair again. Leonard shook with anger, his wrists red and aching from her grip. He felt as helpless as his mother did, and it enraged him.

"I'll go to work! I'll take care of you!" he said. Fiona reached for his clenched fist and cradled it in her hands, rubbing it to soothe him.

"My sweet Leonard. I know you would gladly take care of your sister and me. But you're only eighteen—and there are so many men out of work."

Leonard knew then what he had to do. The idea had been simmering in the back of his mind for days, but now he was certain.

"I'm going to enlist in the army," he said quietly. "I'll send you my pay every month."

"You can't enlist!" she said in horror. "Europe is at war. What if America gets involved in it, too?"

"I believe we will get involved. I think it's inevitable. But like you said, this is the only way I know to get by. I have no other choice."

She leaped to her feet and threw her arms around him, clinging to him as if she could hold him back.

"No . . . No, please don't do this. I couldn't bear to lose you, too."

"I'm sorry, Mother." He pried her arms away. "I can't stay around here, knowing that you're . . . I have to get away. Besides, it'll mean one less mouth for you to feed." He turned and raced up the stairs, taking them two at a time, eager to start packing before he changed his mind.

Eleanor took the news very hard and did her best to talk him out of it. Leonard had always felt close to his sister, protective of her, in spite of her indifference to the labor movement and all of his other causes. In many ways she was very sophisticated—dressing well, wearing makeup, and fixing her hair in the latest styles. She considered herself middle class or even a notch higher, unaware that they were, in fact, poor and forced to survive in a society that abused the poor. He felt sorry for her. Eleanor didn't know the truth about their father or Lorenzo Messina, either—and Leonard would die before he told her. Let her live in her fairy-tale world. The only regret he had in leaving was that he wouldn't be around to protect her from men like them.

"Listen, Eleanor," he said as he prepared to say good-bye. "And I want you to really hear me and not just shrug it off, okay?"

She nodded tearfully, gazing up at him from where she sat cross-legged on his bed.

"Every summer all the snobby rich boys come to town to stay at their families' cottages. You're a pretty girl, and they're going to fall for you—and I won't be here to look after you. Don't trust them, Eleanor. Don't listen to their lies. They'll promise you all kinds of things to get what they want and have their way with you, but none of it is true. You're just a summer fling to them. They'll go back to Philadelphia or New York or wherever and marry snobby rich wives and never give you a second thought."

"They're not all that way—"

"Yes!" he cut in. "Yes, they are! I don't care if you don't believe anything else I ever tell you, but believe this. Don't trust rich men! Stay away from them!"

She leaped up to hug him, and he felt her tears on his neck. "I'll miss you so much! Do you have to go?"

"Yeah," he sighed. "Yeah, I have to go."

Chapter

33

Nothing is the same, Eleanor thought. She sat high in her lifeguard's chair, scanning the nearly deserted beach. Ever since Pearl Harbor last December, everything had changed. She adjusted the angle of the umbrella that shielded her from the warm summer sun and glanced at her watch. Only one more hour to go.

The last six months of high school had gone by in a blur, with everyone focused on the war that America was now fighting. Every last boy in her graduating class had enlisted, as had most of the men in town between the ages of eighteen and thirty-five. And while Deer Falls was usually bursting with summer people this time of year, the beaches and cottages were nearly deserted. The town was always boring enough during the wintertime, but at least Eleanor had always had summer to look forward to—when there would be dances and parties and interesting new people to meet.

She had never forgotten Leonard's warning, though, and had quickly discovered that he'd been right. She'd learned these past two years not to trust the wealthy "summer boys" who blew into town with their fancy cars and smooth words. They were fun to dance with, fun to build bonfires with on the beach and join for an afternoon sail. But she knew better than to fall for one of them in a summertime romance. She had bigger plans in mind for her future. Her mother had always encouraged Eleanor to be independent, to get a good education, to be her own person—and that's exactly what she intended to do.

By the time Eleanor's shift as a lifeguard ended, there was no one left on the beach at all. Other years, she usually could count on a handsome guy or two to offer her a ride home. Instead, she would have to walk. She climbed down from her perch and turned the sign on her chair around to read: *No Lifeguard on Duty*. Then she went inside the beach house to change into street clothes and prepare for the mile walk home.

She hadn't hiked very far when a shiny black car glided to a halt beside her and someone called to her from the open window. It frightened her until she saw that it was Mr. Messina, her mother's landlord.

"Can I offer you a ride home, Eleanor?" he asked. "I'm headed that way."

"Sure. Thanks." She climbed into the passenger's seat, the leather upholstery hot beneath her thin summer shorts. She wondered how Mr. Messina could stand to wear a three-piece suit on a hot day like today.

"So, have you been out for a swim?" he asked casually.

"No, I don't get to swim—unless someone decides to drown," she said, laughing. "I'm the lifeguard."

"The lifeguard! I'm impressed!" he said with a grin. "That's a lot of responsibility for a young woman to take on."

"I'm eighteen. I graduated last month."

"No kidding? I remember the first time I saw you—you were just a little girl. But if you'll forgive an old man like me for noticing, you've turned into a very beautiful woman."

"Oh . . . well . . . t-thank you, Mr. Messina," she stammered. She felt herself blushing. A few of the "summer boys" had called her pretty, but no one had ever told her she was beautiful before—much less called her a woman. And Mr. Messina was a grown man, a city man who had surely seen a lot of women. She glanced at him to see if he was serious and saw nothing but admiration in his gaze. He was a very good-looking man, even if he was old and a little overweight.

"Hey, please don't call me Mr. Messina," he said, making a face. "It makes me feel old. You're an adult now. Call me Lorenzo, okay?"

She shrugged. "Okay." But she was too timid to try it out. She liked being called an adult, though.

"So what else are you doing this summer besides working at the beach?" he asked.

"Nothing. That's the problem. There's nothing to do around here now that all the men have gone off to war. It's almost as boring as in the wintertime."

"Do you like to sail?"

"Sure—but there aren't any 'summer boys' around to go sailing with, either."

"We'll have to see if we can do something about that."

Eleanor wondered what he meant, but she didn't have time to ask; they had reached her apartment. She gathered up her beach bag and opened the door.

"Thanks a million for the ride," she said. "Bye!" She didn't quite have the nerve to say "Lorenzo."

She was halfway home from work the following afternoon when Mr. Messina happened to drive by once again and offer her a ride. This time they got on the topic of food. "What's your favorite restaurant?" he asked her. She laughed.

"It's hard to have a favorite restaurant when I've never eaten in one."

"You're joking, right?"

"No," she said, laughing again. "We can't afford to eat at any restaurants in Deer Falls. And I've never been anyplace else. You can't count the diner, can you?"

"You have a beautiful laugh," he said, gazing at her. "I would tell jokes just to hear it again, if I knew any. But seriously, what about all your boyfriends—don't they take you out to nice places?"

"I don't have any boyfriends, L-Lorenzo." She said his name, just to see how it felt, and was embarrassed when it came out hesitantly. He didn't seem to notice. They pulled to a stop in front of the apartment again, but he touched her arm to stop her from climbing out.

"Wait, Eleanor. You don't mean to tell me that a beautiful, charming young woman such as yourself doesn't have any boyfriends? I refuse to believe it."

"It's true," she said, smiling as she leaned back against the car seat. "The boys from high school are all clumsy and boring. Their idea of a romantic date is to go to the movies and buy a milkshake afterward. And I know better than to get involved with the 'summer boys.'"

"Why is that?" He turned toward her, stretching his arm across the back of the seat, behind her head.

"My brother warned me about them before he joined the army—and he was right. They're all a bunch of spoiled rich boys who flirt and lie and tell me things to get their way, but they really look down on me. I'm just a local-yokel to them, a summer fling. Their families have 'old money' and they'll marry wives who have 'old money.' I hope I'll get to meet a real gentleman, someday—someone who'll take me to fancy restaurants and treat me like a grown-up instead a summer fling."

"I envy that man. He'll be lucky indeed."

On the third afternoon, Eleanor saw Lorenzo's car parked outside the beach house when she'd finished dressing after work. "I can't believe this is a coincidence," she said, laughing. "Are you trying to spoil me, Lorenzo? I'll forget how to walk."

"It isn't a coincidence today," he said. He looked like a movie star when he smiled. An older Clark Gable, in fact. "I waited for you on purpose because I wanted to ask you a question." She climbed in beside him, intrigued. Once again he turned to her, his arm stretched behind her head. "Would you have dinner with me tonight?"

"You're kidding, right?"

"I'm perfectly serious."

She felt her heart do a funny little flip as he studied her face, waiting for her answer. It was the same feeling she sometimes got when a good-looking 'summer boy' flirted with her. But Lorenzo was a grown man, a handsome man—and he found her attractive.

"I . . . um . . . Listen, I didn't say what I said yesterday about never eating in a restaurant so that you'd feel sorry for me and—"

"I don't feel sorry for you at all."

"W-why are you asking me, then?"

He laughed and somehow moved a little closer to her. He smelled good—like cigars. "Because I've eaten in restaurants so many times they've lost their novelty . . . their charm. But if I take you, I'll get to experience all the freshness of it through your eyes. It will be like the first time for me, too. So . . . will you have dinner with me tonight, Eleanor?"

"I . . . I'll ask my mother—"

"Of course. And I'm sure Fiona will approve. But I have to say, I'm a little surprised that a young woman of your wisdom and maturity is still required to ask permission to eat with an old friend."

"I'm not *required,* exactly—"

"Good. Then I'll leave it entirely up to you. But I hope you'll say yes." He started the engine and swung the car around for the drive home.

Eleanor's head spun. She wanted to go in the worst way, but something about the offer didn't seem quite right. She was pretty sure he was married, even though she'd never actually seen his wife. But Eleanor brushed the troubling feeling aside. Lorenzo was an old friend of the family. And he'd made her feel as though she was doing him a favor by accepting—and hurting his feelings by refusing such a generous offer.

"I would love to have dinner with you," she said as they pulled to a stop in front of her apartment.

"Good. I'll pick you up at seven-thirty. We'll go to Sanderson's for steaks."

Eleanor didn't tell her mother. It seemed as though all the magic would fade away from this special evening if she had to explain that the landlord was treating her to dinner because she'd told him she was bored this summer and that she'd never eaten in a restaurant before.

And the evening was magical. Lorenzo treated her to a leisurely six-course meal by candlelight, with soft music playing in the background and a fairy-tale view of the shimmering lake from the restaurant window. But it was more than her first taste of restaurant food that made the evening so memorable. It was the mannerly way Lorenzo treated her, making her feel like a woman for the first time in her life. And the way he looked at her, making her feel all fluttery inside.

"Let's do this again . . . soon," he said when he brought her home close to midnight.

"It can't be too soon," she laughed. "I won't be hungry again for at least a week."

"You make me wish I was young again, Eleanor. In fact, being with you makes me feel young. Thank you so much." He lifted her hand to his lips and kissed her fingers. "Good night."

Eleanor walked on air all week, even when she had to walk home from work. Lorenzo only happened to be passing her way twice, and the second time he asked her which afternoon she had off.

"I'm off this Thursday—why?"

"Would you go sailing with me?" He looked so eager, so hopeful, she couldn't refuse. She didn't want to refuse. She told her mother that she was going to the lake with friends—which was true enough. Lorenzo spent the entire afternoon with her on his magnificent sailboat. All they did was swim and sunbathe and talk, but he was so attentive, asking her hundreds of questions and listening with genuine interest to everything she had to say, that by the time the day ended she felt as though she had gone on an exotic vacation.

Eleanor had lived in Deer Falls most of her life, but she'd never seen Lorenzo Messina's summer home before. It was at the end of a long, gated driveway, hidden within dozens of acres of woodland. He had his own private boat launch and dock, and a secluded beach. It seemed like paradise, right outside Deer Falls.

"Are you hungry?" he asked her as two servants ran outside to help him tie up the sailboat. "Of course you are. Come in, and I'll have my chef fix us something."

She agreed, curious to see what the inside of his magnificent home looked like. What she saw of it was dazzling. And the meal his servants served—by candlelight in the mansion's dining room—was even better than the dinner at Sanderson's had been.

Once again when Lorenzo dropped her off at the apartment, he thanked her. Then he leaned close, the scent of sun and sand and fresh air on his skin, and gently kissed her on the cheek. Eleanor barely felt the pavement beneath her feet as she stepped out of the car and watched him drive away. But when she turned to go inside, she saw her mother standing in the store window holding the blackout curtain in her hand, her face a mask of horror.

Eleanor had never felt more afraid. Fiona moved like a woman in a dream, opening the shop door to let Eleanor inside, the expression of shock and revulsion never leaving her face. She trembled from head to toe as she stood in Eleanor's path.

"What in heaven's name did you think you were doing! Where did you go with that man? What did he do to you?"

"N-nothing—"

"Don't lie to me!" She slapped Eleanor across the face. "I saw you together! I saw him kiss you!"

"I-it was nothing. It didn't mean anything." But Eleanor knew as she rubbed her stinging cheek that she was lying to her mother. She remembered the wonderful, giddy feeling she'd had all day when she'd been with Lorenzo on the boat. She wanted to be with him again tomorrow and the next day and the next. If her mother was upset about the age difference between them, then she'd have to make her understand that it didn't matter.

"Don't you ever go near him again, do you hear me?"

"Why not? Lorenzo respects me, Mom. He treats me like a grown-up, which is more than you or anyone else around here does. He's the only person in the world who listens to me." Fiona looked as though she might faint.

"No, Eleanor, no! He's not listening to you, he's trying to seduce you!"

"He is not! How can you say such a thing?"

"Because I know what kind of a man he is. I know exactly what he's trying to do. He'll flatter you and make you feel special and win your trust, and then . . . then—" A cry choked off her words.

"You don't know anything about Lorenzo. He's kind and sweet, and he laughs with me—"

"I know everything there is to know about him! I'm his *mistress*, Eleanor! That's how I've been able to support you all these years."

Eleanor went cold all over. "That's a lie!"

"It's the truth, God help me. I wish it wasn't. And now it seems he wants you for his mistress, as well. I'll never let him have you, Eleanor. If I have to lock you in your room to keep you away from him, I swear I'll do it!"

Eleanor pushed past her mother and ran up the stairs to the bathroom, slamming the door, locking it behind her. She was afraid she was going to be sick, that she'd throw up the wonderful dinner that Lorenzo's chef had prepared. She sat on the toilet seat in the darkened bathroom and sobbed. She didn't know which was worse—the thought of what Lorenzo Messina did to her mother or of what he'd nearly done to her.

After a long time, her mother knocked on the bathroom door, pleading with her. "Eleanor, please. Open the door."

She didn't answer, didn't move.

"Please, Eleanor." Fiona was crying, too. "Please forgive me. I did what I had to do." She begged for what seemed like hours, but Eleanor didn't reply. She couldn't face her. She was ashamed of her mother, ashamed of herself.

Eleanor knew that she would have to leave Deer Falls. She couldn't risk running into Lorenzo Messina ever again. And she could no longer face her mother, knowing what she was. As Eleanor huddled in the bathroom, waiting for dawn and the first bus out of town, she planned what she would do.

Her mother was sitting at the table, staring blindly into the distance, her beautiful face swollen and red, when Eleanor came out to tell her of her decision. "I'm leaving. You won't have to worry about me." She drew a breath to steady herself and to keep from crying. "I've decided to go to New York City. I'm going to look up some of my father's relatives, and—"

"What? You're doing *what*?"

"Leonard found one of our father's relatives, a man named Russell Bartlett. He directs plays on Broadway—"

"No. . . . no . . ." Fiona moaned. "Don't do it, Eleanor. Don't go there. They won't have anything to do with you."

"Of course they will. I must have aunts and uncles and cousins and grandparents on my father's side. They can't all be dead. Just because you didn't get along with them doesn't mean that I won't. I'll call every Bartlett in the phone book."

Fiona scrambled to her feet, gripping Eleanor's arms, shaking her. "Don't go to New York! You'll get hurt by those people!"

"Why? Why won't you tell me about my father? What happened to him? He isn't really dead, is he?"

"Yes he is, I swear. He died thirteen years ago."

"How did he die? I want the truth!"

Fiona looked as though she'd rather die herself than tell her, but she finally did. "He killed himself. He lost everything in the stock market, and he killed himself."

Eleanor swayed as she absorbed the shock. "Well . . . well, he must have had parents, sisters and brothers. Some sort of family. I'll look them up. I already know I have an uncle—Russell Bartlett."

"No . . . you don't! Please don't make me do this, Eleanor. Please don't make me tell you—"

"What? What are you hiding?" Fiona was so pale that Eleanor thought she might faint.

"He isn't your uncle, he's your half-brother."

"How? Was my father married once before?"

Fiona sank down on the chair and covered her face. "No . . . your father and I were . . . were never married. He was married to Russell's mother."

Eleanor groped for the edge of the table to steady herself. "What are you saying? That I'm . . . *illegitimate*? You were my father's mistress, too?"

Fiona didn't answer. She didn't have to. Her cries of grief and despair told Eleanor the answer. She walked away from her mother, hating her, and went to her room to pack. She locked the bedroom door behind her, but this time her mother didn't stand outside and beg.

Eleanor took all day to pack, deliberately choosing what she would take with her, what she would leave behind. She was leaving home for good. She would never return. She would go to a place where no one knew who she was or where she had come from. She would start all over again.

When she finished late that evening, Eleanor walked down to the drugstore and bought a root beer float and a New York newspaper, then sat at the soda fountain to read it, praying that she wouldn't run into anyone she knew. The paper was filled with advertisements for jobs in defense industries, pleading for women to come forward and do their part. She circled three or four of them in towns she'd never heard of, then went to the bus station to ask about fares and schedules. She didn't want to go home yet, didn't want to face her mother again, so she decided to walk around the lake until she ran out of energy, saying good-bye to the place that had been her home for thirteen years.

The streets of Deer Falls were pitch-black with all the streetlights turned off and blackout curtains in all the houses, but Eleanor knew the way to the lake by heart. She took off her shoes and waded along the shoreline, letting the sound of lapping waves soothe her, crying and crying for all she had lost. An hour later she came to a stretch where the sand ended and the woods met the shore. She sat down on a rock and put on her shoes, then walked on. She had walked only a quarter of a mile farther when she heard a car approaching. The woods were so quiet, she could hear each sound distinctly, and the purr of the engine sounded like Lorenzo's car—or at least an expensive car like his. She thought of him with her mother and felt sick again.

Headlights winked through the trees as the car came closer, and Eleanor ducked down, instinctively trying to hide. When she peered through the trees again, the brake lights lit up the woods behind the car, and she was horrified to see Lorenzo's house nestled among the trees. Somehow she had ended up on his property. It was his car that was driving toward the lake, heading toward the boat launch.

It stopped behind an older model car that was already parked near the dock, and a moment later Lorenzo stepped out. He quickly walked around to the passenger side and opened the door and hauled a man out of his car, dumping him to the ground. The man was bound hand and foot, and was begging. "Please, Mr. Messina. Please . . . I'm sorry!"

"Nobody steals from me, Tony. Nobody."

Lorenzo reached into his jacket, and a moment later Eleanor heard a loud bang as he put the gun to the man's head and shot him. The sound echoed through the woods like an explosion, and she curled up in a ball in terror. He had killed a man! Charming Lorenzo Messina had just killed a man in cold blood! Eleanor stuffed her fist in her mouth to keep from screaming, fighting hysteria.

A moment later, she heard the engine of the second car start up, the motor revving loudly, as if something heavy was pressing the accelerator to the floor. She forced herself to look up and watched as Lorenzo dragged the dead man to the second car and stuffed him into the trunk. Then he put the car in gear and released the brake, and it shot down the boat ramp and tore into the water with a splash. She saw it faintly in the darkness, slowly sinking to the bottom. The entire scene had taken no more than two or three minutes.

Eleanor huddled in the bushes, scarcely daring to breathe, waiting until Lorenzo's car drove away. Then she stood on quaking legs and ran blindly through the woods.

Part
9

KATHLEEN AND JOELLE

2004

Chapter 34

Kathleen stared at her uncle, astounded by what he had just told her. Joelle was sitting very close to her, holding onto Kathleen's arm as if to ground herself from a terrible shock.

"Did she ever tell the police what she'd seen?" Kathleen asked.

Leonard shook his head. "She was scared to death. You have to remember that most of the men she knew were away at war, and the ones who'd stayed behind to serve as police and so forth were pretty old. She didn't know who to trust. Eleanor knew that Messina was a powerful man, and she was afraid that he'd harm our mother if she told anyone what she'd seen. She didn't even tell me about it until years later."

"No wonder she never went back," Kathleen murmured.

"I don't know everything that happened to Eleanor here in Riverside during the war," Uncle Leonard continued, "but when I came home, your mother was a different person from the girl I'd left behind. It came out during the trial that she'd been married and that her husband had been killed in the war, and that explained a lot."

Kathleen was about to interrupt and tell Leonard that Rick Trent hadn't died after all, but he continued with his story too quickly.

"She was very depressed. Your father lifted her spirits. Made her laugh again. It was little wonder that she fell in love with him. And poor Donald was smitten from the first moment he met Eleanor. He never stopped loving her."

"If he loved her so much, then why—?"

"Why did he kill her?" Leonard interrupted. "You'll never convince me that he did."

"I was going to ask why he didn't take better care of her. Why he never got a steady job, why he let her live in squalor."

"This house was much nicer than the one your father grew up in—but I understand what you're asking." He sighed and rubbed his forehead, as if the pain of recalling the past had made his head ache. "Your father made more than a few mistakes, Kathleen. But he's changed. You'll see."

She struggled to recover from the shock of hearing that her mother had witnessed a brutal murder—and to make sense of everything else she had learned in the past two days. "Maybe Lorenzo Messina murdered Mom. He was obviously capable of such a thing."

"But why would he do that?" Leonard asked. "He didn't even know she'd been a witness."

"I don't know," Kathleen said with a shrug. "It was just a thought. . . . So you and Daddy never knew about her marriage to Rick Trent?"

"No. The police found the letters in her purse, along with the final letter that said he'd been killed in battle. Donald wouldn't have cared, though. He loved your mother."

"Her first husband didn't really die in the war, Uncle Leonard. Cynthia Hayworth told me the story last night. Rick's father was very wealthy, and when he found out that his son had secretly married Mom during the war, he did a background search. He must have found out that she was illegitimate. He used that, and the fact that Grandma Fiona had been the mistress of a wealthy New York banker, to have the marriage annulled. He accused Mom of being a gold digger, and he abandoned her. That's why she was so depressed."

Leonard shook his head sadly. "She never told us. But you don't suppose she was going back to this man, do you? Is that what the train tickets were for? I'll never believe that your mother was having an affair. Can you picture Eleanor having an affair? She was too ill, for one thing. If it weren't for the theater tickets, I would have thought she was going to New York to see a specialist."

"What do you mean? What was wrong with her?"

"Your mother had a condition called Myasthenia Gravis."

"What on earth is that?"

"It has something to do with the immune system and causes progressive muscle weakness. It started with slurred speech, trouble swallowing. . . . That's why her eyelids drooped the way they did, and why she was always so weary. It got to the point where she was too embarrassed to go out in public, afraid that people would think she was drunk. Besides, the least little thing, like heating up a can of soup, would tire her out. Medication might have helped, but she couldn't afford it. It was hard enough to feed and clothe four kids, even with public assistance. I helped as much as I could, but I was supporting my mother until she died. She closed the store after Eleanor left home so she could break free from Lorenzo Messina."

For a long moment, Kathleen couldn't speak. "W-why didn't Mom ever tell me she was ill?"

"You were a child, Kathleen. Would you really have understood? And then you left home at such a young age."

"And I didn't even come back to go to Daddy's trial. I feel so bad about that."

"Don't. I'm glad you didn't come back, and so is he. There was no need for you to hear all that ugliness. In fact, we had Connie take Annie and the boys away for about six months to keep them from hearing all about it. They still don't know the details, and they don't want to. You had a chance at a new life, and I'm glad you took it."

"I found all the clippings about the arrest and trial that Connie saved. I read them last night."

"She didn't save those. I did."

"Oh." Kathleen drew a deep breath to ask the question that had been stewing in her mind all day. "Well, if Daddy didn't kill her, then who did? And why?"

"I've been trying to figure out the answer to that for thirty-five years. The police never even considered another suspect."

Kathleen felt a surge of grief for her mother that was as painful and raw as if she'd died only yesterday. "I feel so guilty for arguing with her the last time I saw her," she said through her tears. Leonard reached to take her hand, and she felt Joelle's arm around her shoulder. "I never had a chance to say I was sorry. We argued over money for college, of all things. She wouldn't cosign a loan for me. But she swore that she would get the money for me somehow, and I said, *'How? Are you going to steal it, like Daddy?'* Those were my last words to her."

"I knew she was upset," Leonard said, "but I didn't know why. She said, *'I've let Kathleen down, Len, I've let her down. I've been so bitter toward Mother because of all the ways she failed us, and now I've failed my own daughter.'*"

"Mom!" Joelle said suddenly, "Maybe the money in Eleanor's purse was for you."

Kathleen stared at her, afraid she was right. "But how did she get it? Where did it come from?"

"I wish I knew," Uncle Leonard murmured. "We spent it all on lawyers, but it didn't help. . . . Our lives certainly got all tangled up, didn't they?"

"They sure did," Kathleen agreed. "As Rory Quinn would say, *'We made a blooming mess of things.'*"

They were silent for a moment, and Kathleen heard Connie and Annie and the other women laughing about something in the kitchen. Then a car horn began beeping outside, and a white van pulled to a stop behind Kathleen's Lexus. It had *Gallagher's TV and Appliances* painted on the side.

"He's home!" Annie squealed, running from the kitchen. "Daddy's home!" JT hurried through the house from the backyard, his face red with emotion. Kathleen sprang to her feet and offered her hand to Uncle Leonard to help him.

"You go on," he told her. "I've seen your father over the years—you haven't."

"What do you mean? Did you go up to Attica to visit him?"

"We all did. But he's dying to see you. Go on."

Kathleen couldn't hold back her tears as she followed the others outside to greet their father. He didn't look like a convict or a hardened criminal at all as he climbed from the van, just an elderly, white-haired man—thinner than she remembered, but with the same happy-go-lucky smile and freckled arms. He still had a spring in his step as he hurried toward Annie and JT and drew them into his arms. Prison hadn't beaten him down. Kathleen halted on the porch steps, stunned to realize that he was seventy-nine years old. A sob escaped from her throat when she saw that his shirt and pants and shoes were brand-new.

"Oh, Daddy," she cried. He looked up, his face wet with tears as he went to her and hugged her tightly.

"Kathy! My Kathy! I didn't think I would ever see you again."

"I'm so sorry, Daddy—"

"Shh . . . shh . . ." he soothed. "None of that, now. We're going to look forward from now on, not back." He finally released her and held her at arm's length for a moment to study her. "What a lovely woman you are. As beautiful as your mother."

As she fell into her father's arms again, weeping on his shoulder, Kathleen knew with fierce certainty that he was not her mother's murderer. The knowledge gave her no comfort. Not only had the guilty person gotten away with it, but Daddy had spent thirty-five years in prison—nearly half his lifetime—for a crime he didn't commit.

"Welcome home, Daddy," she murmured. She couldn't think of anything else to say to convey her sense of injustice. "Welcome home."

He laughed when he released her, as if trying to lighten everyone's mood. "Wow! Will you look at this place! The house looks better than it did the day we bought it. Who fixed it all up?"

"We all worked on it, Daddy," Annie replied. "Donny and JT and me. And a whole group of people from church helped, too. It was our mission project."

"Well, I'll be," he said. "You mean your Uncle Leonard let a pack of Christians run loose on this place?"

Annie laughed. "He bought fried chicken for everyone the day they put the new roof on. Come see what they did inside. . . . And your grandkids are waiting to see you."

As Annie took his hand and led him through the front door, Kathleen noticed her brother Poke for the first time. At the hard-to-believe age of fifty, he resembled their father but was stockier, with thick shoulders and arms—probably from lifting TVs. He opened his beefy arms to her. "Hey, Kathy. How you doing?"

"Great. I'm great, Poke." She started crying all over again as she hugged him.

"Hey! You better not call me that again if you know what's good for you."

"Listen, I'm the one who had to hold your hand and drag you to kindergarten every day. Believe me, you earned that name a hundred times over."

"Gee, it's good to see you." His eyes were bright with tears. "We have a lot of catching up to do."

They went inside, and Kathleen could never remember a time when the little bungalow had been filled with so much laughter and joy. She sat back and watched her family as if viewing strangers, awestruck by the change in all of them.

"If I didn't see this with my own eyes, I never would have believed it," she told Joelle. "I'm so glad you talked me into coming."

"Even with all the other awful things you found out about your family?"

"Yeah, even with all that."

"Come on, everybody!" Connie finally called above the commotion. "I've got the food on the table, and we need to sit down and eat it. This is a celebration, for goodness' sake, and what's a celebration without food?"

Everybody heaped their paper plates with food, then found places to sit in the living room, on the floor, or around the dining room table. Kathleen sat at the table between her father and Joelle. Uncle Leonard sat across from them.

"Wait! Nobody eats until we say grace," her father said. He cleared his throat and waited until everyone was quiet. "Lord, I thank you—" He couldn't finish. He covered his eyes with his hand and gestured to Poke.

"Yes, Lord . . . we thank you for this food . . . and for . . . for Dad—" He shook his head, overwhelmed, and nudged JT with his elbow.

"L-Lord, God . . ." He couldn't get any further, either.

Kathleen didn't care if they all knew she was crying. The sight of her father and brothers with their heads bowed, giving thanks to God, was nothing less than a miracle. "Heavenly Father we all thank you," she said. "Thank you for bringing Daddy home . . . and all of us together again. Amen."

"Amen," everyone echoed. There was a burst of laughter all around, and they began to eat. Kathleen thought there must be more food on the table and spread out on the kitchen counters than there had been in the house during her entire childhood. She was almost too overwhelmed to eat any of it.

After most people had finished or gone back for seconds, her father rapped on his water glass to quiet everyone down and get their attention.

"I want to say a few words to all of you while I've got you all in one place," he began. His smile faded and his eyes glimmered with tears. "I didn't kill your mother. But I was guilty of a lot of other things—stealing and teaching you kids to steal, not being a very good father or husband, cheating people out of their money. God knows I deserved to go to jail. I brought shame on myself and on my family because I was a thief and because of the way I made all of you live. I didn't do right by your mother and you kids. But I didn't kill her. I would never lay a hand on her." His voice grew hushed, and it was a moment before he could go on.

"When the justice system declared me guilty of murder, I was pretty angry about it. After all the appeals were exhausted and I realized I was in it for the long haul, well, I figured there was nothing else I could do except appeal to God. I wanted Him to set me free—and He did. But not in the way I expected." He smiled.

"The chaplain taught me about Jesus—how He was unjustly accused and executed for a crime He didn't commit. Yet Jesus submitted to God's will and saved all of us in the bargain. In fact, He took the punishment for my crimes. The chaplain said that our only purpose in life is to glorify God—and I wasn't doing that. I was doing the opposite, in fact. Never mind that I wasn't guilty of murder, I was guilty of so many other things— mainly, wasting the life that God had given me. And so, as I got to know God, I came to the conclusion that if I had to go to prison in order to find Him . . . then it was worth it."

Kathleen stared at her father in amazement, scarcely believing what she was hearing. Her father—her entire family—had become Christians and turned their lives around, and she'd had nothing to do with it. She professed to be a Christian, yet she had cut herself off from them so completely that she'd never even thought to pray for them. She knew that she would have to ask God to forgive her for that. It didn't matter how many great things she'd done for God, how many charities she'd contributed to over the years. If she couldn't even show compassion and love—and forgiveness—to her own family, it meant nothing. It occurred to Kathleen that she had been as much a prisoner as her father, locked away from her family emotionally all these years.

"I didn't murder your mother," her father repeated, "but I didn't help her any, either. And now I want to make sure my accounts are paid with all of you. I want to ask you all to forgive me. Donny. . . ? JT. . . ? Annie. . . ?" he asked, looking at each of them in turn. They all nodded, murmuring their assurances. "Leonard and Connie. . . ? And you, Kathleen?"

"Of course, Daddy. Of course I forgive you."

"Thank you," he whispered.

The room was quiet for a moment as he wiped his tears on his sleeve.

Then JT said, "You probably didn't know it, Kathleen, but Dad has turned into a fire-and-brimstone preacher."

"So I see." She couldn't hold back a smile. Neither could her father.

"I'm proud to be one, too," he said. "God gave me a ministry to the other inmates. They saw the change in me and wanted to know why. The chaplain told us we should have a life verse, and mine was 1 Timothy 1:16: 'I was shown mercy so that in me, the worst of sinners, Christ Jesus might display his unlimited patience as an example for those who would believe on him and receive eternal life.'

"Now the funny thing is, if I had been imprisoned as just a common, ordinary thief, none of the others would've listened to me. But the fact that I was a convicted murderer—well, that gave my testimony real clout among all the other murderers. So you see? God really does know what He's doing. He put me in prison to bring Him glory, and I gotta tell you, we had a genuine revival up there in Attica. Got everybody reading the Bible and going to prayer meetings and everything."

Connie brought out a cake and half a dozen other desserts, and everybody started laughing and talking again. But her father turned to Uncle Leonard, and Kathleen heard him ask quietly, "What about you, Leonard? Did you read those books I gave you?"

"I read them."

"So? What do you think?"

"I think Jesus would have embraced Communism if He'd lived in today's world—well, at the very least He'd've been a socialist. He cared about the poor and the helpless in society. That's all I ever wanted—fair treatment for the poor."

"It doesn't do much good to feed and clothe and house the poor," her father said, "if their souls aren't saved. Jesus wasn't just a good man, Len. Either He's the Son of God or He's a lunatic for saying that He was."

Kathleen saw that Joelle was listening to the conversation, too. She leaned close to her and whispered, "Joelle, Jesus wasn't a socialist."

She smiled and said, "I know what he means, Mom."

Later, when the feast finally ended and everyone sat around talking or dozing, Kathleen joined her sister, Annie, in the kitchen to help her and the other women clean up. She was pleasantly surprised when Joelle picked up a dish towel, too. Kathleen had so much to be thankful for, and she'd felt so many old wounds healing on this remarkable day. But she still felt there were unsettled matters in her heart.

"Annie, I'm trying to remember Mom. I know it was a long time ago, but what do you remember, especially about those last days?"

"You mean . . . when she died?"

"No, no. I don't want you to relive that. . . . I'm wondering . . . I-I'm worried that Mom was angry with me when she died. We had a terrible fight before I left home—"

"She wasn't angry with you at all! Just the opposite, in fact. She said she wanted to help you."

"Help me? How?"

"I thought she was planning a party or something for you because she swore me to secrecy. Even Daddy and Uncle Leonard and the boys weren't supposed to know. But I don't suppose it matters if I tell now."

Kathleen stopped drying the pot in her hands. She held her breath, waiting, while Annie gazed into the distance as if seeing the events all over again.

"Mama borrowed Connie's car and we went on a trip—well, two trips, actually. Both times we left as soon as Daddy and Uncle Leonard went to work in the morning and hurried to get back before they came home. It was summer, and I was home from school. I don't know where the boys were. I asked Mama where we were going and she said, 'We're going to help Kathleen. She deserves my help.'

"I knew you had just left for college, so I thought we were going up there to help you move in or something. But we didn't. First we went to Brinkley's Drugstore, and Mama got a whole pile of change. She told me to pick out my favorite candy bar while she went into the phone booth there in Brinkley's and made some calls. I don't know who to or how many.

"When she came out, we got in Connie's car and drove a long way. Well, it seemed like we went halfway to California because our family never went *anywhere* in the car except to Bensenville. But it was probably just a couple of hours."

"Do you have any idea where you went?" Kathleen asked.

"I think it was only to Albany, but I can't be sure. We finally stopped in front of a building that had red-white-and-blue flags all over it and a sign that said 'reelect somebody or other.' I remember that because I asked Mommy what reelect meant, but she never answered me. She made me wait in the car while she went inside. After driving all that way I was dying to get out, but she said no, she wouldn't be long—and she wasn't. She came out right away with an envelope. I know it had money in it because she took me to a restaurant and pulled out a twenty-dollar bill and bought us lunch. It was the first time I ever ate in a restaurant. I wanted to order dessert, too, but she said, 'We can only spend a little bit. The rest is for Kathleen.' I was really mad at you!" Annie laughed.

Joelle grabbed Kathleen's arm. "Rick Trent! Mom, it had to be! Remember what Mrs. Hayworth said about him going into politics?"

"Yes! I was just thinking the same thing. That must be where the three thousand dollars came from. She probably threatened to go public with what he had done to her. That's why she dug out his old letters."

"What are you talking about?" Annie asked.

"I'll explain later," Kathleen said, brushing away her question. "What was the second trip you took?"

"Well, we did the same thing the next day—leaving right after breakfast—only this time we drove to a pretty little town by a lake."

"Oh, no!" Kathleen covered her mouth with her hand, afraid of what Annie was about to tell her.

"What?" Annie asked.

"Go on, please. I'll explain later."

"She met someone by the lake, an older man with gray hair. She made me wait in the car again, but this time I was glad she did because the man got real angry at her. I saw them arguing. When Mom came back, she was shaking so badly she could hardly shift the car. I was hoping we'd eat in a restaurant again, but she tore out of town like the devil was after her. And she didn't have an envelope this time."

"Lorenzo Messina!" Joelle said.

"She wouldn't be foolish enough to try to blackmail him, would she?" Kathleen breathed. "The car in the lake?"

"Oh, Mom!" Joelle cried. "He must be the one who murdered her!"

"Who? Would you please tell me what you're talking about?" Annie said.

"What's going on out here?" their father asked, coming into the kitchen.

"Get Uncle Leonard," Kathleen said. "He needs to hear this, too."

He thumped into the kitchen with his walker to join them, and Kathleen made both him and her father sit down.

"I think Mom was trying to get money from people in her past to help me pay for college. That's what we fought about the last time I saw her, and she swore she'd get it somehow. I never imagined . . ." She couldn't finish, horrified by the thought that her mother's death might have been instigated by her.

"Aunt Annie just gave us another piece of the puzzle," Joelle continued when Kathleen couldn't. "She and Eleanor drove somewhere, maybe Albany, and someone in a campaign office gave them an envelope with money in it—probably the three thousand dollars Eleanor had in her purse when she died."

"It had to be Rick Trent, her first husband," Kathleen continued. "That's why she dug out his old letters—to bribe him. Mrs. Hayworth said that he ran for Congress or something, but if Mom had ever revealed what a dirty, rotten thing he and his father had done, nobody ever would have voted for him."

"So he killed her?" Uncle Leonard asked.

"Maybe. But I think it was probably Lorenzo Messina. Annie said that Mom took her to a little town by a lake the next day and that she argued with an older man with gray hair."

"What was she thinking!" Leonard cried. "You don't try to blackmail a man like him!"

Once again, the knowledge that her mother had taken such a terrible risk for her sake, made Kathleen feel sick inside. She had to sit down.

"I think I know what the two tickets to New York City were for," Joelle said. "I'll bet she was going to find that Bartlett guy who worked on Broadway and try to get money from him, too."

"But she never got a chance," Kathleen's father said. "She died before she could go."

"I feel awful!" Kathleen wept. "Why didn't I come home? We could have pieced this all together thirty-five years ago if I had spoken up. I'm so sorry, Daddy! It's my fault you were in prison!"

"That's not true, sweetheart," he said, taking her into his arms. "You'd never even heard about this Rick fellow or the other guy."

"We each had a piece of the puzzle and didn't even know it," Annie said. "I'm as guilty as you are, Kathleen. I never told anybody about the two trips Mama took."

"You were nine years old," Kathleen said. "Mom made you promise."

"Listen, now," their father said, "no one is to blame except the guy who did it. Don't you think the Good Lord could have brought out all these facts thirty-five years ago if He'd wanted to? But then where would we all be today, and what kind of people would we be? I'd still be a thief, I know that for sure. No, I meant it when I said that it was worth going to prison to find the Lord."

"Well, I want to get to the bottom of it," Leonard said. "It had to be Lorenzo Messina. I'll go to the police and get them to reopen the case."

"The police won't care," Kathleen said. "As far as they're concerned, it was solved. Dad served time for the crime. Besides, wouldn't Messina be long dead by now? Wasn't he in his forties when you moved to Deer Falls in 1929? He'd be, like . . . 115 years old by now."

"You always were a math whiz," her father said proudly.

"I'll help you, Uncle Leonard, if you want me to," Joelle said. "I can go on the Internet and Google Richard Trent. We can find out what years he ran for office. And we can try to find out about the mobster guy, too.

Maybe we can even find out who the poor guy in the bottom of the lake was."

Annie shook her head as if the conversation was making her dizzy. "The bottom of the lake? I don't even want to ask!"

"I'd be grateful for your help, young lady," Uncle Leonard said. "We'll file a lawsuit. Donald deserves compensation from the blasted government for wrongful imprisonment all these years."

"Good luck with that," Kathleen said wryly.

"I'll bring my laptop next time we visit," Joelle said. "We can find all kinds of things on the Internet. We are coming back to visit again, aren't we, Mom?" she asked, turning to Kathleen. "Like for Thanksgiving and Christmas and stuff?"

"I would like that," Kathleen said, with a smile. "And speaking of Christmas, Daddy . . ."

"Oh, no," he groaned. "You're not going to mention the stolen Christmas tree, are you? I was hoping you'd forgotten that."

"How could I forget?" she laughed. "I was your accomplice!"

"Well, what I remember," Uncle Leonard said, "was how those men from Kathleen's church came to the door with all the presents . . . and me in my underwear, gaping at them like they'd just landed from Mars. One was the bank president, and the other was one of the Brinkleys, from the drugstore. I couldn't imagine why two capitalists would bring presents like that. What was in it for them? But back to your lawsuit, Donald—"

"No, no, no," he said, holding up his hands. "We won't talk about lawsuits today. Do what you want another day, Len, but today we're going to sit down and feast and enjoy this day and each other. Let the past stay in the past. It doesn't do any good to rake it up. The truth is, we each have a chance to start all over again, every day of our lives, if we know the Lord."

"Is this the start of another sermon?" Uncle Leonard asked. "Because if it is . . ." He tried to act grumpy, but Kathleen saw him smile.

"Yes—but I'll make it brief. If you pack up and run away from your problems, they tend to come with you. I think some of you know what I mean. The only way we can really start all over is to do what I did: become a new man in Christ. The Bible says old things are passed away then, and all things are new. You still have to deal with the past and ask for forgiveness, of course. Repentance is part of becoming a new man in Christ. But only He can make all things new."

"You mean to tell me," Leonard said, "that you can just forget all about being in jail for a crime you didn't commit?"

He thought about it before answering, and Kathleen saw his eyes fill with tears. "There's a prayer I learned to pray in Attica—I think it's part of a longer prayer. But the part I like says, 'Let what we suffer teach us to be merciful—let our sins teach us to forgive.'"

Kathleen reached to squeeze his hand and said, "Amen, Daddy. Amen."

Chapter
35

They were almost home, and they were stuck in a traffic jam. Kathleen drummed her fingers on the steering wheel, trying not to grow impatient. She glanced over at Joelle, who had headphones on and was nodding in time to one of her CDs. She was in her own world, yet Kathleen felt so much closer to her than she had when they'd left home just a few days ago. She had reluctantly agreed to this journey, hoping it would bring them together—and she had gotten so much more than she had ever wanted.

Joelle turned to her suddenly and pulled off the headphones. "Are you going to look for another job when we get home?" she asked.

"I thought I would wait until the fall. Why?"

"We should go to Mexico, Mom."

Kathleen laughed. "You mean now? Just keep driving until we get to Mexico like Thelma and Louise or something?"

"No, not like that." She made a face. "I was thinking, you know, they need chaperones for the youth group trip to Mexico, remember?"

Kathleen stared at her. "Do you really want to go? The living conditions will be pretty primitive, you know."

"I know." She smiled and held out her hand, admiring the sapphire ring on her finger. "I really like Uncle Leonard. He's awesome!"

Kathleen laughed out loud.

The traffic started moving again, and twenty minutes later they were off the interstate and nearly home. The sight of all the opulent homes made Kathleen feel a little guilty—but also very grateful. She thought of her father's prayer and recited it to herself again: *Let what we suffer teach us to be merciful—let our sins teach us to forgive.*

"Joelle. . . ?" she said suddenly.

"Yeah, Mom?" She pulled off the headphones.

"On the way there I asked you what you wanted to do with your life, and you said you wanted to do something that mattered, remember?"

"Yeah."

"I've been thinking about Grandma Fiona and my mother, and my own life, too—the dreams we had, the choices we made. Something was missing. When we were figuring out what we wanted out of life, we forgot to ask God what He wanted. That's what I hope you'll ask. A clue to His answer is usually in the gifts He gave us—for me it was something to do with my abilities with numbers. But my father was right when he said that our only purpose in life is to bring God glory. I should have used my gifts for that, not to get a fancy house and cars and things like that. Maybe it's good that I lost my job. I can start all over and do it right this time. You're just at the beginning of adulthood. I hope you'll give your life to Him and seek His dreams for you. I'm sure they're more wonderful than anything we can dream of."

"I know, Mom," she said quietly. Kathleen glanced at Joelle and saw her wipe away a tear.

"Mom?" she said a few minutes later. "The men in Grandma Fiona's and Grandma Eleanor's lives weren't very nice, were they—Rory Quinn, Arthur Bartlett, Rick Trent. Even Grandpa wasn't always very nice."

"No, they weren't. I imagine that Fiona and Eleanor just wanted to be loved, and instead they allowed men to use them. I remember how lonely I was when I was a teenager. I was pretty vulnerable back then, too. All that most people want is to be loved. But don't start hating men, Joelle. There are a lot of good ones out there. I recommend you start by making sure he's a man of faith."

"You made a good choice, Mom. Dad is really great, isn't he?"

"Yeah, he really is."

They pulled into the driveway, and Kathleen felt choked up when she saw all that God had given her.

"Dad's home!" Joelle said.

They saw his car parked in the garage as the automatic door went up. He was sitting at the kitchen table, eating Thai takeout and reading the *Wall Street Journal* when they walked in the door. He had his sleeves rolled up and his tie loosened; Kathleen thought he'd never looked more handsome to her. Joelle threw her arms around him first.

"I missed you, Dad!"

"Me too," Kathleen said. He looked from one to the other, as if unable to comprehend why they were both in tears as they greeted him.

"What's going on with you two? I mean, I'm flattered, but . . ."

Kathleen who was always so controlled, always afraid to say how she felt, always so afraid of rejection, vowed that things would be different from now on. She wrapped her arms around his neck and looked into his eyes.

"I love you, Mike."